KEEP THE HOME
FIRES BURNING

KEEP THE HOME FIRES BURNING

The war was not 'over by Christmas' after all and as 1915 begins, the Hunters begin to settle into wartime life. Diana, the eldest daughter, sees her fiancé off to war but doesn't expect the coldness she receives from her future mother-in-law. Her brother David and his battalion are almost ready to be sent to the front. Below stairs, Ethel, the under housemaid, is tired of having her beaux go off to war so she deliberately sets her sights on a man who works on the railway. Eric turns out to be decent and honest – is this the man who could give her a new life?

KEEP THE HOME FIRES BURNING

by

Cynthia Harrod-Eagles

Magna Large Print Books
Long Preston, North Yorkshire,
BD23 4ND, England.

British Library Cataloguing in Publication Data.

Harrod-Eagles, Cynthia
Keep the home fires burning.

A catalogue record of this book is
available from the British Library

ISBN   978-0-7505-4260-9

7/16

First published in Great Britain in 2015 by Sphere

Copyright © Cynthia Harrod-Eagles 2015

Cover illustration © Rekha Garton by arrangement with
Arcangel Images

The moral right of the author has been asserted.

Published in Large Print 2016 by arrangement with
Little, Brown Book Group

Magna Large Print is an imprint of Library Magna Books Ltd.

Printed and bound in Great Britain by
T.J. (International) Ltd., Cornwall, PL28 8RW

In memory of my friend Joan Bindloss –
sadly missed

THE HUNTER FAMILY
of The Elms, Northcote

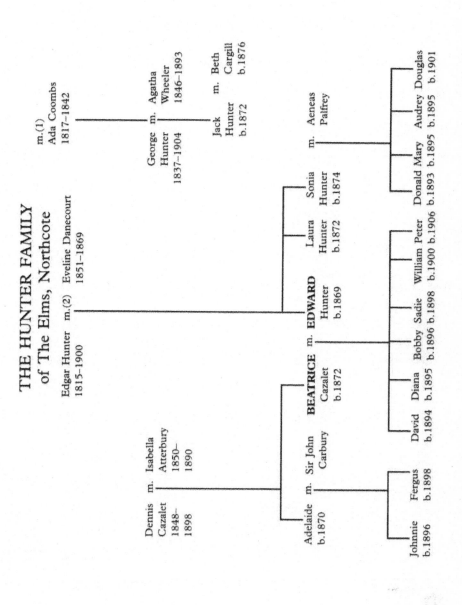

CHAPTER ONE

The December of 1914 had been mild but wet, and Flanders was a flat place. Here, at Ypres, the British army had ended the Race to the Sea, denying the Germans that last crucial fragment of Belgium and the Channel ports. The salient in front of the city was criss-crossed with streams and dykes. Now they were full, and as the water continued to fall from the sky, it made no distinction between a drainage channel dug by farmers and a trench dug by soldiers: it poured into both.

There was little movement beyond the occasional flight of birds from one battered stand of trees to another, or a wisp of smoke from one of the few farm cottages still occupied, climbing reluctantly into the damp, foggy air, grey on grey. The thousands of soldiers who invested the landscape were invisible, gone to ground. On both sides they had dug in to try to make the best of things, shore up their defences and wait for better days.

There wasn't much to do in the trenches. Apart from dawn and dusk stand-tos, there were only routine inspections and maintenance duties. For the rest of the time Jack Hunter read anything he could lay his hands on (books were precious in the front line, but also fragile in the relentless damp) and wrote long letters to his wife. In fact, it was more like one long letter, sent off in sections as chance, the postal collection or running out of paper dictated.

I've been re-reading your account of Christmas [he wrote on New Year's Day]. *Glad to know London is still humming. I can just imagine all those restaurants and clubs bursting at the seams, the dances and parties, the taxi-cabs crammed with revellers.*

The top brass were furious about our 'Christmas Truce', but our colonel was glad of the chance to mend the barbed wire, bail out the trenches and bring in the dead. They've been mouldering out there since November, making us all feel rather fed up. Orders from on high say 'no more fraternisation'; we must all shoot to kill from now on. In fact, hardly anyone shoots at all. What Tommy in his right mind would poop off at an invisible enemy, when it means hours of cleaning the rifle afterwards? I expect the Boche feel the same, because they've been quiet all week.

So we were surprised last night when there was a sudden ferocious fusillade from the trenches opposite. Couldn't think what had come over them, unless they had some choleric general visiting. There was nervous speculation on our side about a new campaign of night raids, until some wise person (yes, it was me!) remembered that our 11 p.m. is their midnight. They were ringing in the New Year, and courteously firing well above our heads so that we shouldn't get the wrong idea. An hour later we returned the compliment, after which it all went quiet again.

By one of those unsought miracles familiar in army life, we had a new pump delivered despite not having asked for one. It is much more efficient than the old one and we are finally pumping out more water than

14

is coming in, so we can see the duckboards again. I have a decentish dugout, and only two more days in the front line, and two in support, before I can get back to the heaven that is Poperinghe, and a bath. The child Jack would never have believed how much the adult Jack would long to be in hot water!

Gibbs has just poked his head in to say that, in honour of the New Year, the commissariat have sent up currant duff with dinner, which has just arrived. Also he has acquired a piece of cheese (best not to ask how) to go with the thimble of port he's been saving for just such an eventuality. So tonight I can report I am fairly comfortable and shall be well fed, and inconvenienced only by the dampness of the writing-paper. That and being so far away from you, dear love. Not much to do but sleep (good!) and reflect Janus-faced (not so good!) as one is obliged to do at the opening of a new year.

It has been a strange war so far – mistakes, setbacks, heroic exertions, swings of fortune, desperate dashes, tremendous stands. Our tiny army has cheated the mighty German machine of what it must have thought was certain victory. And now here we are, where we are, dug in, waiting to see what happens. It occurs to me that the war we all expected and prepared for is actually over. We fought it, and no-one won. Now we are facing a new, different, war, one that no-one imagined, and that no-one really knows how to fight. We shall find out, I suppose, when spring arrives and we come out of hibernation. Let's hope 1915 will see a victory as unequivocal as 1815. Then I can come home to you and sink back into the delicious reverie that is our marriage. Dear love, for nothing less than war would I have broke that happy dream, as Donne almost said.

The whole of Northcote was wild with excitement over the engagement between Charles Wroughton, Viscount Dene, and Diana Hunter. Diana had been the acknowledged local beauty for too long for anyone to resent her success. Besides, the Wroughtons had always been viewed as rather standoffish, and it had been assumed that Charles would eventually marry a titled girl, so it was gratifying that one of their own, so to speak, had conquered the citadel. Visits of congratulation to The Elms began the very next day, and went on for the whole week before Christmas. There were even newspaper reporters, polite at the front door and shifty at the back, looking for comments and the 'story' that would appeal to their readers.

The servants were thrilled about the engagement, and no amount of extra work answering the door and carrying in trays of tea for visitors dampened their enthusiasm. Cook and Ada were talking about making a scrap-book; Emily sang 'They Didn't Believe Me' over and over as she scrubbed floors; Nula had started collecting illustrations of bridal gowns from the magazines and making her own drawings.

Beattie dispensed tea, received congratulations, answered questions, and tried to protect her daughter from the more impertinent intrusions. She found it hard to tell what Diana was thinking. Charles had had to go straight back to his regiment, which lent an air of unreality to the rejoicing. It was no surprise that Diana drifted about like a sleep-walker. Kind visitors had murmured that she was in a daze of bliss; to Beattie it seemed more like shock.

Boxing Day at Dene Park had been a difficult occasion. The earl, who had a certain efficient charm, raised a toast to 'our lovely future daughter-in-law', but Lady Wroughton had spent so much of her life putting people in their place that it was hard for her to stop now. Her kindest address to Diana had been an undertaking to 'see what they could do about making her an asset to the house'.

In addition, there had been Charles's sister, Caroline, and her husband, Lord Grosmore, who seemed unflatteringly astonished about the whole thing; Charles's younger brother, Rupert, who managed to make a smile look like a sharp weapon; and a number of Wroughton relatives, who simply didn't know how to talk to people they didn't know and, worse, had never heard of. The older ones appeared to be wondering how on earth such people had managed to get into the house.

As the Hunters descended from the motor-car that had been sent for them, Beattie had seen her daughter stop and look up at the portico. With its four massive Corinthian pillars and stark, un-decorated pediment, 'imposing' was the adjective most often used by guidebooks. Dene Park dated from 1680, and the Wroughtons of the time had chosen the least fancy of Palladio's designs, with the intention of intimidating visitors rather than enchanting them. As Diana stared, rather white, Beattie could guess her thoughts. To Charles, it would just be the entrance to his home, and he would notice it no more than Diana noticed the porch over the front door at The Elms. The gulf between their two worlds was there before them, encapsulated in solid, undeniable Portland stone.

It was not just Charles, not just the earl and countess and sundry other stiff relatives, but the whole of his world: friends and endless tiers of cousins all brought up like him, with habits and language and expectations quite different from those of a banker's daughter. Not just Dene Park but a house in Norfolk, an estate in Ireland, a hunting-box in Leicestershire and two houses in London. How was Diana, *their* Diana, to fit in with all of that?

Beattie did not confide her doubts to her husband. Dene Park held no fears for him: he dealt daily with the mighty and visited many great houses in the course of business. Besides, he knew the earl – one of his clients – tolerably well. He had even been invited once or twice to shoot at Dene Park. It would not have occurred to him that there were social pitfalls, even less that his wife and daughter might fear them.

But the day after that terrifying Boxing Day had brought relief. A telegram from Charles was followed rapidly by the man himself, bearing apologies for his absence and an engagement ring for Diana. It was a family heirloom, had been his grandmother's: a large, round ruby, set about with diamonds, on heavy gold. Now, suddenly, the engagement became real: the ring was there, Charles was there.

Best of all, he said that as it was only fifteen miles from camp to The Elms, and he had a fast motor-car, he would come and visit whenever he had a few hours off-duty – if Mrs Hunter would allow him.

'Come any time,' Beattie said. 'You don't need to give notice – we're always glad to see you.'

When Beattie was not worrying about the wedding – with the added complications of the war, and how the Wroughton element was to be meshed with the Hunter – she was thinking about David. It was hard not to feel hurt that he had planned to spend his leave with the family of his friend Oliphant. He had said it was because the Oliphants' home in Melton Mowbray was closer to camp, so he would not have to waste his leave travelling. Beattie couldn't help feeling there were other influences at work, which boded her no good.

Highclere Farm, as the name suggested, was at the top of a hill, but still the constant rain had created an ocean of mud.

Sadie did not normally do the rough work, but with eight muddy horses to prepare that morning she insisted on pushing up her sleeves and pitching in. She was excavating the second subject of the morning from its carapace when John Courcy, the veterinary surgeon, appeared at the stable door.

'My goodness! I didn't recognise you for the moment. Is it really Miss Hunter under there?'

Sadie straightened, and pushed her hair back with a forearm, adding another streak to her brow. 'They went and *rolled*, the wretches!' she said. 'They were put out in the top paddock overnight, but there's a weak place in the hedge, and they broke through and found the lowest, wettest spot

19

in the whole field, and down they went.' John Courcy was laughing now. 'They all looked so pleased with themselves when they were fetched in. I swear this one had a smirk on his face.'

'Which one is it?'

'Conker,' she said. The sergeant, Cairns, who had been assigned to them had warned her not to name them in case she got fond of them, but she had done it anyway. Conker was her favourite. She slapped his neck affectionately, and he turned his head and nuzzled her.

'It might have been wiser to keep them in overnight,' Courcy said.

Sadie looked stern. 'I think we know that now,' she said. She glanced down at herself, then shyly up at him. 'Do I look very dreadful?'

'Not at all. Mud becomes you,' he said solemnly.

He had come to examine the eight horses that were leaving today for the Army Remount Service depot. Two of the original intake of ten had been pronounced not ready by Mrs Cuthbert – after nearly four months of schooling by her, Sadie and the grooms, they were still unreliable, particularly in the face of loud noises. Teaching the youngsters to bear having firecrackers let off near them had been the wildest part of the training process. In the consequent rodeos, Sadie had taken several falls. She'd had to conceal the bruises from her family, for fear she would be forbidden to help any more.

Courcy was looking at her with sympathy. 'You're going to miss them,' he suggested.

She tried to brazen it out. 'I'm just pleased we've got the first batch ready to go.'

'Of course you are,' he agreed kindly. 'Well, I'd better give them a going-over.' He glanced at Conker. 'Perhaps I'll start with the clean ones.'

'Conker's the last,' she said. 'The others are all ready.'

'Do you want to leave him for a moment and come with me?' he asked. 'You can hold them for me while I look them over.'

She agreed readily, pleased that he had asked. She loved the way he treated her as an equal, not as a child. At home, they would have disapproved of her muddiness; he just laughed. It was only a pity they didn't see more of him at Highclere. He was attached to the Army Remount Service, so he came whenever they had a veterinary problem, but the Irish horses had been pretty healthy so far. He was also on call for any army units in the area, so she saw him from time to time, buzzing about in his little car. Sometimes he would stop and have a chat with her, but if he was in a hurry he would only wave as he passed.

Now she went with him from box to box, holding the horses while he looked at their ears, eyes, teeth and feet, and listened with his stethoscope to their hearts, lungs and stomachs.

'You're very good with them,' Courcy said. 'You make my job much easier.'

'They're good fellows,' she said, deflecting the praise. She was not used to being complimented.

One of the grooms had finished Conker when they got to him. He shoved his nose under Sadie's arm and sighed a great gusty sigh of content as he leaned into her. Courcy thought that, despite her plucky words, she *would* miss them.

'Well, they're fit enough, anyway,' he said, rolling up his stethoscope. 'When are they leaving?'

'The ten past two train. There's a railway box waiting for them in the siding at Northcote. We're hacking them down.'

'You're going with them?' Courcy asked.

'Me, Podrick, Bent and Oxer – ride one and lead one. Mrs Cuthbert will follow in the motor to collect the tack.' They stepped outside. Just for the moment the rain had stopped, though the sky was grey and threatening. Courcy leaned an elbow on the box door and seemed inclined for conversation. 'I don't suppose it'll be long before you get a new batch in,' he said. 'There's nothing much going on in France at the moment, but they'll want to get up to full strength before any spring offensive.'

'Will there be a spring offensive?' Sadie asked quickly.

'Oh, I haven't heard anything,' he said. 'It's just the way armies work. They can't fight in the current conditions, so both sides will hibernate until spring.'

'It seems awfully silly,' Sadie said slowly, 'to be fighting by rules, like that, when fighting itself is such a... I can't think of the right word.'

'Such an anarchic thing?' he offered.

'Yes,' she agreed.

'I suppose it's as well there *are* rules, or it would be even worse than it is,' he said. 'You have a brother who's volunteered, I believe.'

'David, the eldest.' She nodded. 'He's in training somewhere near Nottingham. He's longing to get out to France.'

'Good for him.'

'He wants to do something noble to serve his country,' Sadie said with pride.

'You're very fond of him,' Courcy noted.

She nodded. 'I miss him. Father calls it "leaving the nest" – he says we'll all hop out sooner or later. I hate the idea of that. I suppose it has to be, but you always hope nice things will stay the same for ever, don't you? Christmas was strange without him.'

'You're lucky to have brothers and sisters,' Courcy said. 'There was only ever me at home. The high point of Christmas Day was my father playing a game of chess with me after dinner. Not exactly riot unbounded.'

'That's sad for you,' said Sadie. 'Brothers and sisters are not always *completely* lovely but, on the whole, I'm glad to have them.'

'And your sister is engaged to be married?' Courcy said.

'How did you hear that?'

'Everyone seems to be talking about it,' he said.

'I can guess what they're saying – how amazing that Lord Dene's chosen a nobody instead of a duke's daughter.'

'I'm sure they don't say that.'

'I'm sure they do, behind our backs.'

'Well, not to me, anyway,' said Courcy. 'And what do *you* say?'

'That he's in love with her, and that's all that matters, isn't it?'

'To you and me, perhaps. I believe in Lord Dene's world other things are usually taken into account. What do you think of him?'

'I've only met him a couple of times, but I like him. He talked very sensibly about dogs, and he was nice to Nailer. Nobody's ever nice to poor Nailer.'

'Except you,' said Courcy.

'And you.'

'It's my job,' he said.

She knew he hadn't been kind to Nailer only because it was his job. 'But you like dogs, too,' she said.

'I like *yours*,' he said.

She met his eyes shyly and had to look away. She had never been shy with grown-ups, but there was something *about* John Courcy... At the end of a rapid chain of thought that wouldn't bear inspection, she blurted out, 'It's my birthday on the twentieth. I'll be seventeen.'

He raised an eyebrow. 'Should one say "congratulations"? I'm not very knowledgeable about such things, but I believe seventeen is something of a milestone.'

'I don't know,' she said. 'I'm not officially "out" – but I don't suppose, with the war and everything, there'll be the old sort of "coming-out" any more. At least until the war's over.' She looked up at him. 'I do think it's changed things, the war – don't you?'

'Yes, but whether the changes are permanent... I suppose it depends rather on how long it goes on.'

At that moment Mrs Cuthbert appeared. 'Everything all right?' she called to Courcy as she approached. 'How did you find my charges?'

'In tip-top condition,' Courcy answered. 'I've

never seen such a happy bunch of four-year-olds. You must have been tucking them in every night with cocoa and a bedtime story.'

'Then I take it you're signing them off. Good-oh. There's a train for them this afternoon.'

'So Miss Sadie was telling me.'

Mrs Cuthbert turned her eyes on Sadie and noticed the state of her. 'My dear girl, you must go indoors and get some of that mud off you at once! I can't have you riding through the public streets like that.'

Sadie was embarrassed. 'I don't see that it matters.'

'Everyone in Northcote knows you, and it'll matter if it gets back to your parents and they forbid you to come again. You're not a child any more.'

'So I've just been told,' said Courcy. 'Seventeen is a young lady, Miss Hunter.'

'"Young ladies" don't do interesting things,' she complained. 'It's nothing but clothes and dancing.'

'I'm sorry you don't like dancing,' said Courcy. 'I imagine you'd do it rather nicely.'

She thought about dancing with him, and was confused. 'Of course I like it. But it can't be *all* dancing. There has to be something else to life as well.'

Courcy was sorry to have teased her. 'I agree. Dancing is far from everything. But it's pleasant while it lasts.' He turned to Mrs Cuthbert. 'I'd better complete the documents for this lot.'

'Yes, of course,' said Mrs Cuthbert, and added to Sadie, 'Go up to the house and have a wash, and ask Annie to brush your clothes and clean your boots. I'll be up in a minute and look you out one of my clean shirts.'

Sadie escaped gratefully, but still couldn't help looking back when she reached the gate for a last sight of John Courcy. But he had turned away with Mrs Cuthbert and she only saw his back view.

She felt proud bringing up the rear of the cavalcade, leading Ginger and riding Conker for the last time. The horses were enjoying being out as a group and were trotting nicely, carrying their heads well and keeping pace with each other as if they were on parade. How different they were from the wild bunch delivered back in September! She was particularly proud when a motor-car idling at the kerb backfired explosively just as they passed, and none of the horses missed a beat.

As they rode through the streets of Northcote, people turned to look, and those who knew her called out and waved to her. There were quite a few soldiers about. After five months, it no longer surprised her, though she always noticed them. The Tommies gave a cheer when they saw she was a girl, and she smiled in response.

There were other reminders of the war, too: red-white-and-blue bunting round the window of Stein's, the butcher's; portraits of the King and Queen in Hadleigh's window; the words 'BUSINESS AS USUAL' on the side of a Simpson's Dairy cart going by. On the railings by the police station there was a recruitment poster, and the advertisement for the Electric Palace in Westleigh had a new sticker across it saying 'Service Men (in uniform) Free'. And as they reached the station yard, the Charrington's coal dray pulled out, drawn by a pair of mules, instead of the lovely shires that had been commandeered by the army. Yes, she thought, clattering into the yard, though most things seemed much the same as always, you wouldn't have any difficulty in remembering there was a war on.

She helped untack and box the horses. They were offered water, but they wouldn't drink – there was a little hay in the rack along one side and they were more interested in that. It was time to say goodbye and, despite her good intentions, Sadie felt tearful. She left Conker till last; but when she caressed him he gave her only a perfunctory nudge and continued tugging eagerly at the wisps of hay.

Podrick, the head man, was waiting at the foot of the ramp. He gave her a sympathetic look. 'They'll be all right,' he said.

'I know,' she said, swallowing the lump in her throat. Podrick, Bent and Oxer were standing by the heap of tack, waiting for Mrs Cuthbert to arrive and take them back. She felt a sudden desire to be alone, and said, 'There won't be anything for me to do at Highclere this afternoon. I think I'll go home.'

'Missus'll give you a lift,' Podrick said.

'Oh, no, thanks. I'll walk. Will you tell her for me?' And with a nod to the grooms, she set off.

It started to drizzle when she was halfway home, and a glance at the sky told her proper rain would be setting in soon. She hunched into her collar, put her hands into her pockets and increased her pace. As she turned in at the gate of The Elms she spotted Nailer sheltering under the laurels. He stuck out his whiskery white muzzle when he saw her, and when she stopped and spoke to him he came out.

'You're soaking!' she said, and he swept his tail back and forth in apologetic agreement. It was getting colder, too, and she could see him shivering. 'Come on,' she said.

She managed to sneak him in by the scullery door, and used the towel from the sink there to dry him. He went limp in her hands, his eyes closed in bliss and his jowls flopping as she rubbed him vigorously to warm him up. 'You're such a fool,' she told him. 'Why didn't you shelter?'

Too much to do, he said in her head, in the growly voice and Hertfordshire accent she always imagined for him. *Places to visit, things to sniff. Don't forget the ears, my girl.*

'I'm not your girl. I'm about the only friend you've got, however. Except for Mr Courcy.'

Those are the only ears I've got, so not so rough, my maiden, if you please.

'How's that?'

Better. So you've been talking with Mr Courcy, have you? I hope you're not getting spoony on him.

She stopped abruptly, having managed to confound herself. 'What a ridiculous suggestion,' she said aloud.

CHAPTER TWO

David sat at the dinner table at the house of his friend Oliphant with the rumble of conversation rolling gently over his head. Mrs Oliphant had invited guests: the neighbours from next door, Colonel and Mrs Fentiman, and their daughter Penelope. David was seated next to her, and on Mrs Oliphant's left. Dinner at the Oliphants', when there were guests, was always rather formal, and Mrs Oliphant did not approve of talking across the table, which meant that David had to divide his attention between Miss Fentiman and his hostess. Miss Fentiman was slightly gingery, with a plump chin and sandy eyelashes, and whether she was dull or merely shy he didn't know, but it had been hard work to prise anything out of her except *yes* and *no*.

He had managed to get over his guilt about not going home. His excuse, that the Oliphant house was closer, was true, but he knew his mother would be upset even so, and he didn't like to upset her. He had missed them all at Christmas, but he belonged to the army now, and Mother had to realise he was a man and made his own decisions. Anyway, the slight discomfort at the back of his mind where his conscience lived was no match for the pleasure of being in the same room as Oliphant's sister, Sophy.

At last the sweet plates were removed and the

dessert put on, which meant that general conversation could take place. David abandoned the unrewarding Miss Fentiman and lapsed into silence so he could gaze across the table at Sophy. He thought her the most beautiful girl in the world, and her beauty was only enhanced by comparison with the neighbours' daughter.

Sophy was small, delicately made, with dark hair and dark eyes that seemed large in her pale face. Her neck was long and slender and swan-white. He adored her neck. There were one or two tiny curls at the nape, escapees from the confines of her chignon, and he found them utterly distracting. A few weeks ago, some of the men at camp had passed round illicit photographs of women in their underwear, some with their breasts almost uncovered. David had been unmoved by them, but those little curls, with their suggestion of *déshabille*, could make him go hot and cold in quick succession.

Now and then her eyes would meet his across the table, to be quickly averted, accompanied by a faint blush. It was all the encouragement he needed to keep looking at her, until he accidentally caught Oliphant's eye instead, and his friend gave him a smirk of amusement and a pitying shake of the head, after which he pulled himself together and listened again to the conversation.

'The newspapers are full of nonsense these days,' Oliphant *père* was saying. 'No proper war news at all. I suppose that's the government's doing, eh, Fentiman? Censorship for our own good?'

'What the people don't know can't hurt 'em,'

said Fentiman. 'Better to keep up morale.'

'Hence all these heartwarming stories, I suppose,' said Mrs Fentiman, 'about missing sons turning up, and acts of heroism at the front.'

'I like to read of such things,' Mrs Oliphant pronounced. 'There was an account in the newspaper about a soldier who went into a barn to fetch straw and found two armed German soldiers hiding there. He had no weapon with him but a pair of wire-cutters, but most bravely and resourcefully, he pointed them at the Germans and shouted, "Hands up!" The Germans threw down their rifles and surrendered.'

'Oh, Mother, that's an old chestnut,' Oliphant junior objected. 'It's been around so long it's got whiskers on it.'

'I don't like that sort of talk, Frederick,' Mrs Oliphant said sternly. She was a large, solid, well-corseted lady, with iron-grey hair tightly waved in old-fashioned parallel crinkles. Her spectacles magnified her pale eyes to alarming size, and she bent them reprovingly on her son. 'I'm quite sure the story is true, or it would not have been published in the newspaper.'

Mrs Fentiman stepped in, accustomed to her neighbour's literal cast of mind: 'At any rate, it illustrates how plucky and quick-witted our fellows are. A Tommy is worth two Fritzes.'

'Quite right,' Mr Oliphant said. 'We can all agree about that, at least. But, Fentiman, you have a better source of information than any of us. What's the plan for rolling up the Germans this year?'

'It's a tricky situation,' said Colonel Fentiman. 'My friend at Horse Guards says the War Council's been considering pulling out of France altogether.'

'Surely not!' said Mr Oliphant.

Fentiman nodded. 'The front stretches from the Swiss border to the Channel without a break, and the enemy everywhere is on higher ground. There's no German flank to be turned, and we've already seen that frontal attack is bloody and futile. Those casualty lists in the autumn have rattled the government. It's not at all clear what can or should be done.'

'But, sir,' said young Oliphant, 'the New Army will be ready this year. I know we were heavily outnumbered last autumn, but once we Kitchener chaps are ready, surely they'll send us to France to knock Jerry for six? Or what are we training for?'

David wondered the same thing, and looked at Colonel Fentiman with painful urgency. From the beginning they had all been afraid the war would be over before they got out there.

The colonel recognised their eagerness: if he had been their age, he'd have felt the same. 'You'll get your chance all right,' he said, with sympathy, 'but it might not be in France. From what I hear, they're thinking of opening up a new front, out in the east.'

Mrs Oliphant looked puzzled. 'In China, do you mean? I didn't know we were at war with the Chinese.'

'No, no, dear lady, not quite so far east as that,' said Fentiman, kindly. 'Against Turkey. You must be aware that the Turks have come in on Germany's side? It's unstabilised the whole region. We can't afford to lose the Levant. Greece. Romania.

Bulgaria's wavering. We need a show of strength to keep them on our side.'

'So what's the plan, sir?' Freddie Oliphant asked.

'To attack Turkey, take Constantinople, and open up the Black Sea route to supply ships. The Russians are up against it, and that will relieve the pressure on them – and, it's hoped, draw the Germans away from France.'

'If they take the bait,' said Mr Oliphant. 'I never heard that the Germans had any liking for the Turks. They might just decide to let them stew.'

'But the Danube, you see, is a back door into Germany. They'd be forced to defend it. At the very least,' he finished, with a faint shrug, 'opening up a new eastern front would divide their forces three ways.'

'It would divide ours too, sir,' David said. He had no wish to go to Constantinople and fight Turks. *That* was not what he had volunteered for. 'Surely our priority *must* be to drive the Germans out of France?'

'That's Sir John French's view,' the general said. 'But Lord Kitchener is an easterner by instinct. And Churchill and young Lloyd George are heart set on it, and between them they may carry the argument. Hard feller to argue against, Churchill. And the government wants to avoid another heavy butcher's bill in France. A naval action in the Dardanelles and a quick victory would give them good headlines in the press.'

David was shocked at this cynical reasoning. 'But, sir,' he protested, 'we *have* to knock the Germans out, after what they've done.'

'We can't just leave them holding half of

France,' young Oliphant agreed.

Mr Oliphant smiled. 'You see, Fentiman, how this cub of mine is eager to get to grips with the enemy. He and young Hunter were among the very first volunteers.'

'Well done!' said Colonel Fentiman. 'I like your pluck. But tell me, why aren't you in officer training? Fellows of your calibre ought to be aiming for a commission.'

David and Oliphant exchanged a glance. 'We did talk about it–'

'–but some of the chaps said ordinary soldiers would get out to France sooner, and if you wanted to have a bash at the enemy you should stay in the ranks.'

'I don't know if that's true or not,' David said, with sudden doubt.

'I shouldn't think so for a moment,' said the colonel. 'They're desperately short of junior officers, and educated men like you are just what's wanted. You'll get to France all right, but you ought to go as officers. It's your duty.'

'It wouldn't make us popular with our CO,' David said, with a smile. 'He hates losing his prime men, doesn't he, Jumbo?'

'Jumbo?' said Miss Fentiman, looking at him with interest.

'Oh, it's a nickname – some of the other fellows have started calling me that,' said Oliphant.

Mrs Oliphant turned her gaze on him. 'I don't understand why.'

'Well, Mother, Jumbo is what you call an elephant, isn't it?'

'But our name is Oliphant, not Elephant,' she

objected uncomprehendingly.

'Yes, Mother, I know,' said Oliphant, patiently. 'It's – um – a sort of joke, I suppose.'

'I don't see how it can be a joke, when our name is *not* Elephant. And I don't believe Elephant is a name at all. I never heard of anyone called it. Certainly not an English person.'

David caught Sophy's eyes across the table. They were glinting with laughter, and she was biting her lip, trying not to let it out. He felt a surge of love. He wanted to do something heroic so that he could lay the deed at her feet as a tribute. He wanted to ride into battle for her with her favour tied round his arm, her *chevalier sans peur et sans reproche.*

'Perhaps we ought to put our names forward when we get back,' David said to his friend.

'If you think so,' Oliphant said, glad to be rescued from his lexical difficulties. 'We can but try.'

'I'd love to see you in officer's uniform,' Sophy said. 'I think the Sam Browne looks so manly. Officers are much more attractive, aren't they, Penny?'

Miss Fentiman murmured something in agreement. But Sophy had been looking at David as she said it, and he had no attention for anything else. There was no more doubt in his mind. It was clearly his duty to put down for officer training.

Charles came whenever he had a few hours of leisure, and The Elms grew tolerably used to his presence. Even Ada managed to smile and call him 'Your Lordship' when she opened the door to him, instead of becoming scarlet, rigid and tongue-tied. The cautious consensus in the

35

servants' hall was that he was nicer than he first appeared, though to curious outsiders (there were plenty of those – back-door traffic had never been heavier), they pretended airily that he was like an old family friend now.

He came one afternoon and, as it wasn't raining for once, he, Diana and Sadie took Nailer for a walk in the woods. Sadie noticed that Nailer was a different dog in his presence, a meek, seemly, respectful individual, trotting along beside him with the occasional upward glance, as if eager to obey his every whim.

Diana noticed that Charles was a different person in Sadie's presence. The dog made a useful bridge between them: from dogs they went on to talk about horses, hunting, country matters in general. Diana had plenty of opportunity to observe him. Though he rarely smiled, there was about him, as he conversed with Sadie, an un-affected kindliness. With Diana he was still rather grave and stiff. Was it possible, she began to wonder, that his reserve was not *hauteur* as every-one supposed? Was it *possible* that he was merely shy? She had had shy suitors before, but had never supposed Lord Dene in all his glory could fall into that category. But if it were true, it put a different complexion on things altogether. She walked in silence, deep in thought.

They made a loop through the woods and, coming out onto the main road, Charles suggested they walk into the village. 'If you're not tired?' He gave Diana a solicitous look. 'It's so good to be out of doors,' he added. 'I seem to spend so much time at a desk, these days, with reports and records.'

It was Sadie who said, 'It must be awful for you. I hate being cooped up indoors.'

Where did Sadie's ease with him come from? Diana wondered. Why didn't *she* find him overwhelming? When Diana sat with him in the morning-room he was so tall and broad, so very much *there*, that he seemed to suck all the oxygen from the room. She was suffocatingly aware of his size and presence – and of the silences that often fell between them. It was better out of doors: the open air suited him. And she liked to have her hand on his arm and have people look at them admiringly as they went by.

He and Sadie were talking now about the state of agriculture, and what Charles would like to do about it when he took up his seat in the Lords one day. Sadie was striding along in her usual way, swishing at the verges with a stick she had somehow managed to pick up. Diana thought about what she would be able to do for Sadie when she was Lady Dene – bringing her out properly, teaching her how to behave; the right clothes, meeting the right people. She could make sure Sadie made a good marriage. She would have her to stay with them as often as possible. It was a cheering thought. She had not previously considered the power to help others that would come with her title.

As she watched Charles talking to Sadie, marrying him seemed less daunting. Certainly he did not smile and joke and tease in the easy way her other suitors had done, but she could imagine him at the other side of the breakfast table, politely pouring her coffee and telling her what he had planned for the day. Not fun but dignity was what she could expect from this union. She lifted her chin a little, and smiled graciously as Hicks, their postman, touched his cap to them. And across the road Alicia Harding and Lizzie Drake stared enviously. They would come to call later, she knew, to tell Diana again how lucky she was. It was all quite gratifying.

Nailer left them, in his sudden way, disappearing under a hedge. 'He says he has important business,' Sadie explained.

'I had a terrier a bit like him when I was a boy,' Charles said.

'What was his name?' Sadie asked.

'Rags. He was a fiery little fellow.'

'Was he always getting into fights?'

'He used to fight with my sister's French poodle.'

'Well, one can understand that,' said Sadie. 'There's such a thing as self-respect.' Charles made no response to this. Sadie wished silently for John Courcy, who would have picked up the comment and made fun with it. Charles was nice, she thought, but rather hard work. She tried a new tack. 'Have you had any news, about going to France? Diana said you thought it might be in January, but here we are, halfway through.'

'We did think that,' Charles agreed. 'Now they're saying it might be February. But we know nothing for sure. I'm afraid we survive on rumour and hope.'

'You must be anxious to be going,' Sadie said.

'The men are itching to be off,' Charles said. 'They're tired of training. They feel they're absolutely ready and can't understand the delays.'

'And are they ready?' Diana asked.

'The old hands are. But we were nowhere near full strength when the war broke out, and about a fifth of our men are new volunteers who've only been with us a few weeks. We've been knocking them into shape as fast as we can.' He paused as if in doubt. 'However,' he went on more surely, 'we'll manage all right, once we're out there. They're all splendid fellows.'

'When do you think it will be over?' Diana asked. 'The war, I mean.'

'It was supposed to be over by Christmas,' Sadie put in. 'Now I hear people say next Christmas.'

'Well,' Charles said, 'even once we've beaten them, mopping up will take time. The spring of 1916, I should say, at the earliest.'

Diana said, 'That seems so far away.'

'Yes,' he said. Sadie dropped behind to look at something in the hedge, and he added in a low voice, 'It was the most wretched luck, this war coming just when I'd finally met you. I wish...' He didn't seem to have the words to finish that.

Diana felt a little thrill of warmth. He so rarely referred to his feelings for her. 'But,' she said at last, 'we will be married before then?'

He looked down at her. 'Of course we will. We talked about June, didn't we?' He hesitated. 'For myself, I'd like to marry you at once. A lot of our fellows have had a register-office wedding, to be sure of fitting it in before we go abroad.'

Diana was dismayed. 'Oh, I don't think I'd like that. Wouldn't it seem, well, rather make-do?'

If he was disappointed, he hid it. 'Oh, quite,' he

said. 'Besides, my mother would never countenance it. You shall have a proper wedding.' He added awkwardly, 'I'd like you always to have everything you want.'

Sadie rejoined them, so there was no opportunity for Diana to pursue this happy thought. 'It's starting to rain,' Sadie said, holding out her hand. A large drop fell obediently onto it. 'It'll be cats and dogs in a minute. Good job you brought a brolly.'

'It's not really big enough for three,' Diana said, with a frown. Charles would be sure to insist the two girls used it, and she didn't want to walk arm in arm with Sadie. She could do that any time. 'We'd better take shelter.'

Charles glanced around. Sadie was disappointed to see his eye pass over the Windmill Café. It alighted instead on Evanton's photographic studio next door.

'Would you come and have your photograph taken with me?' he asked Diana. 'I'd love to have one to keep in my pocket book.'

Diana was pleased and touched. 'I'd like that too,' she said.

'I think I'll go home, then,' Sadie said.

'You'll get wet,' Diana said reprovingly.

'I don't mind,' said Sadie. 'Anyway, my hat's jolly strong. And there are trees nearly all the way.' And, with a smile to Charles, she was away.

The rain suddenly arrived. Diana and Charles ducked into Evanton's, where two soldiers with their female friends were about the same errand. As soon as they saw an officer they jumped out of the way and effaced themselves, begging him to take their turn. Mr Evanton reinforced the request, gesturing Diana, with a bow, towards a chair. After a short discussion, he changed the backdrop to a Tuscan landscape, arranged a red velvet armchair and a parlour palm in a pot, and invited Charles to sit while Diana stood with her left hand, gloveless, on his shoulder, showing the ring.

Charles did not like to sit while a lady stood, but Evanton explained that as he was so much taller than Miss Hunter, this would make a better composition.

The photograph was taken, and Charles ordered two at three inches by two (what Evanton called 'wallet-sized') – one each for himself and Diana; and two twelve-by-eights, one for each of the sets of parents. He paid for them in advance and asked for them to be delivered to Miss Hunter when they were ready, 'as I'm not sure where I shall be'.

'Oh, quite, sir,' Evanton agreed, this being not an unusual set of circumstances in his world.

But the words struck Diana, and she was silent, contemplating the sobering truth of them. Just for a moment she wondered if it wouldn't have been better to marry quickly at a register office after all.

CHAPTER THREE

Ada had a cold, and when she got a cold she always got ear-ache. 'I've always been subject to ears,' she said miserably. 'Ever since I was a child.'

'Nasty things, ears,' Cook said, as she packed the offending orifices with cotton wool soaked in warmed oil of cloves, her patent remedy. 'You don't want to take chances with 'em.'

Emily, leaning her elbows on the table and watching the process with interest, said, 'There was a girl back home died of an earwig in her ear.'

'Don't tell such stories!' Cook reproved her.

Emily looked hurt. ''Tis true! An earwig got in her ear while she was asleep, and it ate its way right into her brain, and she went mad and dashed her head against a wall and killed herself.'

'What's she saying?' asked Ada.

'Nothing. Go and wash up those breakfast things, Emily,' Cook said sternly. 'No-one's interested in your silly tales.'

Emily dragged herself slowly upright, then was galvanised by the sound of a bell. 'Back door!' she cried, and was off.

'That girl!' said Cook.

The bell sounded again. Cook looked at the board. 'Front door, now.' Ada started to rise. 'You stay put. Keep out of the draught. Let Ethel go.'

'She's upstairs. I'll do it,' said Ada, and went.

She opened the front door to a thin, elderly man carrying a parcel done up with brown paper and string. He had a clerical collar peeping out from the neck of his overcoat. He lifted his hat politely and offered his card. 'May I speak with your mistress?' he said, trying not to stare at the cotton wool.

Collecting for something, Ada thought. But you couldn't leave a man of the cloth standing outside. She admitted him to the hall, and went to the morning-room where Beattie was writing letters. Newly deaf, she had no idea how loudly she was speaking, so Ethel, coming downstairs, quite clearly heard her say, 'The Reverend Mr Treadgold asking to see you, madam.'

Ethel's foot froze in mid-air, and she backed up a few steps until she was hidden by the turn. *What was he doing here?*

In the morning-room, Beattie received the visitor patiently, suspecting, like Ada, that he was collecting for something – though his card said he was from Holy Trinity, Gosford, so he was casting his net rather wide. Still, Gosford was a small place, and perhaps his local geese had all been plucked out.

'How can I help you?' she asked, but without asking him to sit down. She managed not to stare at the parcel he was clutching.

'Are you the lady of the house? I beg your pardon, but I do not know your name,' Mr Treadgold said.

Beattie chilled a fraction. He looked the image

43

of a clergyman – lean of face, silver hair, gold-rimmed pince-nez, coat collar a little worn, boots old but well kept – but that did not prove his *bona fides*. 'I am Mrs Hunter,' she said.

He waved a hand, embarrassed. 'You must think it very odd of me to call in this way. I do beg your pardon, but it is a Christian mission, of that I do assure you. I am looking for a Miss Lusby, a Miss Ethel Lusby, and I was informed that she resided at this address.'

Oh, Lord, now what's she done? Beattie thought. 'She is a housemaid here,' she told him, and saw enlightenment creep over his face. 'Perhaps you had better sit down, Mr Treadgold, and tell me what it is you want.'

Five minutes later she rang the bell and, when Ada answered, told her to send Ethel in. There seemed a longish delay, as though Ethel could not be found, but eventually the door opened and the maid came in, her chin defiant and her eyes apprehensive.

'Ethel, this gentleman is the Reverend Mr Tread-gold from Gosford. He wants to talk to you,' Beattie said, in gentle tone.

Ethel said nothing. Treadgold rose and stepped towards her. 'I don't suppose you remember me,' he said. 'You must have been a small child when I last spoke to you, though I have seen you passing once or twice when you've come to the village to visit your mother.' Ethel's gaze sharpened and her lips tightened, but she said nothing. *Least said, soonest mended* was her motto. 'I'm afraid I have some very sad news for you, my child,' Treadgold went on. 'Your mother has passed away. I'm sure

44

you know she had been ill for quite a long time, so you should look upon this as a blessed release.'

Ethel blinked, but all she said, turning her head slightly towards Beattie, was, 'Will that be all, madam?'

Beattie looked at her, puzzled. 'Do you understand what the gentleman said?'

'Yes, madam.'

'I understood that her neighbour, Mrs Clark, had sent a note to you, informing you,' Treadgold pursued, 'but perhaps it went astray. I have one or two things I have been holding for you, thinking you would be coming to collect them, but when you did not... Things belonging to your mother.' He gestured towards the parcel, on the table by the sofa.

Ethel said nothing, and her eyes were fixed straight ahead.

Treadgold examined her doubtfully. Reactions to this news – which he had often had to impart in the course of his duties – had been many and varied, but this was the oddest. A thought occurred to him. 'She was buried on the parish, my dear, there being no money to pay for a funeral, but it was very reverently conducted – I undertook the ceremony myself – and the plot is in a quiet part of the churchyard, over by the old mulberry tree. There is no stone, of course, but any time you wish to visit, I or the sexton can show you where it is. There will be – ahem – no question of recovering the expense from you, I assure you.'

Still nothing from Ethel. Treadgold smiled apologetically at Beattie. 'Perhaps I had better take my leave. No, no, dear lady, don't trouble to ring –

45

I can see myself out. Good day to you – and my apologies again for disturbing you.'

Ethel seemed on the verge of following him, but Beattie called her back. Now the girl merely looked sulky at being detained, but Beattie tried to be kind. 'I'm sorry to hear this, Ethel. I had no idea your mother lived in Gosford. You never mentioned her.'

'She wasn't my mother!' Ethel said fiercely. 'She was–'The ferocity died away. 'Just the person who brought me up.'

'Well,' said Beattie, 'that's the same thing, really, isn't it?'

Ethel's look asserted it wasn't, by a long chalk, but she said nothing. Beattie gave up. 'Very well,' she said. 'You may go. And, again, I'm very sorry.' Ethel turned away. 'Take your parcel,' Beattie reminded her.

'I don't want it,' Ethel said, without turning.

Beattie's lips tightened. 'Take it, please,' she said, in the voice maids didn't disobey.

Ethel picked it up, as though it might bite, and left the room.

Outside, she found she was trembling. She looked at the parcel, and wanted to fling it from her, like something loathsome. But, in the end, curiosity won, and she carried it up to the room she shared with Ada. Sitting on her bed, she untied the string and unwrapped the paper. Inside was a cardboard box. And inside that... She picked out the crumpled newspaper that had been used to pack the items, and drew out the china shepherd that had stood on Ma's mantelpiece. He had a crack down his face and no nose and a chip off his base. Obviously one of a pair, he had lost his shepherdess back in the mists of time – perhaps before Ma had even acquired him. He was grubby, too, from a thousand smoky fires. Vicar could have saved himself the bother, she thought, bringing the mouldy old thing all this way.

Second item: Ma's tea caddy, a square black tin with Union Jacks on the sides and a picture of Queen Victoria on the lid, with the words 'Golden Jubilee' above and the dates below. She opened it. It smelt of tea, but there was none in there. That old thief Mrs Clark must have emptied it. Wonder she didn't take the tin as well. Maybe she'd thought Ethel would miss it – some hopes!

Third item: a little brown milk jug. It was so familiar to Ethel that tears actually pricked her eyes. It had stood in the coolest place in the scullery and always had a round muslin cover weighted with little blue beads to keep the flies out. When Ethel was tiny she had sometimes put the muslin circle on her head and pretended it was a veil, or a hat, or a crown. In a life starved of beauty, she had thought the blue beads the loveliest thing she had ever seen, and imagined them threaded into a necklace.

She rummaged among the newspapers, but the cover was not there.

Ethel stared at the three objects, Ma's total accumulated riches. She felt tears prickling again and *would not* cry them, not for that woman who had never said a kind word to her in all her life. Three pieces of rubbish. That was all there was to show that Annie Lusby had ever lived.

No, wait. She threw out all the rest of the crumpled newspaper, and there *was* something else, lying flat on the bottom underneath it. Three envelopes, tied up with a thin piece of string. She stared at them as though they were a snake that might strike. Turning her head sideways, she could see the postmark. Northampton. And the handwriting clumsy and untutored. Addressed to Annie Lusby, 2 Deedes Row, Gosford. She knew who they were from. There was no-one in the world who would write to Annie Lusby except her daughter Edie, no-one in the world who knew she existed, apart from Edie and Ethel.

She finally got up the courage to pick up the bundle, and held it in her lap, staring at it. Three letters, only three. But inside – what? Why had Annie kept them? Did they tell something important, or had she just forgotten to throw them out? At least, Ethel thought, there would be an address in there, Edie's address. A way to trace her. And ask her...

She shook herself. She didn't want what was in these envelopes. She opened the top drawer of her chest and, with a repelling movement, thrust them inside, under the clothes, and slammed it shut. She'd get rid of them later, when there wasn't any-one to see and ask questions. *You're dead, Annie,* she addressed the shade of the milk jug. *You can't do anything to me now.*

She heard thumping feet on the stairs, and Emily appeared in the doorway, panting. 'Whatever are you doing up here? Cook sent me. She wants you right away.'

'All right,' said Ethel.

Emily's eyes went to the objects on the bed, and her face lit. 'Oh, would you look at the darling little man! Isn't he a treasure! Where'd you get it? I never saw it before.'

Ethel didn't want any questions. She picked up the shepherd. 'D'you want it? You can have it, if you like.'

Emily looked suspicious. 'What's the trick?'

'No trick. I'm trying to be nice, that's all.'

'D'you mean it? I can have it?' Emily took it flinchingly, and when it didn't explode or bite or cut her, her thin face curved into a smile. '*Thank* you!' she breathed. She stroked the damaged china face. 'Oh, isn't he a love! The handsome prince.'

'It's not a prince, it's a shepherd,' Ethel said impatiently. Emily was going daft again.

'He's a prince,' Emily insisted dreamily. 'He looks exactly like – somebody. He's my prince and he'll come on his white horse and take me away.'

'*Someone*'ll come and take you away, that's for sure,' Ethel said, shoving her out of the way as she went out. 'And it'll be in a van.'

Downstairs, Cook gave Ethel a suspicious look as she came in. 'What was you sent for to the morning-room? Are you in trouble?'

Ethel didn't answer. 'Emily said you wanted me, urgent.'

'I want you to do the bread and butter.' Ethel moved towards the table. 'Well?' Cook insisted.

'Well what?'

'There was some clergyman came to see the missus, and you was sent for. Had a parcel when he arrived and no parcel when he left. What was in it?'

Emily chirped up. 'Oh, there was a lovely little–' Ethel pinched her, hard, and the sentence ended in a small squeak.

'It was just some things,' Ethel said, seeing some answer had to be given. 'An old woman died that lived in Gosford. She left me some things, and Vicar brought 'em. That's all.'

'Who do you know in Gosford?' Cook demanded. 'What old woman?'

'Nobody you knew.'

'Don't you be pert with me,' Cook said. 'You're up to something. I know that look.'

Ethel shrugged. 'A person's got a right to have things, if a person leaves 'em to her. How many slices you want?'

'Emily!' Cook said sternly. 'What was in that parcel?'

Emily squirmed, looking sidelong at Ethel. 'Ah, no, don't ask me! Sure, I don't want to say, and she'll pinch me again.' Cook fixed her with a gimlet eye, and she said, ''Twas a little china man, ever so lovely – and Ethel give him to me, I swear to God she did. I never took him. And there was a little jug. That's all I saw, honest.'

Cook shook her head, looked at Ethel, head bent over the loaf and knife, and gave it up. 'If I find you're in trouble and haven't told me...' she said warningly. 'No need to cut so thin, it's only our lunch. Emily, get the jam out, and lay the table. Ada, fetch the cake tin.' There wasn't time to investigate now – Munt would be in any minute and the missus had two ladies coming for

50

luncheon. She'd have a go at Emily later. You could always make Emily talk. That girl's tongue had wheels both ends.

Sadie was woken on her birthday by Ada with a smile and a tray. Sadie sat up, and saw there was a cup of tea and a plate bearing a slice of bread-and-butter.

'Oh, Ada!' she said, moved. 'I've never had tea in bed before. It's just like you read about at country-house weekends.'

'Just this once. It's a special day,' Ada said. 'Happy birthday, Miss Sadie. Seventeen – you're a young lady now.'

So John Courcy had also said. 'I don't feel any different,' she said

'Give it time,' said Ada, going out.

She passed Diana in the doorway. 'What's going on?' Diana said. 'I heard voices.' Her front hair was in rags and she was wearing her most unglamorous but warm dressing-gown, inherited from David – yet still, Sadie noted wistfully, she looked beautiful. 'What's that?' Diana went on, staring at the tray. 'Tea in bed?'

'Because it's my birthday,' Sadie explained.

'Birthday! I'd forgotten. Wait a moment,' Diana said, and whisked away. She was soon back, with a small, tissue-wrapped object in her hand. 'For you,' she said. She climbed up onto Sadie's bed and tucked her feet under her. 'Goodness, it's cold in here. I wish Father would let us have fires in the bedrooms. When I'm married, I'm going to have a fire in my bedroom all the time.'

'Oh, so grand!' Sadie teased. There wasn't even

a fireplace in her room, which was the smallest of the bedrooms. 'I suppose you'll have tea in bed every day as well.'

'That's what's done in great houses,' Diana said loftily. 'They always have tea and bread-and-butter. And then their maids run their baths. Aren't you going to open it?'

Sadie put down the cup from which she had been sipping appreciatively, and turned her attention to the present. She unwrapped it slowly, wanting to make it last, a habit that always annoyed Diana.

'I saw it in the window of Tinnington's last week, and thought it was just right for you,' Diana said. She made an exasperated noise. 'Open it, open it!'

It was a small brooch made of mother-of-pearl, in the shape of a rose. 'Oh, it's lovely!' Sadie cried. 'Thank you so much. You *are* kind.'

'It's about time you had some jewellery,' Diana said, absently eating Sadie's bread-and-butter. 'You're not a child any more now, you know. You'll have to start dressing properly and behaving like a lady.' She shivered. 'I'm going back to my room. It's so cold in here.' She took the other half-slice with her, and left.

Sadie drank the tea, putting the brooch on the tray so she could admire it. It was funny that when Ada had said she was a young lady, it had sounded like a treat, but when Diana had said it, it had sounded like a threat. And then she reflected that it was interesting how those two words, which were opposites, were the same except for the letter *h*.

Birthdays were not made a great deal of in the Hunter household, but there were presents for Sadie at breakfast: a new pair of riding breeches from her parents, and a book, jointly from Bobby, William and Peter, called *The Horse in Sickness and Health*. And beside her plate were cards from the Carburys in Kildare, the Palfreys, Aunt Laura, and Cousin Beth. She noted with a little pang that David had not sent one. She'd thought he might have, as he was not at home. Perhaps something might come in the second delivery.

But whatever anyone might have intended, Sadie's birthday was completely overshadowed by the newspapers, which had arrived since Ada brought her the cup of tea, and which were full of the awful events of the night before. Two German airships had crept silently across the North Sea under cover of darkness and dropped bombs on the sleeping towns of Great Yarmouth, Shering-ham and King's Lynn, and their surrounding villages. At least four people had been killed, with many more injured, and thousands of pounds' worth of damage had been done.

The papers enjoyed in the kitchen were full of sensational reports, awful photographs of blasted houses, and spine-chilling prognostications of horrors to come. Cook was completely undone. Ever since the Germans had shelled Scarborough and other east-coast towns on the 16th of December, she had been in fear of an invasion. But this was in some ways worse. At least you could have a go at an invader, even if it was hopeless – you could go down fighting. But what could you do about bombs dropped on you from the air? Especially in the dead of night. The idea of being killed in your sleep by an enemy you'd never even seen was horripilating.

'You can't hear 'em coming,' she said, quivering over the *Daily Mail*. "Silent death", that's what they call it here.'

'Not so silent when they explodes,' said Munt, who had called in for a cup of tea to take to his shed. He'd come to work early to get away from home, where his wife was equally overthrown by the news, only to find the same scene here. 'Make a bloody big noise then, wouldn't they, when they're a-blowing of you to bits?'

'It's too late then, isn't it?' Cook countered. 'If you could hear the Zeppelins coming you could run away. Now we'll all be killed in our beds! Why don't they do something about it? They have to cross the sea, don't they? Why don't the navy shoot them down?'

'Toast's burning,' Ethel said, coming in with the coffee pot to refill.

Cook was still glued to the newspaper, and it was Ada who said, 'Emily! Stop daydreaming and mind that toast! You'll have to scrape that for us and put some more on for the dining-room.'

'Weren't there supposed to be mushrooms?' Ethel said, peering at the stove.

Cook roused herself at last from the horrors. 'Oh, Lor'! I forgot. Quick, pass me that saucepan. I'll have to do 'em unpeeled. They taste better that way,' she comforted herself.

Later, when their own breakfast had been eaten, Ethel, succumbing to the relentless topic over a second cup of tea, said, 'I can't see why they want to bomb Sheringham and Great Yarmouth anyway. They're just seaside places, aren't they?'

'To strike terror into our hearts, my girl, that's why,' said Cook.

'They probably got blown off course,' said Ada. 'That's what the butcher's boy said. Probably meant to bomb the docks at Hull and lost their way in the dark.'

'But that only makes it worse,' Emily said. 'If they can't even hit the things they want to hit, none of us is safe.'

Henry, the boot-boy, had arrived, and joined in eagerly: 'They don't want us to be safe,' he said. 'My dad says they're going to bomb the 'ole country, kill everybody, near as they can, so they can walk in and take over. It's cheaper than fighting with the army, my dad says. Them Zepps can fly so high nobody can't shoot 'em down, and they'll just come night after night a-bombing of us until we're all dead.'

Emily gave a little shriek, and Cook, though she blanched at the thought, felt he had gone too far. 'Never mind what your dad says, just get started on last night's knives and don't talk so much. Emily, clear the table.'

Mrs Chaplin, the charwoman, came in that day, and brought more information from her son, who was the blacksmith on Rustington Road. 'My Jack says they've known this was coming for ages. Ever since the New Year. They say Mr Churchill reckons there'll be a big raid on the Kaiser's birthday, a hundred Zeppelins coming to bomb London.'

'And when might that be?' Ada asked.

'Twenty-seventh o' January,' said Mrs Chaplin. 'Jack says rich people in London are sending their children away to be safe.'

'Safe where?' Cook said. 'Nowhere's safe from things that can fly like that.'

'How do they see where to go in the dark?' Emily asked.

'From the lights down below,' said Mrs Chaplin, their new expert. 'Street lamps and people's houses and suchlike. When you're up in the sky and everything's dark, the lights stand out like anything.'

'*I* heard,' said Henry, lingering by the scullery door, 'they got German spies in England what signal the Zepps with their car headlights to show 'em where to bomb.'

'My Jack heard that, too,' said Mrs Chaplin.

Henry nodded portentously. 'Anyone you see out in a car at night, he could be a German spy, signalling the Zepps to come. An' I heard there's people live by the seaside what flashes their lights on and off at night so's the Zepps know where the coastline is. There's spies everywhere,' he concluded, round-eyed.

'My Jack says the same. He says we all gotter be on our guard. But it comes to something when you're not safe in your own home,' Mrs Chaplin said indignantly. 'The guv'ment oughter do something about it.'

CHAPTER FOUR

Mrs Fitzgerald refused coffee. 'No, no, thank you, my dear. I have a great deal to do this morning.' She did sit down, however, casting a sharp look around the morning-room as if to discover what Beattie had been doing before her arrival. Beattie folded her hands and tried not to look guilty. 'I've come to speak to you about the Zeppelins,' Mrs Fitzgerald went on. 'The rector feels very strongly that, should the invaders come here, we must have a means of warning our people to take shelter. As you know, the bells of All Hallows have been silenced for the duration of the war. But the rector feels that an exception should be made for a tocsin.'

'A toxin?' Beattie said vaguely, thinking of poisons.

'The tenor and treble rung together as a warning. Now, of course, our ringers have volunteered for the army,' Mrs Fitzgerald said. They had gone all together to join as 'Pals', which was the real reason the rector had silenced the peal – making a virtue of necessity. 'We have old Mr Fields, our reserve ringer, but he's getting rather frail, and it would take him some time to get out his bicycle and ride to the church. So I'm hoping to recruit a number of young ringers, prepared to take on the duty, should the worst happen.'

'Oh, Mother, please, can I?' It was William,

lingering at the door in his Scout uniform, on his way to the Saturday meeting.

'You don't know how to ring a bell,' Beattie said, frowning at him for eavesdropping – though the door was open and he had probably come to say goodbye.

'Fields will train the new ringers,' Mrs Fitzgerald said. 'There will be no great skill required: simply to pull the rope without hurting themselves or damaging the bell.'

'Then *please* can I?' William begged. 'You know us Scouts are supposed to make ourselves useful and help the war effort.' He saw himself sleeping in the bell-chamber every night; keeping watch from the top of the tower; spotting the looming menace and rushing down to save the village by his vigorous ringing. In an ambitious extension he saw himself having a medal pinned on him by the King. *Well done, my boy, you're an example to us all*, said His Majesty. YOUTHFUL HERO SAVES HUNDREDS was the headline in the newspaper the next day...

'I'm afraid you won't do as a ringer,' said Mrs Fitzgerald, shattering the dream. 'Suppose a Zeppelin came when you were at school? You would not be able to reach the church in time.'

'I thought the Zeppelins came by night,' said Beattie.

'So far they have, but we have no idea how they may operate in the future. The essence of the tocsin ringers is that they must be close to the church at all times. So I have come to ask you if I may have your boot-boy, Henry. He seems to be a strong enough lad, and working here and living

58

in Lychgate Close, he will be always on hand.'

'You can ask him, of course,' Beattie said, aware of a faint groan of disappointment from the doorway, 'but I'm not sure that you'll find him very reliable.'

'We can knock him into shape,' said Mrs Fitzgerald, with a certain relish. 'I shall, of course, recruit more than two ringers, to allow for absences. Probably six or eight, to be on the safe side.'

'Yes, well,' said Beattie, 'let's hope the necessity never arrives.'

'Indeed,' said Mrs Fitzgerald, rising to leave, 'but one must be prepared – is that not the Scouting motto, William?' She ruffled his hair kindly as she passed, and William bore it very well, considering the time he had just spent slicking it down with water in an attempt to look like Wallace Reid.

Henry enjoyed a brief moment of celebrity in the kitchen, after his first visit to the bell-tower to be instructed by Mr Fields. Fields was a familiar figure around Northcote. He was not only a ringer and former sexton but, as a veteran of the Crimean and Sudan campaigns, with medals to prove it, he had become latterly a self-proclaimed expert on war. His comforting contention was that the British soldier could not be beaten, and since the current conflict had broken out, he had been stood many a pint of beer by those who wanted reassurance.

'He took us all over the tower,' Henry said. 'The ringing-chamber first, but then up to see the bells, an' all. Gor! That wasn't half good! You have to climb up this ladder, and it's all dark and creepy, like in Frankenstein at the pictures. And the bells are so big and kind of creepy too, like they was looking at you.'

'Daft,' said Ethel, scornfully.

'No, but it was sort of interesting,' Henry protested. 'Mr Fields told us a lot about them. They've all got names. The big one's called Big Tom, and the other one we'll have to ring is Little Penn. They're the lowest and the highest, so you'll hear 'em better. And there's stuff carved on 'em, like mottoes.'

He struggled to remember the mottoes, wanting to make the most of his audience while he had it, but the language was out of his usual experience so it had not stuck. Munt, who had been a ringer in his time, could have told him that the great tenor, which was rung when people died, was inscribed around the soundbow, *Unto the Church +* *I do You call + Death to the Grave + will summon All*; and the treble was inscribed *Least not last yet may I winne + I as trebell doe beginne*. But Munt did not trouble himself to educate fools.

'And then he give us a demonstration, Mr Fields. Down in the ringing-chamber. Gor, they don't half make a noise, them bells, when you're close up! He just rung the treble a bit, to show us. We'll have proper lessons next time.'

'You must be really strong, to pull one of those great big things,' Emily said.

Henry puffed out his non-existent chest. 'Oh, I'm stronger'n what I look,' he said; and then, catching Munt's eye, deflated a little and said, 'You don't really have to be strong. Mr Fields says it's just a knack. The wheel does all the work.'

'A bit different from you, then, ain't it?' said Munt, standing up. 'Well, I got things to do, even if the rest of you haven't.' And he stumped off down the garden.

In fact, he didn't really have a lot to do. January and February were the quiet months. It was a time for fumigating the greenhouse, washing pots, sharpening spades and oiling shears. It was a time for sorting through the packets of seeds he had collected, and examining the apple stores and potato clamps to throw out any that had turned. Most of all, it was a time for sitting in his shed, peacefully planning his growing year. He had a little stove in there which he lit in this part of winter, and with his battered old chair and his pipe going, he was cosy and comfortable and as near to perfect happiness as a man of his misanthropy could hope to be. He had a perfectly good home where he could have sat when he wasn't working, but he and his wife had been married a long time on the understanding that they would keep out of each other's way as much as humanly possible.

It was the one time of year when he not only tolerated but even welcomed Nailer. The dog always knew when the stove was lit and headed unerringly for the warmest, fuggiest place on the premises. There was no rug on the floor of the shed, just bare, splintery floorboards, but it was funny how often there was a bit of old sack covering the space in front of the stove when Nailer arrived, where he could settle down, curled like a cat, and dream, eyebrows twitching, of the rat-chasing, bitch-frolicking days of summer.

It was here Sadie found them on Saturday afternoon. After her birthday the weather had turned, and there had been a heavy snowfall, the remnants of which were still lingering along the line of walls and hedges, but since then it had been dry, though very cold. Cold and dry, she thought, was preferable to mild and wet when it came to horses.

Mum nodded to her, and removed the pipe from his mouth to point with the stem to an upturned orange box in the corner. She pulled it forward a little and sat down. Even though she was only just seventeen, she had always been treated with a certain amount of formality by servants, and anyone else would have stood up when she came in. But Munt lived in his own world, where he ruled alone, and he truckled to no man. And here in his shed, especially, he was lord and she was supplicant. She took the orange box and, rightly, felt it an honour.

Nailer got up, though, and came to her, pausing on the way to bow at the front, arch his back and yawn hugely in greeting, before proffering his head for her to scratch. Munt puffed his pipe in silence. If she had something to say, she would say it. It wasn't for him to prompt her.

At last she said, 'Do you really think the Zeppelins will come here?'

'No knowing,' he replied, through the pipe.

'But there's nothing here of – what do they call it? – strategic importance. And it's not on the way to anywhere. They'd have to get awfully lost to get this far.'

He removed the pipe to say, 'In a war, the only thing you know is that you don't know nothing.'

She gave him a troubled smile. 'That's not very comforting.'

'Weren't meant to be.'

'We had a visit from Mr Begum, about air raids – what to do if the alarm sounded,' she went on, after a pause. Tom Begum was the church warden. 'He said everyone should go down into the cellar for safety. That would mean you as well,' she added. His eyes gleamed sardonically, and he didn't need to say, 'Catch me!' for her to know he was thinking it. 'I suppose it's sensible,' she sighed, 'but I hate the idea of it. Suppose a bomb fell on the house and it collapsed and you were trapped down in the cellar? You might suffocate, or starve to death. They might never be able to get you out. I'd sooner be outside, where at least you could see them coming. If I have to die, I think I'd prefer to die out in the open.'

He nodded. He'd be the same. Better to run than be cornered.

'But I suppose I'd have to go down there, if Mother and Father said so.' She was thoughtful a moment, then smiled. 'Mr Begum was obviously sent by the rector – or, at least, by Mrs Fitzgerald – but the funny thing was we had another visit about the air raids, from Mr Miles, and Mrs Fitzgerald obviously didn't know anything about that.'

Albert Miles had been Northcote's police constable until forced to retire after losing his leg to a train one night when pursuing a poacher, who ran down the track in a confused desire to foil his scent. He found no longer being the constable difficult to accept, and liked to take an active part in the village's official life, sometimes to the annoyance of the current incumbents.

'What'd he want, then?' Munt asked, in a rare burst of encouragement.

'The same as Mr Begum – what to do in an air raid. But he had lots more to say, what to take down into the cellar with us, having emergency supplies kept ready at all times, and so on. He said he was our air-raid warden, and he had an armband round his sleeve, but do you know?' She lowered her voice. 'I don't think he was official at all. I think he just appointed himself.'

'Wouldn't be surprised,' Munt said.

'It's strange, this war,' Sadie went on thoughtfully. 'I mean, all the other wars, the soldiers have gone off abroad and eventually come back victorious. It was never anything to do with *us* – you know, us at home. But now there's air raids, and people coming round with armbands, and the Belgian refugees, and–'

'–and you and your 'orses,' Munt finished for her. 'Slip of a girl like you, training army 'orses 'stead of the sojers doing it, and that Mrs Cuthbert an' all. And your brother joining up.'

Sadie nodded, glad he had got the point. 'It's sort of an amateur's war, isn't it? Everybody's war.'

He looked at her for a long time. 'It'll get professional soon enough,' he said. 'The Jerries'll see to that. You enjoy it while it lasts.'

'What do you mean?' she asked, but he would not expand.

At last he said, 'You got your new 'orses, then. What're they like?'

'Just eight this time, but we've got the two left

over from the last batch. They came from India, so we're told. We were shocked when they arrived, they were so thin. The poor things had been seasick, I expect. But they're settling down, and we're feeding them up. People say the army will be moving in spring, so if that's the end of March, we might have them ready by then.'

There was a silence. Nailer's head had grown heavy in her hands. Munt examined his pipe, prodded the contents, then knocked out the dottle into the lid from a tin of tree grease that served him as an ashtray, and started to refill it. Sadie took this, correctly, as a sign of dismissal. She let Nailer go and stood up.

'One thing Mr Miles said – there should be someone in every household who knows about first aid. I was thinking it would be a good thing if I learned it. Diana's going to be married soon, and Cook and the rest are too busy. I thought I'd find out where there's a class.'

Munt gave a grunt that she could take as approval, if she was so minded. She turned and went. Nailer stood for an agonised moment, torn between following her and frowsting by the fire. But his stomach told him it was nowhere near teatime, and frowsting won hands-down.

When Lady Wroughton wanted to speak to someone, she did not go to see them, she sent for them. Beattie received the note in the spirit in which it was meant, as a summons, and duly presented herself, though it was not convenient. She had linen to check and a meeting at Mrs Oliver's of the Soldiers' Relatives' Hardship Fund committee, and it was a half-hour walk each way. But at least it was dry.

The door was opened to her by a very young footman, who seemed no more than fifteen and very nervous. She remembered Edward talking about his clients complaining that the war was sucking footmen into its maw and that replacements were becoming harder to find. She supposed this must be a new fellow: it might be his very first job. She guessed how scared he must be and threw him a reassuring smile, but it produced no effect other than a spasmodic bobbing of his Adam's apple.

She was led this time to a different part of the house from the Red Saloon and State Dining-room, which they had seen at Christmas. She was shown at last into a sitting-room, which was not even twice as large as the drawing-room back home, and was furnished with chintz-covered sofas and chairs and a multitude of little tables, footstools and other comforts. Every surface was cluttered with ornaments and framed photographs, and behind the array on the mantelpiece were dozens of cards of invitation. There was a good fire, and Lady Wroughton was sitting on a sofa sideways on to it, with a writing-case on her knee and what looked like a heap of correspondence beside her.

She stood when Beattie came in, setting the writing-case aside, but did not advance or offer her hand. She was wearing a tailored coat and skirt, with a lace jabot and multiple layers of pearls at her neck, pearls at her ears, and her hair dressed as only a superior lady's maid could do it. Beattie did her best not to feel intimidated. The grim, unsmiling face did little to assure her that the countess viewed her as an equal partner in the business of uniting two lovers.

'How kind of you to come,' said Lady Wroughton, perfunctorily. 'Please sit down.' She glanced towards the door, which the callow footman was still holding open, and a maid came through it with a tray. The countess gestured furiously with her eyes, and the maid threw an equally stern look at the footman, who at last fathomed his duty and hurried forward to place one of the little tables before the countess, onto which the maid lowered the tray. Beattie smelt coffee, and there was a plate of little round yellow cakes dotted with currants. She felt less penitent, but still waited for Lady Wroughton to lead the conversation. She didn't quite dare to initiate anything.

After pouring coffee and offering cakes, the countess opened with, 'I thought it was time you and I had a discussion about the wedding. There are many details to be decided. If we settle everything between us, I am sure all parties will be satisfied.'

Beattie merely nodded and sipped her coffee, and Violet Wroughton examined her carefully through the pause that followed. A handsome woman, she thought. You could see where the girl had got her looks. And she seemed composed – a point in her favour to the countess, who was used to intimidating people, and reluctantly admired anyone who could face her without trembling. All the same, it was a wretched business: this woman, of whom she knew nothing, to be admitted as an equal into the affairs of Dene Park?

She had said as much to the earl the previous evening while dressing for dinner, when she explained her intention of sending for Mrs Hunter. 'A wretched business. But we must simply put a good face on it,' she had concluded.

The earl, who was already doing so, saw his wife's face reflected in the looking-glass as she sat at her dressing-table putting on rings. He thought it even grimmer than usual. Violet, he knew, was furious at having been handed a *fait accompli* at the ball: a public announcement of that sort simply could not be retracted. She could not bear not to be in control. She felt Charles had deliberately jockeyed them into it.

The earl was not so sure. It had *looked* calculated, but he had studied his son's face during the rest of the evening. He'd concluded that Charles had fallen in love, and had simply acted on an uncharacteristic impulse. It was a nuisance, but perhaps no more than that. The worst thing would be to let people know they were disconcerted. 'I don't see any harm in the girl,' he said mildly. 'At any rate, she's very pretty.' It was an understood thing among men, a bargain that had subsisted throughout history: beauty in exchange for rank and fortune. Beauty, the reward for success.

But the countess snorted at the idea that looks were in any way relevant. 'We don't *know* her. She's not from our circle. It's quite inconceivable that he should be marrying someone like that. She doesn't know *anyone* we know.'

The earl was more sanguine. Edward Hunter was his banker, and he valued his advice. And the fellow was a damned good shot. Of course, it was odd that Charles had picked on his banker's daughter to propose to but, frankly, Charles *was* odd.

'I think we must be grateful, my dear,' he said, 'that he's made up his mind to marry at last. The sooner he gets on with it, the better. I've been wondering lately if he was ever going to produce an heir.'

'I've *said* we must put a good face on it,' the countess said irritably, meeting his eye in the glass. 'But as to feeling *grateful*... And what about Cousin Helen? She's been waiting for him these eight years or more.'

'He was never really likely to marry Helen,' the earl said, with the wisdom of hindsight. 'Perhaps it's just as well. She's a difficult girl, and they'd have had terribly plain children. Might be a good thing to introduce some new stock into the bloodline.'

'We are not horses, Wroughton. And Helen knows she was *my* choice for him. It's going to make things very awkward, very awkward indeed. You know how I dislike unpleasantness.'

'He's never given Helen any encouragement. In fact, he's always *said* he didn't want to marry her.'

'He's as stubborn as a donkey,' Lady Wroughton grumbled, scowling at herself in the glass. It always amazed her. Charles *seemed* so quiet and biddable, but every now and then he dug in his heels and would not be moved.

'It's time we went down,' the earl said. 'Good face, my dear – remember? If we do anything to suggest we're not delighted with his choice, it is *we* who will look foolish.'

The countess rose with dignity. 'I shall do what must be done. I know my duty, even if Charles doesn't. But it's my opinion that he's been "caught".'

'He wouldn't be the first,' the earl had said.

She remembered that conversation as she stared at Beattie and, for a wild moment, wondered if there was yet any way out. A plea for common sense? A sum of money? But, no, the notices had gone into the newspapers. The thing was beyond mending.

'Charles will be going away to France very soon,' she began.

'Oh? Has he been given a date?' Beattie asked quickly.

Lady Wroughton frowned slightly at the interruption. 'No, but it will be soon. You may be sure of that. And, of course, we go up to Town as soon as he leaves. We've only kept the house open this long to accommodate his visits. So it is best that we agree everything straight away, don't you think?'

'If you say so,' said Beattie, wondering what there was to agree. A vague idea about dowries and settlements drifted across her mind, but she dismissed it. Anything like that was for the fathers to discuss.

'Very well,' said Lady Wroughton. 'Now, the date – I think the twelfth of June would be appropriate. It's a Saturday, which makes travelling more comfortable for the guests.'

'Do officers know so far in advance when their

leave will fall?' Beattie asked. It was not what she had heard from Beth: Jack was due leave in February, but could not get any assurance of when it would actually be.

Lady Wroughton said, with a hint of impatience, 'The earl has sufficient influence to be able to secure leave at the right time. Sir John French is a personal friend.'

'Supposing,' Beattie couldn't help asking, 'there's a battle going on at the time? He wouldn't just be able to abandon it, would he?'

The countess lowered her eyelids in a very superior manner. *Really, these people were very stupid!* 'Battles do not just "happen". They are planned and known about in advance, and I assure you that if anything of that sort were planned for the date in question, Charles would be withdrawn to some other duty. You really need not concern yourself about the date. If I say the twelfth June, he will be there on that day. Now, as for where the wedding takes place, I think All Hallows Church.'

'Of course,' said Beattie, surprised. Where else would a girl marry but from her home and in her own church? *Really, these people were very stupid!*

'In summer, a country wedding is so much more pleasant than a Town wedding, don't you think?' said the countess. It was her justification, but it was hard for her to say it. St Margaret's, if not the Abbey, would have been her choice. But one could not expose the girl – not to mention her relatives – to such cultural strains. 'And afterwards we will have the reception here. Given that it's wartime, I think it best to limit the numbers. A certain restraint and modesty is expected of

71

our better families at such times. So if you would like to submit a list to me of, say, fifty guests, I will review it. The floral decoration of the church you may leave to me. Fortunately in June there will be plenty to choose from on the estate, and the maids who do the flowers for the house are quite efficient. Now, bridesmaids. I dare say Diana will want her sister – what is her name?'

'Sadie.'

'Yes, quite – Sadie. You may leave the others to me. There are several cousins who will be quite suitable and, indeed, who will expect to be chosen. Four, I think, will be sufficient for a small church like All Hallows. One must keep things in proportion. And I shall speak to Mr Fitzgerald about the sermon. It won't do to have him please himself. References to Africa would be *quite* unsuitable on such an occasion. I shall choose the hymns, and there should, I think, be an anthem. The choir is adequate, provided we don't lose too many more of the tenors to the recruiting officer. Diana will require a proper lady's maid when she is married. You may leave that to me. I shall make enquiries about a suitable woman. She had better be engaged in time to dress Diana for the wedding. These details should not be left to chance. Now, as for the wedding breakfast...'

So it went on. Beattie sat bemused, almost in a state of shock, watching a well-rehearsed plan being unrolled before her and seeing no point at which intervention would be possible, let alone welcome. Lady Wroughton had been getting her own way since she had put her first governess in her place, and practice had made perfect. Afterwards, to Edward, she said, 'I don't know how it was, but all I could do was nod. I felt almost hypnotised.'

'Like a rabbit before a snake,' Edward said.

'It isn't amusing,' Beattie reproved him. 'We can't have her organising the whole thing. It's for the bride's parents to arrange the wedding.'

'Perhaps it isn't, in their world. Besides, as long as she does it well, does it really matter?'

'How can you ask? Every girl dreams of her own wedding – and every mother dreams of planning it with her. It's humiliating to be ridden over like that.'

'You still have charge of the wedding dress, I presume,' Edward said.

'But not the bridesmaids' dresses. And why should *she* have the choice of three of them? They're *brides*maids, not bridegroom's-mother's-maids. It really won't do,' she concluded crossly. '*You* must talk to them.'

'Me?' He looked horrified.

'If you are to pay for the wedding, I don't see why they should make all the decisions. At least talk to the earl about it, if you're afraid of her.'

'I'm not afraid of her.'

'Everyone's afraid of her.'

Edward looked awkward. 'The fact is, my dear, that I *have* spoken to the earl. He came to see me to discuss financial settlements. He said he quite understood that in our circle dowries were not customary. The implication was that they were being very generous, in return for which we should go along with anything else they proposed. I think,' he added, 'that *he* is rather afraid of the countess as well. It will be much easier for everyone if we just let her have her way. And it's bound to be tastefully done – will that be so bad?'

'That isn't the point,' Beattie began angrily.

He stepped closer and laid a hand on her arm. 'Couldn't we make it the point?'

'But it's treating us with contempt. Don't you see that? How will this marriage go for Diana, with such a gulf between the two families?'

'She's marrying Charles, not his parents.'

'But still–'

'She may have some awkward moments at family gatherings, but our Diana has enough character to weather those. And what young married person *doesn't* find their in-laws a bit strange?' He could see he wasn't moving her. 'Look here,' he said, 'let's just leave it for now. There's time to change things. Apart from the wedding date, nothing will be fixed for several weeks. Talk to Diana, and if she's not happy about the arrangements, let her talk about it to Charles. He's the one to tackle his mother. It would just cause bad feeling if you tried to tell her you don't like her ideas.'

He looked tired, and anxious, and Beattie forbore to continue the argument, but she suspected there would not be many opportunities to change the countess's mind, if any: once she closed the house and decamped to London, she would be effectively out of reach. And the plan that had been unveiled to her seemed to have been thought out in such detail, she would be surprised if Lady Wroughton, who was nothing if not efficient, had not started to put it into action already.

But later, when she broached the matter delicately with Diana, she found her daughter not at all upset by it. To have the reception in the splendour of Dene Park seemed to her in every way preferable to trying to cram everyone into The Elms, or one of the rooms at the Station Hotel, which had been as far as her imagination had taken her before. And to have the countess make the arrangements, she felt, ought to guarantee a certain sumptuousness, besides saving her mother many hours of work and worry.

Her only sticking point was the bridesmaids: she, like her mother, felt they ought to be chosen by her. 'I'll speak to Charles about it,' she said. 'I'm sure he'll agree with me.'

But when Charles came to see her the following day, it was with the news that the battalion had finally received its orders to go to France. Everyone had their forty-eight hours' embarkation leave, and the question of bridesmaids went right out of her head.

Charles's priority for that last visit was to be alone with Diana. Had it been summer, a picnic or a walk in the country would have done the trick. As it was, the best he could do was to take her out to luncheon at a country hotel. Diana was rather thrilled at the idea: she had never eaten in a restaurant with a man before, and half expected her mother to frown and veto it. But the ring on her finger, she discovered, conferred certain freedoms. As an engaged woman she might be seen alone with her fiancé in public places, so she put on her smartest hat and sallied forth with a shining face of anticipation.

Charles had put the top up on his Vermorel, but even so it was too noisy for conversation on the journey. He drove her to the King's Arms in Amersham, a place large enough to be respectable, but at this time of year quiet enough to give them privacy. A discreet half-crown to the waiter secured them a table a little apart, in an alcove. He was touched to see how excited Diana was about the whole adventure. Underneath her veneer of sophistication, she really was innocent and unspoiled. He felt again his astonishing luck in having won her.

Diana read the menu from start to finish, but then asked him to order for her. When that was done, and they were alone, she said, 'Do you know where you will be going?'

'Not exactly,' he said. 'However, I'm sure we'll be sent to a quiet sector to begin with, so that we can complete our training.'

'I thought you said the men were ready.'

'There's still a lot to learn about trench warfare. And, no doubt, other things I don't know about.'

'Are you nervous?' she asked, looking at him frankly.

He thought about it. 'Not nervous, exactly, but – keyed up. I don't want to let anyone down. Especially you.' He laid a hand over hers on the table. 'I want you to be proud of me.' She blushed, looking up at him, and he was emboldened by his imminent departure to speak his mind as men of his background and upbringing rarely did. 'I love you so much, Diana,' he said, low and awkwardly. 'I'm a stupid, clumsy fellow and not very good at expressing myself, but I hope at least you know how very much I love you.'

She was too moved to respond, except to nod. The waiter came with the wine he had ordered, and they withdrew their hands hastily. She sought for a neutral subject. 'Will you be taking your motor-car to France?'

'Yes, I shall – and Randall, too, fortunately.' His chauffeur had volunteered and joined the battalion as his servant. 'It will be good to have him around – a friendly face. He's tremendously excited about going abroad for the first time.'

'You've been abroad before, though, haven't you?'

'Only to the South of France with my parents. And once to Marienbad. My father was one of King Edward's circle.'

'Where's Marienbad?'

'In Bohemia.'

'Is that Germany?'

'It's between Austria and Germany.'

'I've never been anywhere but England. I should like to go abroad.' Diana sighed.

'And you shall,' Charles said. 'As soon as the war's over. I'd like to travel a great deal more. Italy. Switzerland. America.'

'America!' she exclaimed. 'Mrs Oliver has a nephew from California. He says it's the best place on earth.'

He gave her one of his rare smiles, which made him look almost handsome. 'Everyone thinks that about his own place. But I'd like to see it. We'll go together. I'd like to see as much of the world as possible before I have to settle down and run the estate.'

He became fluent, as he could be on that one subject. Repetition was making her familiar with some of the concepts and vocabulary, and while she couldn't say she was yet really interested in it, she did at least understand better what he was talking about.

Afterwards, they drove home, again constrained by the noise of the car. Then, suddenly, he turned off onto a track into some woods and, after driving between the trees for a short distance, came out into an open space at the top of a hill, with a view over a narrow valley. At the bottom a red-roofed farmhouse was snugged down, the chimney emitting a pale wisp of smoke; sheep grazed over the green hillsides, and the bare woods opposite looked violet-blue in the afternoon light.

He stopped the engine, and the silence flooded in. 'This is one of my favourite spots,' he said. 'England is so beautiful. Worth fighting for,' he added, so low it was almost to himself.

In the car, in the silence, he felt very close, very large, very much *there*. Diana was acutely aware of his masculinity, his otherness from her; how different his experience from the cloistered life of a girl, which she had lived until now. He turned to look at her, but she dared not meet his eyes. Then he laid his big, warm hand over hers, and she started like a deer.

'May I kiss you?' he said. His voice sounded different.

'Yes,' she said, in a tiny voice, still looking down.

His hand came and cupped her face, turning it towards him. She had been kissed only once before, on the occasion when he had proposed to

78

her. She felt instinctively that this would be different. He had her now; he would not be so cautious. She closed her eyes as his face came nearer, smelt the wine on his breath as its warmth touched her skin, and his cologne, and under that the scent of his skin. It was the latter that undid her. The smell of a man – of *her* man. Something completely outside her range of experience. Her heart was beating crazily, and she felt a strange pang, like an ache, in a part of her she had never known to have feelings.

Then his lips were laid on hers, and his arms came round her, and tightened, and she sensed something in him that frightened her. He was no boy, to be teased or frosted into submission. This thing in him, if it was let out, would be something she could not control. Her thoughts of marriage had never gone further than the wedding: beyond that was a locked room into which one could not even peek until the time came. This, surely, was the door; and she was afraid of it opening. Yet half of her longed for it, whatever it was. She gave him her lips and felt something loosening in her.

It was he who drew back. He put her gently from him, straightened, looked out of the window away from her, breathing fast. Then he said, 'I'd better get you home.'

She was disappointed that he didn't speak then of love, but afterwards she thought it probably better, a sign that it meant too much to him for words. Rattles were amusing, but it was better, surely, to marry someone solid and worthy.

And the next day he was gone.

CHAPTER FIVE

Edward's sister Sonia invited the family to spend Sunday in Kensington. The letter included the words, 'if you are not afraid of being bombed'.

'It could come at any moment,' she said, as she welcomed them in out of the February gloom. 'It says in the paper that experts believe a raid is certain within the next few weeks.'

'But the experts also say any raid would be doomed to failure, Mumsy,' said Mary, the sensible one.

'I don't know why they should say that,' Sonia retorted indignantly. 'The government has done *nothing* about protecting us.'

'Well, the Zeppelins seem to have other fish to fry at the moment,' Edward said soothingly. 'Tyneside and Humberside and the east coast.'

'And poor old Calais,' said his brother-in-law Aeneas. 'In any case, as I've told you many times, my dear, we're too far west here to get caught up in it. The Germans want to knock out our docks and warehouses, not Derry & Toms.'

Sonia turned to Beattie, hoping for a more sympathetic audience. 'All the same, *I* don't intend to be caught out. I must show you my preparations later. I've made the cellar into our air-raid shelter – lots of blankets and rugs, and tinned food, and a first-aid box. We've each prepared a basket of our most precious belongings to bring down with us.'

'Mine's mostly full of books,' said Audrey, Mary's twin. 'And a torch to read them by. If we have to stay a long time...'

'And we each have a bucket of water ready in our bedrooms in case of fire,' Sonia concluded.

'I tripped over the damned thing the other night,' Aeneas complained. 'Caught a frightful hack on the shin.'

'The Wallanders down the road have a sign outside their house saying anyone can shelter in their cellar in case of a raid,' said Douglas, the youngest, usually known as Duck. 'Mr Wallander says everyone with a cellar ought to have a sign out saying, "You may shelter here." He says the police should be telling people.'

'That's going too far,' Sonia objected. 'I hope one would always do one's duty, but one is *not* a public convenience.' She changed the subject. 'Beattie, dear, how are the wedding plans going?'

She drew Beattie away for a good gossip; the girls took Diana and Sadie to their bedroom, and William and Peter went to see Duck's latest invention, a special kind of rattle for Zeppelin warnings. It was supposed to light up as well as rattle, for the convenience of deaf people. 'But I can't get the dynamo to work properly yet,' Duck confessed.

Aeneas took Edward and Donald, the eldest son, to his business-room, where there was a good fire and a decanter of fine sherry.

'How's business?' Edward asked, settling himself into an armchair.

'Tremendous,' said Aeneas. 'We all thought at the beginning that the war was going to depress things.'

'A lot of companies did close down,' said Edward.

'Yes, the piano works next door to our factory closed in the first month. No new orders coming in.'

'And there was the furniture factory, Poppa,' said Donald. 'The one in Westbourne Grove.'

'But now business is booming. The hardest thing is to find enough labour. You won't believe it, but the Kensington workhouse emptied practically overnight! The same thing with the Salvation Army hostel. They're going to turn the workhouse into an extra hospital for the wounded, and the hostel's going over to housing refugees. I'm minded to point out to the government that all we needed for full employment was a good old-fashioned war!'

'But the biscuit business in particular – how's that going?' Edward prompted.

'I'm almost thinking I was too quick to take on the government contract for hard-tack,' Aeneas said. 'We'd so many orders for tins of fancy biscuits at Christmas, we had to work double shifts. And they're still coming in.'

'People send them to their men at the front,' said Donald. 'And it's not only biscuits. We're getting enquiries for all sorts of foods – cakes and jams and plum puddings and so on.'

'You won't like turning away business,' Edward said to Aeneas.

'How well you know me!' said Aeneas. 'I've decided to expand into special parcels for the fellows at the front. Palfrey's Comfort Hampers, we'll call them. Three different sizes, from the standard to the deluxe. There's a little workshop in Fulham that will make the baskets for me, and I've made an offer for the piano works so we can expand next door. We're going to make jams and marmalades, lime cordial and bottled fruits there.'

Edward was fascinated. 'And what else might I find in a Palfrey's Comfort Hamper?'

'Our own biscuits, of course. Fussell's in Golborne Road will produce cake for us at cost, plus a small margin. They also make fudge and toffee. Tea and coffee – there's a depot in Portobello Road. And we'll buy in things like pickles, calf's-foot jelly, soup squares, Horlicks tablets.' He smiled happily. 'We've already had a couple of dozen advance orders, and we haven't even got the machinery installed.'

'Won't that be hard to find in the present climate?' Edward wondered.

Aeneas looked triumphant. 'I'm having it shipped down from Edinburgh. There was a jam-maker went out of business last year, and I bought the plant at a good price at the closing-down sale. Thought there'd be a use for it some day. I've always had a notion that jam and biscuits went well together.'

'Not cake?' Edward asked, amused.

Aeneas shook his head. 'Too variable. Too many things to go wrong – ask your cook! But there's not much can fail about a batch of biscuits or jam.'

'How will you manage for finance?' Edward asked.

'That's where you come in. I shall need a short-term loan to cover the setting-up costs.'

'I see no difficulty,' said Edward. 'It sounds

supremely profitable.'

'And who knows what may happen in the future?' Aeneas went on. 'Soldiers eat jam, and if I were to get a government contract...'

The talk turned eventually to the war. 'What do you think of this business of opening up an eastern front?' Aeneas asked.

'I'm afraid it's a mistake,' Edward said. 'It was supposed to be a naval-only show, but now Admiral Jackson's said there has to be a military force to follow up the bombardment.'

'*Is* there a military force to be sent?' Aeneas asked. 'I understood we were short of men.'

'There's the Twenty-ninth Division, but that was promised to Sir John French for his spring offensive. A joint exercise with the French to puncture the salient near Arras and cut the German supply line where it's at its longest. I understand that without the Twenty-ninth the French won't agree to it.'

'When does the New Army arrive out there?' Aeneas asked.

'Not until late summer at best. And even then...' Recruitment over the last few months had fallen off. His client Lord Forbesson at the War Office had told him in confidence there was a strong feeling in the War Council that conscription would eventually have to be considered. But it was such a contentious issue it could not be discussed publicly. 'We'll need a lot more men to come forward,' he said instead. 'Kitchener's talking about another half-million. There'll have to be a big recruitment drive this spring.'

Donald was looking uncomfortable. 'I did think

of volunteering,' he said, 'but with things so busy at the factory...'

'I couldn't possibly manage without you,' Aeneas said firmly. 'Your uncle wasn't casting at you – were you, Edward? There are plenty of others who need to be shaken out of the carpet first. How's David doing, by the way?'

'He's put his name down for officer training,' Edward answered. 'We're waiting to hear if he's been accepted.'

'I'm sure he will be. He's just the right sort of youngster. Though it's odd that he didn't join the OTC at school.'

'He was more interested in poetry,' Edward said. 'A scholar, where the OTC fellows were sportsmen.'

'Poetry might come in handy at the front, you never know,' said Aeneas. 'There was a letter in *The Times* the other day, suggesting the troops should be taught to sing English folk songs, like "Greensleeves" and "The Lass of Richmond Hill", rather than leave them to make up their own vulgar ditties.'

Edward laughed. 'People have some odd ideas about the war.'

Edward's other sister Laura arrived in time for dinner, looking very smart in a tailored navy two-piece with a skirt that showed not only her feet but two inches of ankle. Sonia noticed at once and pronounced it daring.

'We active women can't afford to be hampered by trailing skirts and heavy petticoats,' Laura said briskly. 'By summer, skirts will be calf-length, you'll see.'

'How is your war work going, Aunt Laura?' Sadie asked, eager to move the conversation away from clothes.

'We've acquired several more motor-cars,' Laura answered. 'Lady Truscott has just lent us her two, because her chauffeur has enlisted. She's going to stay in London and take taxis. She's a stalwart of the Chelsea Club, undertakes most of the fund-raising. For such a mild-seeming lady she can be quite ruthless in a good cause. She rarely comes away empty-handed.'

'So with more cars you must need more drivers,' Sadie said, perhaps a touch wistfully. She thought her aunt tremendously dashing.

'Oh, yes – particularly as the men leave. Some of our motors are driven by the chauffeurs or husbands or sons of the Chelsea Club ladies, but every month it seems *someone* gives us that apologetic look and says he's joined up. Mind you,' she went on, 'even the female drivers aren't safe.'

'Oh, my dear,' Sonia said in alarm, 'you don't mean... We've heard so much about frightful traffic accidents, with the street lamps being turned off and no lights in the trams.'

'No, dear, it's not that,' Laura said comfortingly, 'though I must say this "blacking out" adds to the fun. It was never easy driving around Piccadilly Circus, even when there were policemen with flares to control the traffic... What I meant was that drivers are in such demand that ours are being poached. Miss Gurnard has gone to drive for the London County Council. And Lady Lugard has stolen Miss Phipps for the War Refugees Council

– disgraceful, when we're supposed to be working for the same end.'

'Do you think you might be poached, and go and do something even more exciting?' Sadie asked.

Laura smiled. 'Oh, I'm happy enough where I am – for the moment. But if this war goes on much longer, I can see all sorts of opportunities might arise.'

'How's Louisa?' Beattie asked.

'Enjoying herself,' Laura said. 'Unfortunately, we don't often drive together, except on "convoy days" when we pick up a large batch of refugees. Otherwise we're usually on separate tasks, and only see each other when we take the motors back to the garage after work. It's such a nuisance that she has to go back to Wimbledon every evening. I wish she would come and live in my house, but she says she has to wait for the right moment to broach it with her aunt.'

'Does her aunt think you not respectable?' Sonia said indignantly.

'I expect Louisa's aunt thinks it's not respectable for two unmarried young women to live together without supervision,' Edward suggested.

'Especially women with such *outré* opinions,' Laura offered, with a twinkling look at her brother. She pulled a shocked face. '*Suffragettes!* How dreadful!' Edward took the teasing in good part, though he had often been made uneasy by her unconventional behaviour. A banker had to be above reproach, which meant his family had to be, too.

'Have you been to any more meetings, Auntie?' Audrey asked.

'Oh, one or two, when Louisa doesn't have to be home too early. Now the militants have a truce with the government for the rest of the war, they're desperate to find a role for themselves.'

'And an outlet for all that pent-up energy,' Aeneas suggested.

'Some of them are more patriotic than Lord Kitchener,' Laura said, with a grin. 'They lurk on street corners urging any man not in uniform to sign up at once and do his duty. And they stand outside factories and protest against the strikes. Strikers are Bolsheviks and traitors, according to them.'

'A man came to our school to give us a talk about German spies,' Duck put in eagerly. 'He said they're everywhere. They want to sabotage the railways and poison the drinking water.'

William nodded. 'We had a talk like that at the Scouts. The man said you can't always tell them from patriotic Englishmen, but if you watch them closely there's always a clue.'

'Oh, the militants are terribly keen on sniffing out traitors,' Laura agreed. 'But they do good work too, you know. Sylvia Pankhurst is helping destitute women in the East End, setting up a mother-and-baby clinic. And she wants to start a canteen to provide cheap midday meals for the poor. We shouldn't forget our home-grown hardship cases just because of the Belgians.'

'I must say,' Sonia said, 'I can see the day when one will become quite tired of the Belgians. One keeps giving money and old clothes and so on, but they never seem to be satisfied.'

'There are an awful lot of them,' Laura said

gently, and saw it was time to change the subject. 'Tell me about your wedding plans, Diana dear. I'm so excited for you. What a pity it's wartime, so he won't be able to take you somewhere thrilling for your honeymoon. Where *will* you go, do you know?'

'I think we'll stay in London,' Diana said. 'He'll only have a few days, so one shouldn't waste them travelling.'

'Ah, well, there'll be the shops and all the shows and so on,' Laura comforted her. 'I was afraid things might get a bit dreary in London, but it's livelier than ever.'

'But *do* be careful if you go out after dark,' Sonia urged. 'It's so dangerous, with half the lights out. A neighbour of ours, Mrs Amberley, stepped off a kerb by accident and badly twisted her ankle. Dr Ferris said it was a miracle she didn't break it.'

The first-aid class that Sadie joined was held in the village hall. It was recommended to her by William, because his Scout master – the same Mr Miles who had appointed himself air-raid warden – had told him it was instructed by a real Red Cross member. The other one close by, held in the church hall, was run by Mrs Fitzgerald and the instructor was Mrs Frobisher's sister, Miss Osborne. 'You might as well learn from someone who really knows what's what,' William advised her earnestly.

They were coming out of the village hall after one of the lessons when a toot on a motor horn made them turn, and John Courcy's little car pulled up alongside them. 'Hello!' he said cheerfully. 'What have you been up to?'

'First-aid class,' Sadie said. 'This is my brother William, by the way. Mr Courcy, William.'

'Hello, sir,' William said politely, and, as he was in his beloved Scout uniform, gave him a smart salute.

'Are you taking the class as well?' Courcy asked.

'Oh, no, sir. We provide the bodies,' William said, and added, to clarify, 'for them to practise on. We have to pretend we've got cuts and broken legs and suchlike, and let them bandage us.'

Courcy grinned. 'How is your sister doing? Man to man.'

William had no need of discretion. 'She's tremendously good at bandaging,' he said. 'Not too tight so it cuts off your circulation, but they always stay put. Some of them, the bandages just fall straight off.'

'It's because I've had a lot of practice bandaging horses,' Sadie said.

'I'd expect her to be good at first aid,' Courcy said. 'She's a great help to me with the horses.'

'Horses aren't the same thing,' William objected.

'A jolly sight harder than humans,' Courcy said. 'Humans can tell you where it hurts. Would you like a lift home? I'm going past the end of your road.'

'Golly, yes, please,' William said, before Sadie could answer. He opened the door and climbed into the back, leaving her to get into the front beside the vet. 'Are you going to the army camp?' he asked, as they set off again.

'Yes, one of the draught horses has gone lame.

Sounds like thrush. I could leave it until tomorrow, but I'm going right past the camp anyway...'
The centre of the village had street lamps, which had had their tops painted, so that they each threw an oval of light downwards onto the road. But where the shops ended, so did the lamps, and the high street became in effect a country lane, with hedges to either side. It was quite dark.

'I say,' William noticed, 'you've covered over your headlamps.'

'Sticky paper, with a hole cut in the middle,' Courcy agreed.

'Is that because of the blackout?'

'Mm. It's like driving by the light of a pocket torch, but I suppose it's necessary.'

'Mr Sowden got knocked down the other night,' William confided, 'on his way home from the Red Lion. He says a car knocked him off his bike.'

'It's quite hard to see someone in dark clothes against a dark road and dark hedges,' Courcy said.

'In Mr Sowden's case,' said Sadie, 'I expect the Red Lion had a bit to do with it. In fact, I wouldn't be surprised if there *was* no car. He wobbles about all over the place when he's been in the Lion.'

'Was he hurt?' Courcy asked.

'Sprained wrist,' said Sadie. 'He'll be off work for a few days.'

'From what I hear about him, he won't mind that,' said Courcy. 'But I hope you're careful when you're walking about these lanes.'

'Oh, we are.' Sadie answered for them both. 'Anyway, it's so dark away from the street lamps you can see a car coming for miles.'

'You can even see the light of a pocket torch,' William said excitedly. He was bursting to tell his news. 'Our troop is helping to guard against spies, sir, did you know?'

'No, I hadn't heard. But I know the Scouts do a tremendous job in many areas,' Courcy said seriously.

William puffed with pride. 'Mr Miles says the police asked for us to help, because there's so many places to guard and not enough of them. So next week I'm going to be guarding the reservoir in White's Lane. To make sure the Germans don't poison it.'

'Just you on your own?' Courcy asked. 'That's a big task.'

'No, we'll patrol in pairs,' William said. 'I'll be with Gus Ellison. We walk round in opposite directions. It takes about half an hour to walk right round so we'll pass each other every fifteen minutes and exchange the "all's well".'

'And what if it isn't well?' Courcy asked.

'You mean if we see someone? Well, we each have a whistle. If he whistles, I come running, and vice versa. Golly, I do hope we catch a German! I'm best at boxing in my class, and Gus is pretty handy too. We'd soon overpower him. I always have a length of rope coiled around my waist, and we'd tie him up and bring him back to the police station. The trouble is,' he confided, 'that Gus and I will be doing the nine-till-midnight patrol, and then two older chaps take over, and it's much more likely a saboteur will be out after midnight. I mean, I would, if it were me.'

He sounded disconsolate, and Courcy said bracingly, 'Well, you can but hope. But it's good to know someone's out there patrolling, keeping our womenfolk safe.'

William felt emboldened to ask, 'I've been wondering, sir, why you aren't in uniform. I mean, you treat the army animals and everything...'

'William!' said Sadie.

'No, it's a fair question,' said Courcy. He glanced at her. 'In fact, it looks as though I shall be in uniform soon. I've rather enjoyed my semi-detached status, but the rumour is all we freelance vets will be taken into the Army Veterinary Corps.'

'You mean – they're making you join the army?' Sadie said.

'Oh, it won't be too bad,' he said. 'We're officially part of the Army Medical Service, and we'll go in as officers, just as the doctors do. Given my age and experience, I'll be a captain straight off.'

'Oh, I say, sir!' said William, impressed.

'The army is beginning to regularise various aspects of the service. It's all been a bit haphazard so far, and whatever worked was accepted for the sake of getting on with the war. But sooner or later the great khaki machine will want to straighten everything out and put it in nice straight lines.'

There was a silence, as Sadie imagined him in khaki, and hoped it wouldn't mean he'd go away.

Then he said, 'By the way, I heard an amusing story the other day. There's a chap I know from Edinburgh, a medical officer, McHoul is his name. He's gone out to France already. He drew a horse for himself from the depot at Étaples, fine animal, except that its coat was pure white. Well, of course, everyone pointed out that it would be a prime target for enemy snipers, so he and his groom dyed its coat with permanganate. It was supposed to make it brown, but something went wrong, and it came out bright canary yellow.'

'Oh dear,' said Sadie. 'Poor thing!'

William hooted with laughter. 'What did he do?'

'Well, he was even more of a target now, so he tried a weak solution of bleach on his yellow horse, but that didn't work. Then a farrier sergeant said he could make up a new dye that would turn the beast into a chestnut. Unfortunately, the dye reacted with the bleach, and instead of brown it ended up a deep shade of purple.'

Laura and Louisa were leaning against their motors, waiting outside the station for the next refugee train to come in.

'I wish you could come to the meeting tonight,' Laura said.

'I told you Auntie's having a bridge party, and I promised to be there. Besides, I'm not sure she'd approve of the meeting.'

'The National Council of Public Morals?' Laura exclaimed. 'What could be more respectable than that? In fact, it's so respectable, I'm not even sure we'd enjoy it.'

Louisa didn't laugh. 'Anything about illegitimacy and drunkenness is bound to strike her as improper.'

'Dearest, the meeting won't be *advocating* them!'

'You don't understand how difficult it is for

me,' Louisa said crossly.

'Oh, I do, I assure you. You're always having to rush off and catch the last bus. We've hardly had a moment to talk for weeks. If you came to the meeting we could have a spot of supper afterwards. You know you can always stay the night if you miss the bus.'

'But she worries so,' said Louisa. 'I can't help it, you know.'

'You can,' Laura said. 'The answer's in your hands. Come and live with me.'

'I am trying,' Louisa said. 'I have to get Auntie used to the idea. She does seem to be softening.'

'You've said that before.'

'Well, you must help me work on her. Come to tea on Sunday, show her what a respectable, sensible person you are.'

'I shall come and be positively horn-rimmed,' said Laura. Then she straightened up. 'Oh. I say, Lou, look at that!'

Two women had come into sight, walking slowly side by side. They were dressed alike in what was evidently some kind of uniform: a dark blue serge skirt, a Norfolk-style jacket of the same material, with many useful pockets, a white shirt and black tie, topped off with a dark blue felt hat that looked like a cross between a riding hat and a panama. Long leather boots showed below the skirt hem, and on the front of the hat were the silver letters 'WPS'.

'WPS – what's that?' Louisa queried.

Laura frowned in thought. 'Wait a minute – I've heard something about it. There were two men talking on the bus behind me the other day,

95

laughing their silly heads off at the idea of "lady policemen". WPS – it must be the Women Police Service!'

They watched, fascinated, as the two approached. It was a severe look, not at all feminine: their hair was concealed under the hat with not a curl in sight. One of them had a silver chain running from one button into the breast pocket. 'Do you think that's a policeman's whistle?' Laura whispered. 'Oh, I die for a policeman's whistle!'

'I die for the uniform,' Louisa whispered back. 'How do you suppose one joins? What do you think they do?'

'I've no idea. They *can't* be official, surely? I can't imagine the Metropolitan Police Force allowing women in. But wouldn't it be fun if they did?'

'More fun than driving for the Chelsea Club,' said Louisa, then clapped her hand over her mouth. 'I shouldn't have said that.'

'Truth will out, my girl. And, you know, there's been a slackening of refugee numbers lately. I wouldn't be surprised if all the Belgians who are coming are here by now. Then what will we do?'

'There'll always be good work,' Louisa said.

Laura watched the two women walk slowly and grandly away. 'I bet we could put the white slavers to flight if we were dressed like that.'

'And the drunken soldiers would heed us,' Louisa added.

'And perhaps those idiotic girls who hang around them would listen to us when we tell them it's not a good thing to do,' said Laura. She made up her mind. 'I mean to find out all about them and, if it's possible, to join... Are you game?'

96

'Oh, yes,' said Louisa. 'We could–' She broke off. 'That's our train coming in. We'd better go. Let's ask Mrs Erskine when we take the motors back.'

CHAPTER SIX

Mary and Diana were shopping. Loder's in Burlington Arcade had received a special consignment of French silk undergarments, and Mary said Diana would be a fool to miss out. 'I know that when you're Lady Dene you'll probably have everything hand made, but until then...'

They had just emerged onto Piccadilly with a satisfying number of parcels when Diana said, 'Oh, Lord, there's Rupert!'

'What – the brother? Where?'

'On the corner.' He was standing talking to another man, their heads close together. 'Quick, let's cross the road!'

'Too late, he's seen you.' The two men separated. 'He's coming this way. Goodness, he's handsome! Stand still, silly! You can't run away now.'

Rupert reached them, raising his hat. 'Ah, the lovely Miss Hunter, if I don't mistake.' His sharp eyes raked the parcels. 'Spending money, eh? How the ladies do love shopping.'

'Mary, may I present Mr Wroughton?' Diana said woodenly. 'My cousin, Miss Palfrey.'

'Enchanted to meet you,' Rupert said, with a wide smile and a glittering look that seemed to bode mischief. He gave Mary a sort of bow that Diana took to be ironic, but did not offer to shake hands.

At the same moment Mary caught sight of her own naked hand half offered, and made an exclamation of annoyance. 'Oh, my gloves! I must have left them in Loder's.'

'You took them off when you were looking at the stockings,' Diana remembered, seeing a chance for escape.

But Mary said, 'I'll run back and get them. No, you stay, I shan't be a moment,' and hastened away, leaving Diana with Rupert.

'Well, well, Diana the Huntress,' Rupert said. 'Was that monumental tact, I wonder, or abject cowardice?'

'She left her gloves, that's all,' Diana said, wondering what was coming next.

But he asked, not unreasonably, 'Have you had a letter recently from my brother?'

'Yes,' she said. 'He doesn't say where he is, but he says it's in a quiet sector.'

'Armentières,' Rupert said.

'How can you know that?' Diana demanded.

'Contacts at the War Office,' said Rupert. 'You'd be surprised at what I know. What else does he say?'

'That they're learning trench craft.' Charles's letters were frequent, but as uncommunicative as the man himself. He wrote in a style even more formal than his speech, as though it had been taught him at a young age by a Victorian governess. The letters were like exercises. A weather report, a few lines about what his company had been doing, some words of praise for his men, and a paragraph about the flora and fauna of the area. And at the end, he always said that he thought about her constantly, and that her photograph in his pocket book was his dearest possession.

She wrote back, of course, but wondered what comfort her own stilted epistles were to him. She had never been good at writing letters, and it took much chewing of the pen-end before she could complete a single side, even in her large, careful handwriting. Sadie contributed bits of village news, otherwise she would have had nothing to say but *we are all well,* and *it is still raining.*

'How romantic. The words of the consummate lover,' Rupert exclaimed admiringly. '"My adored goddess, we are learning trench craft."'

'He's at the front,' Diana said hotly. 'You aren't even in uniform. Why haven't you volunteered?'

Rupert scowled. 'I don't answer to you!'

'And I don't answer to you!' Diana snapped back.

His eyebrows shot up and he stared at her for a moment before saying, with a twisted smile, 'Well said. Showing a little spirit. I respect you for that. However,' he went on, just in case she should begin to relax, 'don't presume to defend my brother to *me.* You're not part of the family yet. There's many a slip 'twixt cup and lip, as Nanny used to say. Tell me,' he said, suddenly serious, 'are you really intending to go through with it?'

Diana became aware of the weight of the ring on her hand, the great ruby distorting the line of her glove-finger. There wasn't anything Rupert could do now – was there? 'I'm engaged to your brother. You may as well get used to the idea,' she said.

'Oh, I don't think I shall be doing that,' he said thoughtfully. 'Savour your little triumph while you can, dear.' He looked over her shoulder. 'Here comes your friend.'

'My cousin,' she corrected, turning her head to see, with relief, that Mary was coming out of the arcade again. When she looked back, Rupert was already several paces away.

'Oh, he's gone,' said Mary, disappointed, when she reached Diana. 'I thought he might take us to tea. I'd like the chance to get to know him. He looks amusing.'

'He thinks he is,' said Diana.

'Golly, that sounds intriguing. What *can* you mean?'

'Oh, nothing. I'm longing for a cup of tea, aren't you? Shall we go to Rich's?'

Mary laughed. 'There's the Ritz right opposite. I think you should start to practise being Lady Dene, don't you?'

The officer training school was housed in what had been a girls' boarding school in Hampshire, called St Monica's. The original occupants had slept some in dormitories and some in shared rooms. David and Jumbo had been lucky enough to be assigned to a three-bedded room. The third occupant was a former railway booking clerk from Birmingham called Dunkeln, who introduced himself with the qualifier, 'You might as well know right off I'm not a gentleman. I wangled my way in by telling 'em I was a Scout master. Officers get

100

better grub, I reckon.'

He had an older brother who was a regular and was full of army expressions and army lore. He looked upon the 'young gentlemen', like David and Jumbo, as innocents abroad and treated them with a mixture of contempt and protectiveness. He said he knew all the 'wheezes', vowed to 'show them the ropes' and boasted that he could 'wangle' anything they wanted. David and Jumbo had never come across anyone yet who had volunteered for reasons other than patriotism. They were fascinated by him, half shocked and half admiring.

The school had been rather shabby to begin with and was growing shabbier by the day under the influx of hearty, heedless young men. It still smelt faintly of chalk and rubber, and there were reminders here and there of the previous occupants: the honours board in the front hall; the sign on the door of what was now the orderly office that said 'Miss M. Deane, Headmistress'; the inappropriately low coat hooks in the cloakroom; the pale green curtains and bedspreads in the bedrooms.

David imagined the ghosts of schoolgirls past lingering unseen, their chatter and pigtails and hand-holding and pashes a softening influence on the large, noisy beings who defiled their hallowed spaces. He had found an exercise book in the drawer of his bedside cabinet, with the words 'BEN, THE ADVENTURES OF A CIRCUS PONY' written in careful capitals on the cover. Inside, on the first page, was written, 'Chapter One. Ben was a lovely little pony of thirteen hands. He was bay with a long black main and tail.' The rest of the book, to his intense regret, was empty.

The day at St Monica's began at six when, yawning and befuddled, the young gentlemen attended their first lecture in the two hours before breakfast at eight and parade at eight thirty. After dinner in the evening they were expected to write up their notes and sometimes prepare written work for the next day. In between there was a mixture of lectures and practical lessons. They still had a good deal of square-bashing, when they would take turns to give the orders while the rest played the part of the platoon they would command. They did route marches and PT to keep themselves fit. Lectures were on subjects as diverse as regimental history, the origins of the war, military etiquette, keeping up morale, personal hygiene, diet and nutrition. They had lessons in map-reading and reconnaissance. Fieldcraft included camouflage, how to build a shelter out of branches and leaves, how to find drinkable water in open country, how to build a fire, and how to skin a rabbit. They learned first aid and care of the feet, and how to tell one carcass from another so that a wily local butcher in some foreign part could not cozen them when they had to buy food for their men. They learned signalling, morse code and semaphore. There were classes for specialist sections, such as machine-gunners, wireless operators, artillery-spotters and stretcher-bearers; and every now and then a number of Tommies from the nearest army camp would be bussed in for them to practise on, either drilling them, lecturing to them, or trying to teach them the practical skills that the young officers had only just learned themselves.

It was hard work, and David sometimes felt his head was ready to explode with all the new information. But he found it intensely satisfying. 'I'm so glad we put down for officer training, aren't you?' he said one day to Jumbo. 'I don't know why we held off so long.'

'I'm not so sure,' said Jumbo. 'I sometimes wonder what some of it's got to do with killing Germans.'

'I suppose we'll find out when we get to France,' David suggested.

'Come to think of it, I wonder why they don't give us French lessons,' said Jumbo. 'You and I did it at school, but my French is frightfully rusty, and some of the chaps don't have a single word of it.'

'I suppose they're training us to be officers anywhere, not just in France,' David said. 'I'm enjoying it all, aren't you? I like the idea that we'll be prepared for any eventuality, that we have to take care of every aspect of our men's welfare.'

'Well...' said Jumbo, doubtfully. He met David's eyes, and David knew exactly what he was thinking.

The one lecture they had found hard to listen to and even harder to have to give was the one on personal hygiene, which started off, straightforwardly enough, about keeping your feet clean, not eating unwashed fruit and boiling water or milk when in the field, but it had gone on to the multiple hazards of associating with ladies of uncertain virtue. When they came to give the lecture themselves, some of the rankers winked and sniggered, and were expert at asking innocent-sounding questions designed to put the young gentlemen to the blush; others, more strictly brought up, looked puzzled or occasionally shocked, which was almost worse.

And some of the young gentlemen found it impossible to refer to such matters and resorted to euphemisms so ambiguous as to leave the subject virtually untouched in the minds of their audience. One of their colleagues, young Agar, whose cherubic face was disastrously prone to blushing, had not understood himself what it was all about until Dunkeln took him aside and made it graphically clear. Thereafter, he found the whole business so distressing that his advice in lectures was to have nothing whatsoever to do with any female for as long as they were in uniform. 'Not even lady typists?' one wit among the Tommies asked.

Agar, unaware that this was a Tommies' euphemism for 'prostitutes', said firmly, 'Not even lady librarians!'

'Not even librarians!' became something of a catch-phrase around St Monica's.

Dunkeln's own lectures were so brutally frank that the rankers could never raise so much as a knowing grin, and one or two tottered out looking distinctly pale. David tried to steer a middle course, but he found the whole subject both shocking and depressing. It did not fit into his view of what they were fighting for. It was beyond his comprehension that men and women should behave like that. Therefore, while touching as lightly as he could on the medical complications, he laid the emphasis of his own lecture on treating all women with honour and respect, 'just as you would treat your own mother, or your best friend's sister'.

David thought about his own best friend's sister a lot, and in the absence of being able to write to her, he had appropriated the blank pages of BEN, THE ADVENTURES OF A CIRCUS PONY to try his hand at poetry. He was lying on his bed one evening, labouring over what he hoped would come out as a Shakespearean sonnet and had therefore entitled 'To His Dark Lady', when Jumbo walked in unexpectedly. David shut the book quickly, but Jumbo caught sight of the title, and went to lie on his own bed and light a cigarette with a thoughtful look. David put the book aside, folded his arms under his head and gazed at the ceiling.

Finally, Jumbo said, 'I say, old fellow, you know I look on you as my best friend?'

'I should hope I am, after all this time,' David said, wondering what was coming. Chaps did not habitually refer to their love for each other.

'Well,' said Jumbo, 'it's about Sophy, you know.'

David took time over his response. 'I know I'm not good enough for her,' he began at last.

'Oh, Lord! It isn't that.' In fact, Jumbo, with a brother's lack of romantic bias, thought David a great deal too good for her. 'It's just that, well, I know you were starting to think a bit about her, and I feel I ought to give you a hint. There's a chap, you see, that she's fond of. Fellow called Humphrey Hobart, parents have a place about half a mile from us. She's known him for ages but just lately... Well, last time the mater wrote she said Sophy's started walking out with him.' He

105

glanced sideways at David, who was still studiously gazing at the ceiling. 'So I thought it only fair to warn you.'

'Yes,' said David, at last. 'Thank you. I should have realised...' Should have realised that such a heavenly creature would not remain uncourted just because he had fallen in love with her. Especially now he was far away. The image of her white neck, dark, wistful eyes, and the little unruly curls came to him and he felt the usual tug at his heart. 'Is he in uniform, this Humphrey fellow?'

'Not so far,' said Jumbo. Of course, he thought, that gave him the edge. It was hardly fair for chaps like him and David to be competing with chaps who were right there on the spot. He thought he heard David sigh, and sought for something to say to cheer him up. 'Saturday tomorrow,' he said. 'Free afternoon. Let's get the transport into the village. I've heard there's going to be a film-show in the church hall. Someone said it was Lillian Gish,' he added beguilingly.

The lure of Lillian Gish was so strong that the transport was full by the time David and Jumbo reached it. 'Never mind,' David said. 'Let's walk. It's only three miles.'

'More like four,' said Jumbo, but without concern. To veterans of the route march, like themselves, four miles each way held no terrors. They swung along, keeping time with each other, at a regulation 120 paces to the minute that cost them no effort. It had been dry now for several days, rather cool, but today the clouds were broken and there was a hint of sunshine, transient and thin.

The countryside was very pretty, grassy downland with some fine oak woods, little rivers and the occasional thatched cottage. David was noticing the signs that the year had turned at last. Birds were singing, buds were swelling on the trees, and there were primroses and little asphodels in the hedgerows.

Coming into the village on foot, they passed a square red-brick house that stood apart from the main row of thatched cottages running into the green at the centre, where the transport stopped. The house had a home-made notice beside the gate that said 'ST HUGH'S SOLDIERS' CLUB'. The front door stood hospitably open. David had noticed it before when they had passed on the transport, and now on a whim said, 'How about going in here for a cup of tea? All this walking has made me thirsty.'

'If you like,' Jumbo said. 'If it's too deadly we can always leave.' On their village visits so far, they had usually stopped at the Four Corners Café, which stood on the green opposite the church hall, or one of the two pubs, the Half Moon or the Spread Eagle.

The front path led through a tidy if rather dull garden, and inside the front door was a large hall. A sign with an arrow on it pointed the way into what must once have been the morning-room, and now had a number of small tables and chairs, a writing-desk, and a side-table bearing a selection of newspapers and magazines. There was no-one else there, and the silence was emphasised by the slow ticking of a long-case clock in the corner, which seemed to hesitate between its tick and its tock as if it wasn't sure it was worth going on.

'I say, this is ghastly,' Jumbo muttered. 'Let's hoof off.'

But before they could move, a young woman came in from the other end of the room. She seemed to be in her middle twenties, with curly brown hair and a clear, sensible face. She wore a plain blue blouse and a plain dark brown skirt with a hem that showed two inches of ankle. She was in every way unremarkable, except that when she saw them, her face creased into a smile that was so welcoming, she might have been waiting for them and them alone to appear.

'Hello!' she said. 'Come and sit down. Don't worry, you won't be the only chaps here. There'll be plenty of others in a little while.'

David was impressed that she had read their minds. 'We thought – um... Can one get a cup of tea?'

'Of course,' she said. 'Something to eat with it?'

'Um...'

'How hungry are you? Sandwiches, or just a scone?'

'Scones would be nice,' David said.

'We've not long had dinner,' Jumbo added.

'I'll be back in a moment,' she said. 'Make yourselves comfortable.'

She vanished, and the young men looked at each other doubtfully for a moment, then selected a table near the window and sat down. A stray band of sunshine found its way in between the curtains. The window was a bay with a padded window-seat, and as they waited, a large ginger cat stalked in and jumped onto it, turned round twice and settled down. David reached out to stroke it, but it gave him a squinty look and a hitch of the shoulders that said, *No blandishments, please,* so he withdrew.

'Why did you say scones?' Jumbo grumbled, in a low voice. 'We'll only be stuck here longer.'

'I like it,' David said. 'It's like being back home.'

'That's what I joined the army to avoid,' Jumbo said.

The young woman was back very quickly with a tray, and David stood automatically to help her. 'No, no, I can manage,' she said, with another warm smile. 'You sit down. You've been working so hard all week.'

There was a pot of tea, and a plate of six scones, with butter and jam to spread on them. The scones were warm and smelt delicious. 'Did you make them yourself?' he asked politely, as she finished arranging the crockery.

She laughed. 'No, I'm afraid my scones never come out like this – with the help of a catapult, you could use them to kill squirrels. These were made by our cook, Mrs Bates. She's a genius in the kitchen. My name's Weston, by the way, Antonia Weston.'

'David Hunter,' he said, offering his hand. 'And my friend Oliphant, known as Jumbo.' They shook hands and he said, 'Would you sit down and join us?' He liked the original way she talked. 'Are you allowed to? We're pining for company.'

'Company that's not in uniform,' Jumbo qualified.

'I'd be delighted to,' she said, 'until the rush starts. How are you finding St Mon's? I used to re myself, you know. It's strange to think of those burly men instead of little girls in gym-ps.'

'I've been thinking the same,' David said. 'What became of them – the little girls?'

'The school closed at Christmas,' Miss Weston said, 'when the army requisitioned the building, and they went home.'

'But what will they do now?'

'The little ones will go somewhere else, I expect. And the older ones will stay home and help Mother.' She shrugged. 'It was never very much of an education, you know – more a way of keeping girls out of circulation until they were ready to marry. I was lucky that my father taught me at home as well. Everything useful I've learned came from him. He was headmaster of St Hugh's, you see – that's the boys' school, companion to St Mon's.'

'That's why you called this place St Hugh's, then?'

She nodded. 'Father's been retired a few years now, working on his treatise, but I think he missed the boys. This is his war work, providing comforts to soldiers, but it's also a way to have his boys around him again.'

'We're a little older,' David pointed out.

'Not by very much, in some cases. You're his new sixth form.'

'And what about you?' David asked. 'Are we your war work too?'

'You are,' she said. 'It's good fun, being big sister to hundreds of chaps, but I also think it's some-thing worth doing. Some of them have never been away from home before. I'm a sympathetic ear, a reassuring presence – sometimes even a shoulder to cry on.' She said it lightly, but David had heard the seriousness underneath.

He wanted to find out more about her. She had mentioned her father, but what about her mother? Brothers and sisters? If St Hugh's was a boarding-school, had she lived there when her father was headmaster? But just then through the open door came a group of four khaki-clad figures, and Miss Weston said, 'Ah, the rush is starting. I'm afraid I must leave you. Let me know if there's anything else you want.' And she stood up and went to greet the newcomers.

'Nice girl,' Jumbo said. 'These scones are jolly good. I wonder what else they have?'

'I thought you weren't hungry,' said David.

'I didn't say I wasn't hungry, I said we'd only just had dinner. I'm *always* hungry. Anyway, now some other chaps have come in, it doesn't seem so deadly. Here come some more – oh, there's Tomkins. I wonder if he knows what time the picture starts. Don't want to miss the beginning.'

He jumped up to go and enquire. David bit dreamily into a well-jammed scone (blackcurrant, one of his favourites), leaned an elbow on the table, and felt so comfortable he wouldn't have minded staying all afternoon. The cat stood up, stretched, and lay down again, purring, in the little band of sunshine. Even Lillian Gish did not seem too much of a draw just then.

CHAPTER SEVEN

Ethel was quite pleased with life at present. She was still seeing the inexplicably attractive Alan Butcher, the young assistant at Hetherton's, whose shyness caused him to blush whenever he clapped eyes on her, making his spots stand out on his fair face. There was something in his absolute devotion that was balm to her spirits, which had been bruised by the discovery that the sergeant of whom she'd had high hopes had been married all along. Ethel was not only after a good time, though that figured high in her priorities, but she did not intend to be a housemaid for ever. She wanted a husband, who would be able to keep her decently, with a little house and no need to go out to work. The sergeant, a print worker in civilian life, had seemed a likely candidate. Alan Butcher was only an assistant in a bakery.

She kept him in her hand, though, to fill in the times when she had no-one else. But she had recently started walking out with one Phil Addis, who worked at Darvell's factory at the far end of the village, on the Westleigh road. Darvell's made brass door furniture, fire irons, ornaments and so on. Phil was a section leader, which meant he was paid slightly more than a machinist – who was, in any case, paid more than a shop assistant. And Phil was obviously bright, with the prospect of one day becoming a foreman, at which point, she reckoned, he ought to be able to afford a wife.

She liked him, though he did talk rather too much about fishing. At their first meeting he had asked her if she liked fishing and, to show willing, she had foolishly said yes, not realising how deep the obsession went. But she was adept at letting her mind wander when bored and was able to say, 'Yes' and 'No' and 'Goodness!' at appropriate moments without actually listening.

He took her to a dance at the Station Hotel on March the 10th, one of a regular series of mid-week dances the Weavers were giving, largely so that the servicemen from the local camp had something to do in the evening. Their son, Ken, had been a reservist and was now out in France, so they were tender towards all soldiers.

The band was not what it had been, in Ethel's opinion. The Happy Harmonists, who had provided the music for most local events, had lost their pianist, their drummer and their clarinet player to the army. A schoolboy, young Gordon Howells, was doing his best on the clarinet, though distracted by classmates, who would peer through the windows to shout, 'Gordon Howls! Yes, I know he does!' at every break.

The piano was now played by an old man from Westleigh called Mulligan. He had been a good pianist but his sight was failing: he tended to slow down when he couldn't decipher the notes and pause altogether to turn the page.

The Harmonists had been lucky enough to be able to borrow a drummer from the army camp on Wednesdays and Saturdays, a Tommy who had been in a band before volunteering. He did his

113

best to keep things going, thumping the rhythm ever louder to counteract the drag of Mr Mulligan, as he peered at pages on which generations of pencil additions, rubbed out and rewritten, had laid a fog over the printed notes reminiscent of a London pea-souper.

But the couples dancing were more interested in each other than the quality of musicianship, and learned to slow down and speed up without interrupting their pleasure. Ethel found complaining about the band a useful way to break into Phil's piscine monologues, though this quite often led to his talking about his other obsession, Marconi radio. He had been trying to build a wireless receiver at home for years, and no matter how often he explained what it was to Ethel, she could not grasp it.

'Radio's going to be important in this war, you know,' he said to her, during a waltz.

'Oh, is it?' she said, as discouragingly as possible. His hand in the middle of her back was firm, and he danced well, steering her competently and never treading on her toes, so she tried to be patient with him.

'You've only got to think of the possibilities,' he said enthusiastically. 'I mean, on a battlefield, information is everything, isn't it? The officer in the front line, say, suddenly needs reinforcements. How does he send a message to the commanders at the rear? He has to send a runner, and by the time the runner's got back there – even if he doesn't get injured on the way – the situation could have changed again. Now, with a Marconi, he can get the message through and have a reply

114

within minutes.'

'Mmm,' said Ethel, feeling the muscle in his shoulder through the jacket of his suit. He was nicely built, all right.

'You can tell the government agrees with me, because they took over the Marconi factory as soon as the war broke out. I've heard they're starting up a training programme for wireless operators there.' The music came to an end and they stopped and applauded. 'I wouldn't mind doing that,' Phil concluded. Ethel didn't know what he was talking about, and smiled distractedly. She had just seen, through the crowd, the back of a head she thought she recognised.

'Ladies and gentlemen,' said the Harmonists' leader, 'please take your partners for – a foxtrot!'

There was a murmur of excitement and pleasure. It was the very latest dance, only invented the year before in America, and most people had only ever seen it done on the cinema screen. The numbers on the dance floor thinned rapidly as people stepped back to watch. 'I don't know how to do this one,' Phil confessed. 'We shall have to sit it out.'

'If you'll excuse me,' said a familiar voice. A large hand came between them, palm up, inviting. It emerged from a khaki sleeve decorated with sergeant's stripes. 'I believe this young lady would like to dance.'

Ethel looked up at the handsome, feral face of Andy Wood and was torn between annoyance and excitement. How *dared* he assume she would dance with him, after what he'd done? But how much more full of life he seemed than every

115

other man in the place.

'Do you know how?' she snapped.

'Of course I do,' he said superbly. 'Come on, let's show these yokels how it's done.'

Phil, correctly divining that he was one of the yokels, bristled and said, 'The lady is with me.'

Andy Wood winked at him. 'I'll bring her back, don't worry. Stand aside, laddie, and let the dog see the rabbit.'

Ethel found herself whisked onto the dance floor, one of only half a dozen couples waiting there for the music. 'What do you think you're doing? I'm not a parcel, to be handed about,' she berated him, though in truth she hadn't really resisted. The thing that radiated from him, the attraction, the spirit – she had no word for it – made her feel weak at the knees. She'd missed him, that was the truth.

'Missed me, have you?' he said, with that uncanny ability to read her mind. The band played an opening chord and he took her in his arms.

'I don't know how to do this,' Ethel said belatedly.

'Don't worry, I do. Just follow me. You were always good at following me.' The music started and he was off.

He held her so closely that she could feel which way he was going, and they had danced together often enough for her to have an instinctive sense of his rhythm. There were a few clashes of feet, but he was strong enough to carry her over them and, being herself a good dancer, she quickly got the hang of it. Soon they were flying round the floor. It was exhilarating. A number of couples, having watched for a minute, were joining in to try for themselves, with varying success, but Andy Wood steered her through the hazards, humming the tune into her ear as he danced.

'Who was that long drink of water you were dancing with?' he demanded, after a moment. 'Dull bloke, isn't he?'

'What's it to you?' she retorted. 'You're a married man.'

'Don't hold it against me,' he begged comically. 'I was trapped. He was boring you to death, that bloke, wasn't he? I could tell from your face. What was he going on about?'

'Fishing, mostly,' she confessed, and he gave a shout of laughter.

'What a slow-coach! Hasn't he got anything better to talk to a cracking girl like you about?'

'At least he's got the right to dance with a girl,' Ethel said.

'If you call what he was doing dancing,' said Wood, whisking her round the end of the floor. 'You've got the hang of it now, haven't you? You and me, Miss Ethel Lusby, we're naturals together. What say we ditch Mr Codfish and find a nice quiet corner somewhere? We can take up where we left off.'

'Oh, no,' Ethel said, feeling her resolve weakening, 'there'll be none of that.'

She felt his hot breath on her ear as he combined a whisper and a kiss. 'We'll see about that.'

The music came to an end and he brought them to a halt right next to Phil, who was looking annoyed and ready to plunge in.

'Look here,' he began, sticking his jaw out,

'what do you mean by dancing like that?'

'It's called the foxtrot,' Wood said genially. 'Latest thing from America.'

'I mean, you were holding her much too close,' Phil said.

'You have to do that in the foxtrot. You should try it, mate.'

Ethel stood between them, looking from one to the other. A little knot of people was gathering with interest, wondering if there was going to be a fight.

'You think just because you're in uniform you can do whatever you like,' Phil said hotly.

'There's an answer to that, cocky,' said Wood. 'Get into uniform yourself. I wonder a well-set-up chap like you hasn't thought of volunteering. What's up? Flat feet?'

Ethel looked at Phil for his answer. He saw several other people doing the same thing. His face flamed. 'I'm *going* to,' he said angrily. 'I'd have gone before, only I had to train someone to take my place at work. But I'll be joining up very soon, in the next couple of weeks.'

'You didn't tell me that,' Ethel said. She was annoyed now. Were all her beaux going to desert her?

The music was starting again.

'I was going to,' said Phil. 'When the time came. Come on, let's dance – shall we?'

'What do you say?' Wood interposed, looking at Ethel with that devilish smile. 'Fancy a change of partner?'

'Now look here!' Phil cried. 'She came with me. You clear off. Get your nose out of it!' His fists had bunched instinctively, and there was a little gasp from the onlookers.

'Don't try and take me on, son,' Andy Wood said provocatively. 'You'd come off worse.'

'Leave off, both of you,' Ethel said, delighted to be fought over.

At that tense moment the music stopped again with a drum roll and cymbal clash designed to catch the attention. For an instant, Ethel thought the band was trying to prevent the fight, but turning to look, she saw that Don Weaver himself had come up on the stage and was standing at the microphone. He looked excited.

'Ladies and gentlemen!' he called. Gradually the hum of voices fell silent. 'Ladies and gentlemen, I'm sorry to interrupt your fun, but I have an announcement. A very important piece of news has just come in, which I know you'll want to hear. Our brave soldiers out in France have fought a great battle today, at a place called Neuve Chapelle. It's a tremendous victory for our forces! The German line has been broken! The enemy is on the run!'

Cheers and applause broke out all around, drowning his next words. People looked at each other, hope and joy mingling.

Weaver managed to make himself heard again: 'The Germans were soundly beaten. They've suffered heavy losses – thousands killed. Our boys have captured hundreds of their machine-guns. Thousands of Germans have been taken prisoner.'

More cheers. Some couples were hugging each other. One or two were in tears. On either side of her, Ethel's companions stood silent, jerked out

119

of their personal concerns by the national importance of the news.

Mr Weaver turned and murmured something to the Harmonists, then turned back to the microphone to say, 'I think we should all join together now in singing the National Anthem, in honour of our brave lads who have brought us this tremendous victory.'

The drums rolled again, then the music and the voices crashed out together, everyone singing lustily, and in some cases tearfully. At the end, someone shouted, 'Three cheers for the BEF!' and they were heartily given. After that, it seemed wrong to start dancing again; by an unspoken agreement, the evening was over.

Ethel found an empty space on her right: Andy Wood had disappeared. She was only partly sorry. He was trouble, that one, and it was better if she wasn't tempted.

She thought Phil would quiz her about him, but as they joined the crowd leaving the room his mind was on other things. 'I wonder where this Neuve Chapelle is. The German line's been broken, he said. Does that mean the Germans are in retreat? I wish we had more news. I suppose it'll be in the papers in the morning. Is this the end of it now? I shall be rotten fed up if I've missed it all.'

She drew him out of the stream heading for the cloakroom, and said, 'Are you really going to join up, or were you just saying that?'

He looked down at her. 'I really am. I always meant to, but it's true what I said. Mr Darvell himself asked me not to go until I'd trained a new section leader. They've already lost two foremen, you see, and it's important to have supervisors who know how the process works. I thought it'd be quite a few more weeks before I could go, but what with this news, and that sergeant chap... I don't want people to think I'm a coward.'

Ethel laid a hand on his arm, feeling the muscle with automatic pleasure. 'Nobody thinks that,' she said impatiently. 'But what you said, about two foremen leaving – does that mean if you stay, you'll get one of their jobs? You'll get to be a foreman straight away?'

'Yes, probably,' he said, 'if I was staying. Mr Darvell thinks a bit about me,' he added modestly.

'Well, then, you loony,' Ethel said, 'why *don't* you stay? You don't have to volunteer. That's why they call it volunteering.'

'You don't mean that. *You* must want me to go, to do my bit for King and country. Haven't you seen those posters? *The Women of England say "Go!"*'

This was a tricky one. 'Of course I want you to do your bit, but you can do that at Darvell's. Someone's got to make things.'

He was looking puzzled, not knowing how to take her words. 'Making door-knockers and things isn't as important as killing Germans,' he said at last. She didn't reply. 'I'm going to talk to Mr Darvell first thing tomorrow morning,' he went on. 'I could finish up the week and be on my way Monday.'

'Bully for you,' Ethel said, a touch listlessly. He'd be no use to her at the front, and even if it was all over by next Christmas, that was the best part of a year away. What she needed, she suddenly realised, was someone in a job of 'national importance', who wouldn't therefore be seduced by the lure of the uniform and the killing-Germans thing. Even as she looked at him, Phil Addis was fading like a ghost at cock-crow.

'You'll be proud of me, if I volunteer, won't you?' he was asking.

'Of course I will,' she said, but her heart wasn't in it. She suddenly wondered if Andy Wood was hanging around outside, waiting for her, then thought it would be better if she didn't find out. 'There's no hurry to leave, is there? How about buying a girl a lemonade? And you can tell me all about your plans.'

Then he could walk her home, and she'd probably let him kiss her. In her eyes he was pretty much gone already, and a girl had a responsibility to send a soldier off to the war happy.

They went to the bar, where he bought a light ale for himself and a lemonade for her. She listened to his war talk and wondered if he knew which were the important occupations, and how to introduce the question in a natural way.

Diana met Lady Wroughton at the house in Clarges Street. Charles had told her about it before he left for France. It had belonged to his grandmother, who had given it to him so that he would have a London house of his own before he came into the title. A young man, she had said, does not always want to be tied to his parents' apron strings. Wroughton House in Belgrave Square was the family's London base. Lady Wroughton had not entirely approved of the gift, seeing no reason for Charles to stay anywhere but at home, and Caroline had been sniffy, since Lord Grosmore was not as wealthy as she would have liked, and if the house had been given to her she could have let it for some welcome extra income.

But Lord Wroughton was pleased with the idea of a 'cadet house', as he put it, and remembered the wild-oat-sowing days of his youth, and how useful a small, discreet house would have been to him – indeed, still would be, he added, in a wistful footnote to himself.

As it happened, Charles had hardly ever used it. He preferred to be in the country whenever he could, and when obliged to be in Town he was happy enough to use Wroughton House or his club. To his father's gloomy observation, he didn't seem to have any interest in wild oats. His agricultural leanings were all towards wheat, hay and such mainstream crops. A dull dog, Charles, in his father's opinion.

But now the cadet house was to come into its own. It was to be Diana's home after she was married, and Charles had also suggested that, as they would have so little time for a honeymoon, they ought not to waste it in travelling but spend it in Clarges Street. 'We'll be private there, but we'll have all the pleasures of London on hand, if we should want them – the restaurants and theatres and so on. And it's always nicer to be at home than to stay in a hotel.'

Diana had little experience of staying in hotels, and would have liked to sample the delights of a Ritz or a Claridges. But she felt obliged to agree with Charles. Lady Wroughton had suggested that she and Diana meet there at some point to inspect the place and discuss any essential refurbishment. Diana was afraid of the countess and wished she might take someone with her for moral support – Cousin Beth sprang immediately to mind – but the invitation had not been worded in that way, so on the day she presented herself nervously at the address.

It was a narrow street opening onto Piccadilly opposite Green Park. The house was part of a terrace, tall and narrow, four storeys plus the semi-basement and attic rooms. The façade was white stuccoed, three windows wide, and those on the first floor had tiny wrought-iron balconies. It was identical to any number of houses in the area, and Diana felt a comfortable sense of familiarity.

While she was standing looking up at it, the earl's Rolls-Royce came along the street and drew up beside her. The chauffeur jumped out and opened the door, and Lady Wroughton emerged, in a dark grey coat, a large sable cape and a Persian lamb hussar hat with a hackle. She moved her head slowly to look at Diana as though the movement pained her. Perhaps, Diana thought unhappily, she has difficulty in seeing anyone not wearing fur. She felt instantly small, insignificant and in the way, and had to stop herself curtsying. Somehow, whenever she saw Lady Wroughton up close, she wanted to bob like a housemaid.

The countess did not say anything, merely stood, like a monument. The chauffeur hurried past her to ring the bell, and Diana wondered how long it had been since she'd had to ring a doorbell for herself. It was one of those telling little dif-

124

ferences between their worlds. The door was opened almost immediately, and the countess gave Diana a summoning sort of look and swept in.

The door was being held by an elderly woman in a black dress, clutching a large bunch of keys; in the background an equally elderly man in a black suit hovered bare-headed, obsequiously hunched.

'This is Rudd, and Mrs Rudd. They are the caretakers,' Lady Wroughton said. 'My future daughter-in-law – she will be your mistress.'

Diana tried to smile, and the two old people bent their heads politely, their faces stiff, leaving her to wonder who among them was the most afraid.

'You need not accompany us,' Lady Wroughton told them, and they shrank back gratefully into the shadows. There were plenty of those. The front door opened straight off the street into a narrow hall with the stairs straight ahead. The paintwork was brown, which made it look darker and somehow dingy.

'The entrance is very bad,' the countess observed. 'I had forgotten how small it is. But I suppose there is nothing to be done about it. These London terraces...'

The air felt stale and cold, and there was a smell of damp under the furniture polish.

'No-one has lived here,' Lady Wroughton went on, 'in, oh, ten years at least. Charles really ought to have done something with it. If he didn't want to use it himself a tenant could have been found. However, what's done is done. Dining-room here.'

It was off to the right, with two windows onto

the street, and stretching all the way to the rear, divided unequally into two with an arch in between. One end was furnished with a long table and chairs, some sideboards, and oil paintings in heavy frames on the walls. The wallpaper was dark green, rather rubbed in places, and there were claret velvet curtains.

'A reasonable size,' the countess pronounced. 'You could close off the smaller end for a breakfast-room, perhaps. There will be no morning-room, of course, in a house like this.'

On the first floor there was a double drawing-room, with folding doors between. Here the wallpaper was dark red, and clashed with the same claret curtains. There was a dim, brownish Turkish carpet on the floor and the room was furnished with heavy Victorian pieces and more of the oil paintings.

'Quite adequate,' said Lady Wroughton.

On the next floor there was a large bedroom, a small bedroom, and a dressing-room. In the large bedroom, there was more dark red wallpaper. In the cheval glass the white counterpane on the high mahogany bed shone unnaturally against all the gloom, as if it were drawing attention to itself. *This is where it would happen,* Diana could not help thinking. She tried for an instant to imagine herself and Charles in here, getting into that bed together, and failed utterly – which was something of a relief. Incongruous as it seemed, this was the entrance to that locked room beyond the altar.

On the next floor up there were three smaller bedrooms – unfurnished – and a bathroom that contained nothing but a bath, with a separate

126

water-closet next door in what had obviously once been a cupboard. Diana, having lived most of her life in a modern house, looked at it with dismay. The bath, she noted, had only one tap.

Lady Wroughton did not seem concerned. 'Quite adequate for Charles's use,' she pronounced.

Diana dared to speak up. 'What about me?'

The countess gave her a look of surprise. 'Bathrooms are for gentlemen,' she said, as if Diana should have known *that*. 'Only servants' bedrooms above – no point in looking at those. And the kitchen and the Rudds' quarters are in the basement.' She began to lead the way downstairs. 'Apart from the entrance, it's better than I expected. With a good cleaning, and perhaps some of the paintwork refreshed, it will do very well. You'll have everything you need. What do you think?'

The last was added as an obvious afterthought, but it was the first time the countess had sought her opinion of anything, and Diana was moved. Apart from the smell of damp – which she supposed was because no fires had been lit for a long time – she loved it. True, it was rather sombre and the decorations and furniture were old-fashioned, but it was to be her first very own home, and she was thrilled by the thought of possessing all this. After just one bedroom at The Elms, she would be mistress of dining-rooms, drawing-rooms – a multitude of rooms! – and staircases and servants and chandeliers and bells. When she pulled one of those bells, her own servants would answer her. At nineteen, the thought was dazzling.

'I like it very much,' she said, with her heart in her voice.

Lady Wroughton looked at her with a hint of approval. She had expected the girl to have inappropriate middle-class tastes that she would demand to have fulfilled (though what those might be Violet Wroughton had no idea). In the kindest voice she had yet used, she said, 'I think I have found a lady's maid for you. She has been recommended by an old friend of mine, Lady Doulton. I shall interview her and see if she's suitable. You won't need her until the wedding, of course,' she concluded, looking Diana up and down again, and sighing faintly.

'We wouldn't have anywhere to put her,' Diana said, and instantly wished she hadn't.

'You must discuss with Charles whether you need more servants,' Lady Wroughton went on, ignoring her. 'With the addition of a housemaid, the Rudds might do, while he is away – you won't be entertaining.'

'Have you heard from Charles lately?' Diana asked bravely. 'I was wondering – with the news from Neuve Chapelle...'

The news had continued to be good. The British line had been advanced by a thousand yards along a front of two miles, and had it not been for bad weather – thick, disabling fog – the army would have swept through all the way to Lille and the war would have been as good as over. As it was, at the end of the third day of the battle, the army had been forced to abandon the attack and dig in to consolidate its gains.

'He wasn't in the fighting.' The countess answered her unasked question. 'He and his battalion are still at Armentières – or near there, at least. Some unpronounceable place. They are holding the line to release more experienced troops for the battle.'

Diana didn't ask how she knew. People like the Wroughtons always had ways of knowing things. 'I'm glad he's safe,' she said. 'But I know he really wanted to be fighting. He'll be disappointed, perhaps.'

'His turn will come soon enough,' the countess said. She studied Diana with a faintly puzzled air. 'You care about him,' she said, and it was not quite a statement and not quite a question.

Diana didn't know how to answer, or whether an answer was even required. At last she said, 'I will do anything I can to make him happy.'

'Hmm,' said the countess, still staring. She seemed to come to a decision. 'Is there anything you want to ask me?'

Diana swallowed. Perhaps such an opening might never come again, and the countess was evidently trying to be nice. 'About the bridesmaids,' she began.

The brows snapped together. 'I have told your mother that you may have your sister,' said Lady Wroughton. 'I have already chosen three very suitable girls for the others.'

'But I really would like to choose them myself. They are *bride's* maids,' Diana said.

'That,' said the countess with finality, 'is mere semantics.'

Diana didn't know what that meant. 'My cousins Mary and Audrey – my Aunt Sonia's daughters –

I'd always planned to have them when I got married.'

'Out of the question. The arrangements have been made.'

Diana saw ahead a lifetime of having everything decided for her. But it was her wedding, the only one she would ever have. She straightened her back and made herself meet the countess's pale eyes. 'I beg your pardon,' she said, 'but I would like to have Mary and Audrey, and my sister Sadie. I am really quite determined about that.'

Lady Wroughton looked rather as she might had a piece of furniture spoken. '*What* did you say?'

'My cousins and my sister. I'm – I'm determined to have them.'

Lady Wroughton pondered long and thoroughly. She perceived that the girl was trembling slightly, but that she was not backing down. There was a line of determination to the mouth. The girl was really quite extraordinarily beautiful, she noticed for the first time. Not just pretty. And, while she might not approve of it, she too knew the age-old custom by which beauty was the reward for power and achievement. Charles, she realised, had not done as badly as she had been thinking in securing this girl.

Violet Wroughton had always been set on having her own way, but she had a faint and backhanded admiration for anyone who stood up to her. They were not many. And she suddenly thought of Charles's streak of stubbornness, and wondered if it had come up against Diana's yet. They would have fun as husband and wife, she thought cruelly, clashing their heads together, like two rams. It would be amusing to watch – from a distance.

'Very well,' she said. 'You may have the three you wish. I cannot take back the invitations I have given, but I dare say six bridesmaids will look well enough.'

She walked past Diana towards the door, and Diana followed, feeling hollow with fear and relief. She thought suddenly of Charles and wished he was there so he could have seen how she had triumphed. She hoped so much he would be in a battle soon. In the warmth of her success, she wanted him to have everything he wanted, too.

She called in at Kensington on the way home and found Cousin Beth there, having called for tea with Sonia and Mary. Audrey was visiting a friend and the boys were at school. Another cup was sent for, and Diana sat down with them, gratefully buttered a teacake (she felt need of sustenance) and told her story. In describing the house aloud, she was aware that it was not coming across very well. The darkness, dinginess and damp seemed to be registering with her listeners rather than the thrilling fact of so much *space*.

'You'll have to make sure these Rudds keep good fires going in all the rooms,' Aunt Sonia said, 'not just the ones you're using, until the house is properly dried out. I wonder Lady Wroughton didn't say something to them.'

'You don't understand,' said Beth. 'Your aristocrats don't give a fig about comfort. Cold, damp, terrible beds, terrible food – they simply ignore them all. It's a point of pride with them.'

'But what did she mean about the bathroom?'

131

Diana asked, and repeated the comment.

Beth laughed. 'Oh, don't worry about that. She didn't mean you to go dirty! I've known a lot of old houses like that – lived in a few. They weren't built with bathrooms. In the olden days everyone bathed in their bedroom in front of the fire. Then when they did put a bath in, it was for the gentlemen only, and only cold water. Ladies continued with the old system.'

Diana was relieved. 'But,' she said, 'it seems like such a lot of work, carrying all that hot water upstairs.'

'Even more difficult getting rid of it afterwards,' said Beth. 'You must talk to Charles, tell him what changes you want made.' She saw Diana looking worried. 'He won't expect you to live without the comforts you're used to just because he's abroad.'

'Won't it cost an awful lot of money?'

'Darling,' said Beth, 'he will have taken all that into consideration. He won't have proposed to you without knowing he could afford to provide you with an establishment.'

Diana was relieved. 'I shouldn't like to live there for long without a bathroom.'

'Well, if it gets too horrid,' said Beth, 'you can always come and stay with me when he's at the front. We'll keep each other company.'

'Jack wasn't at Neuve Chapelle either, was he?' Diana asked.

'No, he's still stuck at Ypres. I was extremely grateful he wasn't caught up in the battle. But, of course, like all these men, he's longing to have a biff at the Boche and doesn't think a thing about his safety.'

'I think Charles is the same,' said Diana.

Beth gave her a sympathetic look. 'But we wouldn't love them if they were different, would we?'

CHAPTER EIGHT

After the euphoria over the victory at Neuve Chapelle, the casualty lists started to come in. At the same time the first letters home arrived from survivors of the battle, at last out of the line at rest. Rumour travelled faster than news. The cost of the battle, it was said, had been shockingly high. Men coming home on leave had stories to tell, and they jumped from mouth to mouth like a grass fire. Dressing-stations had been overwhelmed. Men had lain for hours without attention. Stretcher-bearers had gone back and forth until they dropped in their tracks from exhaustion, their uniforms stiff with other men's blood.

And when Sir John French's official despatch was finally published, it seemed that the victory had not been as overwhelming as first reported. It was clear that the intention had been for the cavalry to pour through the breach in the German line and get the enemy on the run, but the reserves had not been brought up in time and the advantage had been lost.

'WHY NOT TRUST THE PEOPLE?' demanded the *Daily Mail*. 'Our authorities would be well advised not to try to blind the public, even for a time, by telling of the victories and glossing over reverses.'

The casualty lists came in piecemeal, and few people added up the numbers. Only those with information from official circles knew they came to more than twenty-four thousand; but it was clear to everyone that the price of that 1000-yard advance had been high. A new wave of resolve washed over the country, and many who had hesitated to enlist now rushed to volunteer.

Alan Butcher was one of the first. He hurried out from Hetherton's in his apron when he saw Ethel go by to tell her. 'Mum's really upset about it,' he confessed, 'but I told her I've got to do my duty.' His eyes were shining, fixed on more distant horizons. Ethel thought his spots had almost disappeared. He seemed to have grown an inch taller, too. He'd got the makings of a good-looking man – much good would it do her!

'I'm sure Lord Kitchener will be grateful to you,' she said sarcastically.

He took it as encouragement, not really listening. 'What an adventure!' he said, softly but urgently. 'I've never been anywhere. Mother and Dad have never even been to London. It's my chance to see a bit of the world. Think of it! Going abroad, setting foot in a foreign country... And they pay you, too!' He glanced over his shoulder, saw a customer waiting and left her abruptly. Ethel wondered if he had really known she was there.

And then Phil Addis volunteered. Her exasperation knew no bounds when he came to the back door of The Elms to tell her, with the clear expectation that she would be thrilled and encouraging.

'They've opened a new recruitment centre in Westleigh, in the stables next to the police station, and I went there. I say,' he interrupted himself, 'you look pretty in that uniform. I like those dangling things.'

She was in her afternoon guise, the black dress with the muslin apron and muslin cap with streamers. 'Uniform!' she said. 'Don't talk to me about uniform!'

'I won't have mine until I get to the camp, of course,' he apologised, misunderstanding her. 'I wish you could have seen me in it.'

'I shall just have to get over the disappointment, shan't I?' she retorted.

'I have to catch the train tomorrow,' he went on. He looked wistful. 'You couldn't get off tonight, I suppose? I'd love to see you one last time before I go. We could go to the pictures. There's one on at the Electric – *Brewster's Millions*. Supposed to be very good.'

'I've seen it,' Ethel snapped. But he looked rather handsome standing there, turning his cap nervously round in his hands. And who said you had to watch the picture just because you were in a picture palace? Her options were shrinking, anyway. 'Shouldn't you be at work?' she asked, in a softer tone.

'Mr Darvell let me off early so's I could go home and pack and suchlike. Will you come out with me tonight?'

'I'll have to see,' she said. 'You can wait for me at the bus stop. If I can get off, I'll meet you there at seven.' He stepped towards her, smiling with gratitude, but she glanced behind her and said,

'I've got to go. You'll get me in trouble.'

What next? she thought, as she hurried back inside. Billy Snow, Alan Butcher and now Phil Addis – just when she was starting to like him... Her thoughts strayed to Andy Wood and she hauled them back, like an unruly dog. She wouldn't give *him* the satisfaction. Cook looked up as she came back into the kitchen. Trying to sound casual, Ethel asked, 'What d'you suppose an occupation of national importance would be?'

Cook, rolling pastry, thought about it. 'Coal miners,' she said at last. 'And what d'you call 'em that work in docks – stevedores, is it?'

'Fat lot of use that is to me,' Ethel muttered, as she passed.

Diana took the letter up to her bedroom to read it in private. It was different from his usual rather stiff epistles.

My dearest Diana,
We are out of the line and gone back to rest, so I can write to you at last. We were not in the recent fighting. I can tell you now that we are at a place called Plug Street Wood. It is a quiet sector. There is some shelling, but always at the same times, and they fire a few rounds into the air as a warning before they begin so we can take cover. We are learning our trench-craft – to be vigilant on sentry duty, to keep our heads down, to be silent at night and to show no lights. Even so, I have lost two of my men. Hipkiss was killed by a sniper while on listening patrol, and Parsons was wounded by a shell and is not expected to live. It is very hard, when I have known them for so many

years – Parsons, all my life. His wound was quite terrible. But the men are remarkably cheerful and seem to look on the danger as a relish. They long to get to grips with the enemy. Here behind the line we can see that spring is coming, the woods are growing green again. But in the distance the guns pound all the time, a sullen rumble that makes it hard to rest.

One day soon we will go into battle. I cannot look forward to it as the men do. Despite OTC and years in the Territorials, I am not naturally a soldier. I do not glory in the uniforms and guns and fighting. Even as a child I never 'played at soldiers'. I had always sooner be rambling about in the fields and woods. To see things grow is my joy. But war means destruction – not just buildings shattered but trees blown to bits, crops ruined, green spaces torn and gouged.

Soon my job will be to kill other human beings, too. How can man have reached the twentieth century and not have found a better way to resolve differences? I shall do my duty, my dearest, and I am not afraid, but there will be no glory in it for me. It is a hateful ordeal I must pass through before I can return to you and our life together.

I have your dear picture before me as I write, and I kiss it, and bless you every night in my prayers. I will strive every moment to be worthy of the two things I love more than life itself, England, and you. I will make you proud of me, my very dearest.

Ever your
Charles

She sat in thought for a long while when she had finished it. She picked up the photograph that she kept on her bedside table. His unremarkable face

137

looked back at her; she remembered the timbre of his voice, the touch of his lips, his strong arm beneath her hand. She wished passionately that she'd had more time to get to know him; yet with an unwelcome access of self-knowledge, she wondered whether she would have used the time to do so or thought only about the wedding.

Her long-held intention of marrying well seemed now childish and shallow. This was a real man, an older man, a grown-up, with complex thoughts and feelings, and she had viewed him simply as an objective to be secured, like the school essay prize. He loved her, she suspected, in ways and to a degree she knew nothing about. His letter revealed him to her as never before, and she understood suddenly that to do that was hard for him. Here he had given her a greater gift than rubies or great houses: his inmost thoughts.

She was humbled by it. He would strive to make himself worthy of her? She must take a large step into adulthood, and make *her*self worthy of *him*.

'I love him,' she said aloud, surprising herself, and for the first time, it really meant something. She got up and fetched her writing-case to start a reply.

Mrs Fitzgerald had been at a disadvantage since the war broke out in not having any sons who could volunteer and bring her glory. There was more than a touch of triumph about her, therefore, when she paid a visit to The Elms one day in the company of a very young-looking young man, whom she introduced as 'my nephew Adolphus, my sister Beamish's son'.

138

Beattie looked at him with interest and a little sympathy, for he was slight and fair, with the sort of fine skin that showed every blush, shy blue eyes and a vulnerable mouth. He seemed altogether too delicate to cope with Mrs Fitzgerald as an aunt. 'How do you do?' she said kindly. 'Are you paying a long visit?'

He didn't get the chance to answer. 'No,' said Mrs Fitzgerald. 'He'll be here only a few days. He's going to volunteer.' The triumph in her tone demanded a congratulatory murmur. 'My sister and brother-in-law thought it better for him to go to one of the London depots, where he'd have more choice of regiment. And, of course, the benefit of our advice, mine and the rector's, until he has to join his unit. So we shall have a pleasant weekend enjoying his company, and then on Monday – off he goes!'

The young man blushed and lowered his eyes. Beattie took pity on him and said, 'How splendid. I'm sure you are doing the right thing, Mr Beamish, and will be very happy, whichever regiment you join.'

'The right thing?' Mrs Fitzgerald answered for him. 'Of course he is! He knows very well where a man's duty lies, and would have volunteered sooner had he been older – but he is only just nineteen. And there was a certain reluctance to overcome on the part of his mother – wasn't there, Dolly? But I suppose that's natural,' she concluded, with faint scorn, as though it was not, in fact, natural at all.

'I was very reluctant to part with my son David,' Beattie said. 'Any mother is bound to be

139

torn between her public and private feelings.' Young Beamish looked up at that, and met her eyes with perhaps a hint of gratitude. 'Are you intending to go for the infantry or the cavalry?' she asked him.

'I – I really don't know,' he said.

'Oh, we shall discuss all that sort of thing with him before Monday,' Mrs Fitzgerald said briskly. 'We came here this morning merely to introduce him to you, and to ask you to favour us with your company at a little dinner party tomorrow night. Short notice, I know, but we didn't know he was coming until yesterday. You and your husband, and your dear daughters – I hope you will all come? We want to make these last days as enjoyable as possible.'

They happened not to be engaged, and Beattie accepted for all of them, while smiling reassuringly at the nervous young man and thinking the phrase 'these last days' sounded unpleasantly ominous.

They sat down twenty to dinner at the rectory – their dining-room would not comfortably hold more – but Mrs Fitzgerald had invited a lot more people to come after dinner, so even with the doors between the drawing-room and the parlour thrown open, there was quite a crowd. There was little danger that anyone who mattered in Northcote would not know the Fitzgeralds had a nephew in the army.

Adolphus looked, Beattie thought, even more vulnerable in evening clothes, and very young for his nineteen years. Though shy, he had nice manners and had been properly brought up, so he did the rounds of the guests, and if he tended to let them talk at him rather than talk to them himself, it did him no harm. Most people like a listener, and most people have helpful advice ready to give anyone who will stand still for long enough.

Beattie was glad of a social occasion for the girls, for things had been a little quiet recently, and she thought Diana in particular was feeling something of a let-down: it was hard for a girl to enjoy her engagement when her fiancé was so relentlessly absent. She was soon the centre of a lively group of her female friends and such of the male satellites who had not heeded the siren call of the colours.

Sadie, enjoying the novelty of the first proper dinner party she had been invited to, was happy to efface herself in a corner to watch and listen, and was surprised, but pleased, to find herself suddenly sharing it with the star of the evening. She had liked the look of him, understood his shyness, thought it pretty hard cheese that he had to endure being lionised by such an overwhelming force as Mrs Fitzgerald. He looked at her uncertainly as he joined her in her seclusion, as though afraid she would shout, 'Here he is, everybody!'

'So much talk,' she remarked. 'How can people find so much to say to each other – especially as they've all known each other for years and years?' She smiled. 'You've had your ear chewed off this evening, I think?'

'Oh,' he said. 'Well, it couldn't be helped, I suppose. Aunt Honoria wanted to introduce me to everyone.' Sadie blinked, never having thought of Mrs Fitzgerald as having a Christian name. 'It's rather horrid, though, being shown off as if I've done something wonderful. I mean, thousands of other chaps have done the same.'

'Never mind,' Sadie said. 'It's just one evening. It won't kill you. I'm Sadie Hunter, by the way.' She offered her hand.

He shook it, enlightenment in his face. 'Oh, then – Miss Hunter, over there, would be your sister?' He looked across to where Diana was talking and laughing. 'She's very beautiful,' he added, with a hint of wistfulness.

'Yes,' said Sadie.

His fine skin flushed. 'Oh! I'm sorry – I didn't mean... I'm such a clumsy ass.' He looked at her, properly, for the first time. 'You're very pretty, too.'

'It's all right,' Sadie said. 'I'm quite used to the comparison.'

'No, I mean it,' he said earnestly. 'You really are very attractive. A person could look at your face over and over. Don't you think perfect beauty would get a bit boring after a while?'

Sadie laughed now. 'I think you're getting yourself into more and more of a tangle. You'd better stop. Let's talk about you instead. Are you very excited about volunteering?'

A look of gloom came over his face. 'Not really. I say, you won't tell anyone I said that, will you?'

'Of course not. Cross my heart and hope to die. But why are you doing it, then?'

'Aunt Honoria,' he said. 'She talked Mother and Dad into it, pi-jawed them until they couldn't do anything else but throw me to her, like–'

'Like a Christian to the lions,' Sadie suggested.

142

'But don't you want to do your bit for the war effort?'

'Oh, of course,' he said hastily. 'I mean, I suppose I'd have had to go eventually. And I know it's King and country and everything, and naturally I'll be proud to do my duty, but – well – I suppose I'm not really the soldiering type. I'm not looking forward to it.'

Sadie observed his suffering look with interest. She didn't *think* it was simple cowardice. 'What is it you're not looking forward to?' she asked.

He met her eyes. 'Being with all those men. Having to join in, never being able to get away and be on one's own. It was bad enough at school, but the army will be much worse – must be, when you think of it. The talking, the laughing – the way men are when they get together. Perfectly decent chaps change when they're in a group. They become coarse. And cruel. I don't like the smell of them. And the noise – that's worst of all.'

Sadie was receiving startling images, but her quick imagination could see how it must be for a sensitive person. She was fond of solitude herself, but was able to shut out what she didn't like when she could not be alone. It must be awful for someone who couldn't.

'What *do* you like?' she asked.

'Music,' he said, his eyes lighting. 'I play the violin. Are you musical?'

'I learned the piano,' Sadie said, 'but I wouldn't say I was very good at it. Are you good?'

'Competent,' he said. 'I will get better, if I'm allowed. It's all I want to do – play music. I'd like to be a professional musician, but Mother and

Dad won't hear of it. They want me to go into Dad's business.'

Sadie was not surprised. It was like a daughter saying she wanted to be an actress. 'I don't suppose you can earn much money as a musician,' she said. 'Isn't it rather a drudge?'

'It used to be. But things are different now. There's the new orchestra, the London Symphony Orchestra. The players run it themselves and take a share of the profits. Oh, you'd never be rich, but you could earn a reasonable living. I *know* I'd be good enough to get in. And then – just think! To do nothing all day, every day, but play the greatest music that's ever been written! Under the greatest conductors! They even go abroad now. In 1912 they did a tour of America – New York, Boston, everything. What bliss!'

'Well,' said Sadie, sorry to bring him down to earth, 'I expect it'll be different now there's a war on. I mean, everything seems to get cancelled, doesn't it? The hunting, the football – they're saying there'll be no cricket this summer. Probably there won't be many concerts until the war's over.'

'I expect you're right,' he said, the light dying. 'And it won't matter if there are, because *I* shan't be playing in them. I've got to go and be a soldier.'

'Probably the other musicians will, too,' she said. 'But there's always after the war. Once you're twenty-one, you can do what you like.'

'That's true,' he said. 'Though I'd hate to upset the parents. But once I've done my duty in the army, perhaps they'll feel differently and let me follow my own path. Except,' the gloom again, 'I shall be so out of practice by then.'

144

'But you can get back *in* practice, can't you?' Sadie said, with a touch of impatience.

'I suppose so.' He brightened. 'I can take my violin with me to the army, and practise when I'm not on duty. I say, you are a brick to listen to me like this! I wish I had a sister like you. And I'm a selfish brute, talking about myself. Now *you* tell me all about what you like.'

Sadie had only drawn a preparatory breath when she was blasted aside by the power of an arriving personality, and Mrs Fitzgerald's hand came past her to seize Beamish's arm. 'There you are! What are you doing, hiding in the corner like this? Come and talk to Mrs Colonel Barry. I'm sure she'll have some very good advice for you.' He was carried away, able only to cast an apologetic glance in Sadie's direction as the crowd swallowed him up.

CHAPTER NINE

Rustington was a village in a valley, at the confluence of three small rivers, and the road to Northcote was up a very steep hill. Sadie had to push the bicycle. When she paused for breath, the pedal swung round and rapped her smartly on the shin. Like an unwilling horse, it frequently bit and kicked her, and occasionally threw her off. As she wrestled it into position again, she heard an engine coming up the hill and turned to look. John Courcy's car was approaching, and to her surprise

145

Nailer was sitting very upright on the front seat, his eyes half closed with bliss at the movement.

Courcy waved when he saw her and drew to a halt beside her.

'How did you come by a passenger?' Sadie called.

'I saw him running up the road. I was worried he might get run over, so I stopped and called him, and he jumped in as though he'd been riding in cars all his life.'

'He looks as if he's enjoying it,' Sadie said.

'Are you going home?' asked Courcy. 'Can I give you a lift?'

'I've got the bicycle,' Sadie demurred unwillingly.

But he said, 'It can go on the back seat. This hill's too steep for pedalling.'

In a moment they were on their way again, the bicycle in the back and Sadie sharing the front seat with Nailer, who sat to the outside of her and stuck his head into the wind of passage. 'Funny old dog,' she said, but he was enjoying it too much to answer. 'He must trust you to get into the car so readily,' she remarked to Courcy.

'Animals like me,' he said. 'Good thing, too.'

'Are you going to the camp?' she asked.

'No, to Rice's,' he replied, and gave her a significant look. 'This may be the last time you see me in civilian clothes.'

She caught his meaning. 'You're going to get your uniform?'

'Yes, my captain's commission's come through. I'm in the army now.'

'Captain Courcy,' she said. 'It sounds very fine.

Your father must be pleased.'

'I think it's taken a lot of the sting out of having a vet for a son,' he admitted.

'Will you have to go abroad?' She thought that, like all men, he must want to, but she would miss seeing him around Northcote.

'I expect so. They haven't said anything, but I understand there's going to be a big battle soon, and they're bound to need vets in the aftermath, if not the preparation.'

'For the horses.' Sadie thought with a pang of horses being wounded; perhaps those she had helped train.

'They have messenger dogs, too, and carrier pigeons.'

'Do you know a lot about pigeons?'

'Nothing at all,' he admitted. 'I imagine if they're wounded it will be a matter of despatching them humanely.' He saw her frown of concern, and went on, to distract her, 'Of course, there are other animals. Goats, for instance.'

'Goats?'

'Regimental mascots. And behind the line there are often pigs and chickens and so on, kept for food, so I expect I shall be able to keep my hand in.'

'But it's mostly horses.'

'Most of a vet's training is in horses. I dare say we spent four-fifths of our time at the Dick School on equine anatomy and ailments. Speaking of equines, how are yours up at Highclere?'

Warren came in with some papers for Edward to sign, and said, 'Would you like your tea now, sir?'

147

'Hm? Oh, yes, thank you,' Edward said.

He looked up with a smile, and seeing he was receptive, Warren went on, 'I think I mentioned that my cousin Robert was home on leave at the weekend?'

'You did.'

'I went with him to visit our great-aunt in Godalming on Sunday, for tea. Robert was trying to tell her what it was like at the front, and when he paused, she said, "Tell me, dear, are there any picture palaces there, where you and your friends can go when you get back from the trenches in the evening?"'

Edward laughed. Warren liked to bring him amusing little anecdotes to brighten his day. 'I don't suppose anyone who hasn't been there can really know what it's like.'

'No, sir,' said Warren. 'Which brings me to the question—'

'No, Warren,' Edward interrupted. 'I know you're eager to do your bit, but there's more than one way to help England to victory. Without banking, everything would stop.' He saw the resistance in the young man's eyes. 'I really could not manage without you,' he concluded sincerely.

'Thank you, sir,' said Warren, though his tone was wistful. 'I'll bring your tea.'

He was back sooner than Edward expected, and empty-handed. 'There's a lady to see you, sir,' said Warren.

There was something about the quality of hesitance in his voice that warned Edward. 'Evidently we don't know her,' he said. 'What sort of a lady?'

'A foreign lady. She gives her name as Madame de Rouveroy, but she doesn't have a card.'

Edward examined his secretary's face. 'And you feel I should see her?'

'I don't think she's collecting, sir,' Warren excused himself. One or two grand ladies had got past him on pretence of wanting to do business with Edward, only to ask him for a donation to their pet cause. Everyone was collecting for something, these days. 'She has a maid with her. I think she is – *sérieuse*.'

'Very well,' Edward said. If she turned out to be just a refugee in need he would direct her to Lady Lugard or Mrs Alfred Lyttelton of the War Refugees Council at the Aldwych. But he trusted Warren's instincts, and his lapse into French was only because there wasn't a direct translation. *Of serious purpose – not light or frivolous*, perhaps came near it. 'Show her in.'

She was all in black – a black woollen coat to the ankles, and a black hat with a full veil. The hat was large, not in the latest style, and it and the coat were a little shabby. But Edward's practised eye took in the boots, which were well made and polished, and the gloves, which were fine.

He stood and went towards her, and said, 'Madame, how may I be of service to you?'

She threw back the veil, then carefully removed one glove before looking up at him. She was small, a little smaller than Beattie, and slenderly made. The hand she extended to him was white and fragile-looking as a china doll's; and the face was thin, pale and delicately carved. Her eyes were blue, with heavy white lids like magnolia petals;

149

the lips full under a straight nose; the hair revealed at her temples lay in heavy curves of dark gold, caught up under the hat. She stood before him very erect, and offered her hand with a kind of authority. The eyes and lips seemed to promise sensuality, but the nose and chin had determination about them, and she looked directly into his eyes in a way very few women ever did. It was not coquettish, nor was it challenging. It seemed to say, *Here I am. Deal with me as I am.*

'I am Élise de Rouveroy,' she said. 'It is good of you to see me.' Her voice was pleasant and musical, and her slight accent, to Edward's undiscerning ear, sounded French. He took her hand. It seemed very small in his, and felt cold. April had come in much drier than March, thank God, but with the wind from the north, much colder. And that coat did not look very thick.

'Won't you come to the fire, Madame?' he said, leading her towards the pair of armchairs where his favoured clients chatted to him over sherry while toasting their feet. A movement caught his eye and he saw that Warren was lingering at the door in case his instinct had proved wrong and his master wanted her ejected. 'Bring some tea, will you, Warren?' he said.

'You are very kind,' said his visitor, going to the fire with a suppressed eagerness, taking off her other glove. He thought she was shivering, but couldn't be sure. She moved with unusual grace, and seated herself in a way that reminded him of something, or someone, though he couldn't quite determine what, or whom. 'Of course, England *is* kind, to take us in,' she went on, 'and to fight for

150

us. But one cannot depend too much on charity, for one might wear it out.'

'You are from France, Madame?'

'From Belgium,' she corrected him. 'Allow me to warm myself for a moment, and I will tell you my story.' She was stretching out her hands to the flames. 'I am aware, sir, that you are a man of affairs. I will not take more of your time than I must.'

'Please, take all the time you wish,' he said, and for once in his busy life he really meant it. He was quite happy to wait, and have the opportunity to look at her. There was something almost ethereal about her, so delicate and pale and graceful, as though she had come from a much more distant bourne than the prosaic-sounding Belgium.

Warren came in with the tea tray, on which he had thoughtfully placed a plate of biscuits – Palfrey's assorted, of course: there was always a tin of them in the outer office, thanks to Aeneas. The visitor seemed to have stopped shivering. She straightened up as Warren placed the tray, and her gaze was avid as she looked at it. Edward was intrigued by her. She was hungry, she was thin, she was unsuitably dressed for the weather; but her clothes had been good, and there was refinement in every line and gesture. A lady, who had had to leave everything behind to flee her country: so far, so understandable. But there was also that directness, which did not fit into the story.

Warren withdrew, Edward poured tea and placed the cup and the biscuits within her reach. She gave him almost an apologetic look, sipped thirstily, selected a biscuit, which she demolished

151

rapidly, and took another. Then she sighed, straightened her back, and said, 'You are remarkably patient, sir. I will not cause you to wait longer. I am ready now to give explanation of myself.'

Edward crossed his legs and leaned back, signalling receptiveness.

She was the widow of Guillaume de Rouveroy of Tournai, a wealthy man whose fortune stemmed from the manufacture of bicycles and motor-car parts. 'I was his second wife. His first wife died, poor lady, many years before, and I inherited from her a grown-up step-son, Émile. When the Germans invaded, Émile went at once to join the army. Within the month, the enemy reached Tournai. Guillaume and I fled across the border to Lille, where he had a house.' She looked at him. 'Of course, you must know the history of Lille.'

'It fell in October last year,' said Edward.

'Many people fled. Perhaps we should have – Lille was not our first home. But there was a small garrison, and they were not giving up, so Guillaume said we should resist. He would not leave, and I would not leave him. For ten days we held the Germans off. We endured their bombardment – much was destroyed. But, in the end, they won. Then they were angry that we had resisted and burned a whole section of the town as punishment.'

'The *Schrecklichkeit*,' Edward murmured. 'We read about it here.'

'They were afraid of the Francs-tireurs, and the resistance of Belgium.' She shrugged. 'It was not as bad as in Liege, or Louvain, or Dinant. But it

152

was no longer a place to stay. I had almost left it too late. A friend of my husband helped me to get away.' A pause. 'Guillaume was killed in the fighting at the end. He would not let the *sales Boches* come without a struggle.'

'I'm so sorry, Madame.'

She gave him a clear look that held no self-pity. 'Our house was one of those burned. I was not able to save anything from it. But one does what one can. I escaped with my maid Solange and what we could carry, and we made our way at last to England. Here we have met with great kindness.'

Edward hardly liked to ask. 'And your step-son, Émile?'

'He was killed at Ypres in November. The news found me here. I am glad only that Guillaume did not have to hear it. It would have broken his heart.'

He poured her more tea. 'And in what way can I be of service to you, Madame?' he asked gently.

She squared her shoulders as to an unpleasant task and gave him again that direct look. 'The money I managed to bring with me has run out. I must raise somehow enough to live on. I have documents that Guillaume brought from the safe in our house in Tournai which relate to stocks – as I believe they are called. He said they were valuable, and so I wish now to sell them. Lady Lugard told me that you were a sympathetic person who would understand and be able to help.'

'I will certainly try,' Edward said. 'May I see these documents?'

'Solange has them in a bag, downstairs.'

153

The maid was elderly, with a lined face, thick, pitted skin, and a heavy underlip that made her look sullen. She peered at Edward suspiciously, clutching the carpet bag to her, until Madame de Rouveroy addressed her sharply in rapid French. Then she yielded the bag reluctantly to Edward, who placed it on his desk to examine the contents. Inside were bundles of stock certificates. He invited his guest to take more tea while he examined them, but his heart had sunk at the name on the topmost one. Halbach's were a large munitions manufacturers in the Wupper Valley in Germany.

When he had gone through them all, he sat for a moment in silence, wondering how to break the news. Madame de Rouveroy looked at him anxiously, and at last said, 'Do not keep me in suspense. I think from your face it is not good news.'

'I'm afraid, Madame, that the investments represented by these documents are worthless,' he said.

Her cheeks trembled. 'How can that be? Guillaume was a wise businessman. He told me the stocks were valuable.'

'They were, at one time, but the war changed everything. German munitions manufacturers were valuable businesses and paid good dividends. Your husband invested wisely. But the German government has nationalised the companies, and suspended the shares.'

'Is it – is it all German munitions?'

'Not all, but the bulk of the investments is in German companies. The rest is in companies in what is now occupied territory. No dividends will be paid to foreign holders, like yourself, and the shares cannot be sold. I'm afraid what was once

154

a fortune here,' he tapped the pile of certificates, 'is now turned to dust.'

Her eyes were fixed on him painfully, and she was trying valiantly not to cry. He hoped she wouldn't cry. He didn't think he could bear it. He looked instead at the maid, whose ugly face was thrust towards her mistress, frowning, trying to understand.

After a moment Madame de Rouveroy regained control. 'Thank you for telling me,' she said, in a voice that wavered only slightly.

'You may, of course, take another opinion,' said Edward.

'No, I am sure you are right.' She sighed. 'Poor Guillaume. He always said he would leave me well provided for. He was many years older than me, and was concerned how I should live if he died. He would be heartbroken to think all his care was for nothing.'

Edward wondered if she was now destitute. 'Have you anything else you can sell, Madame?' he asked. He couldn't imagine her going out to work. An insane thread in his mind trembled on the edge of inviting her to come and live in his household…

'My jewels,' she said, and sighed again. 'I did not manage to bring everything away, but Solange and I brought the best pieces. I shall be sorry to part with them, for Guillaume gave them to me, but I suppose it must come to it.'

'I'm sure your husband would understand. Would you like me to negotiate a sale for you?'

She raised her eyebrows. 'Can you do that?'

'I have done the same thing many times in the

155

past for other families. I have good contacts in both jewellery companies and auction houses. I feel sure I can get you a good price. May I see the pieces?'

Now she smiled, and the effect was devastating. 'But of course. They are at home – in what we must call home now, though it is but a small apartment. Solange and I can bring them to you.'

'No need, Madame. I will not put you to the trouble,' he said, thinking that the streets were not the safest place these days for a woman to be carrying a bag full of jewellery. 'It will be my pleasure to wait on you at home, whenever is convenient to you. And, if I might suggest, the jewellery ought to be kept here, in the safe, until a sale is arranged. We live in uncertain times.'

'Ah, yes, I comprehend you,' she said. 'You are very kind. Please come whenever is most convenient to you. I know you must be busy. I, alas, have nothing to do.'

'Tomorrow morning, then – will that suit?' Edward asked.

She bent her head graciously.

CHAPTER TEN

Beth invited Diana to stay with her in Town for a week or so. 'We'll do some shopping, see a show or two – what do you say? It will be a kindness to me. I'm not used to being without Jack. I don't think we ever spent more than one night apart in

156

all the years we've been married.'

'Mind you,' said Beth, on the first evening, as they sat down to supper in her elegant dining-room with its dark green Regency-stripe wallpaper, 'I'm surprised that your future mother-in-law hasn't invited you to stay. She *is* still in Town, isn't she?'

'She isn't at Dene Park,' Diana said, 'so I suppose so. I'd sooner stay with you, anyway. It wouldn't be much fun at Wroughton House. Lady Wroughton terrifies me.'

'All the same, she ought to have asked you. She must be a strange woman. Especially with your fiancé away at the front, she owes you the attention.'

'Ought I to call on her?' Diana asked doubtfully.

'No, darling. Not unless she invites you. But we can leave cards, if you like, to say you are in Town.' She took a reflective sip of wine. 'I must say, it seems odd to be worrying about points of etiquette, cards and suchlike, when our men are engaged in war. But you're going to belong to her set, so it's better to be correct. You wouldn't want it thought you didn't know how to behave.'

Diana was ready to enjoy herself. Beth was an easy companion, and so extremely elegant that her advice while shopping was invaluable; and London was lively with plenty to see and do. There were more signs of the war there than in North-cote: lots of men in uniform everywhere, and a disturbing number of wounded in their hospital blue, hobbling about or being pushed in wheel-chairs. There were posters about recruitment, forthcoming meetings and speeches, and exhortations to do one's bit in various ways. There were ladies collecting for pet funds at every strategic point; and a few with hard eyes and uncompromising hats handing out white feathers to any man who did not move quickly enough to avoid them. Cinemas were showing war newsreels and offering free admission to men in uniform, and Lyons Corner Houses advertised a special Patriotic Tea.

Diana also saw for the first time a woman driving a motor-van, and turned her head to stare, though from the fact that no-one else did, she gathered that lady drivers were not so rare in London.

And then there was the blackout, as people were calling it. It was strange not to see the usual gay lights at night. Houses and clubs were muffled with curtains, shops were dark, trams ran with their internal lights off, headlights were partly painted over, street lamps had their tops painted black and their power turned down so that the cones of light no longer joined up. An electric torch, Diana learned, was the first thing a lady put into her handbag and a man into his pocket when going out for the evening. It was said that for the first time you could see stars in the sky above Piccadilly, but though Diana passed through it often enough she was always too happily occupied to look.

The other big change wrought by the war was the rather aggressive urge to morality that had sprung up. The newspapers were still full of letters and appeals by the teetotallers to ban all alcohol, and men with sandwich boards paraded in front of pubs, social clubs and music halls with messages such as 'Are you forgetting there's a War on?'

Beth told Diana there was a campaign, started by the Evangelicals, to shut down the music halls, or at least to rid them of the 'salacious' revues, 'vulgar' comic turns and 'indecent' dancing girls that were the delight of working-class Londoners and of soldiers and sailors. And a similar campaign, carried on relentlessly since the previous autumn, had finally driven the Football Association to announce that professional football would cease for the duration of the war. The Cup Final between Chelsea and Sheffield United on the 24th of April would be the last match until peace returned.

'I don't understand what they've got against football,' Diana said. 'Surely it's an innocent enough thing.'

'I gather the puritan element believe that any frivolous activity is a waste of time and money and a moral affront in time of war. We should all be straining every fibre of our being at every moment to defeat the enemy.'

'Surely men on leave from the front have the right to enjoy themselves,' Diana argued.

'Ah, but puritans don't believe in enjoyment,' Beth said gaily. 'It's a sure sign you are sinning. What do you say to coffee and cake at Gunter's? I don't know about you, but I feel I've hardly sinned at all today.'

Lady Wroughton sent a typed note that said, 'The Countess Wroughton thanks you for the kind information of your presence in Town,' but it was not followed up with any further communication. Diana was relieved, though Beth was indignant on her behalf.

In fact, the countess had been about to invite Diana to stay, but Rupert had talked her out of it.

'Why encourage her?' he demanded. 'You don't want this marriage to go ahead, do you?'

'Nothing would please me more than if the engagement had never happened,' said her ladyship, crossly, 'but it's been announced. There's nothing to be done now.'

'Of course Charles can't jilt her,' Rupert admitted. 'That would be disgraceful. And he wouldn't do it anyway.'

'Charles has a high sense of honour,' said the countess, though not as if it gave her any pleasure.

'No, the poor fish thinks he's in love with her,' Rupert said. 'But what if *she* jilts *him?* He'd be free and clear with no disgrace.'

'But why should she do that?'

'Because she doesn't care a jot for Charles. All she's interested in is the money and the title. She's a fortune-hunter, plain and simple.'

Lady Wroughton looked a little shocked. 'You surely don't mean that.'

'She's as cold and rapacious as a spider. And how do you distract a spider that's bent on eating a fly?'

'Really, Rupert, how on earth should I know? Speak sense, if you must speak at all.'

'You dangle an even fatter, juicier fly in front of it,' said Rupert. The countess shuddered at the imagery. 'Miss Hunter doesn't care for Charles.

She wants to marry a lord, and it can't matter to her which one. So suppose *I* make a point of bumping into her and befriending her. And then I introduce my friend Saint-Henry to her. *Much* juicier than poor old Charles, you see. Saint-Henry's not just the son of a duke, and rich, he's also charming and very good-looking, which we can't claim for Charles, much as we love him.'

The countess considered. It was true that Lord Saint-Henry was very handsome – tall, dark, with a Byronic profile and a smile that had impressed itself even on her. Still, 'I don't understand you,' the countess said impatiently.

Rupert explained. 'Saint-Henry is a terrible flirt – and a good sport. If he makes a play for Miss Hunter, and does it convincingly enough, she'll drop Charles and make a grab for him. A bird in the hand, you see, poor old Charles being far away in France. I know Saint-Henry will play if *I* ask him.'

The countess shook her head. 'It smacks of underhand dealing. I don't like it. It is not the sort of thing a Wroughton would stoop to.'

'Dear Mama, you needn't stoop to anything. *I*'ll do the dirty deed. All you have to do is not encourage her.'

'All the same, it isn't right. No, Rupert, you shall not trick the girl.'

Rupert scowled, not liking to be thwarted, but quickly cleared his brow and put on his most reasonable face. 'There's no trick to it, Mama. If the girl is true and honest, Saint-Henry won't have any effect on her. He'll flirt and she'll brush him off. It's only if she's a bad lot that she'll go for the lure – and if she does, aren't we well rid of her?'

'And all you want me to do is not invite her to stay?' Lady Wroughton said doubtfully.

'That's all.'

I ought to pay her the attention, the countess thought. It was proper – and she had always done what was proper. But the Season hadn't fully started yet. There was no harm, perhaps, in delaying a few weeks. If the engagement still persisted in May, she could ask her then. If not... Her mind moved on to the pleasant prospect of cancelling the wedding. Very little money had yet been expended. The bridesmaids' dresses – probably a cancellation fee if they had been cut out already. There would be notices to send out. Presents would not start arriving until next month, but any that did would have to be sent back. And the work being done on the house in Clarges Street would not be wasted: if Charles didn't want a separate Town house, it could always be rented out.

'I wish to know nothing about it,' she said at last. 'I do not authorise you in any way, Rupert. Do you understand?'

'Oh, yes,' said Rupert. He understood very well. Mentally he rubbed his hands with relish. No-one could resist Saint-Henry, who was the worst flirt – or, say, the best flirt – in London, and he loved a dare. The Hunter female would fall right into the trap.

Soho Square was not the most salubrious address, but it was at least within easy walking distance of Piccadilly. Edward had made his first call at Madame de Rouveroy's flat on the day after her visit, to inspect the jewels and take them away. The flat was in a big, five-storey tenement, built about twenty-five years ago and in need of painting and some repair. But the rooms inside were of a decent size and had high ceilings. Madame de Rouveroy had a two-bedroom flat at the top, high up enough to enjoy cleaner air than that found at street-level. It was furnished with the usual utilitarian ugliness, but she had done a lot with small touches to make it more pleasant. The curtains were tied back with ribbon to let in as much light as possible; there were gay shawls thrown over the sofa and arm-chairs to conceal the shabbiness of the upholstery; bunches of dried flowers and grasses in tall vases brightened dark corners; and to supply the bareness of the walls (and to conceal as much of the wallpaper as possible) she had hung up pictures cut out of magazines, mounted on card and framed with *passe-partout*, of thin and elongated ladies in fashionable outfits.

Solange answered the door to him on this, his second, visit, with no melting of the sullen look. He hoped it was inveterate rather than indicating mistrust of him.

'Is your mistress at home?'

He gave the maid his silk hat, gloves and umbrella, and followed her down the narrow passage to the sitting-room. Though it was a sunny enough April day, it was cold out, and there was a bright fire. Madame de Rouveroy was sitting on the sofa in front of it, reading, one foot tucked under her in a delightfully informal way, her chin propped on her hand. She was wearing a dark red skirt and a holly green woollen top, and the curves of her gold hair caught the moving firelight. It was a lovely scene, full of colour and warmth. He wished in that instant that he was a painter.

'Do I disturb you, Madame?' he said.

She jumped up, smiling, and came towards him, her hand outstretched so welcomingly that when he took it, he covered it with his other hand in a spontaneous gesture. 'I am delighted to be disturbed. This house is too quiet and I spend too much time reading. It is, at least, a way to pass time that does not cost money, but I know the books too well. You bring me good news?'

'I hope you will think so,' said Edward, obeying her graceful gesture and sitting down on the sofa. She sat beside him, but turned sideways to face him. 'I have an offer for all of your jewellery, and I think the price good. I have the details here.'

He began to produce the sheaf of papers, but she placed the tips of her fingers briefly on his hand in a staying motion. The touch made him jump, and not because they were cold. 'Oh, no, please,' she said. 'Let us be civilised. First to drink a glass, and to talk – that was the way Guillaume conducted business. The pounds and guineas should wait – don't you think so?'

'As you prefer, Madame,' he said, putting the papers down again, and then, thinking he had sounded cold, added, 'It will be my pleasure.'

'Ah, you think so! Good! Then let me beg you to have luncheon with me. Ah, no, don't refuse – I see it in your face. But only think – I have been used to be a great hostess, before I was reduced to this little place. So it will be a kindness to let me perform once more, even in this small way, to pretend things are again as they were. Let me entertain you.' She surveyed his expression keenly and added, with an impish smile, 'Solange is a good cook.'

He could not hold out against such pleading – it would have seemed like a snub. 'I accept with pleasure, Madame.'

'Good, good! Then first, with sherry. It should be champagne to celebrate your good news, perhaps, but sherry we have, and so–' She gave a funny little shrug and got up and went to the table by the fireplace to pour sherry from a bottle into two glasses. 'A toast,' she said, handing him one. 'To good business – and good friends.'

Edward drank the toast, wondering what they were to talk about. He took luncheon not infrequently with clients, but they were men and the talk was of business and politics. His conversations with women had always been on social occasions and the subjects were usually local affairs or friends and family. Neither of those would apply to the present situation. It might be rather awkward.

But Madame de Rouveroy began without the slightest unease. 'Now, Mr Hunter, tell me about you. Because you arouse my curiosity. You are not at all like a banker.'

'And what are bankers like, Madame?' Edward asked.

'Old,' she said. 'And dull. And always – the *embonpoint*.' She described a curve with her hand from chest to lap, and laughed infectiously.

Edward had to smile. 'In time, Madame, I hope to acquire the appropriate shape.'

165

'No, no, you must not. I like you as you are.'

'But a hungry banker does not inspire confidence. He must look prosperous – as though he takes care of his own money very well.'

'I prefer the intellectual appearance. Tell me of yourself. Did you always want to be a banker?'

It was so easy, so comfortable, that somehow he found himself talking about himself in a way that he had never done in his whole life. When he was courting Beattie, it was she who had been the interesting one. Struggling in the web of her own personal disaster, she had known as much about him already as she needed to, without further questioning. And since then, there had been no need or opportunity.

At some point in the conversation the sherry was finished and they moved without interrupting it from the sofa to the drop-leaf table, which Solange had been quietly setting up behind them in the window. The meal that the maid served to them was simple but tasty: grilled sardines with lemon juice and bread-and-butter, followed by a dish of mutton braised in what his hostess called a *casserole,* with onions and vegetables and a rich liquor, and finally a dessert of cheese and dried apples. She apologised that there was no wine – 'But one day soon I think I shall afford it again, no?' – but they had another glass of sherry with the cheese.

And the conversation never flagged. When they were settled with their dessert and Solange had left them, he felt enough at home to say playfully, 'And now, Madame, you must return the compliment and tell me about *you.* My curiosity is also aroused.'

'Am I not like a wealthy man's wife?'

He searched for a polite way to say it. 'I cannot at all account for you.'

'Perhaps that is because I was out of my place. Guillaume inherited his fortune from his father, and never went near the factories that were the source of it. He wished to live the life of ease and pleasure, as was his right. Tournai is a pleasant place, but perhaps not the best for those seeking *la vie mondiale*. The ill-health of his first wife made him stay at home a great deal, and when her death released him, he travelled. Brussels, Paris, Berlin, London, Rome – wherever the lights were brightest. But it did not answer. In his heart, Guillaume was a man who needed someone to care for. Madeleine was dead, Émile away at the university. He had money to spend but no-one to spend it on except himself. It did not answer.'

'I can understand that,' Edward said. The thought of life without Beattie and his children...! All the wealth in the world would be useless.

She looked kindly at him. 'Yes, I know you can. I see it. So, Guillaume was *désolé*.'

'And then he found you,' Edward said.

She nodded. 'In Paris he found me.'

'So you are French, not Belgian?'

She eyed him with a bright, curious look, like a bird. 'Do you wish to know where he found me?'

'If you wish to tell me.'

'At the Opéra!' She laughed gaily. 'Do I shock you? *Bien sûr*, gentlemen do not meet ladies at the Opéra – but I was not a lady. I was a ballet girl. *Now* I have shocked you, I think?'

167

'Not at all, Madame,' Edward said. He really meant it, but from the fear that she would not believe him, he sounded awkward.

'I will tell you,' she said, pouring more sherry. 'When you know all, you may be as shocked as you please. I was from a poor family. My father died when I was a child, my mother struggled to care for us. I had three younger brothers. She found a place as a concierge, she took in sewing, but always, always it was a struggle. I was a pretty girl, and one of the residents, who owned a ballet school, took a fancy to me and taught me free of charge. My mother thought it would be a good way for me to earn my living and would take me off her hands. But you know, I am sure, the reputation of ballet girls.' She shrugged. 'Well, one must live. To find a good, generous keeper is one's dream. I was luckier. I was dancing in *Orphée aux Enfers* when he saw me. He came backstage and invited me to dinner. I thought it would all go as usual. But I encouraged him to talk, and at the end of the evening, he took me home in a taxi – to *my* home. He kissed my hand and asked if he could see me the next night. In three weeks more we were married.'

'He fell in love with you,' said Edward.

'One cannot explain these things. It was as you say. He married me and took me back to Tournai and the travelling was done. Like Odysseus, he wanted to go home. But he took his Penelope with him.' Edward could not help looking surprised at the reference. She smiled. 'You thought me uneducated.'

'I beg your pardon– I didn't mean–'

168

'Ah, but so I was. An ignorant ballet girl. But Guillaume had a large library, and there was not always much for me to do. So I read.' She laughed happily. 'I began at one end and read all the way to the other. And now I know many things.'

'Were you happy together?' Edward heard himself ask, and was astonished. Such a personal question, on such a brief acquaintance, was impertinence, and not at all like him. But nothing about this lunch was like him.

'Yes, I was happy. He was good to me. I was safe for ever.' Another shrug. 'The *grandes dames* of Tournai turned up their noses at me – is not that a good English phrase, "turned up their noses"? I speak English very well, don't you think? Yes, when they found where I came from I was not good enough for them. But as Guillaume's wife I was invited everywhere, and everyone wanted to be invited to his dinners, which were my dinners. And Émile – there might have been difficulty there. But his mother was too long dead for jealousy, and he liked me, *tout simple.*' Suddenly her smiling face changed, seemed to grow older in one instant, drawn and pale as it had been when he had first seen her. 'And now they are dead, my kind Guillaume and my sweet Émile. And I am alone, and have nothing.' She tried to smile but it was a travesty. 'I cannot even dance now, for my living. I am too old.'

Edward was horribly touched. He had, in the course of business, been told many sad tales and faced many men who were all to pieces, but it was not his business to feel emotion in their cases. He must remain detached in order to do the best for them, for the bank, and for his career, on which his family depended. But this delicate-looking creature dragged painfully at his heart. He cleared his throat awkwardly, and said, 'I hope, when you see the price I have been able to secure for your jewels, that you will feel more comfortable. The sum raised should keep you and Solange for a long time – for years, if you are content to live in a modest way.'

'What other way can I?' she said, and smiled at him. 'Ah, Edward, do not look so sad. May I call you Edward? I feel as if I have known you for such a long time. Do not be sad. I shall manage, me. And if I cannot dance, I can teach. Though,' she added, with a frown, 'I wonder, with the war, if people will still want dancing classes.'

'It should not be necessary for you to work, Madame. The money, properly invested – and there I hope to be able to help you–'

'I know you will,' she said, 'but I wish that you will not call me "Madame". I am Élise.'

Edward drew himself back from the edge of some unsuspected precipice. 'I fear that would not be proper, Madame,' he said awkwardly.

She looked at him a moment, as though she were reading his thoughts, and then she said, quite comfortably, 'It is as you please. And now, will you take some coffee while we talk business? Solange makes excellent coffee.'

Edward assented, and fetched out his papers, feeling that he was back on safe ground – and also, oddly, as though he had missed something, a turning or signpost, without even knowing it had been there.

CHAPTER ELEVEN

'How is your wedding dress coming along?' Beth asked at breakfast.

'Nula is being very secretive,' Diana said. 'I'm not allowed to see it until the first fitting, which she says won't be until next month. Even Mother hasn't seen it. Once I've had a fitting, Mother and I will come up to buy the veil and the shoes.'

Beth heard something in her voice, and said, 'Poor dear, it must be hard for you. I expect it all seems rather unreal, with Charles away. A girl's engagement should be a wonderful time for her. This horrid war! Never mind, we'll have a lovely time shopping today. I'm going to take you to Lucile's in Hanover Square.'

Diana's eyes widened. Every young woman who loved clothes had heard of Lucile's, the fashion house belonging to Lucy Duff-Gordon, wife of Sir Cosmo. They had been survivors of the *Titanic* sinking, having been on their way to visit the New York branch of her business; there was a branch in Paris, too. Lucile Ltd made evening gowns of fabulous beauty and expense for the very wealthiest in society, including film stars and royalty. 'But that's where the aristocracy buy dresses,' she said.

Beth laughed. '*You* are going to be aristocracy,' she said. 'You seem to forget.'

It was true – she did. Diana blinked a moment at the thought. 'But I'm sure I can't afford a

Lucile gown,' she said. Her father had given her a very generous allowance for her trousseau – more money than she had dreamed of. He knew very well that his daughter would be observed and judged, and wanted her to have the best he could afford; and having her wedding dress made at home had relieved him of the most expensive item. All the same, a Lucile gown must cost hundreds.

'We shan't go there for gowns,' Beth said, to Diana's simultaneous relief and disappointment. 'I'm taking you to buy lingerie.'

'Lingerie?'

'Nightgowns, peignoirs, petticoats, chemises, drawers,' said Beth. 'Underthings must be chosen with due regard for the wearer's future position in life, and you will be Lady Dene and the future Countess Wroughton. A great deal can be done with dresses and costumes in the way of economy – as long as the cut and fit are excellent. But your lingerie must be of the very best.' She gave Diana a twinkling smile. 'It's an outlay that you will see the return on when you are married. A collection of exquisite things to astonish and delight your husband and make him your abject slave. Men are *very* susceptible to lingerie.'

Diana could not answer. Her cheeks felt hot at the thought of Charles seeing her underthings. At the moment she was decently clad under her skirt and blouse in the sort of fine white cotton relieved by white ribbon and little bits of broderie anglaise that she had been wearing since she was fifteen and had come out of combinations and into corsets. But at the thought of what Beth was describing, a sort of lust entered her soul for silk and lace.

Beth went on, 'And, my dear, when they know whom you are marrying, we may get an invitation to one of the private showings of the collection. I've never been to one, but I understand they have a proper stage with curtains, just like a theatre, and you sit below and take tea, and the mannequins walk out to music and show the gowns. You're given a souvenir programme and a gold pencil to make notes of the ones you like, and there's always a beautifully wrapped gift for each guest to take away. Even if you don't buy anything, it's a wonderful occasion.'

With this tempting vision before her, Diana went off to her bedroom to prepare to go out. She was pushing a last pin into her chignon when Maud, the live-out house-parlourmaid, came to say that the Hon. Rupert Wroughton had called, asking to see both ladies. Surprise mingled with apprehension: what could he want? Surely not simply to abuse her again. She would rather not see him at all, but Maud said that Beth was already on her way – of course, a courtesy call from Diana's fiancé's brother would seem perfectly normal to her – so she made a face at herself in the looking-glass and obeyed the summons.

But it was plain from the moment she entered the drawing-room that this was a very different Rupert. He was smiling, charming, even diffident.

He began, 'My mother begs me to express her apologies that she is so very much engaged at the moment, and unable to call on you or entertain you. I hope you will accept me as a very poor substitute.'

He addressed himself mostly to Beth, as was proper, and Diana was free to observe him. He seemed bent on ingratiating himself, and was using his natural charm to such good effect that Beth, with no reason to think badly of him, was much taken with him. To Diana he spoke respectfully, and with gentleness, so she finally decided he must have had a change of heart and be wanting to make amends. She was naturally anxious to get on with all of Charles's family, so was willing to forgive him and move on. As she relaxed under his spell, she discovered what good company he could be. They spent a very enjoyable quarter-hour in conversation.

Finally he asked, 'How are you ladies engaged this morning?'

'We're going shopping,' Beth said. 'We must look at the new fashions.'

'Indeed you must. A very proper occupation for ladies.'

'You may laugh,' Beth said, 'but as Diana will be a bride, it is important that she starts off right.'

Diana thought a flicker crossed Rupert's smiling face, but she might have imagined it because his next words were most cordial. 'After so much strenuous activity you will be in need of refreshment. May I have the honour of taking you both to lunch?' Beth hesitated only to look at Diana for her approval, and he hurried on, 'My future sister and my future cousin – now, you can't deny me, can you? Shall we say the Ritz, at one o'clock?'

So it was settled. He went away and Beth said, 'He seems very charming and chatty. Is his brother like him?'

'As different as can be,' Diana said. 'Charles is very quiet.'

'Well, we shall have a lively lunch of it, I imagine,' said Beth. She examined Diana's expression. 'What's the matter?'

'He's never been so attentive to me before. In fact—' But she didn't want to turn Beth against him, if he *had* seen the error of his ways. 'In fact, I thought he didn't like me,' she concluded.

'He seems to like you now,' Beth said. 'Perhaps he was jealous of his brother. Such things happen. But we'd better make a start, or the morning will be half gone.'

Lucile's was everything a girl could dream of. Among the froth of silk, satin, lace, ribbons, tucks and frills, the embroidered rosebuds and French knots, the sprays of fabric flowers and delicate self-covered buttons, Diana drifted in a dream. Everyone was very kind and attentive to her: they spoke of Mademoiselle's brave fiancé serving his country, of his noble old house and illustrious forebears; they praised Mademoiselle's beauty and said what a privilege it would be to dress her; they begged most humbly to know whether Mademoiselle had yet bespoken her wedding dress.

Fortunately, Beth retained her senses and her head and answered for Diana, and oversaw the selection of a dozen nightgowns and a quantity of chemises, drawers and petticoats. One of the nightgowns, in the most delicate shell-pink shade, was of silk so fine it could be drawn through a wedding ring, as the sales assistant demonstrated. To complement it, Beth picked out a white satin peignoir trimmed with ostrich, appliquéd fabric roses on the bodice and a froth of lace drooping from the sleeves. They seemed to Diana too fine to wear. 'For your wedding night,' Beth said, and Diana imagined for one searing instant wearing them in the bedroom with Charles looking on, and confused herself into blushes.

By the time they left, she felt quite drunk, and stepped out into Hanover Square with a feeling of astonishment that it was still daylight. 'We'd better take a taxi,' Beth said, glancing at the clock in the hall as they passed. 'We're already late.'

At the Ritz, they were shown to a table in the lovely pink and gold dining room to find not only Rupert but a strange young man waiting for them. Beth gave a look of cool surprise as both men rose, but Rupert was ready with his charming smile and air of deprecation to say, 'I hope you will not object to my introducing my very particular friend, Lord Saint-Henry. He is an extremely respectable and well-behaved fellow, and a *partie carrée* is always so much more comfortable, don't you think?'

And Lord Saint-Henry, with an apologetic smile that did nothing to detract from his extreme good looks, said, 'I know it's shocking bad form, but Rupert and I were at school together and I've known Charles since nursery days. Lord and Lady Wroughton count me practically as an extra son, so perhaps I might qualify as one of the family? If you please?'

There was no resisting either of them, and as Beth was aware that Saint-Henry was the son of a duke, she thought it just as well that Diana

176

should start getting to know what would be her circle after she was married. And Rupert had obviously meant it kindly. They sat, menus were brought, champagne proposed and poured, and it looked like being a very pleasant lunch. Rupert devoted himself to Beth, which left Saint-Henry to entertain Diana. She was not sorry. She still felt a little uneasy with Rupert, and Saint-Henry proved to be charming. He engaged her in just the sort of light, amusing chat that she had been used to when she was the belle of Northcote and surrounded by a crowd of competing suitors. In truth she had missed that flattering attention, when her every word was hung on and her every whim important. Saint-Henry differed from her old beaux only in being wittier, more urbane, and much more handsome. She thought she had never seen a handsomer man, and he seemed to admire her from first sight. She began to enjoy the luncheon much more than she had expected to, and smiled more than she had for weeks.

Stepping out onto Charing Cross Road from the Alhambra, where they had been to see a musical revue, Beth, with her hand on Rupert's arm, was halted by the sheer press of people on the pavement.

'And all looking for a taxi, I don't doubt,' she commented. Just then, her eye was drawn to two women walking along the pavement on the other side of the road. They were wearing some kind of dark serge uniform with a severe, Boy-Scoutish sort of hat to match, and rather than walking were in fact pacing majestically, like a constable on his beat.

Rupert gave a little crow of laughter. 'My God!' he exclaimed. 'Lady-policemen! I'd heard about them but never really believed in them. What next? Two-headed calves? Cockatrices?'

Beth was about to make a comment when one of them, happening to turn her head, caught her eye through a gap in the traffic, smiled slightly and raised a finger to her hat brim in acknowledgement.

Rupert looked at Beth sharply. 'Good Lord, do you know her?' he asked.

Beth felt some kind of mockery was threatening: having eccentric relatives was not something to be exposed to the likes of these fashionable young men. But at that moment a motor-bus, inching forward, came between them and the women, and at the same time she was able to distract Rupert with a timely cry: 'Is that a taxi? Yes, look, his flag is up. Quickly, Mr Wroughton!'

Rupert knew the value of a taxi at such a moment too well to delay, and leaped forward. Beth glanced behind, and saw that Diana and Lord Saint-Henry were too busy talking and laughing to have noticed anyone or anything else. Their heads were closer together than Beth quite liked to see, but in fairness it was probably only so that they could hear each other over the noise of the crowd and the traffic. She breathed a sigh of relief. The awkward moment had passed, and if she kept Rupert distracted with conversation he might not remember it.

The next morning Diana went to visit the

178

Palfreys, and Beth stayed behind to write letters. While she was thus occupied, Maud came to announce a visitor. Close behind her, with her usual brisk walk, came Laura. She looked entirely normal and feminine in a neat grey tailor-made over a peach-striped silk shirt, and a straw boater with a matching gay striped ribbon.

'Well,' said Beth, getting up to embrace her, 'you look rather different from last night. Much more like the Laura I know. Now, what have you got to say for yourself?'

Laura laughed. 'Only that you've found me out! I'm glad it was you.'

'But why have you kept it such a secret?' Beth asked, inviting her to sit down. 'Maudie, coffee, please.'

'Yes, madam.' Maud departed in disappointment, wondering how she'd find out what the secret was.

'Because,' Laura said, stripping off her gloves, 'you know quite well that Edward won't approve.'

'You'll have to tell sooner or later,' Beth said.

'I know. But I've been under training, and I wanted to make sure I passed before I told the family. No point in provoking all the fuss for nothing. And since I passed, I've been having too much fun and have kept putting it off.'

'So you've given up driving for the refugees?'

'Oh, I might still drive now and then, if they're desperate for someone. We only patrol on three days a week at the moment, so I could fit it in. But there aren't so many refugees arriving any more.'

'Is that why you changed?' Beth asked.

Laura grinned. 'If you want the truth, I took it

up for the heavenly uniform!'

'Now, do be serious,' Beth protested. 'How did you get into it at all?'

Laura explained how she and Louisa had seen the two WPS ladies, and the seed had been planted. 'Finally, Mrs Erskine introduced us to Miss Damer Dawson, who started the whole thing. She's a wealthy, well-connected woman given to good works – animal welfare was her first passion, especially horses. Then she got interested in the fight against white slavery. The slavers are always hanging around the railway stations, waiting to pick up unwary girls.'

'Oh, yes, I remember your talking about it,' Beth said.

Laura nodded. 'They're horribly persistent. Even as you drive them out of one exit, they come back through another, and they're getting bolder all the time. Miss Dawson realised that if they were to be frightened off, it had to be with some kind of official sanction. And that gave her the idea of a body of trained, disciplined, uniformed women: in effect, a women's police force.'

'How do the real police feel about that?' Beth asked.

'They were tremendously hostile at first,' Laura said, with a shrug. 'Not just because men always think females can't do anything but because of the Suffragettes. Relations between the police and anything in a skirt became very strained during the militant period. But the militants have sworn a truce for the duration of the war, as Miss Dawson reminded the commissioner when she went to see him.'

'She went to see Sir Edward Henry? I'm surprised he would even receive her on such a mission.'

'Well, she didn't tell him, of course, beforehand, just played on her respectable background.' Laura laughed. 'He granted her an interview without the faintest idea of what she was going to ask him. She looks nothing like a troublemaker – just a nice, ordinary, respectable lady. But she's wonderfully determined. Sir Edward was no match for her. She asked permission for women to train and patrol in London on a voluntary basis, and when he realised she wasn't demanding they actually be part of the Metropolitan Police Force, he seemed to think it quite a good idea. He knows as well as anyone the slavers are a problem, and the police haven't the time or numbers to do it properly.'

'Did he lay down what the women's duties would be?'

'No, I think he wanted to keep out of it as much as possible. He suggested some textbooks for Miss Dawson to study, and she laid out the guidelines herself. But he did put her in touch with a retired police sergeant to advise her, and he's the one who trains us.'

'What in?'

'Well, drill, you know, like the constables learn. We meet in the gymnasium of a school and we march up and down like soldiers. It's the greatest fun! Sergeant Billings is *such* a dear, so patient with us – but he takes us seriously, and insists everything is done perfectly. He teaches us how to salute properly – and *who* to salute. "Smartly, ladies, one, two three."' She demonstrated. 'And how to take proper notes, and how to give evidence in court. It's all very interesting. Oh, and first aid, and how to walk the beat. The hardest thing was learning to do the slow police walk. It doesn't come naturally to females.'

'I shouldn't think any of it does,' said Beth.

'Don't say that! I haven't told you everything yet. He teaches us ju-jitsu.'

'Oh, my dear! Isn't that awfully rough?'

'We have mats to fall on. Though I must say,' Laura said, thoughtfully rubbing her arm, 'you do go about with interesting bruises until you get the hang of it. That was another reason I held off from telling Edward.'

'Do you really tell me you might use this ju-jitsu on someone? Out in the street? Not on a *man?*'

'One hopes not, of course. The thing is that it makes you more self-confident, and that's often all you need to disarm a situation. But it's as well to have something up your sleeve, just in case things get sticky. We aren't allowed to carry a truncheon,' she said, with evident regret, 'though we do have a police whistle to summon help. Miss Dawson's trying to persuade Sir Edward to let us use the police telephone boxes, but no luck yet.'

'But what exactly do you do?' Beth asked.

'We patrol the railway stations, keeping an eye out for white slavers, and giving help and advice to women and children. A lot of girls come up to London looking for adventure without realising what they're getting themselves into. We try to intercept them, give them a sharp talking-to and put them on a train home.'

'Well, that doesn't sound so bad,' Beth said, with relief. 'I expect it's work the real police don't want to do.'

'Quite. I think it's helping to reconcile them to us. Of course, now that we have the commissioner's sanction they have to put up with us, and some of them are actually friendly and helpful. And even those who aren't are quite glad to call on us to take care of lost children, or deal with drunken women who are getting into trouble with the soldiers.'

'My *dear!* Drunken women? How horrible.'

'The women can be worse than the men. You can usually shame a drunken man into behaving – invoke his mother and sisters, look disappointed in him.' She demonstrated the look, making Beth laugh. 'But the women seem to lose all sense of decency when they get to a certain state.'

'But, my dear,' said Beth, serious again, 'how can you bear it?'

'Some parts of the job are unpleasant,' Laura admitted, 'but the same can be said of any job. It's knowing that it's important work that carries one through. And it does give one a wonderful sense of power, you know, to be walking along in that uniform in places our sort of female usually avoids. Actually to be able to *do* something about those things one used to see and deplore.'

'But is it really war work? Saving drunken women from themselves?'

'Well, that isn't all we do. We help drunken soldiers and sailors, too, make sure they get back to their units and don't miss their trains. There's a lot of *them* wandering around London, you know,

183

quite lost and helpless. The poor befuddled chaps are usually only too glad for someone to tell them what to do. I become distinctly aunt-like – kind but very strict, you know – and they stagger off like lambs. I've never had one threaten me, though I suppose it may happen one day,' she added. 'I must say I rather relish the idea. I'm longing to try out my ju-jitsu in a real situation. Satisfying though it is to fling the instructor to the floor, one can't help knowing he's helping a bit.'

'You couldn't really use it on a man, could you?' Beth asked. 'I mean, he'd be bigger and heavier than you, almost for sure.'

'That's the point of ju-jitsu. You use a person's own weight to unbalance them. And, of course, they're not expecting it, so you take them off guard. I could show you, if you like.'

'No, darling, I'll take your word for it,' said Beth. 'But what were you doing in Charing Cross Road last night?'

'We patrol the streets, too, not just the stations. Piccadilly Circus, Leicester Square and Charing Cross Road, that's our beat – mine and Louisa's. Lots of alleys, courts, yards and passages – dark places where soldiers take girls and express their natural urges. We have to turf them out. Don't look like that, dear, or I shall laugh. Someone has to do it. It's hard luck on them, really, not having anywhere else to go,' she added, 'but they can't be allowed to offend public decency.'

'So your decency is offended to save the public's? Sooner you than me.'

'That's the whole essence of it,' said Laura, cheerfully. 'And, by the way, there are lots of loose women hanging around the music halls and theatres – *especially* the Alhambra. A well-known pick-up place for prostitutes, is the Alhambra. I was shocked to see you there,' she ended, with mock severity.

Beth did not rise to the bait. 'Laura, dear,' she said affectionately, 'I can't help thinking you've gone a bit mad. How you can call it fun... What does Miss Cotton's aunt think about it?'

'We haven't told her everything, for fear of sending her into a fit. Fortunately, she's agreed at last to let Louisa live with me, so there's no reason for her ever to find out – she never leaves Wimbledon. She thinks we give directions, or tell people the time, or help lost children. All very respectable and safe. Louisa's rather too young and pretty, really, for the job, but she's remarkably tough inside, and it's surprising how far a uniform and an air of authority will carry you. And her ju-jitsu is better than mine – I think because she did ballet when she was a girl. She has a certain rhythm and balance that serve her well. She managed to throw darling Sergeant Billings right off the mat once.'

Beth shook her head. 'When I think of all the things you might have done to help the war effort...'

'Like bandage-rolling? Or knitting?' Laura suggested sarcastically.

'No, I never thought you would be content with that. Not once you'd learned to drive,' Beth said.

'One of our members, Mary Allen, said that when war broke out she was invited to join a needlework guild. She was so horrified she went straight out to see if she could sign on as a police

185

"special". Mind you, she was one of the militant Suffragettes, so I suppose she'd already got used to a certain level of excitement.'

'Poor Edward,' Beth said. 'He's going to have quite a shock. You'd better tell him before he bumps into you by accident in your uniform.'

'That's not likely. We patrol from eight till midnight and he's hardly ever in London in the evening. Besides, he's got enough on his plate with the wedding coming up,' said Laura. 'I doubt he'll have any anxiety to spare for my doings. By the way, was that the groom's brother I saw you with last night?'

'Yes, Rupert Wroughton. We've been seeing a lot of him lately. He's been very attentive ever since Diana came to stay with me. He's a very amusing companion – quite adds to the gaiety of the Season.'

'What brought him to your door?' Laura asked.

'Oh, to begin with he came to apologise for his mother's being too busy to call. But he seems to have taken us under his wing. He calls most days, now. Seems determined to get on with Diana's family, which is to his credit. He's even been with us to the Palfreys'. Of course, Sonia's always perfectly happy to lay another place at the table. Her cook must have the temper of a saint, for she never knows until the last minute how many she's cooking for.'

'And who was the other fellow, the extremely handsome chap with Diana? I thought he looked familiar.'

'Lord Saint-Henry. Yes, he seems to have attached himself along with Rupert. Whenever

186

Rupert calls, there he is too.'

'Saint-Henry! I knew I recognised the face. I've seen him in the illustrateds. But, my dear, he's a notorious flirt! I suppose you won't have heard, spending so much time abroad these past years, but he's been an acknowledged heart-breaker these three or four Seasons. I hope he hasn't got designs on our beautiful Diana.'

Beth frowned, thinking of those two heads so close together last night. But she said, 'Oh, I don't think he can have. He knows she's engaged to Lord Dene. It's been in all the papers, and Rupert must have mentioned it, even if he hasn't noticed the ring on her finger. Besides, he's only ever here in Rupert's company, so I don't think Lord Dene can have any reason to object.'

'I'm sure you're right,' said Laura. 'Saint-Henry just seemed an unlikely *chevalier servant.* I wonder what's in it for him. Perhaps he just feels safe paying attention to an engaged girl. A lot of men do. Your hardened flirts are as frightened of marriage as a horse is of pigs.'

'What a charming image!' Beth laughed.

Maud brought the coffee in, and Laura changed the subject. 'Have you heard from Jack recently? Is he still in Ypres?'

CHAPTER TWELVE

Sonia called in at Edward's office one day with a letter from Aeneas about some bonds, and in the course of ten minutes' rapid chat managed to convey most of the news from that branch of the family. Diana's latest visit to Kensington with Rupert and Lord Saint-Henry in tow would have been galloped past had Edward not caught hold.

'Lord Dene's brother? How did that come about?'

'Oh, he's been squiring Diana and Beth lately. Perhaps he wants to make up for Lord Dene not being here,' Sonia said.

'I suppose he's staying with his parents in Town,' Edward said. 'I'm surprised the countess hasn't paid her more attention. I'd have thought we might at least have been asked to dine. But perhaps they don't entertain much.'

'A lot of your top families have given it up because of the war,' Sonia agreed.

'And why was Lord Saint-Henry there?' Edward knew of him, of course, though he had never met him. His father, the duke, banked with Coutts.

'He's Mr Wroughton's close friend, apparently,' said Sonia. 'A very charming man indeed – quite the life of the party. I think Mary might have danced with him once, at the Buller-Fullertons'. She says not, but I'm sure I remember him from some ball or other. Now, Edward, I'm come with

188

an invitation. With Diana staying in Town, it's a perfect excuse to have a dinner party. You and Beattie, Beth, Diana, Laura and a few friends. And I'll ask Mr Wroughton and Lord Saint-Henry, to make it cheerful. Just a small party – twenty or so at table. And perhaps a few more in the evening so that the young people can dance, if they want. What do you say?'

'If the date is clear, of course we'll come. It's been quiet at home without Diana, and with none of her friends calling in.'

Edward was happy to accept for Beattie, who was probably the one to miss Diana most. But he had other things on his mind. It was clear from military intelligence that a big offensive in the salient before Ypres was imminent. The British army was busy moving up troops to reinforce the line. But only the day before Sonia's visit, Lord Forbesson had called in, as he often did on his way to or from the War Office, with some alarming news.

'It seems that some French officers from the northern sector of the salient got talking with some of ours from the Cameron Highlanders. The Frenchies said that they had recently taken prisoner a German, who told them the Boche are planning to use poison gas in the coming attack.'

'My God!' said Edward, aghast.

'We've been hearing rumours for weeks now,' Forbesson said, 'but we didn't give them much weight. Who would have thought even the Huns would do something like that? But this German prisoner was very specific – how many cylinders, what size, where in the line they were being stored. And he said the Hun troops have been

189

issued with anti-gas respirators for the attack.'

'Surely...' Edward said '...surely it's unthinkable! The use of poison gas is strictly forbidden by the Hague Convention. The Germans signed that just as we did.'

'Well,' said Forbesson, 'they haven't always obeyed the letter, you know. Think of Louvain. Even so – chlorine gas! It's barbarous. Still, it *might* just be another rumour. The chap was apparently very forthcoming – eager to tell his tale.'

'You think he was too forthcoming? A plant, perhaps? Sent to spread fear and despondency?'

'It's possible,' said Forbesson, but he sounded worried.

Edward was worried, too, especially as Jack's unit was still in the salient. But there was nothing to be done about it, except to hope that the story would be proved false. Using poison gas would cross a line that it was hard to believe any civilised country would violate.

But the next day he met Lord Forbesson again, both of them on their way to the club for lunch.

'Walk with me,' Forbesson invited. 'I've something to tell you – for your ears only, though it won't be long getting about.'

'You can rely on my discretion,' Edward said.

'I know I can. I can tell you, it's a comfort to me. This war is undeniably getting nastier, and one needs a safe pair of ears sometimes or one would explode. This is it: a queer thing has just come in on Reuter's. Very queer indeed. The German newspapers are carrying a story that the British army has been using poison gas against them.'

'Surely that's not true,' Edward said, startled.

'No, no. It's a lie, of course,' Forbesson said, frowning. 'The question is – why are they saying it? The report's accompanied by a tirade of condemnation, raving about British perfidy, how we're breaking the rules of war and the very laws of civilisation.'

'It must be propaganda,' Edward said, puzzled.

'Oh, quite – but a very specific sort. The thinking at the War Office is that they are publishing this lie as justification ahead of their own gas attack. They'll reason they can't be blamed for breaking the Hague Convention if we did it first, and they can call it retaliation.'

Edward was thoughtful. 'So you think this tends to confirm the gas-attack rumours?'

'It's hard to read it in any other way,' said Forbesson. They walked on in silence for a moment, to the accompaniment of street noises – motor-cars and motor-vans, footsteps and voices, news vendors' cries and the insistent cheeping of sparrows in the gutters above. Everything that was normal and familiar. As far as possible from the horror of poison gas.

'When do you think the attack will come?' Edward asked at last. 'Is there any intelligence on that?'

'It's not a matter of intelligence now,' Forbesson said, 'except of the non-military sort. The wind out there has been steadily from the south for weeks. If you use gas, you have to be sure it blows towards the enemy, not back over your own men.'

'So when the wind changes...?' Edward asked.

'Then we shall see if the rumours were true. I

hope to God they weren't,' said Forbesson.

The German bombardment started on the 21st of April, shelling not just the line but the city of Ypres itself. It was on the following afternoon that they released poison gas, the wind being right to drive it over the line, at a point held by French colonial troops, mostly Algerians. Thousands died within minutes, falling where they stood; others obeyed the natural instinct to flee, but that only kept them within the cloud, and thousands more fell. Those who dived into ditches, shell holes or relief trenches for safety discovered that chlorine gas is heavier than air. It rolled in after them, and they choked.

A four-mile gap was opened up in the front line, but the Germans, perhaps afraid of the gas themselves, did not advance to take advantage of it. The Canadians were able to scramble across through heavy shellfire and extend their line to cover it; reinforcements were moved up as rapidly as they could march across the tortured terrain.

The fighting went on for days. The Germans attacked all round the salient with artillery, machine-guns and more gas. The news came back of heavy casualties and ferocious fighting, of unceasing shellfire – the city of Ypres was an inferno – and, of course, of the hideous effects of the gas: men blinded, men asphyxiated, men writhing in agonised death throes, faces blackened, froth on their lips.

The horror felt back home was almost beyond words. The newspapers were full of furious condemnation of this new 'frightfulness'. But the official War Office reports gave some comfort. The line had held. The Germans had not broken through. Ypres was still in Allied hands, and counteroffensives were being mounted. For all the Hun's wickedness, he had not succeeded. As it said in the more popular papers, favoured in servants' halls, Tommy had been in a tight spot for a while, but he had prevailed, as he always did. There was no doubt whose side God was on.

The casualty lists started to come in, along with the unofficial reports – the word-of-mouth of returning soldiers. The tremendous shelling and machine-gun fire had taken tens of thousands of lives, but it was the gas casualties that raised the most pity. Chlorine gas formed an acid when it came in contact with water, meaning that it attacked the moist tissues, like eyes, throats and lungs. Most of those affected died within ten minutes, choked to death; those who survived were generally blinded, and died within days from damage to the respiratory system.

'The Canadians have discovered that a piece of cloth soaked in urine and tied around the face helps,' Edward said to Beattie, when they were alone one night, preparing for bed. 'The ammonia in the urine apparently neutralises the chlorine.'

'How horrible for them,' Beattie said. 'But thank God there's something they can do. Poor Sadie was terribly upset this afternoon about the horses. I don't suppose they can do anything for them, can they?'

'I don't suppose so. But they don't keep any horses right up at the front line, and the gas is very heavy. There's a good chance it will have sunk below head-height before it reaches them.'

'I wish you would say that to her, then,' said Beattie. 'She minds it very much.'

'Poor Beth must be in agonies, wondering about Jack,' Edward said, taking out his cufflinks. He didn't pass on something else he'd heard – that because of the rapid changes in the front line, thousands of dead bodies lay where they could not be recovered. If Jack was among them, it would be long before they heard anything. He might never be found.

'I wonder if we should bring Diana home,' Beattie said. 'Beth won't want to be bothering with her now – taking her about and so on.'

'I'll call in tomorrow and suggest it. It's a pity Diana's visit should be cut short, but she won't want to be making merry at such a time.'

'She could go to Sonia's,' Beattie said, pulling the pins out of her chignon. 'At least she'd have company there.' She shook her hair loose and picked up the hairbrush. Edward watched her. He loved the ritual of hair-brushing. It seemed to make her open and vulnerable to him, as she rarely was during the day, carefully dressed and coiffed for public consumption.

'Thank God David's safe,' she said, after a moment. She caught her husband's eye in the looking-glass. 'I know you're worried about Jack – I am, too – but it's different when it's one's own son.'

'Yes,' he said, though he didn't entirely agree. Jack was almost like a brother to him – more like a brother than George had ever been. He waited for Beattie's next thought, knowing what it would be.

'I wonder when they'll send him to the front. Oh, I hope to God the war's over before then! Why is it taking so long? Why don't they smash the Germans – *smash* them?' she cried. He laid a hand on her shoulder, but she pulled away. 'You should have forbidden him to go,' she said angrily.

He knew there was no reasoning with her, no words of duty or honour or King and country that would mean anything to her, weighed in the balance against her beloved first-born. He knew it was unlikely that the war would end soon enough to keep David from seeing action. But perhaps he would not see much. And he might well come through completely unscathed. The only way, at least for Beattie, to face the future was to believe that.

'Try not to worry,' he said gently.

She gave him another angry look, and went on brushing.

'Do you want me to go?' Diana asked.

The atmosphere in Ebury Street was tense and sombre. Edward had confirmed through his War Office contacts that Jack's unit was one of those in the fighting. More than that he could not find out, with the battle still going on. He had called with his sympathies, and to hint that Diana might go home, or to the Palfreys', if she was in Beth's way.

Not even for Diana's sake could Beth pretend to take an interest in shopping or shows. Until she heard from Jack, or about Jack, she could only stay at home, walking restlessly from room

195

to room, or sitting staring at nothing, pretending to read, waiting for a telegram or a field postcard, trying not to think. But she looked at the beautiful face, on which grave anxiety seemed so out of place, and attempted to smile. 'You're supposed to be enjoying the Season,' she said. 'You don't need to keep vigil with me.'

'But I'd like to stay – if it comforts you to have me?' Diana said.

Beth hesitated, but then admitted, 'It does, if you don't mind missing the shows.'

'Oh, what do they matter, compared with Jack?' Diana said.

The pleasures of London seemed to her just then as hollow and fragile as Christmas baubles. She had no desire to go out, and when Rupert and Saint-Henry called, she felt not the slightest pang at having them told 'not at home'. She could be useful here, doing what she could to distract Beth, with conversation, card games, music. Mary and Audrey called, and sat for a while, talking quietly and sensibly. Sonia had put off her planned dinner party, but the twins had brought with them her blanket invitation to come and eat *en famille* whenever Beth and Diana liked. 'Just come – no need to let us know in advance.'

But they did not stir out of doors. Laura came to ask if there was any news, and tried to persuade them to take a walk, for a change of air. But Beth was gripped with a terrible inertia; it was almost a dread that doing anything at all might trigger some disaster. She kept still, like a mouse when a hawk is circling. So Laura stayed instead, and they played three-handed whist until supper, which Beth could not eat.

The War Office put out a plea for hundreds of thousands of rudimentary gas masks, to fill the gap until proper respirators could be manufactured, and the nation responded with energy. The Northcote branch of the Red Cross was not behindhand. Mrs Oliver, the chairman, and her committee rushed to organise the village on a large scale.

'We want everyone to turn to,' said Mrs Oliver, when she called at The Elms. 'We're taking over the village hall to get the thing moving. Grand opening session tomorrow, starting at nine o'clock and working all day. Now, I would like you to bring your whole household – servants and all! We need every pair of hands we can get. Will you show the way, Mrs Hunter, set an example?'

Beattie faltered, thinking of various household problems this would throw up. 'I'd be happy to help, and bring the children, but the servants... They'll have their work to do. And Mr Hunter will come home expecting his luncheon. At the end of a week at the office I don't suppose–'

'Of course, of course, some of the gentlemen won't be able to come,' Mrs Oliver interrupted. 'They work so hard, one shouldn't expect it. And I don't expect anyone to stay all day, but if everyone can give an hour or two we can really make a difference. The government has asked for half a million in the next two weeks. They are needed so desperately urgently.'

'Oh, certainly–'

'When one thinks of our poor soldiers in

197

Flanders, and what they are facing... It's the *most* important work of the war so far.'

'Of course,' Beattie said, thinking of Jack, and ashamed that domestic issues should have made her hesitate. 'We will certainly come – everyone I can muster.'

'Thank you, thank you, my dear. I knew I could rely on you. I believe Diana is still in London? Just so. My nephew, Henry, will be sorry not to see her.' She gave a twinkling smile. 'But perhaps it's just as well for him not to be exposed to her.'

'He'll be there, of course?'

'Oh, yes. I'm relying on him to keep our labourers in good heart. Such a cheerful boy, he has the knack of making you laugh. And the Church Women's Guild will be providing a sandwich luncheon, and plenty of tea all through the day. Mrs Fitzgerald is organising that. A sterling character, Mrs Fitzgerald.'

'Yes, indeed,' said Beattie, and read unspoken in Mrs Oliver's eyes the struggle that must have been won before the rector's wife would give up the prestige of organising the whole event and settle for merely the catering.

In the event, everyone from The Elms went to the village hall on Saturday morning. Cook and Emily stayed behind to clear up after breakfast and put the master's luncheon in hand before following on, but Beattie walked up with Sadie and the boys to be there for nine o'clock. Sadie was still fretting about the horses. William was weighed down with the responsibility of being a Boy Scout, while Peter frisked with pleasure at a change in routine. Behind them came Ada, determined to do her duty, and Ethel, wondering who would be there: she had heard that some soldiers from the camp had volunteered to give up their off-duty time in a good cause.

And at the rear of the procession came Nailer, trying to look as if they were nothing to do with him, and that he just happened to be going in the same direction, and thinking, as far as a dog can think, that it might turn out to be a picnic, though there was a disappointing lack of baskets.

By the time they got there the village hall had been set up, by the male volunteers, with rows of trestle tables flanked by benches and chairs. On the platform Mr Garrett, the caretaker from the village school, had erected a blackboard and easel, and on it Miss Snoddy, the headmistress, had chalked the instructions, sent by the War Office, together with a drawing for those of a less verbal intellect. On the platform, too, were tables bearing the stock of gauze, cotton wool and tape. Everything was ready.

Henry Bowers, who referred to himself as 'Hank', came and greeted the party from The Elms, made them welcome and got them started. As more and more people arrived, the room began to buzz with cheerful conversation. Children too young to settle to steady occupation ran about, or sat on the floor in corners to play. Cups of tea soon began to appear from the kitchen behind the stage. The committee members circulated, answering questions, giving advice and praise, and the big box on the edge of the stage gradually filled with completed masks, waiting to be made up in packages of a hundred, and sent to the Royal Army Clothing Department in Pimlico. Platt, the carrier, had volunteered to take them up to save costs.

Cook and Emily appeared, and seeing empty cups standing around, Cook started to gather them up, prodding Emily to help. Soon the two of them disappeared into the kitchen, where the Guild ladies were cutting sandwiches. It seemed a more natural environment to Cook. If she was to make anything that morning, better it was sandwiches.

After half an hour, William came to his mother to say, 'It's more like a party than hard work.'

'Is that a complaint?' she enquired.

He frowned. 'Well, people are having too much fun, I think.'

Beattie looked around. There were smiling faces everywhere, and mouths moving rapidly in eager chat. The village liked to get together, and if it was in a good cause, so much the better. 'If the work gets done just the same, does it matter if people enjoy doing it?' she asked.

'But it ought to be serious,' William said. 'The war is a serious thing.'

'Of course it is. Everybody knows that. But we don't have to be sad and serious all the time. Look at Mr McVey – he's laughing.' Alec McVey was the assistant Scout master, and something of a hero to William. 'So it can't be wrong, can it? Why don't you go and ask him about it?' she concluded, glad to scrape off the philosophical question onto someone else.

William looked over to where Mr McVey was

leaning over the shoulder of Miss Garland, the pretty young assistant schoolmistress, and laughing as he attempted to correct her work. He certainly seemed to be enjoying the occasion. William hurried off to quiz him on the subject.

Sadie was glad to see Mrs Cuthbert arrive, accompanied by her maid Annie bearing a tray of cakes. She hurried over to her to put her question about horses and poison gas.

'I haven't heard anything about it,' Mrs Cuthbert said. 'I don't know whether they've been affected or not, but I will enquire. I know! I'll write to Mr Courcy – *Captain* Courcy, I should say.'

'Oh, will you?' Sadie said eagerly. Her cheeks grew pink. Since he had gone to France, not only was his person missing from the neighbourhood but also his name from conversations. His replacement as the local army vet was an elderly Scotsman brought out of retirement, tall, bony and grim. Captain Mackintosh had enormous hands – he could hold a horse's hoof easily in one of them – and they seemed to know their job, but it wasn't the same. Where John Courcy had let her help, and explained things to her, he gave her a sour look and said, 'Oot o' the way, if ye please, missie.'

'If they *are* in the gas area, I'd like to know if anything can be done for them, in the way of a gas mask,' Sadie went on.

'I don't know how you'd fasten a pad of any sort,' said Mrs Cuthbert. 'You know how they shake their heads if there's anything on their noses, poor things. But Captain Courcy will know for sure. I'll write to him tonight.'

'And when you do,' Sadie said shyly, 'would

201

you – would you give him my regards, please?'

'I shall say everything proper,' said Mrs Cuthbert, with a look of suppressed amusement. First love, she thought, was always painful. But useful as practice, to prime the heart for its real work. When she was Sadie's age there had been a young man, a hard rider to hounds... She remembered he'd had the most beautiful moustaches. She paused for a sentimental moment to wonder what had happened to him, where he was now, then shook herself and said briskly, 'Well, we must get to work. Annie, take those into the kitchen, will you? Oh, there's Mrs Oliver – I must speak to her.'

When Mrs Cuthbert buttonholed his aunt, Hank came to enquire of Sadie, very politely, about Diana's whereabouts and state of health.

'Oh, she's well, but rather worried at the moment, of course, about Cousin Jack. His unit was in Ypres, and Father says it's one of those in the battle. We're all waiting for news of him.'

'It must be difficult,' he said. 'Waiting, when there's nothing you can do, is the hardest thing. Um – her fiancé? Is he...?'

'Oh – no, Lord Dene isn't in that part. I believe he's in what they call a quiet sector.' She frowned. 'Though one can't imagine any part of the war being really quiet.'

'I expect it's a comparative term. Is she staying long in London?'

'Until there's some news of Jack, I think. She's staying with Jack's wife, you see, and keeping her company.'

'I see. Well, please send her my respects, if you speak to her. I'm off to Wales next week to stay with some cousins, so I shan't be around for a while. Fishing,' he added, with a discontented look. 'But what can you do?'

Sadie divined his thoughts. 'It must be annoying for you, not to be able to volunteer.'

'You don't know how much!' he said. 'If I join a British unit, I'll lose my citizenship, but meanwhile my homeland, the great United States of America, is standing back with its hands in its pockets. Keeping out of the biggest thing that's ever happened! It makes me so mad I can hardly stand it. And, to cap it all, every time I go up to London I get accosted by ladies asking me oh-so-sweetly why I'm not in uniform. It's not fair!'

'No, it isn't, I see that,' said Sadie. 'I'm sure you'd join up if you could.'

'Like a shot from a gun,' Hank assured her. 'The biggest adventure in history going on just a few miles across the Channel, and I can't get in on it! I'm hopping!'

Sadie searched about for consolation. 'Well, we can all do some good here today, anyway.' Hank made a disparaging sort of noise, and she said, 'We ought to do whatever we can, even if it's not very exciting.'

He made a rueful face. 'You're right, of course. I stand rebuked.'

Sadie was shocked at the idea. 'Oh, no, I–'

But he shook her hand seriously. 'I shall go and work with all diligence, to atone in advance for my slacking in Wales next week.' The irrepressible grin returned. 'At least I shan't be stopped in the street by the white-feather brigade down there.'

'You won't?'

'No streets!' he said triumphantly.

Ethel's first care was to be as far away from Ada and anyone else from The Elms as possible; her second to get herself in with a lively group. The work, she could see in an instant, was not hard, and it would be perfectly possible to gossip and laugh while doing it, and even flirt if the opportunity arose. There were a few khaki-clad soldiers present, but a quick inventory proved none was of interest to her. There were non-uniformed men in the hall, people from the village. Some were known to her, shop assistants and tradesmen, and some were obviously husbands of the ladies present, but others presented fresh faces. And there was a continuous slow churning as new people arrived and some of the first-comers left. She moved around from group to group, avoiding the supervisory gaze of any of the Red Cross committee, or the Church Women's Guild, or anyone at all connected with Mrs Fitzgerald, settling briefly where there seemed to be a bit of fun going on, and moving on when something better offered.

Gradually she narrowed her interest down to a young chap who was making himself useful, collecting up finished gas masks and handing out new materials, showing newcomers to empty seats, collecting cups and handing out tea, sweeping up and running errands. He was not bad-looking, no film star, but with a pleasant, friendly face, blue eyes and a nice smile; not tall, but with a neat, spare body, and strong-looking hands. She liked strong hands. She worked her way quietly round to him, and when the moment was right, when he was vigorously wielding a broom to sweep up the snips and threads of gauze that would cling to the rough floorboards, she contrived to get behind him and let him hit her with his elbow.

Actually, she misjudged it, and caught a harder blow in the diaphragm than she had counted on. She was winded and staggered back into the wall, almost sliding down to the floor. The young man jumped, turned and caught her by the elbows, his face gratifyingly shocked and apologetic.

'Oh dear! Oh, goodness! Oh, miss, I'm so sorry! I didn't know you were there.'

At first Ethel could only gasp, hoping she did not look too much like a fish. She held on to his forearms, however, to show she didn't object to his support.

'Have I hurt you? Do you need a doctor?' he was asking. She was getting her breath back now. Yes, close-to he was rather nice. As long as he was not spoken for...

'Please say you're not badly hurt,' he was saying now.

'That's a nice way to treat a girl, I must say,' she said archly, lowering her eyelashes at him. 'Knocking her about instead of saying how-do-you-do.'

He saw that it was all right to smile. 'Can I say it now? How do you do, Miss...'

'Lusby. Ethel Lusby.'

'Miss Lusby, can you assure me you're not hurt? Let me find a chair for you.'

That would not suit Ethel's purposes. 'Perhaps you'd escort me outside for a breath of air, Mr...?'

205

'Travers, Eric Travers. It would be my pleasure, Miss Lusby – the least I can do.' He turned her and offered his arm, which she took, then managed a very artistic totter. 'Take it slowly. Lean on me. Are you sure you don't need a doctor?'

He wasn't behaving like a man who was spoken for, Ethel thought, with satisfaction. Outside, she let him sit her on the wall, and by keeping hold of his arm got him to sit beside her. He seemed to be examining her with interest, even admiration. She was glad she had come down to the village hall in her own clothes. Ada had come in uniform, saying it wasn't worth the effort of having to change later – but then, Ada had come to make gas masks and nothing else.

'How are you feeling now?'

'Oh, much better, thank you, Mr Travers, now I've got my breath back.'

'The colour's coming back to your cheeks,' he said. She gave him a fluttering look. 'And a very pretty colour it is, too, if I may say so.'

'Mr Travers! I shall begin to think you knocked into me deliberately, just to get to know me.'

He rose gallantly to the occasion. 'I'm ashamed to say I didn't see you there behind me. If I had, I'd have wanted to get to know you, but I'd have chosen a better way to do it than knocking you down!'

'Such as?' She helped him along.

'Well – inviting you to have a cup of tea with me, perhaps.'

'A cup of tea – that sounds like a good idea. I have had a shock.'

'Course you have.' He jumped up with alacrity.

'I should have thought. Hot, sweet tea is the thing for shock.'

Now was the test, Ethel thought. If he suggested getting a cup from the village hall kitchen...

But he said, offering his arm again, 'The Windmill Café's just down there. Would you let me buy you a cup of tea by way of apology? And a bun, perhaps.'

'Don't mind if I do,' Ethel said, taking his arm. They walked off together. Now she had only to find out that he was not on the point of enlisting...

'I don't think I've seen you around Northcote before,' she said.

'Well, I live in Westleigh, but I'm here, all right, if you look for me. I work on the railway, you see.'

A smile of pure pleasure curved Ethel's lips into their most alluring shape. The railway! Now that must surely be an occupation of national importance...

CHAPTER THIRTEEN

The first news of Jack came in a field postcard that arrived on the 28th of April. It ended a week of anxiety for Beth, though it was not wholly reassuring. All the sentences had been crossed out except *I have been admitted into hospital – wounded – and am going on well* and *Letter follows at first opportunity*. It was dated the 26th of April, and it bore Jack's signature, though the writing looked uneven.

'Wounded' could mean any number of things. An imagination freed from the dread of death was at liberty to roam over a wide field of lesser horrors. Edward came round in response to Beth's telephone call, and applied his logic. 'This comes from France,' he said, 'so he must have been admitted to a field hospital over there. Which means his wound can't be too serious. The badly wounded are sent to hospitals back here. You've heard the expression "a Blighty wound"? Those sent to a hospital in France are expected to recover rapidly and go straight back to their units.'

That was not the whole story. Those so desperately wounded they could not stand the journey were also admitted to field hospitals, but Edward felt there was no point in worrying Beth with the idea. Besides, Jack had signed the card himself, so it was unlikely he was in that category.

Beth wanted to be comforted, but there was so little on the wretched postcard to take hold of. 'But look how his signature straggles,' she mourned. 'He must have been in pain!'

'He might have had nothing to lean on when he was writing,' Edward offered.

'And this stain here,' cried Beth. 'Can it be blood?'

'More likely iodine,' Edward said briskly. 'Now, don't torment yourself, my dear. He says he's writing to you, so he can't be too bad. Wait for the letter before you imagine terrible things.' He pressed her hand. 'Jack sent this postcard to reassure you. It defeats the object if you let it worry you.'

Beth admitted he was right. 'I'm ashamed to be so weak, when I think what he must have been

208

facing. It's just that if I should lose him...' She faltered. He continued to hold her hand until she rallied. 'I wish he *had* been sent home,' she said, in a stronger voice, 'then I could have visited him. I need to *see* him. And he must need all sorts of things – pyjamas, cigarettes, chocolate–'

'Calf's-foot jelly, clean socks, Palfrey's biscuits...'

She managed a smile. 'Now you're teasing me.'

The letter came two days later, scrawled in pencil on horrible cheap paper, but as precious to Beth as an illuminated manuscript:

We were in the line for five days [he wrote], *and in battle for a great deal of the time. I can't give you much idea of the action. It seemed to consist of desperate scrambles from one position to another to plug the gaps, then holding on under the maddest shell-fire until the order came to move again. Lack of sleep gives a sense of unreality, and the sudden moves were mostly in darkness. I have a dreamlike impression of shadowy figures, men moving up and wounded going down, of overturned limbers and dead horses, shell holes and ruined buildings, shattered trees poking the sky, all lit by the lurid glow of fire and the weird star-bursts of artillery. Maddeningly, I was wounded* after *we were relieved. Half an hour more and I'd have been out of range! But as we picked our way down the road towards Ypres, a shell exploded nearby and I was hit by the shrapnel. Now, don't be alarmed! It's only a flesh wound, no bones broken, so I shall no doubt be back with my unit in a week or two. My own men carried me to the dressing-station at Vlamertinghe, then I was taken by ambulance to the number 11 General at*

Boulogne, where I am very well treated. The battle goes on, as you know, but we are holding the salient, though somewhat reduced in area. I was not in the gas zone, though I saw some of the casualties. I won't write of it, but just say it's proof the Boche realise they cannot beat us by conventional means. Now, don't worry about me – I know you will, but I'll say it anyway! A <u>long</u> letter from you will be the best thing to speed my recovery. Please also send pyjamas, shaving soap and safety razors, as my kit is somewhere back with the company. And something to read! We are all so bored, the merest dog-eared magazine is a treasure here, even with the last page of the serial missing!

Once Beth was restored to near-normality, Diana obeyed the urging of her parents and went home to Northcote.

It was strange to be back, still an engaged person without a fiancé, but she was descended on straight away by her usual crowd. There were presents to inspect and new clothes to show off, plays and exhibitions to tell about, and all the local gossip to catch up on. On the Sunday, at church, she learned that the Wroughtons were back at Dene Park, having brought a party for trout fishing: Ada had it from the Gordons' maid, Betty, who had a cousin who was a gardener at Dene Park, who had overheard it from the housekeeper when he took a basket of produce up to the kitchen.

'Well, then,' said Edward, when Diana relayed the news to him, 'we're bound to see them, if they're back in residence. They might throw a dinner for you. It's time they showed you a little attention.' He was worried, though he didn't let her see it. The absence of any contact while Diana was in London seemed odd to him – it was almost a snub. But how could they snub their eldest son's fiancée? It wasn't reasonable. Even though it was wartime, basic courtesy demanded some social interaction. The Wroughtons must be odd people, he concluded. But if they were known to be at Dene, they would, they *must*, invite the Hunters.

They were all at home, sitting down to their roast of beef, when a telegram arrived for Diana, from Charles, announcing that he would be calling to see her later that day. Her immediate reaction was to jump up, flustered, and cry, 'He might be here any time! I must go up and change!'

'You look perfectly nice as you are,' Edward said. 'Sit down and finish your meal.'

Diana had to obey, but her cheeks were flushed and she could no longer eat. Finally Beattie decided the apple dumplings were sheer cruelty and, with a glance at Edward, gave her permission to go.

The rest of the family were just rising from the table when there was the sound of a motor-car stopping outside. William and Peter ran to the window. 'It's an officer,' Peter reported. Then, 'It's Lord Dene all right! And there's another soldier with him.'

'That must be his soldier-servant,' said William. 'Didn't Diana say his chauffeur went to war with him?'

'Don't stare, boys,' Beattie admonished, but this had the effect of driving them from the window into the hall, and as Sadie followed, it was the whole family that was waiting as Ada opened the

211

door. At least, Edward thought, Lord Dene could have no doubt as to his welcome.

'We've just this moment got up from luncheon,' Beattie said. 'Will you take something?'

'Thank you, no,' Charles said. 'I lunched on the train.'

'I'm sure your man would like a cup of tea. Ada, take Mr Randall into the kitchen.' Ada departed with Randall, and Charles tucked his hat under his arm, with a brown-paper parcel he was carrying, and followed the others into the drawing-room.

'This is an unexpected pleasure,' Edward said. 'We didn't think you would have any leave yet.'

'It isn't leave,' Charles explained. 'Our colonel had to come over for a meeting at the War Office, and he asked me to come with him. He's an old friend of my father, so I suspect there was some kind of wangle involved. However, I wasn't inclined to argue, especially when he told me this morning that I wouldn't be needed again until tomorrow.'

'And how–' Edward began, when Charles's eyes went past him and his attention with them. Turning his head, Edward saw Diana, halted in the drawing-room door, her eyes wide, her mouth uncertain.

And then the most extraordinary thing happened. She *ran* across the room, and Charles, hastily dropping his hat and parcel on the nearest chair, opened his arms and took her in.

Beattie hustled the children out before her, and drew Edward after her with a stern look.

The lovers stood for a long time, clasped

together. Diana could feel the roughness of the serge against her cheek, the heat and weight of his body, the warmth of his hands on her back, the rise and fall of his quick breathing. He was there, he was solid and real. She had a piercing sense of his presence, a rush of emotion that made something tighten inside her.

He loosened his grasp just enough to look down at her, and then his head dipped and his mouth was on hers.

They seemed to go on kissing for a long time, and then they were hugging again. At last he let her go, only to take both her hands, as if he was afraid she might escape, and stood looking down at her. 'It seems such a long time,' he said.

'I can't believe you're really here,' said Diana. 'I've missed you so much.'

'Have you? Truly?'

She nodded, lost for words. A great warmth was swelling inside her. He was not Lord Dene, heir to the earldom, he was simply Charles – and, more than that, he was *her* Charles. The sense of him was a revelation, as though she had seen him before indistinctly, through a veil; now, suddenly, he was clear and present. She felt him on her skin; she drew him in with her breath; her eyes seemed to have developed the sense of touch. He was hers, and his name and rank didn't matter. She wanted *him* and, with her hands safely folded in his, would have followed him anywhere, then and there, without question, and left the world behind.

'I love you,' she said, and the words hung on the air with strange, huge significance. She was aware it was the first time she had said it to him. She saw she had been flighty and selfish, and he had given his love before she deserved it, but she knew her faults now and wanted to make up for them. 'I love you,' she said again, and her eyes filled with tears.

He looked down at her, too full for words. He was humbled by her loveliness. He didn't deserve her. He was plain and clumsy and ordinary and had never been beloved of anyone, yet she loved him. His whole life, dedicated to serving her, would not be enough in return.

But he could not speak of these things. Instead, with the side of his thumb he gently moved the tears from under her eyes, and said, 'Don't cry.'

'I'm not,' she said. 'I'm happy to see you.'

'And I am, to see you.'

'It's been so strange,' Diana said. 'Sometimes I wake up in the middle of the night and wonder if I've dreamed the whole thing. I couldn't seem to – *find* you.' She hadn't really the words for what she meant. She had never in her life spoken of feelings like this; had never dreamed that she would be able to speak of them to a man – a strange man, at that. But no, she thought, examining his ordinary, so important face, he was not strange any more. And that was the strangest thing of all.

'I know what you mean,' he said. 'If it weren't for your picture...' He touched his breast pocket. 'I carry it with me all the time. But it doesn't make up for *this*.' He squeezed her hands. 'But it won't be for much longer. In less than six weeks now we'll be married.'

'But then you'll have to go away again.'

'The war won't last for ever. And then we'll

have our whole lives together.'

'I shall like that,' she said. Boldly she lifted her mouth for kissing. When he broke off, he was breathing fast, as though he'd been running.

'Tell me what you've been doing since I went away,' he said awkwardly, as though changing the subject.

'I've been staying in London, with my cousin Beth,' she said, 'buying wedding clothes.' She thought of the delicate under-things, and made herself blush.

'Wedding clothes!' he exclaimed. 'I was forgetting – I've brought you a present.' He released himself to pick up the brown-paper parcel and put it in her hands. She untied the string and opened it to find, neatly folded, a length of exquisite lace.

'It's the very best,' he said hopefully, watching her face. 'All hand-made, smuggled in from Bruges. The shop assistant said it would cost a great deal in the West End. It cost a great deal in Armentières,' he admitted. 'She said it was the fashion now for brides to edge their veils with lace, so I thought you might... I bought ten yards – I hope it's enough.'

'It's beautiful!' Diana said. 'Nula will be delighted. I haven't seen the wedding dress yet,' she added. 'I'll be having the first fitting soon. Nula is such a good dressmaker.' She wondered suddenly if he would mind his bride not being dressed by a couturier. Or if he didn't mind, whether his parents would.

He said, 'You didn't mention in your letters whether you saw much of my mother and father while you were in London.'

215

'No,' she said, 'nothing at all. But we saw your brother several times.'

He was taken aback. 'You didn't see my parents *at all?*'

She looked at him uncertainly, afraid something was wrong. 'Rupert said your mother was very busy. I expect it was war work. Everyone seems to be on so many committees these days, don't they?'

'Yes,' he said. 'That must be it.' He put the subject aside for later and asked, 'What else did you do? Did you see any plays?'

'I'm sure I told you in my letters. Tell me more about your life. I'd like to understand. I want to be able to imagine you there.'

He glanced around him, aware of the presence, close but out of sight, of the household. 'Can we go outside?' he asked. 'It's a shame to waste a fine day.'

So they walked out into the garden, her hand safely tucked under his arm, and he told her about Plug Street Wood, and his splendid fellows, and the trenches they were improving, and the football and amateur dramatics interspersed with fatigues when they were behind the line. She listened quietly, trying to see through his eyes, and his voice, usually rather flat and clipped, took on a musicality as his reserve melted before her interest.

Their stroll brought them to the kitchen garden, where Munt was hoeing his vegetable beds. He glanced up at the movement as they came in sight, and then, to Diana's surprise, he straightened up, grounding his hoe, like a Roman soldier his pilum, signifying his willingness to be spoken to.

Charles halted beside him and said, 'Fine day.'

'Ar,' said Munt. 'No rain in them clouds.'

'My goodness, your peas are well on! How do you do it?'

Munt glanced at him, and straightened a trifle more. 'Sow 'em in September,' he said. He did not say, 'my lord' – perhaps only for the King would he go as far as an honorific – but his tone was polite, something Diana had never heard before. 'Mr Hunter's fond of his early peas. Likes 'em with the first lamb. Sow 'em in the autumn, while the soil's still warm, and they gets a good start.'

'And is that broad beans?' Charles asked, in a wondering voice.

'Same again,' Munt said. 'Don't get so troubled with blackfly. On account their tips is not so tender.'

'Do you favour Bunyard's?'

'That's a good bean, but Aquadulce is better for autumn sowing.'

They had a brief discussion of varieties, before Charles concluded, 'Well, I can see you know what you're about, Mr...?'

'Munt, s'.' The rogue s, barely articulated, was as close as he could come to 'sir'. Mr Hunter had occasionally merited one, when praising Munt's chrysanthemums, but no outsider had been so honoured.

'I wish we had you at Dene Park,' Charles said cordially, 'but I'm sure Mr Hunter would never part with you.' Something passed from his hand into Munt's, and Munt gave a very slight nod of acknowledgement, glanced indifferently at Diana and turned away, setting his hoe again to the rows.

Charles pressed Diana's hand and moved on. When they were out of earshot, she said, 'How do you know all that about gardening?'

He glanced down at her, seeming amused by the question. 'Why shouldn't I know it? We have kitchen gardens as well as farms, and one day the responsibility for them will be mine. Besides,' he added lightly, 'I'm very fond of peas and broad beans. I like to eat them, so I'm interested in how they grow.'

Diana was silent, digesting this. It had never occurred to her to wonder how vegetables arrived on her plate. Munt sent them in, that was all she knew. But the wonder of Munt showing her fiancé such attention! It was not for her sake, she knew. Munt had never cared a jot for her, nor she for him. They had conducted their lives thus far on a basis of mutual indifference that had served them so well there seemed no reason it should ever change. And she didn't *think* it was because Charles was Lord Dene. It seemed to her that it was a tribute to Charles himself, to his character and worth.

'I'd like to see the kitchen gardens at Dene Park,' she said at last.

'I'd like to show you,' Charles said, his pleasure in his voice. The wonder of new shoots coming up through the earth was to him so intense he had always been surprised that the young women he had squired over the years showed no interest – indeed, were actively averse to walking around between damp vegetable beds when they could be indoors on a sofa flicking through *Tatler*.

In great cordiality they walked on until the de-

218

clining sun left the air a little chilly and Charles, in concern for his love, suggested they went in. When they re-entered the drawing-room, the rest of the family was there, and Beattie asked Charles to stay to tea.

Charles refused, saying he must go and pay his respects to his parents, but he accepted, with a gladness that touched Beattie, her invitation to supper that evening.

Lady Wroughton had never seen Charles so angry. She had certainly never been addressed in such a way by anyone, least of all her own son, but there was a pure quality to his anger that held back hers. She managed to say, 'Really, Charles, I will not have you speak to me in such a tone,' but it did not have the force of conviction.

'What were you thinking?' he raved. 'Don't you know how it must have appeared? Everyone will know that you were in Town, yet you let Rupert take her about, making her presence public, and did nothing to show her or her family attention. You could hardly have snubbed the Hunters more thoroughly if you'd publicly cut them!'

'I really don't see–' she began haughtily, but it was no use.

'What were you thinking?' he demanded again. 'Mother, I want an answer. *Why* did you treat my fiancée so shabbily?'

'I will not be quizzed!' She tried to stare him down, with the icy look that had quelled every uprising in her vicinity for forty years, but it wasn't working. He stared back implacably. There was something of her in this son of hers, after all. Suddenly her feelings burst through. 'Your *fiancée!* I cannot bear the sound of that word! Oh, Charles, the thought of you throwing yourself away on someone like that when you might have had any-one – *anyone!* And having to know her wretched family, having them in the house!'

He swallowed a cold rage and felt it slide, thick and unpleasant, into his stomach. 'So you thought you'd ignore them in the hope that they'd go away,' he said quietly.

Even to her, it sounded ridiculous when he put it like that. 'No, not that, of course,' she began awkwardly.

'*What,* then?' he demanded.

'I thought you might change your mind,' she said. She thought of Rupert's scheme with a cer-tain shame – and annoyance. *Damn the boy, why couldn't he make it work?* 'I thought *she* would change her mind.'

'Let me understand – you deliberately snubbed the woman I love, hoping that she would realise she wasn't welcome and call off the engagement? You were relying, in fact, on her having more delicacy and good breeding than you?'

'How *dare* you?'

'No, Mother, how dare *you?* I know you've never much cared for me, but I am your son and the heir to the title and estate. I'm of age and entitled to choose my own wife. I'm also entitled to a little common respect from you and Father. If your affection doesn't provide it, your sense of propriety ought to.'

'I will not be spoken to like that!'

He brushed away her protest unheeded. 'I love

Diana, I'm going to marry her, and she will be your daughter-in-law and the mother of your grandsons, so you had better come to terms with it. I have to go away again tomorrow, and this is what you will do: you will invite the family to dinner, you will arrange appropriate social occasions to present them to your circle, you will show Diana every attention the world expects towards my future wife. You have a wedding to arrange, and I don't want anyone to be able to say that anything was held back. My wedding to Diana Hunter will be perfect, do you understand?'

'You are not speaking to a child,' said Lady Wroughton, indignantly.

'Sometimes it feels as though I am.' Suddenly Charles looked tired. The strains of the past weeks showed in his face, like scars. He was not a born soldier, and warfare, even the limited sort he had so far experienced, bent him out of his nature. It was changing him, and Lady Wroughton saw the change and was suddenly afraid of him. This was not her meek, vague, dreaming, unsatisfactory son: this was a grown man, hardened by experience; this was a stranger, and thus unpredictable. 'Will you do as I ask – as you ought to have done before?'

She reached after a shred of dignity to take her out of the room. 'I think I know what's proper,' she said, turned on her heel and stalked away.

That night Cook pulled out all the stops. Usually the servants had Sunday afternoons off and she'd lay a cold supper ready on the kitchen table to be carried in by the family themselves when they were ready. But with Lord Dene coming... 'Got to put our best foot forward,' she said, 'for Miss Diana's sake. Don't want him thinking we don't know what's what – and him going back to France tomorrow, and not seeing her again until the wedding!' It fulfilled all the criteria for a romantic interlude, and she sighed with satisfaction.

'You can see he's mad in love with her,' Emily agreed, with a sigh of her own. 'When he looks at her, he kind of melts inside, and he says–'

'What are you babbling about?' Cook said irritably. 'You've never heard him say anything.'

'In me mind I have,' Emily said. Lord Dene and Miss Diana were frequent stars in the film that played behind her eyes as she went about her work.

'Never mind that rubbish now,' said Cook. 'Fetch me the big mixing bowl, and the eggs, and start weighing out the sugar. He shall have a sponge cake, bigger and lighter than anything he gets at Dene Park.'

Ada was quite willing to give up her afternoon to help, and nobody asked Emily, but Ethel refused point blank. 'My time off's my own. I don't have to stop in for anyone.'

'Seeing her new best boy,' Emily said wisely. 'He must be somethin' special, so he must, the way she's hardly said a cross word to anyone all week.'

'You keep your nose out of my business,' Ethel said, threatening with the back of her hand, but it lacked conviction. It was true she was extremely pleased with the way things were going with Eric Travers. She really *liked* him – an unusual development in her pursuit of the right man. It made her feel both nervous and strangely good-tempered. 'I'm off to get changed,' she said, and whisked herself away.

'Miss Hoity-Toity,' Ada called after her. 'Never mind. I can manage serving tea on me own.'

'I'll help!' Emily said eagerly. 'I can carry plates round ever so nice.'

'Not with hands like that you can't,' said Ada. 'Black as Newgate knocker! I said, I'll manage.'

'Ah, I'd like to see the young lovers together,' Emily mourned, 'holdin' hands like two turtle doves...'

'Emily! Sugar!' Cook snapped, breaking eggs into the bowl. Emily jerked into action, but the smile on her lips belonged to her inner landscape. 'I don't know what's wrong with that girl,' Cook sighed.

'Emily?' said Ada.

'No, Ethel. She sneaked out of the gas-mask meeting, gone over an hour, and when she came back, she was no more use than the kitchen cat. Leaves her work half done – I could see the dust on the morning-room mantelpiece this morning right from the door as I went past. Won't help out when she's needed, like today. Doesn't have no sense of loyalty. Flighty, that's what she is! We'll have trouble with her before long, you mark my words.'

'She's got a secret past,' Emily said, drifting up to the table with the sugar. 'I bet she was switched in the cradle by gypsies, and she's really a princess.' No-one answered her, and she added quietly to herself, her lower lip pouting, 'You'll see I'm right one day. I know she has a secret. And

223

I know where she keeps the letters.'

Supper was a great success. Charles ate with the appetite of a man long starved of dainties, particularly praising Cook's feather-light Victoria sponge, and the delicate pastry of her mock-crab patties. His mood was delightful. The family had never seen him so relaxed, so forthcoming. Beattie met Edward's eye across the room and her eyebrows asked, *Is this really the same reserved, awkward Lord Dene you can hardly get a word out of?* Edward's smile in return said, *It must be love.*

Whatever it was, Charles was the one who primed the conversation. He asked about William's scouting, talked to Peter about fishing and promised him he should fish for trout at Dene Park when he was next at home. He talked to Sadie about horses and won her heart – not that it wasn't already his – by asking after Nailer. He spoke sensibly about finance to Edward and described French fashions and shopping to Beattie and Diana.

And when supper was finished he seemed to have no desire to go away. It was he who proposed a round game. The boys and Sadie were delighted, and even Diana, who was sometimes on her dignity, fell in with the plan. The cards were fetched for Newmarket, Charles cheating himself with genial openness so Diana should win. Then they played Consequences, which reduced everyone to helpless laughter. Later, the boys asked Charles about France and the war, and he entertained them with descriptions of various warrant officers and senior brass out in France, their mannerisms and foibles. He was no impersonator, but he acted them out with an enthusiasm that made up for it. Sadie and the boys were obviously enchanted by him, and egged him on for more until the clock striking eleven startled Beattie into realising that it was a school night and the boys should have been in bed hours ago.

Charles was to leave the next day. He accepted with evident gladness an invitation to take breakfast with them, and with hearty handshakes all round and a tender smile for Diana, he went away.

'What a *very* pleasant evening,' Beattie said to Edward, as they went upstairs. 'I never imagined Lord Dene could be such a romp.'

'I was surprised myself,' said Edward. 'He was always such a dignified young man.' It boded well for harmony, he thought.

Charles was there early for breakfast, less lighthearted than the night before, obviously having things on his mind. He was not able to stay long. Soon the motor and Randall arrived outside, and he had to put down his knife and fork, wipe his lips and make his farewells. Diana accompanied him into the hall, and Beattie held the others back so that she could be alone with him.

He pressed her hands, looking gravely down at her. 'You'll write to me?' She nodded. 'It won't be long now,' he said.

'Please take care of yourself.'

'I will. Don't worry.' He managed a smile. 'You'll be so busy with the wedding you won't have time to miss me.'

But she said, 'I *will* miss you.'

'I'll see you in June,' he said, glanced round to

see they were alone, stooped to kiss her, and then was gone. Diana watched the motor-car to the end of the road, where it turned out of sight, but he did not look back.

CHAPTER FOURTEEN

A soldier locked in congress with a prostitute up against a wall down an alley was no longer an unusual sight to Laura, but the alley was off St Martin's Lane and they were in full view of passers-by. She stopped Louisa with a hand on her arm, and issued the universally understood admonishment: 'Oy!'

The prostitute whipped her head round. On seeing them, she shoved the soldier away, dropped her skirt and legged it down the alley, which opened at the other end onto Charing Cross Road. The soldier, evidently drunk, reeled a full circle before regaining his balance, stared about him for a moment, as if wondering how his companion had vanished like that, then staggered the wrong way, towards Laura and Louisa. His fingers fumbled a moment with his fly, then forgot what they were doing, and he emerged onto St Martin's Lane with his flaccid penis dangling sadly on show.

Only a couple of weeks ago Louisa would have gone scarlet and covered her eyes; and though she was tougher now, Laura knew she was still not at ease with such scenes and took charge herself. She stepped in front of him. 'Now then, sir, you're not a fireman. Put the hose away.' It was a formula she had heard her male counterparts use to men caught urinating in public places. But the soldier goggled at her uncomprehendingly. 'Tidy yourself up,' she said sternly, with a gesture that pierced the fumes. He looked down stupidly, and stuffed the offending object out of sight, swaying dangerously with the effort. 'Where are you off to?' Laura asked, watching him try vainly to marry fly-buttons with buttonholes.

He looked up, located the source of her voice, and grinned. 'Ladies,' he said. 'Lovely ladies.'

'We're women police, sir, and we want to see you get safely where you're going,' Laura said, in her least encouraging, auntish voice.

'*Two* lovely ladies,' he slurred, though he was probably seeing at least four of them. 'Sh'my lucky day.' He reached out for Laura and missed, almost falling through the gap between them, recovered himself and made a grab for Louisa. 'C'mere, darlin'! Give us a kiss!' Louisa stepped sharply back, and he groped hopelessly after her. 'Two lovely ladies. Where'sh other one gone?'

Laura realised with pleasure that here was an opportunity to use the 'come-along-o'-me' grip that dear Sergeant Billings had shown them. She grabbed the soldier's flailing right hand and, with the twist Billings had demonstrated, whipped it up behind his back. The sergeant had warned them that pushing it too far could break the arm. For a first attempt Laura felt it had been pretty smooth, but perhaps she had been too enthusiastic as the soldier gave a startled cry, though he was probably too drunk to feel the full spectrum of pain. She eased the grip a little. 'All right, Private, stand still and you won't get hurt. Where are you off to?'

The soldier waved his free arm around as if searching for his lost pleasure. ''Snot a nice way to treat a bloke,' he mumbled. 'Wha' sort o' ladies are you?'

'Breast pocket,' Laura said to Louisa, who stepped forward, evading the left arm that waved about randomly as though in a breeze, unbuttoned the pocket and took out the various documents.

'Travel warrant,' she said. 'Charing Cross, eleven forty-eight. He's going back to France.'

'End of your leave, is it, Tommy?' Laura said kindly. 'One last rowdy? I hope it was worth it.' It was a phenomenon they often came across, and though not many of them got so drunk that they missed their trains, the consequences could be serious. 'Let's get you to the station. Come along, this way. Step out. Left, right, left...'

Louisa grabbed his left elbow, and between them they propelled him on his uncertain legs in the direction of the station, half pushing, half supporting. Passers-by stepped out of their way, staring, some amused, some repelled, some dividing disapproving looks equally between the disgusting drunk and the unnatural women. One bowler-hatted gentleman, glaring furiously, went so far as to step in front of them to halt them. 'Women pretending to be policemen? It's an outrage! If you had a shred of decency you'd leave this sort of thing to the proper authorities. You should be ashamed of yourselves. Females like you bring your whole sex into disrepute.'

His face was red with indignation. Laura knew the futility of arguing with such people. She said sweetly, 'I wouldn't stand just there if I were you, sir. This soldier is very drunk and likely to vomit.'

Bowler Hat skipped like a ram out of the way, and they moved on, followed by his disobliging comments about 'women behaving like men'. Laura glanced at Louisa, and saw he had upset her. 'There are plenty of that type about,' she said lightly, to take the sting out of it. 'Very anxious to have their rubbish collected, then complain that the dustmen have dirty fingernails.'

Louisa gave a reluctant smile. 'I suppose that's what we are – refuse collectors.'

'It's a job someone has to do,' said Laura.

They reached the Strand, opposite the station, and paused to cross the road, still very busy with traffic despite the late hour. There were lots of khaki-clad figures about, and one detached itself and came towards them. It was a middle-aged corporal, with a knowing, monkeyish face.

'Hullo-ullo-ullo!' he warbled cheerfully. 'This one's one o' mine. What you been up to, 'Arris? Got yourself a nice coupla companions, ain't you?' He grinned at Laura and Louisa. 'What's the charge – drunk an' disorderly? You're lady police-men, ain't you? I seen a few about, never close up, though. What's 'e done?'

'Indecent exposure,' Laura said. 'Left the rabbit out of the hutch.'

'Deary, deary me. That'll never do.'

'We looked at his papers, saw his train was due to leave, and thought we'd better get him along here.'

229

'Well, that's right decent of you, miss. I'll take 'im from 'ere. 'E don't mean no 'arm miss, not 'Arris. 'E's just stupid.' He surveyed the drooping figure. "E'll 'ave a 'ead like a rotten turnip tomorrow. That'll be punishment enough. I'll take 'im, miss, thank you kindly.'

Laura released the arm and the corporal grabbed the private before he could sink to the ground. His hilarity had given way to somnolence. 'That's a pretty good grip you 'ad on 'im, miss,' the corporal said admiringly. 'They teach you that? Pretty useful, I should think. Well, thanks again. 'Arris'd thank you if 'e 'ad the brains of a glass o' water. Goo'night, ladies.'

The word seemed to wake Harris, whose arm was now slung over the corporal's shoulder. 'Ladies!' he said excitedly. 'Ladies, Corp! I seen 'em.'

'Yeah, you seen 'em,' said the corporal, getting him moving.

'Two of 'em, Corp,' Harris said, with increasing urgency, as he was shuffled away. 'They was givin' me the eye!'

'Yeah, an' I'm the Queen o' Sheba's left titty,' said the corporal, turning his head to drop the women a swift wink. 'There was never no ladies. You imagined 'em. Come on, my lad, one-two-one-two, pick 'em up or we'll miss the train and then the sergeant'll be upset. Don't want to upset the sergeant, do we?'

They disappeared into the khaki throng that was converging on the sighing, steaming troop train.

'So,' said Louisa, 'that was a job well done.' She glanced over towards the clock. 'And it's a quarter to midnight. Our shift's over.'

'So it is. Shall we have a cup of tea at the buffet?' Laura said.

'Stay in the station? No, something else might come up, and I know you, you wouldn't let being off duty stop you. Let's go home. I could really love a hot bath – couldn't you?'

'All right,' said Laura. 'You can go first, and I'll have the water after you.'

'And I'll make some cocoa while you're in it,' said Louisa. She yawned comfortably. 'Isn't it nice that I don't have to go back to Wimbledon?'

'I think the same every single day,' said Laura.

The sinking of the *Lusitania* pushed both the gas attacks and the ongoing speculation about the Brides in the Bath off the front pages. The Cunarder, holder of the Blue Riband in both directions, had continued making her regular crossings of the Atlantic, despite the German warning that ships sailing under a British flag did so at their own risk. It had not been supposed that even the Germans would attack an unarmed passenger vessel. But she was torpedoed not far off the coast of Ireland, in the afternoon of the 7th of May, and sank.

'That lovely ship,' Cook mourned, over the Sunday newspaper at breakfast. There was a photograph of her on the front page, dressed with flags and accompanied by tugs as she left harbour, her graceful lines and four raked funnels the signature of her speed. 'What kind of monsters are they, sinking a passenger ship! Sunk without so much as a warning. They're not fit to walk the same earth

231

as decent people.'

'They're saying twelve hundred people dead,' said Ada, sipping tea.

'I heard it was fourteen hundred,' said Emily. 'She sank so quick they couldn't save 'em, just like the *Titanic*.'

'It's nothing like the *Titanic*,' Cook objected. 'This was deliberate, wicked torpedoes, not an iceberg that nobody could help.'

The sinking had happened in broad daylight and only ten miles off the Old Head of Kinsale, but though rescue vessels had arrived quickly, the ship had gone down in less than twenty minutes, and only around seven hundred and fifty people had been saved.

'Well, there was two hundred Americans drownded,' said Emily, 'and that'll cause trouble. The Yanks won't stand for it. President Wilson'll have to do something.'

Cook heaved herself to her feet. 'Get the table cleared, and less of your opinions, my girl. Then you can start the potatoes. Ethel, you can pod them peas.'

Ethel got up and went to fetch them, and Cook stared after her with puzzlement. Usually Ethel objected to any such jobs, which she categorised as kitchen maid's work. She had sat through breakfast without a word, too, though she generally had something sharp to say about every subject. 'No back-chat? What's going on with her?' she asked Ada, in a low voice.

Ada shrugged. 'Maybe she's in love.'

'In love? That girl hasn't got a heart to be in love with. She must be sickening for something. I just hope it's not catching.'

She was making pastry at the kitchen table when the back door opened, and Frank Hussey came in, carrying a big bunch of flowers wrapped in damp newspaper. 'Hello, Mrs D!'

'Well, look who's blown in,' Cook said. 'A sight for sore eyes, you are. What you got there?'

'For you,' Frank said, displaying his bounty – cornflowers and lilac.

'Not lilac in the house! It's unlucky!' Cook cried in alarm.

'No, no, that's only white lilac. The mauve sort's okay. My lady has big vases of it in the hall, and she wouldn't do that if it was unlucky, would she?' He put the flowers down on the end of the table and kissed Cook's cheek, suppressing her objections and raising a blush of pleasure. 'Pleased to see me, then?'

'Never mind your sauce,' Cook said. 'Kissing people in their own kitchen! We haven't seen you in a while. What you been up to?'

'Busy time in the garden, March and April. Things are settling down a bit now.' He sniffed. 'Something smells good.'

'That's a roast of lamb for upstairs to go with the first peas, and a nice big steak and kidney pie for us. You're welcome to stay.'

'Thanks. I was hoping you'd ask,' said Frank. As second gardener at Mandeville Hall he lived in a tiny two-roomed cottage on the estate, which had few attractions as a place to spend one's Sundays off. It was his pleasant habit to come back to The Elms, where he had once been gardener's boy, whenever he could, and have his Sunday dinner

233

cooked for him by the skilled hands of Joan Dunkley. 'Anything I can do to help?'

'You could put them flowers in something for me, get them off my table. There's vases in the scullery. Ethel's in there – she'll show you.'

Ethel was absently rubbing up the knives and forks for laying upstairs, a job that should have taken five minutes but which at the rate she was going would last all day. She looked up as Frank came in, and felt a momentary pang. He was so big and handsome, and there was something about Frank, something that made things grow when he planted them and made animals come to him trustingly when he held out his hand. But he had never shown her any proper encouragement, treating her, in fact, rather like a younger sister, and an amusingly foolish one at that, so she had long ago given up any hopes in regard to him. Besides, as things were now...

'Here,' he said, 'that's a man's job. Up at the Hall, they've got a pantry-boy does all the cutlery.'

'Henry's s'posed to do it, but he's never been the same since they told him he could ring the bells if the Germans invaded. Spends all his time looking for Zeppelins. Can't get a lick of work out of him,' said Ethel.

'Well, you won't get a shine on 'em like that, not without some elbow grease,' said Frank. 'Why don't we swap? I'll do your knives, you put these flowers in vases. That's more of a girl's job.'

He expected some kind of sharp rebuke, but she only said, 'Don't mind if I do', abandoned the task to him and went rummaging in a cupboard. Frank picked up the cloth and a knife and watched as she got out vases and scissors and set to work with an air of abstraction, a faint smile on her lips. After a moment he realised she was humming softly under her breath. 'Well,' he said, 'you're in a good mood. Come into money, have you?'

Still no sharp retort. She smiled at the lilac she was trimming and said, 'Better than that.'

He waited. 'Got to guess, have I?'

'Hmm?' she said vaguely. 'Oh – no. I've got a new beau.'

'Ah!' said Frank. 'Good one, is he? Tell me about him.'

Ethel didn't need any more urging. 'His name's Eric Travers.' She told how she had met him.

'And what does he do?' asked Frank.

'He works on the railway,' said Ethel, proudly. 'He's a guard, which is a good job anyway, but he's training to be a driver, which is even better. More money.'

'More security, too,' Frank said. 'And the way chaps are joining up, these days, I should think they'll be eager to get new drivers.'

'That's what Eric says. The training usually takes a year, but they're doing it in months now.'

'And I suppose as soon as he's qualified he'll volunteer and waste all that training.'

'That's the best bit. Train driving's work of national importance, so the government doesn't want them to volunteer, and Eric says he's not going to. Someone's got to keep the railways running or there'll *be* no war effort.' She looked at Frank with a faint echo of her old challenge. 'Like you always say, someone's got to grow the peas an' carrots.'

235

'Well, I'm not wrong, am I?' he said. 'So is he treating you right, this Eric-the-train-driver?'

'He's lovely,' Ethel admitted, and Frank was touched at the change in her. She had always spoken of her admirers with scorn and called them silly fools.

Ethel heard her own words on the air and admitted the difference to herself. She had begun by watching for Eric's faults, ready to hector him into treating her as a lady should be treated, but she had discovered it was unnecessary. Once, when she had been flirting and teasing him, he had smiled and said, 'You're a really pretty girl, Ethel, and I like you. You don't need to try so hard.' She had felt put out for a moment, but he had gone on being so nice to her that she had got over it. To her own surprise, she had gradually come to relax in his company. She had never trusted anyone in her life before, and there had never been anyone who hadn't let her down, but with Eric... She hadn't quite stopped wondering what the catch was and when he would reveal his true colours, but there were times when she forgot about it for long periods, when she almost thought...

'So it's serious this time, then?' Frank asked kindly.

She snapped out of it. 'Serious? For him, maybe. I didn't come down with the last shower.'

'I know,' Frank said. 'But sometimes a chap is just a good chap, and...' He hesitated, wondering if advice would push her the wrong way. She looked up at him, her expression wary. He thought he'd risk it. He felt strangely anxious for her to be happy.

'What?' she asked.

'Don't push him away by being too tough. Let him be nice to you.'

She was silent a long moment, as if wondering how much to admit to him. Then she said, 'He is nice. I think–' She didn't finish that thought. She picked up a stem of lilac and started cutting it. 'I'm only seeing him,' she said, in a low voice. 'I've dropped the others.'

'Good for you,' said Frank, and laid a hand on her arm. 'I wish you all the luck in the world.'

Tears jumped to her eyes at his kindness. She wasn't having that. She blinked them back determinedly and set her lips into a mocking smile. 'Luck? What makes you think I need luck?' And she tossed her head in the old manner. 'You mind your knitting, Frank Hussey, thank you very much, and *I'll* mind mine.'

'That's what I'm worried about,' he said, but he had turned away to his knives, and said it too quietly for her to catch it.

It was a surprise to everyone when Bobby's trunk was delivered by Platt the carrier's cart. It sat in the middle of the hall, an object of wonder.

'Oh dear, I hope he hasn't got into trouble,' Beattie said. 'I wonder if he's been rusticated?'

'But he'd have written and told us, wouldn't he?' Sadie said.

'Not him,' said Diana. 'He'd put off the row as long as possible.'

'I hope he's not ill,' Ada said. 'I've heard there's an awful lot of chicken-pox around.'

'But then the college would have written,

wouldn't they?' said Sadie.

They hadn't long to wait. Henry was run to earth watching for Zeppelins from the shrubbery and forced to help Ada carry the trunk up to Bobby's room, and Ada was still unpacking it when the man himself came round the corner at a swinging walk and presented himself at the front door, with a wide and cheerful grin.

'No, no, I'm not in trouble!' he exclaimed, to the babble of questions. 'I've enlisted.' He looked quickly at his mother, and forestalled any comment she might make. 'You see, our college has always had ties with the Middlesex Regiment, and the other day we had a chap – an officer – come to talk to the JCR about this shocking *Lusitania* business, and the poison gas, and how it was now every man's business to do his bit, because there's no knowing what the Hun will do next if he's not stopped. He said he was recruiting for a very special battalion that consists purely of public-school and university men, who will all serve together – an elite battalion that will embody the very best traditions of service and patriotism and what-not. It'll be the finest in the whole army! So a lot of us talked about it very seriously – sat up all night jawing, in fact – and this morning we went up to London to the sixteenth Battalion recruiting office in Panton Street and, well, we signed on.'

Sadie gave him a quick smile and mouthed, 'Good for you!' but everyone was waiting for Beattie's reaction. She was frowning.

'You sat up all night talking to your friends about it, but you didn't think to talk to your father or me,' she said at last.

'I know, Mother, I know I ought to have really, but we were caught up with the excitement of it. We couldn't wait to sign on, and... Well, I was rather afraid you might pour cold water on it. I know you weren't best pleased when David went. But you've got used to it now, haven't you? And I bet you're proud of him really. I mean, naturally you have a mother's concern and so on, but you wouldn't like to feel ashamed of your boys for not doing their duty, now would you?' He gave her his most wheedling smile. 'I could understand last year, when I was only eighteen and nobody realised how serious the war was. But I'm turned nineteen now, and men of nineteen are out there already, fighting for their country. So please say you understand and aren't angry. Please, Mother?'

Beattie did not smile. But she said, 'I can see there's nothing I can do about it. So I suppose I must put up with it. But I don't know what your father will say.'

Bobby grinned. 'He'll be proud of me,' he promised. 'And I'll make you proud, too, before I'm done.'

He seized his mother in a bear-hug and, after an instant's resistance, she put her arms round him in return and said, 'I *am* proud of you.' In truth, she had never felt the same way about Bobby as about David. She loved him, of course, but there was that rubbery quality to Bobby, that happy-go-lucky indestructibility that made it impossible to worry so much about him. As a boy he had been the sort who would fall out of a tree and not even bruise himself, tumble into a river and get washed straight to the bank. Wasps did not sting him; ants did not get into his picnic sandwich. He would cross a field with a bull in it without the bull's even spotting him. Everybody liked him. Old ladies gave him sweets, stray dogs did not bite but smiled at him. It was just – Bobby.

He released her and, with a grin of triumph, received the congratulations of the rest. 'When do you go?' Diana asked.

'We have to report at Waterloo tomorrow for the train to Woldingham, where the camp is. That's in Surrey. It's a super outfit, you know – the very best chaps! They've got a pipe band! Real Scottish bag-pipes. This chap who gave us the talk said it was from the Napoleonic wars, when the whole of the Duke of Atholl's regiment was wiped out except for the pipers, who then attached themselves to the Middlesex. So ever since the regiment's been entitled to a pipe band.'

'But, Bobby, surely you'll be an officer?' Sadie objected.

'Yes, I expect so,' Bobby said. 'Quite a lot of chaps in the sixteenth say they want to stay in the ranks and fight shoulder-to-shoulder, but they need junior officers just as much, if not more, so once I've settled in, I'll put my name forward for officer cadet training. I'll be taken right away, what with being in OTC and everything. David would have done better to join OTC, instead of wasting his time with all those books.'

'Nobody expected there would be a war,' said Beattie, stiffly. 'And it won't last for ever. He'll be glad of his wide reading when it's over.'

Edward's reaction, when he arrived home that

240

evening and heard the news, was more sanguine than Beattie's. He had expected Bobby to want to enlist at some point: the lad admired David and would want to emulate him; and every boy of spirit must long to play his part in such a great endeavour. It would have been more respectful if Bobby had asked his father's permission before volunteering, but there again, he had David's example before him. Bobby – like any boy of spirit – would do what he felt he must first, and endure the consequences afterwards.

Besides, the war had taken on a different character since those heady days of August. It was no longer someone else's responsibility, but was beginning to creep into everyone's lives. Edward took Bobby into his study to give him the same talk he had given to David, and came out with his arm round his shoulders to present him to his mother and siblings, shriven and garlanded, restored with full forgiveness to the bosom of the family as a hero-in-waiting.

Conversation around the dinner table was mostly about the Middlesex Regiment and its proud history, together with what Bobby had so far gleaned about the 16th, known as the Public Schools Battalion. After dinner, Bobby wandered over to Diana, who was pouring the coffee, and said, 'How are things with you, sissy? I got a hint from David in a letter that there was some kind of trouble with your beloved's family.'

'No, no,' Diana said. 'Not at all. Everything's going on very well.' She was annoyed that David had cast doubts in that way. Where had he got that idea? Whatever had been going on in London, the

241

Wroughtons were perfectly civil and attentive now they were back in the country. Diana and her mother had been to luncheon with the countess already, and she and both parents were invited to a dinner party at the weekend, at which Lady Wroughton said she would be 'presenting Diana to the county'.

'I'm glad to hear it,' said Bobby. 'Wedding plans all in order? The one bad thing about my volunteering is that I doubt I'll be able to be at the wedding.'

'Oh, surely they'll give you a day off for something as important as that.'

'I don't know how important they think a wedding is, compared with war against the Germans, but I promise you I'll come if I can. I want to see you turned off in all your glory. Lady Dene! Who'd have thought it? I hope your wedding dress is suitably grand.'

'I haven't seen it yet. I'm having the first fitting next week. Charles brought me some real lace from France last week. I hadn't expected to see him until June.'

Bobby examined her expression and said, 'So you really are in love? I'm glad. I want my big sister to be happy. And you tell this fellow Charles that if he ever makes you unhappy he'll have an irate brother to deal with.'

'He won't ever make me unhappy,' she said.

One day the following week Beattie and Diana were in the morning room, opening wedding presents and making a list of the contents and donors, when visitors were announced, and Mrs

242

Oliver came in, followed by Hank Bowers.

'I hope we're not disturbing you? Ah, what a pleasant occupation!'

'Puzzling, at times,' Beattie said. 'What odd things some people send. Look at this pokerwork object, sent by a second cousin on Mr Hunter's side. I'm not even sure what it is.'

'I think it's a bookshelf, or a bracket for displaying ornaments,' Hank said helpfully. 'Look, it's this way up. You fix it to the wall through these holes...'

'How clever you are to work it out,' said Beattie, doubtfully. 'Will you have some coffee?'

'No, thank you, we won't disturb you for long. We're calling on a few friends this morning with some news. Henry, dear, you tell the story.'

'It's because of the *Lusitania*,' Hank said. 'There's been a terrific fuss back home.'

'There's been quite a fuss here,' Diana reminded him. There had been riots in Liverpool that required troops to be called out to restore order, and a fresh outbreak of anti-German feeling and attacks in several cities on businesses with German names. The German government had claimed that *Lusitania* had been carrying shells and ammunition, as well as passengers, so it was within its rights to attack her; the British and American governments had fiercely denied there was any such cargo on board.

'Ah, but the feeling is extra strong in the old USA,' Hank said, 'because we are a neutral country – I'm sorry to say. Also, there were so many American lives lost. Dad sent me some newspaper cuttings – there's a tremendous uproar all across

243

the country. Still, on the whole the folks back home don't want to go to war. But there *has* been a surge in hot-blooded young fellows running away to fight – either crossing into Canada to join the Canucks, or hopping on a ship over to England.'

Diana frowned. She knew all about Hank wanting to volunteer and the reason he hadn't. 'But–' she began.

'Yes, exactly,' he anticipated. 'The law that says an American who joins a foreign country's military loses his citizenship. But Dad writes that so many leading families have got sons itching to go to war – or actually going! – that President Wilson has told Congress it's got to be repealed. Can't outlaw the scions of the top families, the very people who form the governing classes – or, at least, pay their campaign expenses!'

'Henry! Needlessly cynical,' Mrs Oliver reproached him.

He grinned. 'Sorry, Auntie. At all events, it'll have gone through by next week. Then I shall be free to do what I've wanted to do all along. Dad's going to send me a wire, and that very instant I shall be off to the nearest recruiting office.'

'Congratulations,' Diana said. 'I'm very pleased for you.'

Hank gave her a curious look – accepting the congratulations, but sad that his departure would cause no pang in her heart. She would not worry for his safety – she would not even miss him! Well, once Lord Dene had stepped in, a mere Hank Bowers had no chance.

'And your Bobby's gone, too,' said Mrs Oliver

to Beattie.

'Yes, to some camp at the top of the Surrey Downs. It's lucky that it's May and the weather's mild. Bobby says it's very exposed, and those who were there in the winter say it was bitterly cold and uncomfortable. But he won't be there long.'

'No, he'll put his name forward for officer training, won't he?' said Mrs Oliver. 'I expect Henry will, too.'

'At the first opportunity,' said Hank. 'I understand the food and the frequency of baths absolutely demand it!'

'Well,' said Mrs Oliver, getting up, 'we had better be on our way. I must call on Mrs Fitzgerald. She'd be offended if Henry didn't take a particular farewell of her.' She glanced around. 'I suppose Sadie is up at Highclere, is she? You must be proud of her, doing such sterling war work.'

'I suppose it is that,' Beattie said unenthusiastically.

'I've half a mind to go up there and see the fun,' Hank said.

'Well, do,' said Beattie. 'I'm sure Sadie would like it.'

CHAPTER FIFTEEN

May was an uneasy month. Matters in the Dardanelles were at a crisis point. British troops were clinging perilously to a narrow ledge along the rocky coast and quite unable to dislodge the

Turks on the high ground above. Frontal attacks had proved disastrous. More men and more ships must be sent to Gallipoli – though the whole point of opening the eastern front had been to relieve the strain on the western. On the 15th of May, Fisher, the First Lord of the Admiralty, had resigned in protest, causing uproar in the Palace of Westminster.

Fighting was still going on at Ypres, and on the 9th of May, in a different part of the line, a joint Allied attack, intending to take the high ground of Aubers Ridge, had failed. Sir John French, who blamed the failure on the shortage of shells, broke with protocol by expressing his fury to a newspaper reporter.

'Worst of all,' said Lord Forbesson to Edward, over lunch at the club, 'it was a Northcliffe reporter. You know how Northcliffe hates Lord Kitchener. Now Sir John has given him the ammunition he needs – it will be all over *The Times* tomorrow.' He shook his head in disapproval, though it might have been at the cutlet on his plate, which was proving disappointingly tough.

'That won't be good for the government,' Edward commented. The Liberals were clinging on with a tiny minority in the Commons.

'It could bring it down,' said Forbesson, gloomily. 'Only three weeks ago Asquith made a public speech stating categorically, on Kitchener's advice, that there was no shortage of munitions. Sir John says he's been complaining about it for months. And now, as the last straw, Kitchener's ordered him to release twenty thousand rounds to

246

be sent to Gallipoli. He's hopping mad. The enemy has all the shells it needs, while he's having to ration his guns to so many rounds a day.'

'Is that true?' Edward said.

'Sir John says there's a shortage, Kitchener says there's no shortage. But between you, me and the bedpost,' Forbesson said, lowering his voice and glancing round to see that no-one was near, 'K's out of touch. He cut his teeth on a different kind of warfare, and I don't think he can conceive how such a tremendous amount of munitions could possibly be less than adequate. The man on the spot sees a different reality. Something will have to be done.'

'Such as what?'

Forbesson abandoned the cutlet and took a sip of his claret. 'Lloyd George has been agitating for some time for a Ministry of Munitions, completely independent and with full powers to control supply.'

'And who would take charge of that? Surely not Lord Kitchener.'

'No, of course not. Lloyd George offers himself.'

'He'd be willing to give up the Exchequer?'

'Temporarily. McKenna will keep it warm for him. And it will give him the opportunity to do great things and prove himself the saviour of the country. Men died at Aubers Ridge because of a lack of shells – that's what *The Times* will say tomorrow. Cometh the hour, cometh the man.' He sighed. 'I can't *like* the feller – there's something not straightforward about him.'

This was mild language to Edward: another of his clients, Sir Thomas Bromley, had described

Lloyd George as 'a damned thruster', while Admiral Tenby had said he was 'as twisted as a corkscrew'.

'However,' Forbesson went on, 'he may well be what's needed for this crisis. He's a bustling, active type and might well manage to get things moving. He did pretty well getting the unions on side back in March. We'll need to build new munitions factories, on a large scale and quickly. Buildings, machinery, materials, manpower, transport. And in the face of a lot of established interests. Civil servants can't move like that. Protocols will have to be cut and systems bypassed. Traditions ignored, feelings disregarded. All the things Kitchener would never countenance. Lloyd George may just be our man.'

'And the government?' Edward asked.

'Ah,' said Forbesson. 'There's the rub. Lloyd George won't pull Asquith's bacon out of the fire for the love of him. It's no secret that he wants his job.'

Edward supposed he meant that the government would fall. But the next day Lloyd George and Bonar Law went to see Asquith in a secret meeting that lasted only fifteen minutes, and the evening papers announced that there was to be a coalition government, with Asquith still prime minister. What happened in that meeting would probably never be known – Asquith was a cool hand who could keep his counsel – but Edward was glad at least that Lord Forbesson would still be his source of information.

Lord Kitchener remained Secretary of State for War. He was too valuable a figurehead to be given up. The public adored him: there had been outrage against the *Daily Mail* – another Northcliffe paper – when it had criticised him.

'And there's his birthday coming up in June,' Edward said to Warren, as he signed the day's letters. 'Planning for the Kitchener's Birthday Recruitment Drive has gone too far to have it cancelled now.' He read the light in his secretary's eyes. 'Don't you think of it, Warren. It's bad enough that two of my sons have volunteered.'

'I won't leave you, sir,' Warren said, suppressing a sigh. 'Not until I have to.'

Laura and Louisa had been invited to a supper party at a house in Bedford Square, with a new set to whom they had been introduced by one of Louisa's old Suffragette friends. The Bedford Group was a loose association of friends who got together to discuss art, philosophy, ethics and other similar themes. All were educated, well-to-do, middle class. Many were artists, writers and journalists. Some were also members of the Bloomsbury Group. They were all rather left-leaning, unconventional, and what the general public classified as 'Bohemian'.

They were sitting around the large drawing-room of the house belonging to Lady Frances Webber, who wrote poetry and was married to a publisher. The room was everything to be expected of Bohemianism, full of ferns and Turkish rugs, velvet cushions, mirrors and swathes of drapery. Lady Frances herself was dressed in a pre-Raphaelite sort of gown, her red hair held back by a multicoloured silk scarf. Many of the members, even the women, were smoking, and an urn of Russian tea steamed in the corner.

Louisa knew several of them through 'Baby' Melville, the Suffragette, whose brother was a novelist, and she seemed quite at home, sitting on a cushion on the floor with her arms clasped around her knees. Laura, however, listening to the high intellectual tone of the conversation, found herself wondering why they had been asked – until a pause introduced a rather self-conscious-sounding question from one of the members about being a lady-policeman.

'I mean, I do think it awfully splendid of you,' said the pale, beaky-nosed young man, 'and, of course, one is all for women *doing* things. I think I can safely say we are all suffragists here.' There was a murmur of agreement. 'But don't you find it awfully *unfeminising?*'

'I'm not sure what you mean by that,' Laura said. She knew exactly what he meant but didn't want to have that argument all over again.

'It's not the practical aspect of it that one objects to,' said the young man. 'One must consider the *intrinsic worth,* as opposed to the *instrumental value.*'

'Oh, Freddy, you can't apply Moore to this situation,' another man protested. 'It's a clear case of Ends and Means. As Russell says–'

His words were drowned in a surge of objections, out of which Freddy's rather reedy voice rose again: 'The prime object of life is the creation of aesthetic experience – I think we can all agree on that – and there must be something deeply *un*aesthetic about a woman-policeman. It offends the sensibilities.'

'You surely can't be saying that all women can be allowed to do is sit around the drawing-room being decorative,' Baby objected. 'We've come far beyond that.'

'Of course, of course,' Freddy said soothingly. 'We all agree that women must be allowed to pursue knowledge and beauty, must be admitted to the universities and the professions, must be free to seek out love and personal fulfilment without the trammelling of Victorian conventions–'

'What exactly are you saying, Freddy?' asked a rather solid young woman, dressed in baggy black Turkish trousers and a scarlet jacket, who was sitting with her arm round the shoulders of a slight, fair girl and sharing a thin cheroot with her, puff and puff about. 'Spit it out, old chap, before we die of boredom.'

'I'm saying one's spiritual goals must be paramount. The situations the police find themselves in are necessarily ugly, dirty, unpleasant. Lowering to the spirit. And doubly so for a woman.'

He stopped and looked at Laura, and since everyone else seemed to be waiting for her to answer him, she sighed inwardly and said, 'There aren't enough men to do the police work, now so many have gone to the front. Women can do some of it. Louisa and I are doing useful work. That's all.' She heard how bald her words sounded after his elaborate effusions.

'Oh, but that's so earthbound, so worldly!' Freddy cried.

Some others joined in with what to Laura was mere babble, about greater values and the

251

pursuit of Higher Truth through Art.

In the next pause she said, 'Without the police to keep order, you wouldn't have the freedom to pursue your arts. You can't paint pictures or write books with burglars breaking your windows and stealing your brushes and pens.'

'Police are a necessary evil, one agrees,' said a very tall, thin female in a turban, 'but that's no reason to *plunge* oneself into the horrors of the concrete.'

'There can never be good reason for increasing the ugliness in the world,' said someone else.

'We are all threatened with ugliness by this government's wretched war,' said an older man in horn-rims.

Laura said, 'The war is everyone's war. We all have to play our part.'

Freddy lifted his hands in horror. 'It's not *ours* – we are all pacifists here. We'll have no part in it.'

'War is the ultimate barbarism,' Turban Lady agreed.

'By doing the police force's work,' Freddy continued, 'and releasing police officers to go and fight, I'm sorry to say you are facilitating it.'

'Now, now, Freddy,' said the cheroot woman, 'you can't call her a warmonger. That's not cricket. Miss Hunter, the truth is we're all agog to hear about some of your experiences. We really can't imagine what it's like to tangle with criminals and prostitutes and so on. Do give us the grisly details.'

Laura realised now why she had been invited: as the comic turn to enliven the evening. She glanced at Louisa, who was keeping her eyes firmly on the floor and her lips tightly shut, either with embarrassment or vexation. Very well, she thought, you people have asked for it. So she embarked on a narration of some of the more exciting encounters they had had, embroidering them for maximum effect. Her audience listened in silence, some thrilled, some horrified, and one or two of the younger ones, she could see, even envious.

'Goodness!' said Baby Melville, when she paused, 'I had no idea! Louisa, is it true? It sounds positively gruesome – but terrible fun!'

'I don't know about fun,' Louisa said. 'But it's useful work. And it makes one feel...' She couldn't think of the right words.

'It makes one feel free,' Laura said for her. 'To know one can walk anywhere, and deal with anything that arises, to be afraid of nobody – *that's* freedom.' Not painting pictures of nudes and having affairs with each other's husbands, she added internally.

Fortunately someone latched on to the word 'freedom', questioned its meaning, and the conversation shot off at a tangent into philosophical byways where she couldn't follow – and didn't want to.

Later, when they were leaving, they were accosted by the cheroot lady and her companion.

'Sylvia Partridge,' she announced, holding out her hand. 'And this is Beryl Gibson.' Her handshake was a finger-crusher. 'I thought you held your end up splendidly,' she went on. 'Don't mind what some of the others said – especially that ass Freddy. Some people get drunk on words and lose the sense of them, you know. You must both come to a little *soirée* we're having at our studio on

253

Tuesday, meet some of our friends. Bedfordites, but more fun than Frances's set, and all doing splendid work.'

Laura was framing an excuse, but a glance at Louisa told her that she wanted to go. Perhaps they ought to get out more, she thought. She was happy with a quiet evening at home, but Louisa had been used to being surrounded by people when she was helping with the Cause, and probably missed all the social interaction. 'We'd love to come,' she said bravely, and her reward was the brightening of Louisa's face.

Diana had a letter from Charles, which concluded:

I learn that we are moving from here to another part of the line. I may not tell you where, because I think we are going into action at last. The men are as excited as children about it. They are quite ready, after months of training, and spirits could not be higher. The regulars call us Hyde Park Soldiers, but we are fit, strong, disciplined and steady, and eager to show our people at home that we are as good as the best. The post is going and I must close now, but kiss your dear picture, and trust that when I come home to you next month, it will be having won something, be it only a few yards of ground, for the country and the woman I love.

She took it to her father. 'Where do you think he will be going? Will it be Ypres?'

'I don't know, my dear,' Edward said. 'They are still fighting there. There's also a battle going on near Arras, trying to break the German salient and capture Aubers Ridge. He might be sent there.'

254

'Well, I hope he is,' Diana said. 'I shouldn't like him to have to go to Ypres.' Cousin Jack had been wounded at Ypres. It was a dangerous place.

Edward patted her shoulder. 'We can be sure that, wherever he is, Lord Dene will conduct himself with honour.'

Diana smiled. 'Perhaps he'll be given a medal. That would look well on his uniform at our wedding.'

'Where's my beaver?' Munt demanded, coming in through the back door. 'Ain't you women got nothing better to do than stand around clacking?'

Cook and Ada were bent over the newspaper, spread out on the table. Cook looked up distractedly. 'This awful Zeppelin bombing! First it was Southend, now it's Ramsgate and Dover! Where will it all end?'

'It'll end with you gettin' that kettle on, and my beaver ready. What cake you got for me today?'

Cook wasn't listening. 'A hundred bombs dropped on Southend last week! What do they want to bomb a seaside place for? It's wicked!'

'Southend, Westcliff and Leigh-on-Sea,' Ada amplified. 'Some of 'em were incendiaries. Smashing people's houses, then burning 'em up!'

'A woman was killed,' said Cook, 'and her Dalmatian dog and her cat. The pity of it, killing poor defenceless animals!'

'And now Ramsgate,' Ada went on. 'Just another holiday place, no army or anything there. People going about their lives all peaceful, doing no harm to a soul, and that Kaiser orders 'em to be bombed to death. God'll strike him down if there's any justice!'

'And what about us?' Cook cried. 'When's he going to come for us?'

'Never mind the Kaiser, I'll come for you if you don't get my tea, an' I'm a lot closer than him,' said Munt.

'I suppose you'd like being bombed for no reason,' Cook retorted. 'People getting killed in their beds – it isn't right.'

'It's a war, you daft ha'porth,' said Munt. 'That's what war means – folk getting killed. Gah! I'll go without me beaver. Sooner that than listen to females bleating away.'

'Oh, go and sit down, you old misery. The tea's made and on the table, and the cake.'

Munt was unwilling to be mollified. 'Made already? And gettin' cold and stewed, I don't doubt.'

'Well, it's all you'll get, so make your mind up to it. I don't know how I manage to get meals out at all, with all this bombing and the awful casualty lists – thousands and thousands every day. So many names! All those poor boys. There's Mrs Prendergast's son Harold gassed to death at Wipers, and Mrs Gort's lost her son. She's char to the Gordons – that's only just up the road. It feels as if the war's getting nearer and nearer, and one day it'll be right here on our doorstep!'

'Well, if the Germans come, you can poison 'em with your stewed tea,' said Munt, and stumped away into the other room.

The dinner party at Dene Park was not such an awful ordeal as the Christmas visit had been. For one thing, Diana was more confident now. She knew Charles really loved her, and thus could face whatever disapproval came from other quarters. There were only a few weeks to go before she would be installed immovably in her place, and there was nothing anyone could do about that.

Besides, the Wroughtons were more welcoming now. Nothing could make Lady Wroughton friendly, but she behaved correctly and said the right things; the earl's public face was genial, and he could sincerely admire a pretty girl, so he came across as quite fatherly, which was as much as Diana wanted.

Rupert was not there, and Diana was not sorry. He had been very nice to her in London, but she had not forgotten his earlier unpleasantness, and did not entirely trust his change of heart.

In fact, there were no young people there that night. Diana was being 'presented to the county', and the other guests were luminaries and leaders of the social life. It was a middle-aged and elderly company. They did not scrutinise Diana in the uncomfortable way the younger set had, and they had not the dynastic doubts that had afflicted the Wroughtons' relatives. They greeted the Hunters civilly, then paid them no particular attention.

The talk was mostly of war and politics.

'I understand,' said Sir George Farrow, the MP for the north of the county, 'that Lloyd George and Bonar Law went into the meeting with Asquith to demand a coalition on the grounds of his failure, but Asquith got his word in first – demanded a coalition on the grounds of national interest! He shot their fox, the canny devil.'

Edward repeated his own opinion: 'A coalition

257

might be the best thing in wartime. There are too many opportunities for passing blame, playing party politics with the nation's safety.'

The magistrate, Mr Worthington, said, 'The Unionists won't like being cheated of their turn in the driving seat.'

'What they principally don't like,' said Sir George, 'is Fisher resigning and Churchill staying. Everyone knows the whole Dardanelles campaign was Churchill's idea, and if anyone ought to take the blame...'

'Can't stand the feller,' said Lord Bentley, who owned a large estate over at Coneysfield. 'Too bumptious by half. Rides roughshod over everybody.'

'All the same,' said Admiral Caldicott, 'it's thanks to him that we've got any defences at all against these Zeppelins. Give him his due, he foresaw the attacks right back in August.'

'But what are these defences, Admiral?' Lady Wroughton asked. 'I haven't heard of them.'

'We haven't needed them yet, dear lady. But there's a ring of anti-aircraft guns and aeroplane stations all around London – Eastchurch, Hendon, Hounslow and so on.'

'I hope it will be enough,' Edward said.

'What do you mean by that?' the admiral asked.

'All the best aeroplanes have been sent to France,' said Edward. 'Those reserved for home defence are antiquated – as are the guns. And those Zeppelins fly so high, it's unlikely either will be able to reach them.'

'That's rather defeatist talk, Hunter,' the earl reproved.

'But the Zeppelins will never bomb London,' Lady Bentley objected. 'The Kaiser's forbidden it. Too many of his own relatives there.'

'As I see it,' said Mr Worthington, 'these Zeppelins are more of a propaganda weapon. They can't ever contribute much militarily – too slow, too easily blown off course. Little chance of actually hitting a target. No, I believe they're meant to spread fear and despondency in the civilian population. To sap morale.'

'You may well be right, Worthington,' said Sir George. 'But, if so, the Huns have misread the British character. Any attempt to get us down will only make us more determined.'

'Quite right,' said his wife. 'Stiff upper lip, and all that sort of thing. With the cream of young manhood over there... Have you heard anything from Charles recently, Lord Wroughton?'

'Oh, the boy is about to get his first taste of battle, so I understand,' said the earl. 'Can't say where, of course, but Simpkins at Horse Guards assures me the Terriers are about to win their spurs. Charles can't wait to get to grips with the enemy. What about your boy?'

'Somewhere in Champagne,' Sir George answered for his wife. 'Quiet sector. And the younger boy's in camp up in Nottingham.'

'It must be difficult for you, planning a wedding, in these circumstances,' Lady Farrow said to the countess. 'It's such a shame for the young people.' She bestowed a kindly smile on Diana. 'But wars don't last for ever. I believe you'll have a London house, to begin with?'

Diana opened her mouth to answer, but the

259

countess jumped in first: 'Yes, we're doing up the house in Clarges Street for them. It's small, but it's all they'll need to begin with.'

'You'll be neighbours with a very dear friend of mine, Lady Paulson,' Lady Farrow told Diana. 'She lives in Clarges Street. She's done wonders with the house – extended it at the back, created a garden room with a glazed roof. It makes all the difference – for it must be said, those houses can be very dark and damp.'

The subject of house improvements was taken up with relish; after a while, the other end of the table went back to politics and the current discontent of the back-benchers.

Nula had brought the wedding gown at last, and Diana was having her first fitting. Sadie was home, and was graciously allowed to sit in the corner of the room and watch. It was exciting at first, for no-one had seen it until now, and Nula was enough of a showman to make the unveiling of her masterpiece into an occasion.

It was beautiful – even Sadie, generally indifferent to dress, could see that. It was of ivory charmeuse, with a high waist and natural gathers falling softly to the floor, and a three-quarters overdress of chiffon.

The bodice and sleeves were trimmed with some of Charles's lace 'Beautiful stuff, it is,' Nula said, with approval, fingering it delicately. 'Someone steered him right. I've edged the veil with it – you'll see in a minute – and very nice it looks. *And,*' she added, with a significant look, 'there's enough left over for the trimming of a christening gown.'

260

Diana blushed at the reference, and Beattie answered for her: 'I dare say the Wroughtons will have a family robe they'll want to use. Especially if it's a boy – eventual heir to the title and so on.'

'Well, it'll do for something,' Nula said. 'A fine bit o' lace like that never goes amiss. You can save it for your daughter's wedding, Diana dear. Ah, now, don't be looking like that. It'll come sooner than you think. Time flies like an arrow, though when you're young it doesn't feel like it.'

The women helped Diana into the gown, and she became instantly transformed into a radiant and ethereal figure. Sadie admired in silence. There followed a dull period, for her, as Nula pinched and tugged and stroked at the gown, and discussed with Beattie whether various bits should be taken in or let out and whether a button should be moved or a sleeve adjusted. Her attention drifted. She gazed round the room, saw the photograph of Lord Dene on Diana's bedside table, and thought that he looked better in uniform than in 'civvies'. She supposed most men did, and wondered for a moment why that was. Gosh, she thought, wouldn't it be awkward if he couldn't get leave when the time came? But Diana had said that she had it from Lady Wroughton that the earl had fixed it in advance, and that he knew Sir John French, so it was bound to be all right.

She thought about John Courcy, and how nice he looked in uniform. He had replied to Mrs Cuthbert's letter to assure them that horses did have gas masks, and the soldiers were instructed to make sure they were fitted before they put on their own. At present it was a simple nosebag with a flannelette bag inside it soaked in neutralising chemical, but it seemed to be effective. The War Office and the Veterinary Corps were working hard on the gas problem, and it was hoped men and horses both would have proper respirators by June or July.

His letter had ended with a message for Sadie, hoping she was well, sending greetings to 'his friend' Nailer, and asking if she had read the book they were talking about when they had last met. Sadie was intensely pleased that he had thought of her.

Her thoughts still on khaki, she said, 'Oh, Diana, I met Alicia Harding in the street this morning. She said she called on Lizzie Drake yesterday evening and the Drakes are all upset because their cousin Toby was killed at Ypres. Wasn't he sweet on you the Christmas before last? I remember him and Martin arguing over who was going to sit next to you.'

Nula said, 'We'll have no talk about war just now, Sadie, thank you.'

Sadie went red, realising she had been tactless. But Diana only said, 'Poor Toby. How awful for them. I must go round and see Lizzie this afternoon.'

'She'll like that, dear,' Beattie said, gave Sadie a minatory glance, and went on, 'We haven't decided about gloves yet, Nula dear.'

Diana knew the subject was being changed, and why. But she had no fears. Only that morning she had received a field postcard from Charles, with everything crossed out except *I am quite well* and *Letter follows at first opportunity*. She said, 'I'm wondering what's going to hold on the veil. It looks unfinished without anything.'

'Ah,' said Nula, 'I was rather thinking the countess might offer you a tiara, which would be fitting, seeing as you're marrying a viscount. But in case she doesn't, I'm planning a headband of fresh flowers – white roses. They'll have to be ordered in advance,' she added to Beattie, 'to be sure of getting 'em. I'd like one that wasn't dead white, but just a bit creamy or yellowy in the centre.'

'"Princess Victoria", perhaps,' Beattie said. 'Or "Queen of Beauty". I'll make enquiries.' She smiled at her lovely daughter. 'Luckily, as it's June, there'll be all the roses you want. Imagine if you'd got married in January.'

Diana smiled back. 'Then Nula would have thought of something else.'

CHAPTER SIXTEEN

The news came first by Miss Bleeker, who worked at the telephone exchange. As soon as she was off duty, she got on her bicycle and pedalled as fast as she could to the rectory to speak to Dr Fitzgerald. Mrs Fitzgerald regarded Miss Bleeker as one of her most valuable sources of information, and therefore made sure she was present as she told the rector what she had overheard.

The rector delivered his standard stern homily on eavesdropping.

'I didn't mean to, of course,' said Miss Bleeker,

263

unblushingly, 'but sometimes one can't help it, you know.' She seemed to feel this was sufficient penitence, for she went on, 'But done is done, and now – oughtn't someone to tell them? Don't you think? They ought not to be left in the dark.'

'Quite right. They must be told at once,' said Mrs Fitzgerald, her eyes bright. 'I will go myself. It will come better from me.'

But for once the rector overruled her. Deplorable though it was to act on information that had been come by dishonestly, he knew this particular cat could not be kept in the bag, so the harm must be mitigated as far as possible. He must take responsibility. 'No, my dear,' he said firmly, 'this is a job for the shepherd of the flock. They will want spiritual comfort. I shall go alone. And, Miss Bleeker, I trust you not to spread this any further. It may, indeed, be all a mistake.'

'No, indeed, I am quite sure, considering the source–'

'Miss Bleeker! Not a word to anyone.' The rector rarely asserted himself, but when he did, he could be quite impressive.

Miss Bleeker subsided meekly, and as the rector went away to prepare himself, Mrs Fitzgerald consoled herself by saying to the telephonist, 'You must need a cup of tea after such an unpleasant shock,' and leading her into the drawing-room to be pumped.

As it was a Saturday afternoon, Edward was at home, playing croquet at the far end of the garden with Sadie and William. Peter had been playing with them too, but had grown bored and abandoned the game in favour of swinging on the front gate and hoping something would happen. He was surprised to see the rector approaching, an unusual enough event almost to be interesting.

'Are your mother and father at home, my boy?' Dr Fitzgerald asked, as he reached him.

'Mother's in the drawing-room and Father's in the garden,' said Peter, remembering his manners and jumping down to open the gate.

'I will go to your mother, and perhaps you will just run down and ask your father to come up too.'

Peter read his face, and went haring off full of importance.

Shown into the drawing-room, the rector greeted the mildly surprised Beattie, 'I come on an unhappy errand, Mrs Hunter. I have something to tell you and your husband. But first, where is Miss Diana?'

A cold hand gripped Beattie's heart. 'She's upstairs in her room – reading, I believe. What is it? Not bad news – please not that.'

'I will wait for your husband,' said Dr Fitzgerald.

An agonising pause followed until Edward appeared in the doorway, with Sadie and the boys behind him. The rector threw a look at Beattie, who moistened her lips and said, in as normal a tone as possible, 'Go away, children. We want to be private.'

Edward came in, shutting the door behind him, looked enquiringly at Beattie and received a ghastly look in return. 'What is it?' he asked.

'I have come with, I'm afraid, terrible news. Miss Bleeker overheard part of a telephone call from an officer at the War Office to Dene Park. Normally,

265

of course, I would pay no attention to anything gained by eavesdropping, which I'm afraid is what it comes down to, but given the nature of what she overheard, I felt it was my duty to forewarn you.'

'For God's sake!' Beattie protested. 'What is it?' Edward stepped close to her.

'I'm very much afraid that Lord Dene has...' The rector sought the least hurtful words. 'His name has been entered into the casualty lists.'

It was Edward who asked, 'He's been injured?'

'What was said was that he was wounded and taken to a casualty clearing station, but died soon afterwards. I am very sorry.' He regarded them with the grave, kindly look a clergyman develops for such occasions. He saw they were too bewildered to speak, and went on, 'I thought the kindest thing was to let you know at once, so that you could prepare yourselves and Miss Diana as far as possible. The War Office will not send you an official notification – that will go to Dene Park.'

Of course, thought Beattie. They wouldn't tell a fiancée, only a wife. Otherwise, it would be the parents.

'And there is no knowing when Lord and Lady Wroughton, in their shock and grief, will think to pass on the news to you,' the rector continued. 'But I do believe Lord Dene's fiancée should not be the last to hear. I hope you feel I did right.'

There was no answer. Beattie was staring at nothing, and Edward was looking at her. He had taken her hand, but she did not seem to notice it.

'I know what a shock this must be,' the rector went on, 'and the poor young lady is much to be pitied, only three weeks away from her wedding. It

266

is a consideration of great poignancy. But you must comfort her with the knowledge that he died in the best of causes. *Dulce et decorum est pro patria mori.* I recommend you to seek the consolation of prayer, and the balm that only the Almighty can lay on earthly wounds. I will be happy to pray with you, if it will be of any comfort.'

Edward managed to say, 'No, thank you, Dr Fitzgerald, not now. I don't think it will help now. We must think what to say to Diana.'

'Of course. I am at your service at any time,' the rector said graciously.

When they were alone, Beattie turned her painful gaze on her husband. 'What shall we do? Do you believe it?'

Edward shook his head, trying to clear it. 'The thing is, do we tell Diana?' he said.

'It might all be a mistake,' Beattie said. 'Miss Bleeker is not the most sensible of women, and she loves to gossip. She might have misheard, or misunderstood.'

'Taking it to the rector makes it seem she was sure. Otherwise she'd have spread it around her friends first.'

'But it's not official,' Beattie pleaded, 'until we've heard it from an official source. The Wroughtons—'

'They'll be devastated. It may be days before they think to tell us, and by then the gossip will be all round the village. We can't let Diana hear it in that way.'

'But supposing we tell her, and it isn't true?'

He looked at her steadily, and read in her face his own conviction, which lay at the pit of his

267

stomach like a stone, that it was true.

'If only we had the telephone!' she cried.

Edward came to a decision. 'I'll go up to Dene Park and see the earl. Don't say anything to anyone until I get back.'

When he had gone, the children came back in, subdued, sensing the atmosphere. 'Where's Father gone?' Peter asked.

'What did Dr Fitzgerald want?' said Sadie.

'Never mind,' said Beattie. 'Don't ask questions now. You'll know when it's time. Go out and play, and don't bother me. Go on!' she added sharply. 'I mean it. I can't talk to you now.'

They drifted away unhappily. 'It's bad news,' William whispered, as they trailed back into the garden. 'Do you think Father's lost all his money?'

'I don't know,' said Sadie. Her fears were turning towards David and Bobby. Had there been an accident? She stared around blankly, and saw Nailer watching from under a mock-orange bush. 'I'm going for a walk,' she said. She called to the dog and walked away. William watched her, feeling abandoned, until Peter, less introspective, said, 'Oh, come on, let's play something. We can't just mope around. Let's play croquet.'

'All right,' said William. 'I'll give you a hoop.'

'Two hoops,' Peter stipulated. 'You're nearly twice as old as me.'

Edward was shown into the earl's study. Lord Wroughton was seated at his desk, staring at his hands. The truth was in his face. He looked up at Edward searchingly, as though hoping he brought a reprieve, then sighed.

'You've heard,' he said.

'I heard a rumour,' said Edward. 'I had to know if it was true.'

'Yes,' said the earl. 'We would have told you. One has to – get used to it. It's hard to take it in.'

'So it is true? Lord Dene is – was killed?'

The earl nodded. He did not invite Edward to sit down, but this seemed absence of mind rather than discourtesy so Edward sat anyway. 'What happened?'

'It was near Artois,' the earl said. 'A series of attacks, jointly by the French and the First Army, to reduce the German salient and capture Aubers Ridge. The initial attack was successful. Gained a thousand yards. The second attack went in on Thursday, to capture the village of Festubert from the Germans. The Germans were entrenched – there was heavy machine-gun fire–' He stopped, and began rubbing his hands over and over as if washing them.

'He was wounded,' Edward said. He was surprised to hear his own voice.

'He was shot in the neck,' the earl said. 'They carried him back to a dressing-station. He was still alive, though he couldn't talk. But it seems – they think – that the bullet moved and severed a major blood vessel. He suffered a violent haemorrhage and died.' He stared at his moving hands. 'It was very quick,' he added, in a low voice. 'They couldn't do anything.'

Edward was silent, waiting, but there seemed no more to come. After a while he said, 'I am very sorry.'

Wroughton looked up. 'Yes,' he said. And then

seemed to remember. 'Your daughter–' He closed his eyes in pain, and opened them again. 'It is the most unlucky thing,' he said at last.

Unlucky. The inadequacy of the word seemed to make clearer the loss to everyone. The Wroughtons had lost their eldest son. Diana had lost her future husband. The Hunters had lost their son-in-law. The world had lost a good man and, he imagined, a good soldier. It was – *unlucky.* Luck would have moved the bullet a little to the side and spared them all, but then someone else might have been hit. There was no real luck to be had in war. It was a cruel ledger kept by a heartless clerk.

'So,' Edward said, 'there is no doubt about it?'

Wroughton shook his head. 'It was Simpkins at the War Office who told me. He was telephoned by an aide to Sir Douglas Haig, who was commanding. The official notification is on its way, but he wanted me to be forewarned.' He sighed shakily, as though he was having trouble breathing. 'They'll bury him out there, of course. There was a lot of anger about young Gladstone's body being brought home. The government is clamping down – there'll be no more permissions. That's the part that upsets his mother most. She doesn't understand what right the state has to decide where the dead lie. He ought to rest here, among his ancestors. Why does the fleeting camaraderie of the trenches have precedence over the love of his own family?'

Edward knew the arguments. He thought about it as he walked home. William Gladstone, MP, Lord Lieutenant of Flintshire, had fallen at Ypres in April and had been buried at Poperinghe; but despite the ban on repatriations that had been in force since March, he had been exhumed and brought home after his uncles had made special representation to the King and the prime minister. There had been widespread resentment. Every man, high or low, who fell in France gave up the one thing most precious to him, his life; but a lord lieutenant had been given a special privilege denied those not so well connected. It was a matter of great delicacy: the decision had been made that if all could not be brought home, none should, and it must be enforced. As Wroughton said, there would be no more exceptions made, even for a friend of the commander-in-chief. Charles Wroughton would lie in Flanders, making common cause with his men.

Sadie was waiting for him at the gate, with Nailer sitting at her feet, her face one big question.

'Is it Charles?' she asked bluntly.

He nodded wearily.

'Dead?' He didn't need to reply. She put her fingers over her lips in a curious gesture, as though something might fall out of her. Then she turned away and walked off up the road, Nailer following closely.

He went in. The servants were lingering in the recesses of the hall as he passed through. The family was all gathered in the drawing-room. Beattie had managed not to tell anyone anything yet, but there was apprehension, anxiety, and the first threads of suspicion.

He went straight to Diana, and took both her hands. 'My darling, you must be very brave,' he said.

'No,' she said. 'Please don't–'

'Charles was killed in action at a place called Festubert,' Edward said. He decided not to burden her with more details. This would be enough to take in.

She searched his face. 'It can't be true. We're getting married.'

'I'm afraid it is. I'm so very sorry.'

'No,' she said again. 'We're getting married in three weeks. It must be a mistake. He wouldn't do that.' She seemed to reach for some proof in her mind. 'He sent me a postcard,' she said. 'It said *I am quite well.*'

'I'm so sorry,' said Edward again.

She looked once round the assembled faces, then ran out of the room. They heard her footsteps on the stairs, and the slam of her bedroom door.

The Wroughtons were not at church the next day. 'Why must we go?' Sadie had cried. 'People will look at us!'

'It's expected,' said Beattie. But she excused Diana – indeed, she could hardly have got her along. The rest of them went, and endured the eyes and the curiosity and the kind words.

And afterwards Rupert came to the house. His eyes were red and his face seemed raw, as though stripped of some essential defence. Beattie received him alone, in the drawing-room. The children were mooching about somewhere, waiting for things to be normal again. Diana was in her room, Edward in his study. All were hiding from each other. She imagined it must be the same at Dene

Park. Perhaps that was what had driven Rupert to come here.

He sat, refusing offers of refreshment, looked around the room as though seeing it for the first time.

'How is your mother?' Beattie asked at last.

He shrugged. 'I think she's angry.'

'I can understand that,' Beattie said.

'Can you?'

'When you lose someone very precious to you, you are angry with Fate. Or God. Whatever decided it.'

'It was a German machine-gun that decided it,' he said. 'That makes *me* angry.' He gave a sarcastic laugh. 'What in the world was he doing there? The only things he ever killed in his life were pheasants and rabbits.'

'He was doing his duty,' Beattie said.

'He was no soldier,' Rupert said savagely. 'He was only in the Territorials because it was the expected thing. And now look what's happened. What a farce! What a waste! That's what doing your duty gets you.'

Beattie had no answer to that – and knew, besides, that he did not want one. He needed to rail. She remembered the feeling from long, long ago. It proved, though, she thought, that he had been fond of his brother, and that was to his credit.

He got up and walked restlessly round the room, picked up an ornament from the mantelpiece and examined it, putting it back without seeing it. He stood at the window, shoving his hands in his pockets. 'Is Diana – is Miss Hunter...? I suppose

273

she's upset?'

'She's in her room,' Beattie said, wondering what was behind his question. 'She hasn't stopped crying.'

'Then – she did love him?'

'What are you asking? Of course she did.'

He turned. 'I'm sorry. I don't seem to know what I'm saying. I don't know what I'm thinking most of the time. He's always been *there*, you see. Whether one liked him or not. I didn't always. But he was always – *there*. Solid. Permanent. Like some great – monument. And now...'

He bit his lip, and his face quivered. Beattie saw his Adam's apple rise and fall, and knew he was trying not to cry. Her instinct was to go to him and take him in her arms, but she didn't know him well enough. Yet he seemed just then very young, and needing a mother, and she couldn't imagine the countess was very motherly. She pitied him. Her mind flew to her own David, and flinched away again. She must not think of him in the context of death. It might be unlucky.

'I'm so sorry,' she said – all, it seemed, that could be said.

He dragged in a breath that was half a sob, and got control of himself. He smiled – a most inappropriate smile, but she understood it was all he could do with his face just then. 'So am I,' he said, and turned and left her.

Munt found Sadie wandering disconsolately around the far reaches of the garden, caught in the lethargy of sorrow. She had a stick in her hand, which she idly trailed in bushes and against trees as she passed. Nailer, trotting along with her, staying close, as he had since yesterday, eyed the stick occasionally, as if wondering whether he would be obliged to run after it. She reached a bench down by the wilderness at last and sat, and Nailer sat in front of her, fixing his eyes on her face. She looked beyond the dog and saw Munt, coming towards her carrying a basket.

'It's like having a cold,' she said, without pre-amble. 'That awful stuffed-up feeling when you can't do anything but you can't do *nothing*, and nothing's any good anyway, and you feel as if it will always be like this for the rest of your life.'

'Think of Miss Diana,' said Munt.

'I do. I do try to, but I can't imagine how ghastly she must feel. I think, what if it were me–' She stopped and started again. 'But I can't really *know*, can I?' She looked an appeal at him. 'She doesn't want me. I did knock this morning but she told me to go away.'

'Time, that's all,' said Munt.

'I know,' said Sadie, 'but time's not much help, is it, when you're at this end of it? I wish we could just skip straight to the other end.' Munt kept a useful silence, and into it she said quietly, 'Having to cancel the wedding and everything... But, oh, poor Charles! I liked him so much.'

'She chose better'n she knew,' Munt said.

Sadie stared. Munt never said nice things about anyone. Charles must have been a special person to gain his approval. She remembered that Charles had liked Nailer. He and John Courcy were the only ones who did. She stooped and stroked the dog's rough head. Nailer twitched his bottom

275

against the grass in response. Happiness came so easily to him – it only took someone being nice to him. 'I wish I was a dog,' she said.

'No, you don't,' said Munt.

She looked up at him. 'I wish there was something I could do,' she said.

He took something out of the basket and gave it to her. It was a little straw punnet, stained from last year's fruit – he kept a stock of them in his shed. It was lined with a rhubarb leaf, on which nestled the crimson jewels of wild strawberries.

'Where did you get them?' she asked in surprise. 'Not here – in the garden? You always pull up wild strawberry plants.' He said they were weeds, and pernicious. If you didn't keep on top of them they got everywhere.

His eyes slid away. 'Kep' a little patch, backer my shed.'

'You didn't!'

He looked at her defiantly. 'Can if I likes! Sweetest fruit in the world, wild strawberries. Taste like scent.' He jerked his chin towards the punnet in her hand. 'For Miss Diana.' He turned away, so that she might not say anything about his gesture that he might have to hear.

Below stairs, Emily was the most inconsolable. She had lived on the dream of Miss Diana and her prince. If the dream did not come true for them, what hope was there for anyone else? She wept as she scrubbed the kitchen floor, her tears falling onto the flags and being wiped away with the cloth.

Cook resorted to cookery, worked out her frus-

276

tration in a frenzy of baking, and sent up her sympathy with a succession of delicacies to tempt Miss Diana as if she were an invalid. 'This cruel, wicked war!' she cried, as she wielded the rolling pin.

'I knew it was too good to be true,' Ada muttered, and tripped over the feet of Henry, who for once did not need to be cajoled into staying at his post. He was sitting at the end of the table cleaning silver, but his ears were the busiest part of him. 'Get on with your work!' she snapped at him.

'And keep your polish to yourself,' Cook added. 'I don't want it in my pastry. There's enough trouble in this world...'

'She'll never get over it,' Ada predicted. 'She'll go into a decline. It's not as if she'll ever get another chance like that one. A lord...'

'But she loved him,' Emily sobbed. 'She truly loved him. Didn't matter if he was a lord or a chimbley sweep!'

In the morning room, Ethel was helping Beattie wrap up the wedding gifts for sending back. It was fortunate, Beattie thought, that most of the stuff had gone to Dene Park so that she didn't have to be bothered with it. And then she suffered a pang of conscience. Lady Wroughton, unpleasant as she was, had lost a son: her loss was greater than Beattie's. Perhaps she should send a note, offering to help with the task.

But, then, Lady Wroughton had a secretary and servants, who would probably do it all for her. It was hard to imagine the countess suffering. And that thought caused her a second pang of conscience.

'But I have two sons in uniform!' she said aloud, then remembered she was not alone and clamped her lips shut.

Ethel stored up the outburst to tell Eric when she saw him that evening. One of the nice things about him was that he didn't mind her being a maid. 'It's honest work,' he had said. 'And you get your bed and board – that's worth a lot.' And once he had said, 'Good training for a young woman, for when she gets a home of her own.' It had seemed a delightfully pointed sort of thing to say, though he hadn't elaborated on it. In return for his tolerance of her domestic-servant status, she liked to bring him little titbits of news and insights into the life of the house. Lord Dene's death would make a good talking point on their way to the picture palace.

Might as well be some use, she thought gloomily. The wedding would have given her much more to talk about.

The wedding gown, swathed in protective muslin, was still hanging in the sewing-room. Since the first fitting, and with no further need for secrecy, Nula had meant to work on it there, rather than carrying it back and forth to her own home. It hung now like a faceless, handless bride, a cruel ghost mocking the hopes and expectations of the innocent.

Diana had finally been coaxed out of her room, pale and red-eyed, to the breakfast table, though it was not to be expected that she would eat much, and thence to the drawing-room sofa where Sadie had played cards with her, trying to keep her mind

278

occupied. The game was gin, and Sadie was having to deal both sides as well as keep score because Diana seemed incapable of it.

Finally Diana said, 'You don't need to bother with me. I'm sure you'd sooner be somewhere else. With your horses or something.'

'I want to be with you,' Sadie said. 'I want to help.'

'You can't,' Diana said. 'Everything's over. Nothing good will happen, ever again.'

Sadie found the wisdom not to argue. She shuffled the cards together. 'Come for a walk,' she said. 'The fresh air will do you good. Ah, do! Put your hat on and we'll go through the woods. It'll be quiet there.'

She coaxed her sister and gentled her, like a nervous horse, and got her out of the house at last. She reasoned to herself that everything was better when you were surrounded by nature, and that Diana spent too long cooped up indoors at the best of times. And this was assuredly not the best of times. She could not imagine what Diana was feeling, but understood at least that it was too soon for her to stop feeling it, whatever those who loved her might wish. She had eaten the wild strawberries herself rather than let Munt know they had been rejected; but when she had taken the punnet back to him and said, 'Diana loved them,' she had had the uncomfortable feeling that he knew perfectly well where they had gone. At least, she had salved her conscience. Diana would have loved the idea of them, had she been able to think about anything other than Charles, so it was not really a lie.

It *did* seem to do Diana good to be out, Sadie thought. She did not try to talk to her. The sisters walked in silence under the dappled leaves, but she thought Diana straightened up a little, like a blade of grass when the foot is lifted. Apart from the birds, it was very quiet, but it was a *good* quiet, a growing quiet, not the silence of indoors from which nothing good could come.

I would love to be riding here, Sadie thought. It was a perfect track for cantering. "'You will hear the beat of a horse's feet,/And the swish of a skirt in the dew,/Steadily cantering through/The misty solitudes,'" she quoted.

Diana didn't say anything – perhaps had not even heard. Sadie remembered that Diana had promised her horses and the run of Dene Park; but she remembered it only in the context of wishing that Diana rode, because then she could have suggested a real comfort for her. You could never really be lonely or sad when you were with a horse.

While the girls were out for their walk, Nula, who had been hanging around the kitchen waiting for an opportunity, slipped upstairs, retrieved the wedding dress and took it away with her. Best, she thought, if there was no danger of Diana catching sight of it.

CHAPTER SEVENTEEN

Festubert was captured, and by the 25th of May the attack had resulted in an advance of almost two miles. The newspapers declared it a success – and, indeed, by the standards that had come to obtain in the war so far, it was a resounding one. At Ypres, where the fighting was dying down at about the same time, the best that could be said was that the town had not fallen, though the salient around it had been compressed to half its size and the town itself was in ruins. Yet holding on under such an onslaught, including the use of poison gas, was a triumph, though it came at a terrible price.

Diana cared nothing about Festubert, or indeed any other piece of war news. War was just the place 'over there' that took the young men away and killed them. Toby Drake and Harold Prendergast were dead, and news came that Mrs Oliver's nephew Aldis Crane, who had been one of Diana's admirers, had fallen at Bellewaerde. Young men she had danced with, who had flirted with her. She thought about them because it hurt too much to think about Charles.

Fallen. It made her think of trees – a forest being levelled. Those familiar young men, so full of life, lying in swathes across the landscape, as dead as felled trees. Where would it end? Her brothers were in training, to be sent 'over there' sometime

– in the case of David, perhaps soon. Hank Bowers had enlisted. Alec Gordon and Alfred Harding had volunteered in the wake of *Lusitania,* at much the same time as Bobby. Was every fit young man to be sucked into the monster's maw?

She was no longer an engaged person. She had taken off the ruby ring and stared at it for a long time, before putting it carefully on the bedside table. She had no right to wear it now. There would be no wedding. She would never wear that wedding dress, the veil with the lace Charles had brought for her, the crown of white roses. She would not live in the house in Clarges Street. She would not pass with Charles through that door, and through the other, secret, door into the land of the married. She had just had her twentieth birthday, and life was over for her.

She sat on the edge of her bed, staring at the photograph of Charles, trying to make it into the reality of his big, warm body and strong arms, longing to wake from this horrible dream to a reality where he wasn't dead.

Where would it all end?

Lest Cook and Ada should slip into comfortable indifference, Southend was bombed again by Zeppelins on the 26th of May, when the household was still reeling over the death of Lord Dene and the cancellation of the wedding. There seemed no end to the troubles that the war was to inflict on them. And then on the 31st of May, the moment arrived that London had been dreading since January. One of the monstrous gas bags drifted silently under cover of darkness, following

282

the silvery gleam of the Thames, and bombed the unsuspecting and defenceless suburbs of north-west London. The first bomb had fallen on Stoke Newington, and then the airship looped about over Hackney and Hoxton, and back to Shoreditch, Spitalfields, Stepney, West Ham and Leytonstone. Incendiary bombs and grenades rained down, houses were smashed and burned, people killed and injured.

The next morning Sonia came to Edward's office in a state of trembling. 'It's like the end of the world!' she cried. 'We're not safe in our own beds! Aeneas went to the factory this morning – went as soon as it got light – Donald with him. I begged him not to go and leave us alone. What are we to do? Oh, Edward, what's to become of us? We could see the red of the burning buildings from the top floor. The servants are all in hysterics. Half of them are down in the cellar and won't come up, and the other half have gone out to see the sights and I don't know where they are. The milkman was so late we had to have our tea black at breakfast, and when he *did* come he said that a crowd of people had attacked Hausman's bakery on the corner of Allen Street this morning and broken the windows and ruined all the bread, and the Hausmans have been forced to run away to save themselves. It's not like England any more. I don't understand anything.'

Edward calmed her as best he could, and told Warren to bring in coffee, strong.

'I shall never be able to sleep again,' Sonia said. 'They're going to bomb us every night. You can't hear them coming, that's the worst of it, so you never know where they'll strike next.'

'If you're as worried as all that,' Edward said, 'go down and sleep in the cellar.'

'I'm going to, don't you worry,' Sonia said, 'but you're not safe even there. Suppose the house falls down on top of us, or catches fire?'

'My dear, you mustn't give way like this,' Edward said. 'The Germans want to frighten us–'

'Well, they're succeeding!'

'–but we mustn't let them. Think of our young men in France, and what they're facing. What would they feel if they thought we were in a state of panic over a few bombs? It would take the heart out of them. We must do our bit for them by being brave, and not making a fuss, so that they can concentrate on what they have to do.'

Either his words or two cups of coffee were having an effect because she was visibly bracing herself. 'You're right,' she said at last, after application of a little more of both. 'We must show our grit. Keep a stiff upper lip.' Another sip or two, and she was able to declare, 'Those hateful Huns are not going to throw *me* into a panic.'

'That's the girl,' Edward said, with a pat on the shoulder.

'But what's the government *doing* about it? That's what I want to know,' Sonia said indignantly. 'Letting those things fly about over our heads with impunity.'

'Oh, the government's doing plenty, don't worry about that,' Edward said.

When she had gone, Warren came to remove the tray and said, 'They're saying it was just one airship, sir. Hard to believe it could have done so much damage. At least a hundred bombs, perhaps more. And it got away.'

'It's not so easy to shoot down a Zeppelin,' Edward said. 'They fly at over ten thousand feet, and the poor old aeroplanes assigned to home defence take so long to climb that high, it would be gone before they could make the altitude.'

'The anti-aircraft guns didn't seem to have much luck either,' said Warren.

'Even if they could see the airship – not so easy to spot against a dark sky – the guns couldn't reach that high. And given the shape of them, even a direct hit tends to slide off, so I'm told, rather than penetrate the skin.'

'So, really, they don't do any good,' said Warren, discontentedly.

'Except to help morale,' said Edward.

'And to thrill all the little children, who are even now dashing about picking up shrapnel and digging bomb fragments out of the roadways! I saw a gang of them setting off this morning from my street, as I was leaving for work. Reminded me of the gangs that go off fruit-picking in Kent in the summer holidays.'

'A rather different sort of fruit,' Edward remarked.

It was reported that nine defence aircraft had taken off when the alert was given, but none had managed to make the height, and one had crashed in the attempt, killing the pilot.

'I could hear the AA guns, banging away,' said Eric to Ethel, over a cup of tea in the station café after the cinema. He had been in London on the night of the raid, working a late shift. 'And you could see the searchlights sweeping back and forth. Ever so dramatic it looked, but you never saw a hint of the Zepp. Must have been too high up.'

'Didn't stop it dropping its bombs, did it?' said Ethel.

'No, and coming from that height, they'd get up a bit of speed. Must've been a hell of a wallop – leave aside the explosive. You could hear them hit,' said Eric. 'And see the glow from the flames. Course, it shows up better with the blackout. Poor devils,' he added, with feeling. 'What a way to go.'

'I wonder they want to bomb places like that. You'd think they'd try and hit army places or factories.'

'Don't suppose they're very accurate, not flying that high. Besides,' he added, 'if they were aiming at targets, they'd likely aim at the railway, and you wouldn't like that, would you?'

'Me?' Ethel said, with a toss of the head. 'Why should I care?'

He laid a hand over hers on the table. 'You *would* care, if I was killed.'

'Oh, I'd cry for a week,' Ethel said, with large irony.

But he just grinned, as if he knew what she was really thinking. That was the trouble with him – she couldn't get under his skin. He was too sure of himself – but, oddly, she liked that in him. And there was no doubt, she thought, remembering the picture palace, that he was a good kisser. Much better than Billy Snow – or even Andy Wood... But she wouldn't think about *him*. No, she was quite content with Eric Travers – for the moment. And if he got promoted to driver, well, there was no knowing how she might feel.

'What did you think of the picture?' he asked.

The days immediately following did not bring another Zeppelin attack, but no-one in London could relax, especially as the newspapers for many days were full of reports with all the details of the raid. Cook and Ada pored over every page, giving themselves the horrors.

'Poor little Elsie Leggatt, three years old, killed when an incendiary hit her house,' Ada read. 'A child that age! And her sister May in hospital with burns and like to die.'

'A couple was burned to death in a house in Balls Pond Road,' Cook countered, from her own sheet. 'I knew a girl lived in Balls Pond Road when I was at school. Makes you think.' She had never liked her, as a matter of fact – she'd had *things* in her hair – but still... 'Burned to death! That's worse than being blown up.'

'Dead is dead,' Ada said. 'Here's two children killed in Stepney on the way back from the cinema, blown up while they were sheltering in a doorway.'

'At least blown up is quick,' said Cook.

'You don't know,' said Ada. 'And just coming back from the cinema, poor innocent little things. A happy evening of pleasure, doing no harm to a soul and then – gone!'

Edward gave his speech to the servants about not giving way to panic, and pointed out that no

287

Zeppelin had got this far west, so there was no need for alarm. But more newspapers were sold by alarming the public than by telling them there was nothing to fear, and indulging in the horrors at least took your mind off troubles closer to home, like poor Miss Diana's cancelled wedding.

Peter, like most of boyhood, was downright excited about the Zeppelins and jealous of those further east for having all the fun. Pieces of shrapnel from the 31st of May found their way eventually to his school, and he parted with a substantial number of cigarette cards from his collection to secure one, which he put in a cardboard box under his bed where he kept his treasures. Select friends were invited to see it and even handle it. His friend Willy Andrews offered him his pet frog for it, and he was tempted for a moment, but then reasoned that he could catch a frog of his own and tame it if he wanted, but he might never get another bit of shrapnel.

William was enough of a boy to want to inspect Peter's souvenir, but at fifteen he was too grownup to be fascinated by it. War, he told his brother sternly, amounted to more than a bit of old shellcasing. The Scouts had extra responsibilities now. The reservoir had to be guarded not only against German spies poisoning it, but Zeppelins bombing it as well. He and Gus did their patrol twice a week, and now they had answered the call for volunteers to keep a watch on White's Hill above the railway tunnel. Edward decreed he could do only one stint at that – more than three evenings a week, he thought, would have a detrimental effect on his school work.

'I can get my homework done before I go out,' William pleaded. 'And what use is school anyway, with the war going on? I'd rather be doing something to help.'

'The war won't last for ever,' Edward said, 'and you'll have to earn your living afterwards, just like everyone else.'

But when you're fifteen, the future has no power to compete with the present.

It was Henry, the boot-boy, who made the biggest splash in Northcote in the wake of the Zeppelin attack. In the middle of the night of the 6th of June, he dashed from his bed in Lychgate Close, with a mackintosh over the underwear in which he customarily slept, to the church. The tower was locked but, like all the designated ringers, he knew where the key was kept. It took two to ring a proper tocsin on tenor and treble, but by the time the rector, the rectory gardener and Mr Fields arrived he had been pulling lustily on the treble for more than five minutes.

When they managed to detach him from Little Penn's sallie, they found him bewildered, but stubbornly sure he had done the right thing. The Zeppelins were coming, he asserted, with wild eyes. Three of 'em! Subsequent interrogation, in calmer surroundings, left him even more bewildered, for he could not say how he knew the Zeppelins were coming, or who had called him to his post. 'I *know* they were coming,' he repeated.

He didn't remember getting out of bed, or running to the church, only ringing the bell. Finally he was brought to admit, 'It must have been a dream.' He seemed to shrink as he said it, looking pathetically crestfallen. This had been his moment of triumph, and now it counted no more than a silly prank.

The rector was furious. 'You stupid boy!' he snarled. 'How could you be so foolish?' He had been dragged from his comfortable bed for nothing but, worse, he had been seen by some of his parishioners looking undignified in his dressing-gown with his hair rumpled. A small crowd of them had gathered in the churchyard, wondering what the bell meant; though fortunately it seemed the majority of residents had either slept through it, or decided that such a short ringing of only one bell was not a proper alarm and most likely a mistake.

A calm speech from the rector praised those who had attended for their diligence, told them there was nothing to worry about and sent them back to bed. Dismissal from the ringing team by Mr Fields was considered apt punishment for Henry. He was then escorted ungently from the premises by the horny hand of the gardener, who sent him on his way with a growl and a cuff round the head for good measure. The cuff hurt a lot less than losing his treasured status as a tocsin ringer.

His mother, who was a heavy sleeper, was woken by his return, having heard nothing of the bell, and had difficulty in understanding what had gone on, why Henry had been dismissed and why he would never be able to go back to The Elms, where they would be bound to find out and make fun of him.

The next morning he delivered a note to The Elms resigning as boot-boy, taking it round so early that no-one saw him come or go. It was found on the hall mat by Emily on her way to the kitchen. Afraid that everyone in Northcote would laugh at him, he did not dare look for another place in the village. Eventually he found himself a gardening job in Gosford. It meant a bit of a walk there and back, but it was better than the notoriety.

An odd thing that emerged was that there actually had been an intended Zeppelin raid on the south of England on the 6th of June, but the airships had been turned back by bad weather over the Channel, and a British fighter pilot, Lieutenant Warneton, in pursuit had been able to destroy one of them over the city of Ghent.

'Poor Henry,' said Sadie, always tender-hearted towards dumb animals. 'He was right after all. And there *were* three of them, just like he said.'

No-one knew why the highest point of Northcote was called Mount Olive. From it, there was a wonderful vista, right across the rolling fields and foothills to the next highest point, the pudding-basin shape of Harrow Hill, with the spire of St Mary's sticking out of the trees on top.

In mediaeval times there had been a priory of Benedictine sisters on Mount Olive, but it had been destroyed at the Dissolution so thoroughly that the only physical evidence remaining was the stone footings of the well-house. For its view, Mount Olive had been a much visited local beauty spot, until in 1867 the Metropolitan Asylums

Board had decided it was the perfect place to build one of the ring of fever hospitals it was setting up around London for the sick poor, in an attempt to break the savage cycle of infectious diseases in the slums.

It was a large, square, red-brick building with a campanile-like tower, not unreminiscent of Osborne House. In the 1880s, with falling demand, it had closed, but reopened a few years later as a sanatorium for consumptives, who might hope to benefit from the fine air of that high spot, and the good country eggs and milk from local farms. The new establishment was officially called Mount Olive Tuberculosis Sanatorium. Local people, however, as wary of consumption as of measles, continued to call it the fever hospital.

It was Mrs Oliver who called round to tell Beattie the news: 'I'm here in my Red Cross guise this morning, my dear. I expect you've already heard rumours, but I've called to tell you officially what's happening to the fever hospital. The lungers are going. It's going to be a war hospital.'

It was the day Diana should have been married, and Beattie was sitting with her daughter in the morning-room sewing. Sadie was up at Highclere and the boys were out with friends, and Beattie was trying to think of something to distract Diana from unhappy thoughts, so any visitor was most welcome.

Mrs Oliver was wearing a black armband for her nephew, Aldis Crane. There were a lot more of them to be seen these days. The lack of a funeral left people high and dry, yet the widespread resentment caused by the repatriation of William

292

Gladstone warned against too public a display of mourning. It was beginning to seem almost un-patriotic to make a fuss when so many were in the same boat. To be proud that one's beloved had given their life to the cause seemed the better attitude to strike.

Beattie saw Diana notice the armband, and thought that perhaps wearing something similar might comfort her. As only a fiancée, her right to grieve was almost unacknowledged. She could not wear widow's weeds; the War Office did not know her. Beattie decided to suggest it later.

Now she said, 'A war hospital? I hadn't heard anything.'

'There've been so many casualties this spring that the London hospitals are overwhelmed,' said Mrs Oliver. 'The wounded not needing critical care have to be moved out to make room. Dame Barbara says they're going to set up new hospitals wherever a suitable large building can be requisi-tioned.' Dame Barbara Woodville was the local branch's president.

'I see,' Beattie said. 'Well, Mount Olive hasn't been full for years, and it's a shame to waste a good building. But where are they sending the poor consumptives? It seems rather hard to turn them out of their beds.'

'Oh, they're moving to a place in Sussex,' said Mrs Oliver. 'Up high on the South Downs. Won-derful air. They'll be well cared for. I'm very pleased that Northcote is to get its own war hos-pital. At last we'll be able to do our part in caring for those who've given so much for us.' She looked at Diana as she spoke. Diana's head was bent over her sewing, but Mrs Oliver could see how pale and pinched she looked. Of course – now she thought of it, this was the very day... Perhaps she had been tactless in coming. But, no – she braced herself – they all had to carry on, no matter what.

'Yes, of course,' Beattie said. 'Do we know when they're coming?'

'Very soon – in two weeks' time. And that's what I've come to see you about. There's a great deal to do. The War Office will arrange for the hospital to be disinfected – an army medical detail will see to that as soon as the lungers are gone – but they haven't the time or manpower to do more, and the Red Cross has offered to take up the slack.'

'What slack are we talking about?' asked Beattie.

'Why, to make the place more pleasant. It's sadly shabby at the moment. We need to freshen it up – wax the floors, polish the furniture, clean the windows. I'd like to see flowers in all the wards. And the grounds need tidying up. It would be nice to have a few bright flower-beds where they can be seen from the windows.'

'That doesn't sound too difficult,' Beattie said. 'But the time is short.'

'Yes, we will have to get every hand possible to help. The Red Cross Committee must combine with the other local groups –the Church Ladies, the Soldiers' Relatives' Hardship Fund, the Soldiers' Comforts Fund and so on. Of course, there's a great deal of overlap between them,' she added. The philanthropic and the leading players in the village tended to be on more than one committee. 'But I think we can get enough of us together if we make an effort.'

'I'll do anything I can,' said Beattie. 'And I'm sure the girls will help.'

Diana looked up and said colourlessly, 'Yes, of course.'

'Good,' said Mrs Oliver. 'What I'd like you to do first is help me with the recruiting. Call on as many people as possible and persuade them to pledge their time.'

Beattie had a moment of doubt that Diana would be up to such public exposure. So far she had been loath to see anyone. Beattie understood that it was hard enough to bear pity from her close friends, like Lizzie Drake and Alicia Harding, but there were others not so close, like Betty Fealdman and Sally Sprange, who had been jealous when she had 'caught' Lord Dene, and whose pity might be tinged with triumph.

Still, it would be better for her to exert herself than sit moping; and service to others was a way, if not to heal a broken heart, at least to smother the pain. She determined to talk to Diana seriously when Mrs Oliver had gone.

But Diana had already come independently to the same conclusion. Long thought had brought her to feel that in time of war mourning was a sort of selfishness. Charles had gone to France willingly, offered his life for his country and – in his own words – for her. She must not let him down. She must work in whatever way she could, however unpleasant to her, to bring about the victory he had died for.

Such noble intentions did not always sustain, of course. They were poor comfort in the lonely hours when she could not sleep, and the future lay grey and empty, stretching drearily ahead for the rest of her life. War work was not as good as love, but it was something to put into the hollow inside her, better than nothing at all.

So she said again, 'Yes, of course.'

Mrs Oliver smiled. 'Good girl! I knew you would. And the first people to see, I fancy, are the Belgian Refugees Committee. They haven't had much to do lately, now the flood of Belgians has dried up. And I happen to know they have a number of bales of cloth donated to them by Costin's, for making dresses for the women, that have never been used. Good stout cotton, with nice bright flower prints.'

'What would you need those for?' Beattie asked.

'Bed curtains, my dear. The ones at Mount Olive are in poor condition, the fabric very worn and faded, and they were an unpleasant green to start with. Most depressing. Nice bright screens will help the poor men when they have to endure dressings being changed, which I understand is very painful. There isn't anything else to look at while it's going on.'

Beattie nodded. 'Then we had better get the Sewing Circle involved as well,' she said.

'What a good idea,' said Mrs Oliver. 'I must make a note. Now, I have here a list of people I'd like you to go and see...'

Northcote's many war committees could pull together in a good cause, and an ingress of wounded heroes was as good a cause as there was. The fever hospital was scrubbed and garlanded. The smell of wax polish drowned the reek of disinfectant left by the army working party, as the fine wood panelling and mahogany stair rails of the entrance hall were buffed to a shine. Internal doors were revarnished and the brass knobs polished. The Scouts sent along volunteers to whitewash the walls. Windows were cleaned, and the outdoor party, having cut the grass and trimmed the edges, created new beds to be seen from them, filled with bright zinnias and salvias and geraniums.

In the church rooms and the village hall, as well as various private homes, scissors snipped, sewing-machines whirred, and nimble fingers sewed on the rings as the cheerful bed curtains took shape. And finally vases were donated by the wealthier families, and the various Munts of Northcote took secateurs and walked about their cherished flower gardens deciding what they could sacrifice in the good cause of filling them.

When the time the train would be arriving at Northcote Station was announced, a further push for volunteers was needed, for transport was lacking to carry the wounded up to Mount Olive. The fever hospital had only one ambulance; there was one at the general hospital, the cottage hospital had an elderly horse-drawn one, and the army camp was to provide two. But the newly formed Mount Olive Hospital Committee had to go round asking for volunteers with motor-cars to make them available on the day.

'We ought to ask Lord Wroughton for the use of his,' said Mrs Prendergast. 'It's very roomy and comfortable, and they still have a chauffeur.' This was a material point: in several cases there had been motor-cars available but no-one to drive them.

'It will be awkward, asking them,' said Mrs Ellison, nervously, 'given that their son...'

'Nonsense,' said Mrs Prendergast. 'You can't feather-bed people. Besides, they are not the only people to lose someone. We must all do our duty.' No-one could argue with this. Her own son Harold had fallen at Ypres, but her firm onward stride had not faltered, and it would be a bold person who offered her sympathy. She coped with pain by simply refusing delivery.

'I wonder who would be the best person to send,' said Mrs Oliver, trying not to catch the eye of Mrs Fitzgerald, who was on the brink of declaring herself uniquely qualified for the job.

But before the rector's wife could frame her sentence, Diana looked up and said calmly, 'I'll go.'

There was a little silence, perhaps a tribute to her courage. Then Mrs Oliver said, 'Thank you, dear. If you're sure.'

Beattie, sitting next to her, said quietly into her ear, 'I'll go with you,' and Diana threw her a look of gratitude that proved she was not as brave about it as she seemed.

And so it was that they saw the countess for the first time since Charles's death. She had not been seen in public in that time, had not been to church, and no-one had been invited to the Park. The earl had gone back to London to attend sessions at the House, and Rupert had returned to Town almost immediately after that first terrible weekend. It occurred to Beattie, as they walked up the wearying drive, that the countess had been left callously alone. She had always seemed a hard, even emotionless woman, but she was a mother who had lost a child. It was not possible for her to feel nothing, and however little she might welcome sympathy, it must hurt her to have none offered.

'Most likely she won't receive us,' she said to Diana, as they trudged along the hot gravel through the June sunshine. The trees were in lovely new leaf, the grass was green, and the park looked fresh, beautiful, inviting. Diana thought how Charles had loved it. She remembered the plans he had explained to her for improving the estate, the alterations he had intended to make to the house when he inherited. *This would all have been mine,* she thought. *I would have been mistress of Dene Park.* It was both astonishing and painful.

'No, probably not,' she answered her mother. There was nothing for her here now. She was as much a stranger in Dene Park as the lowliest tradesman.

They presented themselves at the door, enquired if the countess was at home, and sat meekly to wait on the hard little chairs with the heraldic paintings on the back that were all the comfort the great hall offered the uninvited. The house was absolutely silent, once the footsteps of the servant had faded away. There seemed a long wait. They could hear him returning from a great distance, bearing, no doubt, a rejection. The faint sense of dread those approaching feet roused in her reminded Beattie of waiting for the doctor to come out of her mother's room long ago, to give the news they all expected, that there was nothing more to be done.

He came back, the same very young lad she had seen before, but more assured now, growing into his job. How long, she wondered, before he volunteered? He must be about sixteen. They would take him as a boy soldier at that age, though he could not be sent abroad until he was nineteen.

'Her ladyship will see you,' he announced, and they were so surprised that neither of them moved for a noticeable moment. He had to nod and gesture with his gloved hand before they got to their feet.

They were taken to the family part of the house, though not to the cluttered sitting-room Beattie had seen before. It was a more formal room, with a mainly green carpet and green silk on the walls. The chairs and sofas were chintz-covered, in cream with a pattern of large green roses, but looked hardly used. Though it was a bright June day outside, the blinds were drawn half down, as though the housemaid had forgotten to raise them that morning when she dusted; it gave the room a gloomy, forgotten air. The empty grate, undisguised by screen or folded fan of paper, looked black and hostile; the enormous looking-glass over the chimney-piece, and the pictures on the walls, had been covered with gathered black voile; and there were black feathers instead of flowers in the big vases.

Here, then, was mourning in all its old-fashioned display. Everything Diana was not entitled to. Charles's death was here in this room in its terrible finality. And the countess herself, sitting on one of the sofas, was in black from head to toe. She sat, upright as a rod, hands folded in her lap, her chiselled face showing nothing of what she felt, except in the presence of new lines deeply carved into it, and the bags of exhaustion under her eyes.

'Sit down,' she said, before either of them could speak.

They sat on the sofa opposite her and waited. Nothing Beattie could say seemed appropriate – indeed, to offer any conventional words would sound like impertinence. She looked straight at the unflinching face, and wondered, though she hated herself for wondering, whether all this display was sign of a genuinely broken heart, or whether it was meant to disguise the fact that there was no heart there at all.

The countess did not look at her. After a pause, she moved her gaze from the middle distance to Diana. She seemed to examine her, as if noting the signs of sorrow in the pale face, the shadowed eyes. Her gaze flicked over the black armband that Diana wore round the sleeve of her plain white blouse. Diana shrivelled a little, afraid she would be told angrily to take it off.

But when the countess spoke at last, she said, 'You are to be pitied.'

Diana swallowed, and blinked back the tears this unexpected remark brought forward. She felt the countess would not approve of tears.

'I didn't want him to marry you,' Lady Wroughton went on. 'I make no secret. You are not of our station in life. Such unequal marriages rarely prosper. But he persuaded me at last.' She paused. 'I may say that he had never shown such interest in a female before. You were his first love.' Her throat moved painfully, and she added, 'And,

301

it seems, his last.'

Diana had to close her eyes now to keep the tears back.

The countess made an impatient movement of her hand, as if brushing any softness away. 'I do not know you. When he died, I rejoiced that I should never have to. But now I think...' She paused again, and went on with seeming reluctance. 'I wonder if I ought to find out *why* he loved you. There must be more to you than seems. Charles was too old to be caught by mere prettiness.' She stared a moment longer, then sighed heavily, as if tiring of it all. 'What do you want? Why have you come here?'

The request now seemed banal in the extreme, after such a revelation of intimate feelings. Yet what else could Beattie say? She phrased it as well as she could, emphasising the duty owed to the wounded men to make them comfortable, mentioning the word 'sacrifice', at which the countess winced slightly.

She stopped Beattie in mid-sentence. 'I had not heard,' she said, 'that there was to be a war hospital at Mount Olive. I suppose what you ask is reasonable. And we ought – we must do our duty. You may have the motor-car and the chauffeur. Now please leave me.'

They stood, Beattie murmured thanks, and they left the room. Diana, turning to close the door behind them, found the countess still staring at her with a painful, questioning look, but there seemed nothing more to say or do, so she closed it. The footman was waiting in the passage outside to escort them away.

'Poor woman,' said Beattie, as they walked back down the drive.

On the day the train came in, Northcote turned out to welcome it. A crowd with flags clutched in their fists waved it into the siding, and cheered the men wildly as they were carried or helped from the carriages. As well as the ambulances, a motley collection of vehicles was waiting for them, and several local traders had released their delivery men to drive those that had been lent without chauffeurs.

Sadie was delighted to be helping in a practical way, for Breakespeare's Livery Stables – which had pretty much gone out of business since most of the local horses had been taken – had lent their charabanc and scraped up a couple of horses to draw it. Since it had been Sadie's idea to ask them, she was allowed to help drive, and sat up proudly on the box beside old Len Clarke, their head groom, who was too ancient to go and fight. He was so pleased to be driving the old 'sharrer' again, he could not grin widely enough, and would have kissed Sadie for suggesting it, if she had ever leaned close enough. He had groomed the two horses to a fine polish, plaited ribbons into their manes, and unearthed two couple of rather moth-eaten plumes to fix on the hames.

Sadie was pleased when some of the more mobile of the wounded soldiers actually clamoured to go in the charabanc rather than a car. The first to be helped on, a young man with a dark, narrow face, whose heavily bandaged arm was strapped immobile to his chest, took the seat

303

at the front, next to her, and said, with a happy smile, 'I haven't been in one of these since I was a kid! What a treat to be in the fresh air, after frowsting indoors with hospital stink all this time. You can't think how good it smells! The horses, too.'

'I love the smell of horses,' Sadie agreed delightedly.

'You're a woman after my own heart,' he said. He offered his left hand to shake. 'Tom Piper,' he introduced himself. 'My father was also called Tom, so the chaps call me Tom-Tom.'

Sadie got it. 'The Piper's son!' She shook his hand. 'I'm Sadie Hunter.'

'Delighted to meet you, Miss Sadie Hunter. Dare I hope you'll visit me at the hospital? My family lives too far away to come.'

For a man who loved the smell of horses, Sadie would have promised more than that.

CHAPTER EIGHTEEN

Sadie put on her good navy coat and skirt and a clean white shirt for going to visit the hospital and, after a pause for consideration, removed her hair from its usual convenient plaits and did it up into a chignon behind. She was not sure why, except that it seemed more respectful towards Our Brave Wounded. This was not an entirely rational thought, she knew. She inspected her reflection in the glass and thought that, for the first time, she actually looked seventeen. Why the idea should please her she didn't know.

Though she had helped prepare it, the entrance hall of the hospital seemed daunting now. No cheerful, friendly neighbour-workers, but that hospital hush, and the background smell of anti-septic, that seemed to demand frowningly of the outsider, 'What are *you* doing here?' But she had told Lieutenant Piper that she would come, and didn't want him to think she had forgotten. So she enquired of the hall porter – the same old man who had served the function for the con-sumptives – and he consulted a list and directed her up the stairs to Alice Montgomery Ward. It comforted her that he did not appear to think her presence anything out-of-the-way.

At the door of the ward she encountered a young nurse just going in, carrying a carton of something. At Sadie's question she looked anx-ious. 'Oh dear, I don't think you'll be allowed to visit. They've just done the dressings round. I don't know when visiting hours will be. You'd better wait here while I ask Sister.' The tone of her voice implied that Sister was a Gorgon, and asking her anything an act of bravery.

Standing alone outside the door, Sadie felt a fool. The Hunters were a healthy tribe and she'd never had anything to do with a hospital before: she hadn't realised that there would be visiting hours. She wondered why the porter had let her come up. Perhaps they had not had them for the consumptives.

After a moment a quick-moving, red-headed sister in a highly starched apron came out. She was not ancient and warty, like a wicked witch, but perhaps in her thirties, and actually quite personable, with intelligent eyes. She looked Sadie up and down, though not, it seemed to Sadie, with hostility, but rather as if assessing what she might be good for.

'I'm Sister Ryman. You've come to see Lieutenant Piper? Are you a member of the family?'

Sadie stood to attention. 'No,' she said. 'I met him when I helped drive the men from the station. He was one of my passengers. He asked if I would visit him, because his family lives too far away, and I promised I would.'

The sister looked at her consideringly. 'Hospital visiting time is two thirty to four thirty in the afternoon, on Tuesdays and Thursdays,' she said.

'I didn't know,' said Sadie.

'It varies a little from hospital to hospital. But, in any case, it is never, never in the morning.'

'I'm sorry,' said Sadie, and turned to go.

'Wait,' said Sister Ryman. Sadie turned questioningly. 'You drove one of the vehicles?'

'The charabanc,' Sadie clarified. 'Horse-drawn. I can't drive a motor-car – though I'd like to learn.'

Sister Ryman thought a moment longer. She seemed to be weighing various considerations in the balance. 'Will you come and visit Lieutenant Piper again, at the proper time?'

'Oh, yes – if he would like me to,' said Sadie. She thought she had been dismissed.

But the sister said, 'I think, as you are here, you may see him. But only for a few moments. And just this once. After this you must come at visiting time.'

Sadie followed her in, and noted with a feeling of pride the fresh, clean walls, the smell of furniture polish, the vases of flowers on the tables down the centre, the bright floral curtains. It was as pleasant as a hospital ward could be.

Then she noticed the occupants. The curtains were drawn round one or two beds, and some men were in dressing-gowns, sitting at the centre tables, but most were in bed, and as eyes turned towards her, she felt her face grow hot. She had never before been in the presence of strange men in their nightwear. She had seen her brothers in bed on occasion, but never anyone else – not even her father. What had she been thinking, coming here? She wished the floor would open up and swallow her. But she had to go through with it now. Eyes glued to her shoes, face burning, she followed the brisk-tapping sister until she halted before a bed.

The sister's voice said, 'A visitor for you, Lieutenant Piper, if you feel up to it. Only a few moments, now.'

And then the sister moved away, and Sadie had to look up. Tom Piper was sitting up in bed, in striped pyjamas. But she barely noticed them because his face, she saw with a sense of shock, was colourless and waxy, and there was sweat on his upper lip. His eyes seemed somehow to have sunk deeper in his face. He looked much, much worse than the day before. His wounded right arm was no longer strapped to his chest, but was resting beside him, and she realised, with another shock, that it ended prematurely in a thick bulge of bandages. His hand was gone. There were bandages round his chest, too, under his pyjama jacket.

'I'm – I'm sorry,' she managed to say, tears pricking her eyes. 'I shouldn't have come. You're not well–'

The focus of his eyes seemed to come back from a long way away. He seemed to recognise her at last, and said weakly, 'No, please, I'm glad you did.'

Sadie met his eyes cautiously. 'You seemed so much better before.'

'I've just had the dressings changed,' he said. 'It sets you back a bit. Please, stay and talk to me. One's glad to have one's mind taken off.' With his left hand he gestured to the chairs at the centre tables, and she went quickly and fetched one, and sat down. By the time she had done that, he seemed to have gathered himself, and looked a little less deathly.

'Is it very painful?' she asked.

He looked at his bandaged stump. 'Changing the dressings is the worst bit. When you see that trolley approaching, you want to start yipping like a puppy. Some of the chaps… But I shouldn't say things like that to you.'

'You can say anything to me,' Sadie said staunchly. 'Please. I'm not squeamish.' He looked as if he didn't quite believe her. 'I work with horses,' she said, 'and the vet, Mr Courcy, always let me help him when any of them were injured. *Captain* Courcy, I should say – he's out in France now.'

'Tell me about the horses,' he said.

Remembering what he had said, about taking the mind off, she explained her war work, and told him an amusing anecdote or two. He listened, nodding now and then. But after a while she saw his eyelids were drooping. Her voice was sending him off to sleep.

The sister must have been observing too, for she appeared at Sadie's side and said, 'You'll have to go now.'

She stood up, and Tom Piper's eyes opened heavily, his left hand moved towards her in an uncompleted gesture. 'You will come again?' he asked.

'If you'd like me to.'

'Yes, please.'

'Is there anything I can bring you?'

'Some writing paper and a pencil. If I dictate, would you write a letter for me to my family?' He made an effort to smile. 'It's dashed inconvenient, but I'm right-handed.'

Sadie swelled with pleasure. It was good to feel there was something practical she could do to help. 'Of course I will,' she said.

'Thanks,' he murmured, his eyes already sliding inexorably shut again. Sadie felt the touch of the sister's hand on her elbow.

At the door of the ward, Sister Ryman said, 'You've done him good. I hope you will come again.'

'Oh, yes – I promise,' Sadie said eagerly.

'Tomorrow is visiting day. But not before two thirty,' the sister added sternly. 'Never, never in the morning.'

Ada answered the front door to a young khaki-clad soldier. He was smartly turned out, his boots shiny, his puttees immaculate, his face so closely shaved it looked almost painful, his cap badge gleaming with metal polish in the June sunshine.

'Good morning, miss,' he said, with a nervous smile. 'I am here as part of the Lord Kitchener's Birthday Recruitment Drive. May I enquire whether there are any men of military age in your household?'

He had obviously learned it off by heart and was primed and ready to say it at all costs.

Ada was annoyed at being called from dusting the dining-room, so she didn't at first notice his nervousness, and answered witheringly, 'In the first place, I'm the maid, as you'd know if you had eyes in your head. And in the second place, both our young gentlemen that's old enough have volunteered already, so I wouldn't go asking the mistress that question, if I was you. You might get short shrift.'

The lad turned as scarlet as if he had been dipped in boiling water. He began to stammer apologies: 'No offence meant, miss. I didn't know. We was told to knock on every door. I beg pardon if I said anything–'

Ada suddenly saw how young he was. 'You wasn't to know,' she said. 'Not your fault.' Bless the lamb, he didn't look old enough to be in uniform. 'I expect you could do with a cup of tea, eh?' she suggested.

He licked his lips and cast a fearful look left and right, as if the sergeant might be lurking in the laurels. 'Well...' he said.

Ada smiled. 'I should hate to go knocking on strangers' doors m'self. Ah, come on, five minutes won't hurt. Go on round to the back door.'

In the kitchen, kindly received by Cook and gazed at with round-eyed wonder by Emily, who had never been allowed to get this close to anyone in khaki before, the soldier sat at the table, politely removed his cap and told them his name was 'Private Ogden'.

Cook, filling the teapot, was amused. 'Go on! I bet your mum doesn't call you "Private".'

He smiled shyly. 'Sam. My name's Sam.'

'And what did she think about you enlisting?'

'She didn't like it at first,' he admitted. 'Called me a damn – sorry, a bloomin' fool. But she's proud of me now. Dad always was. Him and me worked at the same factory. A recruiting sergeant come round one day at dinner-time and give us a talk, and a whole lot of us joined up together. Five of us from Number Two shop,' he added proudly.

'Good for you,' said Cook. 'Emily, stop gawping and get the cake tin.'

Ethel came in with her housemaid's box in her hand. 'What's all this? Nobody working this morning?' she enquired, peeved.

'We're having our lunch a bit early because we've got a visitor,' Cook said.

'Nice of someone to come and tell me,' Ethel retorted. She inspected the soldier with professional interest. 'You from Paget's Piece?'

'That's right – er, miss,' said Ogden, wary of her prettiness and bright-eyed stare, which reminded him of the cat back home when it was crouching by a mouse hole.

'He came to ask if we had any men in the

311

household of military age,' Ada said.

Ogden started to explain. 'It's part of the Lord Kitchener's Birthday–'

'Oh, I know. We read about that in the paper,' Ethel interrupted. 'The recruitment drive. There's going to be a special show at the Electric Palace tonight, songs and tableaux, and a moving-picture of Lord Kitchener inspecting troops.'

'And a rally in the village hall,' Emily added, putting out plates. 'With a band.'

'Not that *we*'ll get to see anything of it,' Ethel added, 'stuck in this mouldy hole all day and night.'

'You mind your lip. Mouldy hole indeed! Pay no attention to her,' Cook said, placing the largest slice of cake she could contrive on Private Ogden's plate. 'So, you're one of Kitchener's Mob – Kitchener's Army, I *should* say,' she corrected herself graciously. 'The first lot. And they've sent you out to get the next lot signed up, I suppose.'

'I wasn't sent, I volunteered,' said Ogden. He took a large bite from his slice of Madeira, which rendered him speechless for a moment. 'Lovely cake, this,' he said, as soon as he could. 'Did you make it yourself?'

Cook could see he was trying to be polite, so despite Ethel's snigger she didn't bite his head off, but only said, 'No shop-bought cake in *this* house, young man. So why did you volunteer?'

'It makes a change,' he said. 'All we do these days is drills and parades and marches, and you can have enough of *them*. So when they asked for volunteers... Well, anything different's a treat. And if you get so many to sign up, you get a forty-eight. Privilege leave.'

'How many you got so far?' Ethel asked.

'None yet,' Ogden admitted. 'But there's the rest of the day to go.'

They were interrupted as the new boot-boy, Ginger, burst in, took in the general tea-and-cakeness of the scene, and said, 'Wot's all this? Church clock's not struck yet! Only five to.'

'So what are you doing in here, then?' Ethel returned the serve smartly.

Ginger was a more robust character than Henry, and could hold his own. He was also a cheerful and energetic worker, so his 'cheek' was largely put up with. 'Gotta wash me 'ands, ent I? Bin told often enough. Cor,' he noticed the visitor, 'you a real sojer?'

'No, he's one of Kitchener's Mob from Paget's Piece,' Ethel answered scornfully. 'Never been nearer to France than Southend pier.' She saw from the corner of her eye that she had made him blush, and turned on him with a sweet smile and a poisonous question. 'When *are* you going, as a matter of fact? You been there so long you must've all grown roots. War'll be over before you lot get a move on.'

Cook tried to rescue him: 'Now, Ethel, it's not the boy's fault. He's not Lord Kitchener. He doesn't make the rules.'

But Ginger wanted the question answered. 'Yeah, when *are* you going? If it was me, I wouldn't wait to be told, I'd be off to kill some Germans. Pow, pow, pow!' He imitated firing a rifle. 'Got-tim!' he crowed at the clock on the mantelpiece.

Private Ogden looked hurt. It had been a sore

point for some time among the early volunteers that they had – in their own opinion – long since been brought to a peak of military perfection, but were still being kept kicking their heels in England. They were sick of it. They wanted to go to France every bit as much as the Gingers of this world wanted them to, but week after week and rumour after rumour, they woke daily to the same horizon. Some wit had even made up words to a popular recruiting song, which they sang as they endlessly route-marched or polished their boots:

On Sunday they say we'll go to Flanders,
On Monday we're down for Nice or Cannes.
On Tuesday we smile when they hint at the Nile,
On Wednesday the Sudan.
On Thursday it's Malta or Gibraltar,
On Friday they saying it's Lahore.
But on Saturday we're willing
To bet an even shilling,
We here for the duration of the war!

So he could perhaps be forgiven, especially under the sting of Ethel's smile, for standing up for himself. 'As a matter of fact,' he said, catching their attention, 'I shouldn't really be telling you, but we're leaving the camp next week.'

'Going to France?' Ginger cried excitedly.

'Well, no, not right away. We're going to Hounslow Heath for brigade exercises and firearms training. But, soon as that's done, we'll be going to France all right.'

'It's just another rumour,' Ethel said, nibbling daintily at her cake. 'You're not going anywhere.'

314

'No, it's true this time. I overheard–' He went red. 'Well, anyway, I can't say how I know, but it's true all right. We're breaking camp next week, and the person I heard saying it said we'd be in France in the autumn.'

'Well, I'm pleased for you, then,' Cook said. 'France, eh? My goodness, that'll be an adventure! Everything's different over there. They say they eat frogs and snails. And horses.' She shuddered. 'They don't even speak English.'

'I know,' said Ogden, eagerly. 'It's called Polly Voo, what they speak. There's this officer in B Company, Lieutenant Peake, he speaks it, and he's given some of the chaps lessons, so they can ask for things in the estaminays. That's what they call caffs over there,' he added, with a touch of grandeur.

'Go on, then,' Ethel said derisively. 'Say something in French.'

'I can't speak it. It's jolly hard to learn. I only know one thing.'

'Well, say that, then.'

'No, I'm not very good.'

'Oh, go on,' Ginger urged. 'Teach it me. I wouldn't half like to be able to speak French.'

Ogden yielded. 'Oh, all right. But it's hard, like I said. This is what I know to say. *Kelker shows among jay.*'

There was a stunned silence. 'Who shows you *what?*' Emily asked.

'What's a kelker when it's at home?' said Cook.

Ginger said, 'Crikey! Who'd want to say that? Doesn't make any *sense!*'

Ogden went red again. 'I might not have said it

315

quite right. But it's something like that, anyway.'

'All right, what does it mean, then?' Ada asked kindly.

The red intensified. Ada was worried his ears might actually explode. 'I dunno,' he admitted. 'It's something you say in an est – in a caff.'

'If I was you, I'd stick to eggs and bacon,' said Cook. 'If they *have* eggs and bacon,' she added, with large doubt.

'They have sausages,' Ogden said eagerly. 'Lieutenant Peake told us that one.'

'So what're *they* called?' Ethel demanded.

Ogden scowled in furious concentration. 'It's something like ... *sossies.*'

'*Sossies!* That's what little kids call 'em. You can't have grown men going about asking for sossies. Make us the laughing stock.'

'Leave him alone,' said Ada. 'It's not his fault if it's a silly language.'

'All langwidges is silly, 'cept English,' said Ginger, loyally.

Ethel got up and patted Ogden on the head as she passed. 'Good thing you're not going till the autumn, if you ask me,' she said. 'You and your sossies.' At the door, she turned to remark, 'I suppose if this lot's leaving Paget's Piece, we'll be getting a new lot in.'

'More soldiers,' Emily said dreamily.

Cook snapped to attention. 'Never mind soldiers, you get on and fill a mug for Mr Munt. Doesn't look like he's coming in. And, Ginger, you can take it down to him. Time you got back to work anyway, never mind sitting there with your elbows on the table. Go on now! And you'd

316

better be on your way, too, young man,' she concluded, to the soldier. 'The army doesn't pay you for drinking tea in my kitchen.'

The party broke up.

Kitchener's Birthday meant something different to Sadie. Mrs Cuthbert had received an official notification that they were going to be inspected by a party of bigwigs on that day.

'It's a great honour,' she said. 'An acknowledgement that we're doing good work.'

Sadie was thrilled. 'Who's coming?' she asked.

'Well, there'll be a colonel from the Army Service Corps, a Major Hennes from the Remount Headquarters at Woolwich, our own Captain Casimir *and...*' she added, with a dramatic pause, '...he hinted that someone might be coming down specially from the War Office.' Her eyes were bright. 'Apart from anything else, Sadie dear, it's wonderful that the stick-in-the-mud old army should allow females to do anything, let alone praise them for doing it well.'

'What will actually happen, then, on the day? Will we have to line up for inspection, like soldiers?'

'I thought,' said Mrs Cuthbert, 'that we ought to give them a little bit of a show. This last batch is just about ready.'

'Apart from the roan,' Sadie said. 'He's not quite reliable yet.'

'We'll leave him out – and the black that kicks. I thought we could do something like a musical ride – without the music, of course.'

'There aren't enough of us to ride them all at

once,' Sadie pointed out.

'I've an idea about that as well,' said Mrs Cuthbert.

On the 24th, Sadie bicycled up to Highclere very early to help with the stable work. The horses had to be groomed to a very high standard, and the stables themselves had to be immaculate. Then they had one last rehearsal of the display ride. Mrs Cuthbert, Sadie, Podrick, Baker and Biggs were to take part in it, with Bent and Oxer, the stable-boys, helping on the ground.

'I wish we could all be in uniform,' Sadie said to Mrs Cuthbert, a little nervously, as they waited for the visitors to arrive. 'It would look neater. I'm afraid we'll give an untidy appearance.'

'It's the horses that count,' Mrs Cuthbert comforted her. 'We want to show how good and ready they are. They won't be looking at us.'

With military punctuality, Captain Casimir's little motor bumped into the stableyard with two more, much grander, behind, freighted with pressed khaki and polished leather. Casimir jumped out and performed the introductions. In the second car was Major Arnold from the ASC – of which the Remount Service was a branch – a powerful-looking middle-aged man with a small, dark moustache. With him was Major Hennes from the Remount Service, a lean, brisk man, who in civilian life owned a brewery and was an MFH. The Remount Service often drew its officers from gentlemen with experience of horses to avoid taking line officers from their duties: the painters Lionel Edwards and Alfred Munnings were

318

among them. Major Arnold seemed to know Hennes very well and addressed him as 'Dick'.

Most exciting was the presence in the third car of a large, elderly officer, with enormous white moustaches, who came from the War Office. Colonel Bentine was obviously a 'dugout', and from his mahogany complexion might have been a veteran of the South African War. With him were a press secretary and a photographer. 'The War Office likes to make the most of good stories,' Casimir whispered. 'You may see yourselves in the newspaper.'

Colonel Bentine shook Mrs Cuthbert's hand with an air of reluctance. 'I come with Lord Kitchener's greeting and congratulations,' he said, but without warmth. Mrs Cuthbert introduced Sadie. Colonel Bentine's upturned moustaches made him look as if he was smiling, but his pale eyes were cold, and they seemed to sweep over her breeches and boots with distaste. He nodded without offering to shake hands, as if she were not worth noticing, and moved on to the men with a faint air of relief.

Mrs Cuthbert made a funny little rueful face at Sadie behind the colonel's back. A lot of men couldn't stand the sight of women in trousers of any sort; what would he think when he saw them ride across instead of side-saddle? But someone ought surely to have briefed him about what he was inspecting. She was aware of the stories about Lord Kitchener, that he had no time for women. Perhaps Bentine was modelling himself on his boss and – as so often happened – was out-Cæsaring Cæsar.

After an inspection of the stables, Casimir explained to the visitors that a demonstration had been prepared, and showed them to the seats that had been set out at one end of the large paddock, while the stable-boys helped the others to get mounted.

Mrs Cuthbert's idea was that each of the five of them should ride one horse and lead another, as the Royal Horse Artillery did when they were exercising. 'That way, they'll see more of the horses, and it will prove they're good at being ridden in formation.' With five riders, they could leave the two least reliable mounts in the stables.

I wish we had some music, Sadie thought, as she rode into the paddock, second in line behind Mrs Cuthbert. Her two were trotting nicely together. The practice they had put in had paid off. They did one circuit, then rode down the centre and split off at the far end, going alternately left and right as on a musical ride, and at the corners the two files turned in diagonally and they 'threaded the needle' in the centre. They reunited the two files on the next circuit, and went into an extended trot, then a canter. The thunder of forty hoofs was quite impressive.

After this, Bent and Oxer erected three low jumps down the centre, and the whole ride took them in turn at a canter. This was the hardest part, as the led horse tended to want to pick its own take-off, and if the two horses didn't rise together, the rider risked being pulled from the saddle. It had happened a couple of times in practice. Sadie could feel her led horse lagging a little, looking at the jump, and resorted to a tug on the lead and a shouted 'Hup!' as she applied her heels to her mount at the take-off moment. With relief she felt them both rise together, but her led horse pecked on landing and she nearly came off anyway. At the second and third jumps she took no chances and shrieked, 'Hup!' at the top of her voice, and they got safely over.

Finally the whole ride resumed the trot round the circuit, and Bent and Oxer let off the fire-crackers. One or two of the horses tossed their heads, and Sadie's led horse did a sideways canter for a step or two, but not one of them tried to break away, and on the second circuit, with more explosions, they did not even flinch.

They finished by lining up, all ten horses in line abreast, ready for inspection, and Mrs Cuthbert took off her hat as a salute. The bigwigs applauded, and came over. Major Arnold shook Mrs Cuthbert's hand as she leaned down from the saddle and said, with genuine enthusiasm, 'By Jove, dear lady, that's quite a display! You've obviously put a lot of work in on these beasts.'

Major Hennes, grinning, said, 'Wonderful touch, the firecrackers. We need horses out in France who won't shy at sudden noises. Very well done indeed.'

Colonel Bentine said nothing. He walked along the line, hands clasped behind his back, looking only at the horses, not the riders. When he reached Podrick, who was last in line, he ran a leather-gloved hand over his led horse's back, down its legs, and lifted up a hoof for inspection. Then he returned to a place opposite the centre of the line, staring into the middle distance and frowning as the other visitors made a more leisurely and friendly inspection.

When they were all gathered again, Bentine cleared his throat for silence, and said, 'What I've seen is impressive, most impressive. You have done a thorough job, and Lord Kitchener thanks you.'

Looking ahead between her mount's ears, Sadie had an odd moment of standing outside herself. In imagination she could see the line of horses, never quite still: ears flicking against the flies, the swish of tails, the occasional toss of a head. Her led horse turned its head to rub an itchy muzzle against her mount's neck. A breeze was moving the trees in the distance behind the visitors, and a colony of rooks somewhere was cawing. The air smelt of pounded dust and crushed grass and horses, and the sweetness of warm June air. She realised in that instant that she was utterly, completely happy. *Happy birthday, Lord Kitchener,* she thought, and wondered what he was doing. Nothing as nice as this, she would wager.

Colonel Bentine made a few more remarks, about the war and everyone pulling together and working towards a glorious victory and so on – even to Sadie's inexperienced ears, they sounded like routine remarks tailored to fit any occasion – and then the change of his tone revealed he had come to something new.

'In war, we are all called upon to do our duty. For ladies, that has always taken the form of nurturing and supporting our brave soldiers in the traditional, feminine ways hallowed by time. However, this war has already brought changes.' His cold eyes swept the horizon, and Sadie guessed he didn't much like changes of any sort, let alone those that involved 'ladies'. 'You are doing men's work, in order to free men for the front, and the country is grateful to you,' he concluded tersely, and held out a hand to Major Arnold, who put into it two rolled-up scrolls. He walked up to Mrs Cuthbert and gave one to her, shaking her other hand. 'Well done,' he said. 'Well done indeed.' He paused in the middle of this act to turn his head towards the photographer, and the moment was captured for eternity.

He moved on and handed the other to Sadie, without a word, and with the briefest possible shake of the tips of her fingers, before stalking away. She thought the photographer would have had to be quick to capture that moment.

The other officers had gathered round Mrs Cuthbert talking and laughing, and Casimir glanced at Sadie and gave her a wink of complicity. Sadie smiled, but did not in the least mind being ignored by the great man. She tucked her reins under her knee to free her hands to unroll the scroll. It was beautifully written in Gothic script with an illuminated first letter and a wax seal at the bottom. A space had been left where her name had been filled in, and the rest of the writing said that she had performed outstanding war work and that Lord Kitchener thanked her on behalf of the War Office. Beside the clerk's beautiful ink-work, the handwriting of the one word at the bottom was rather mundane, but it meant everything to Sadie. You could clearly read that it said 'Kitchener' – and he had written it himself.

CHAPTER NINETEEN

The occupants of The Elms were very proud when the article appeared in the newspaper about High-clere. There was a photograph of the distinguished visitors sitting watching the display, and one of Colonel Bentine handing the scroll to Mrs Cuthbert.

William was indignant, and Peter disappointed, that there was no photograph of Sadie. 'It's not fair! You ought to have been in there too!'

Sadie said, 'You can *nearly* see me, look. This is my led horse, next to Mrs Cuthbert, and you can just see – that's my hand on the lead-rein, and the end of my sleeve.'

But her name was there, in the text, mentioned along with Mrs Cuthbert's as 'one of our new breed of gallant young ladies ready to do their all to help the war effort', which was fair enough. And there was the scroll. She took it, with the newspaper, to the kitchen to show them, and they were as excited as the boys. Cook was thrilled at the sight of Sadie's name, actually in a real newspaper, and Ada was deeply impressed with Lord Kitchener's signature on the scroll. 'His hand held the pen that wrote this,' she said reverently. 'Oh, Miss Sadie, you've as good as shaken the hand of the Secretary of State for War!'

Nula, who was there that day, said, 'I suppose we'll have to get used to ladies being in the papers, and not think it shocking. Wouldn't have done when I was a girl, but this war seems to be changing everything.' She looked disapprovingly at Sadie. 'I always knew *you'd* be a tomboy, but I never thought it'd get you in the papers.'

'In a *good* way, though,' Ada defended her. 'It's all for the war effort.'

Nula sniffed. 'If there was no war, we wouldn't need a war effort. We got on very well before. If women ruled the world, there'd be no wars.'

'There'd be no motor-cars either,' Ethel said. 'Nor picture palaces.'

'We did all right without them, too,' said Nula.

Sadie took the scroll and the newspaper to show to Munt. He was tending his tomatoes, and welcomed the opportunity to stop and light his pipe. Sadie waited patiently until the time-consuming process was completed – she had long thought he smoked the pipe rather to have something to do than for any pleasure the smoke might give him, since it always seemed to go out after a minute or two. Munt had to fumble out his spectacles, which he hated wearing, so it was a tribute to her that he bothered. He read both pieces of paper slowly and carefully, before handing them back to her.

Sadie knew well enough not to ask him for his opinion. She stood, feet together, hands clasped behind her back, and let him survey her.

'So,' he said at last, taking the pipe from his mouth, 'you're a genuine hero, eh?' Sadie shook her head modestly. 'Says so here,' he said, tapping the paper with the pipe stem. 'Must be true if it's in the papers, eh? Don't read no lies in the papers.'

She thought he was making fun of her. Her cheeks reddened. 'I can't help what they say. I didn't write it.'

'No more you did,' he said. He folded up his glasses and put them away. 'You'll do,' he said, more kindly.

It was high praise from Munt. She beamed. 'Thanks,' she said. 'Though it's funny being praised for doing something I enjoy.' She turned to go.

'Enjoy it while you can,' he said. ''Twon't last.'

She turned at the greenhouse door. 'Why not?'

'They've noticed you now. Army doesn't like things out of line. They move slow, but they'll get to you, take the 'ole thing over. Then you'll be out on your ear. Can't have girls in it. Everything got to be uniform in the army, see.'

Sadie remembered Courcy saying the army liked things in nice straight rows. She didn't know if Munt was right or not, but she wouldn't argue with him. 'Oh, well,' she said. 'I suppose, if that happened, I would have to find something else.'

She went away. Nailer, who had been basking in a dust-hollow on the sunny side of a black-currant bush, jumped up and came to walk with her. 'The important thing,' she told him, 'is that having war work means no-one will send me off to finishing school. In fact, no-one ever seems to notice me at all at the moment. Which is nice. I know war is terrible and everything, but it has its good side.'

Nailer twitched his eyebrows in response. *Like he says, you enjoy it while it lasts,* he said, in the growly voice she had invented for him.

'You think he's right? That they'll take it away from us?' she said.

Nothing good lasts, was Nailer's response.

Ethel came out of Stein's, the butcher's, where she had been to collect a piece of steak for the master's dinner, and saw Sergeant Andy Wood standing on the other side of the road, apparently in charge of a detail of men who were handing out leaflets to the passers-by. She felt herself go hot all over as he looked round and caught her eye. He said something to the man nearest him and started to cross the road towards her. Suppose he thought she had deliberately invited his attention? She straightened her back and put her chin up, determined not to let him get the better of her. She didn't need the likes of *him* any more.

'Hullo,' he said, as he reached her, and his old, slow, too-intimate smile wormed its way through her defences. 'Long time since I've had the pleasure, Miss Lusby. Piece of luck you happening to be here just at the same time as me.'

'Lucky for *you*,' she said haughtily. '*I* can manage to live without seeing you, thank you very much.'

'The tenth of March it was, at the dance at the Station Hotel,' he said, as though she hadn't spoken. 'Burned on my heart, that date. You went off with that pale green type instead of me – and after we'd danced the foxtrot together! What happened to him, anyway?'

'He joined up,' she said.

He grinned. 'So you're not still with him.'

'I didn't say that.'

'No, but I can tell from your voice. Why didn't you let me know? Now you've left it too late – we're off next week.'

'So I hear,' Ethel said, with dignity. 'Not that it's anything to me what you do. Off to Hounslow Heath, aren't you?'

'Oh, you know all about it. So you do care.'

'I do not,' she said hotly. 'I've got myself a new chap now – and a better one than you, Andy Wood, let me tell you.'

He stepped closer, and she could feel the heat of his body and the intensity of his feral force. 'Not possible. You know that. You and me, we've had a few times together, haven't we – Ethel?' The way he said her name weakened her knees. 'We make a lovely pair. Cut from the same cloth, we are. Does he know what you're really like, this new bloke? Is he up to you?'

'Leave me alone,' she said weakly.

'Oh, you don't mean that,' he breathed, only inches from her ear. Why didn't someone in the street notice, she wondered desperately, and come and rescue her? 'The last thing you want is for me to leave you alone. Nobody else gives you a thrill like I do. Now, how about meeting me tonight for a little goodbye party, just the two of us? You and me and the June moonlight. Like a poem, isn't it? Oh, Ethel, my lovely, lovely Ethel. Let me woo you in the woods tonight.' Hidden from view by his body, his hand made a swift pass along her forearm that made her shiver.

She pulled herself away, with a furious effort,

stepping back from him enough to break the spell. 'I'm not meeting you tonight or any time,' she said.

He smiled on, as though she'd said yes. There was no shaking this man. 'You and me,' he said. 'It's got to happen. It's written in the stars. You can't escape it.'

'Stars, rubbish!' she said. 'I've got a new man now, a good one – and you're going to France to get blown up by the Germans.'

He laughed hugely. 'Oh, Ethel, what a tender thought to send a soldier off to war with! Did you read that in a ladies' magazine? Never mind,' he said, smiling down at her indulgently, 'I know you didn't mean it. And I shan't let it put me off coming to see you when I get back. You and me – we've got unfinished business. I'll be back, and then…' He stroked her arm again, winked, and turned smartly away, to march across the road, back to his men.

Ethel turned quickly so that she would not seem to be watching him go, and walked away, head high, inwardly fuming. *That man! The cheek of him!* It did nothing to cool her temper to discover she was walking the wrong way. She reversed direction hastily, and hoped Andy Wood hadn't seen.

The back garden at St Hugh's Soldiers' Club had a wide lawn where round metal tables and chairs were set out. Here, when the weather was fine, the soldiers could sit and take their tea or just smoke and talk. Down at the bottom there was a little stream, on the other side of which was a meadow that, in June, was prettily decorated with buttercups and daisies and red clover. A plank laid across from bank to bank provided a rather wobbly bridge. Across this David followed Miss Weston, and was followed in turn by the ginger cat, stepping daintily, tail erect as a flagpole. Reaching the other side, however, the cat stalked away on important business of his own, and disappeared into the long grass fringing the trees.

David's relations with the St Hugh's household had developed so rapidly over the weeks that he now felt it to be a home-from-home. He and Jumbo had both been favoured at first, but as time went on Jumbo had found other occupations, and David visited more often without him. He had met Miss Weston's father, and got on with him like a house afire. He had been invited to family dinner. Mrs Bates approved of him and often when he left he would carry away a packet of cake or pie to share with his companions at St Monica's.

He had visited any time he was able to get away. He especially enjoyed the times when the club was closed and he and Miss Weston could talk and read together. As the weather improved, he and Jumbo, on borrowed bicycles, had made up sightseeing parties with Miss Weston and her friend from the village, Miss Bertha Dale, sometimes just the four of them and sometimes in larger groups. The surrounding scenery was awfully pretty.

But best of all had been those evenings when he called after dinner and sat with Miss Weston by the fire in their small parlour, talking endlessly, while her father read and smoked his pipe across the room. They read poetry: Dryden and Spenser, Wordsworth and Byron, Browning and Yeats. They read – with translation to hand – Homer and Virgil, and discussed war in the ancient world. They read Racine and Verlaine, and practised French conversation for when he went abroad. And sometimes their exchanges took lighter paths, and they would chat and laugh about nothing in particular, like old friends.

Today was a glorious June day, and when he had called in at the club, not expecting more than to exchange a nod with Miss Weston, who would surely be busy, she had told him that there were enough volunteers today so she was not really needed. Would he like to take a picnic across to the meadow? 'We could carry on with the *Aeneid*.'

An old horse-blanket spread out would counteract any lingering dampness of the grass, and a packet of egg sandwiches and a flask of tea would deal with the inner man, should his importunes disturb an afternoon of reading and conversation. So they had made their way through the garden, past the soldiers, to the wobbly bridge, David carrying a basket containing the victuals and the books, and Miss Weston the blanket.

After the death of Dido and a spirited discussion of the almost universal unpleasantness meted out to female characters in the classics, a pause ensued as they gathered their thoughts. David leaned back on his elbow, gazing at the treetops and the sky. Miss Weston sat with knees drawn up, her arms locked around them, a little breeze stirring the curls that lay on her forehead. The ginger cat reappeared and sat near her, winding his tail firmly around his hind legs as if to stop them wandering off again.

At last David said, 'I must say, it's very decent of your father to let us be alone like this. A lot of fathers would come down sticky about it.'

'Alone?' Miss Weston said, raising an eyebrow. She looked pointedly across the river to the soldiers, coming and going in the garden, being served by the volunteers. 'We're in full view. We might as well be on stage at His Majesty's.'

David laughed. 'That's true. I'd hardly noticed them, but we are most thoroughly chaperoned! In any event,' he added, 'I expect your father knows there's nothing like that going on between us. I mean, he's seen us often enough together to know you're like a big sister to me.'

'Is that what I am?'

'You said yourself he looks on us soldiers as his sons.'

'Yes, I did say that, didn't I?' Her voice sounded cool on the warm air.

'Which makes me your brother,' David said comfortably. He reached in for his cigarettes. 'May I?'

'Of course.' She watched him light up and take a first long draw. 'There's something you're not telling me,' she said, after a moment.

'How's that?'

'You have some news that you're hesitating about passing on.'

'You're awfully uncanny sometimes,' he said, staring. 'How could you possibly know?'

'So there *is* something. Tell me.'

'All right. I would have told you anyway, but I didn't want to spoil today. We'll be leaving next week. Jumbo and I have passed muster and we'll be going back to our battalion. The battalion is moving down to Salisbury Plain for six weeks' brigade training, and when that's finished–'

'You'll be off to the front,' she concluded for him.

He couldn't help grinning. 'Yes! Off to the war! God, I hope we get sent to France! But wherever it is, we'll be seeing action at last.'

'It had to happen sooner or later,' she said.

'Well, it couldn't be soon enough for me.' The words seemed to create an odd echo in his mind, and he looked at her a little awkwardly. 'Of course I'll be awfully sorry to leave here. I've enjoyed our talks so much – and reading together and so on.'

'But you naturally want to get on with the war,' she said. 'I understand.'

'I knew you would. You're a capital girl! Young lady, I should say,' he corrected himself hastily.

'I don't mind being called a girl,' she said neutrally. 'Isn't that a brother's privilege?'

He relaxed, glad he hadn't offended her. 'I say, how *did* you know I had something to tell? Can you read minds?'

'Fortunately not.'

'Fortunately?'

'I don't think it would be a comfortable thing to know what people were thinking.'

'Could come in handy sometimes. Back at school, doing Latin, you could read the construe in the beak's mind, and get it right every time.'

'But would that do you any good?'

'Blessed if I know! What do the Trojan wars teach us anyway? No handy gods and goddesses to intervene for us in *our* war.'

'Education doesn't have to have a practical application. All learning is good. The wider the mind, the better the decisions one makes,' Miss Weston said.

'But how *did* you know?' David reverted.

'Daddy heard it from your CO. They met at dinner at Lady Teale's, and he knew you were a pet of Daddy's, so he told. And Daddy told me.'

'Oh,' said David. He smoked in silence for a few moments, frowning in thought. Then he said hesitantly, 'I say, going to France, you know – I wonder if... Well, do you think your papa would mind if we wrote to each other? I know it's an awful cheek to ask, but as it is–'

'As we're like brother and sister, you mean?'

'Well, yes. Do you think he'd see it like that?'

She looked away, and said, 'You've got sisters of your own to write to you.'

'But they're not brainy like you. I'm awfully fond of them, of course, but they wouldn't write interesting letters. And I couldn't write interesting things to them, either. But I could to you – and I wouldn't have to wrap it up in pretty language, the way I would if you were ... well, like Sophy.' He had told her, in the course of their long conversations, about his hopeless love for Sophy Oliphant. 'You're so sensible. And you understand things.'

'That's true,' she said. 'Well, we can ask Daddy. If he says it's all right–'

'You'll write to me? I say, you are a trump!'

'Yes, that's what I am, all right. A trump.' Head turned away, she drew out her handkerchief and blew her nose.

'I say,' he said with concern, 'are you all right?' Surely, he thought, she couldn't be *crying*. But her eyes did look rather moist.

'It's this old rug,' she said lightly. 'Horsehair always made me sneeze. There must be a bit left on it still.' She put her handkerchief away and turned back to him. 'It used to belong to my dear old pony, Zephyr. Goodness, how I loved him! The first true love of my life.'

'Sophy Oliphant is mine,' he said sadly.

'Talking of ponies,' she said briskly, 'why don't we go on with our story? We won't have many more opportunities to finish it.'

He had told her about the exercise book and the story of Ben the Circus Pony, and she had said it was a great pity to leave poor Ben stranded without his narrative, like a beached whale. Since then, they had been writing the story together, just for fun.

Miss Weston had acquired a new exercise book, since the original contained his poetry. She got it out now, and a pencil, and said, 'Let's see, where had we got to?'

'He'd just seen the robber go into the circus boss's caravan,' said David.

'Ah, yes. And now he's got to give the alarm. How?'

'By neighing?'

'Hmm. That might be missed. I imagine circuses are noisy places, with all those animals roaring and howling. Perhaps he should bite through his rope and go and wake somebody.'

'Right-ho! But who? Oh, of course, his friend, the good clown, Beppo!'

335

He watched her as she bent her head over the book, and wrote in her neat, careful hand, speaking the words aloud for him as she wrote. Really, she was a capital girl, he thought. An absolute trump. And he would miss these meetings with her when he went away. He hoped her father would allow them to correspond. It would be a good, warm thing to have someone back home to tell things to, when he was at the front.

'Wouldn't it be nice if we knew who Ben's owner was, so we could send her the completed story?' he said.

She looked up. 'She might not like it. Everyone has their own way of telling their story. And everyone knows what ending they hoped for.'

The battalion at Paget's Piece had been there long enough to have become a village fixture, and when it marched out, the village made a celebration of it. The shops in the high street got their bunting out again, and the ladies of the Soldiers' Comforts Fund committee (recently formed from the amalgamation of the Soldiers' Families' Emergency Fund and the Soldiers' Relatives' Hardship Fund) drew the bunting from the village-hall store and decorated the approach to the station and the station building itself.

The brass band had lost a euphonium and two trumpets to recruitment, but two boys were lent from the orchestra of Lorrimers' Guild, the local boarding-school, and a very old man who had given up the euphonium long ago for lack of puff reckoned he could manage a tune or two more, as it was in a good cause. A dais was set up in the station yard and the MP, Mr Whiteley, and the magistrate, Mr Worthington, were joined by Mr Woodwick, the chairman of the Rural District Council, the rector, and Mrs Oliver in her largest hat, to bid the boys farewell officially.

Their marching out was a smarter business than their marching in had been: then they had still sported their civilian clothes and had little idea of keeping time. Now they were in proper uniform, and hundreds of hours of practice had their legs and arms swinging as one. Their own band preceded them and, though laden with full kit and rifle, they grinned with high spirits as they swung along to 'Tipperary' and other favourites. Dogs and little boys provided the constant factor, hopping along beside and behind them just as they had when the battalion arrived, just as boys and dogs would always caper about a column of soldiers until the world turned to coal.

The population turned out to line the streets and wave 'their' soldiers goodbye. The village school assembled all its pupils at the roadside to cheer. Some landladies, who were losing their officers, shed a tear for the dear boys, who had been like sons to them. Mrs Wilkins, who had lodged two, was almost melting with sorrow, and not for the loss of income, either, since she had treated them so royally that the allowance hadn't nearly covered her expenses. There were a few tears among the young ladies, too. There had been three hasty marriages in the past week at the register office in Westleigh, and many promises made.

Beattie had given the servants permission to go and watch. Cook, whose feet were her weak point from being on them all day, was content to go no further than the end of the road to see them go by, but Ada and Emily went down to the high street, and Ethel went one further: she slipped round behind the dais and into the siding, where she met Eric Travers for an unexpected tryst. He had sent her a note by the butcher's boy to say he would be the guard on the battalion's train.

'It's a real honour,' he told her now. 'It wasn't really my shift, but once the word got out when it was, I managed to switch with old Arnie Braithwaite. He didn't mind – his teeth are bad again, so it gives him a chance to see a dentist. And I get to help the battalion on its way.'

'Only as far as Hounslow Heath,' Ethel said, with all the scorn left over from her brush with Andy Wood. 'I don't know who's fighting the war, I really don't. All the soldiers seem to be in England.'

'Got to be properly trained,' Eric said. 'Anyway, it's a step on the road, isn't it?'

'Step on the road's about right. All this lot seem to do is march about the country. What time you finish today?'

'I should be back here about half past six. It's not your evening off, is it?'

'No, but once we've done their dinner, I can slip out for an hour.'

'Really? I don't want you to get into trouble.'

'Don't worry about me. I can take care of myself. Well, d'you want to meet?'

'Course I do.' He grinned. 'I've got something to celebrate.'

'What's that?'

'I'm taking my test next week. Supervisor told me this morning. Then I'll be a proper driver.'

'If you pass.'

'Course I'll pass.' He looked hurt. 'Haven't you got any faith in me?'

'The proof's in the pudding,' she said.

The approaching sound of the battalion's band came faintly to them, combined with a roar of many voices cheering. The village band started fidgeting and blowing a few preliminary toots. They were coming!

Someone called Eric's name, and he looked over his shoulder. 'I'll have to go,' he said. 'I'll see you tonight then – at the bus stop?'

'All right. Go on, then. Go and play with your trains.'

He took the teasing in good part. 'I wish I was going with them, though,' he said, looking towards the place where the marching column would appear, his eyes bright and distant with visions. 'Off to war, everyone cheering, waving flags. Girls blowing kisses. Off to serve your King and country.'

Ethel was alarmed. 'Don't you even think of it,' she said.

'Got to *think* of it,' he said. 'It's what every man wants – excitement, adventure, glory.'

'Soft in the head, that's what you are, Eric Travers. Just about to become a real train driver, what you've always dreamed about, and talking rubbish about soldiers!'

'So you *do* believe I'll pass,' he said triumphantly.

'Oh, I expect you'll muddle through,' Ethel said, but she smiled – and, as no-one was looking

339

their way, she leaned forward and kissed him for good measure.

Sadie was passing Diana's bedroom, and heard a distinctive sound. She approached the closed door and listened, and her heart was tugged. She hesitated a moment – Diana disliked being disturbed – but she couldn't leave her. They didn't always get on, but she was her sister and she loved her. She turned the knob and walked quietly in.

Diana was lying on her bed, her face buried in the pillow. The weeping checked an instant as Sadie approached and said, 'It's only me,' then began again.

Sadie was at a loss how to comfort her. She could soothe and calm horses, dogs and cats. She was even quite good with little children. But grown-ups... And Diana's sorrow was one for which no remedy existed. But she knew better than to speak. She sat down at the bedside and waited in silence.

After a time the weeping slowed. Diana's hand, clutching a sodden handkerchief, lay near her. Sadie gently drew the wet hanky away from the fingers and inserted her own. 'It's quite clean,' she said.

Eventually the sounds of crying stopped. Diana blew her nose, then turned her face to Sadie and opened her eyes. Even with red eyes and a swollen nose, Sadie thought, she was still beautiful. She half expected to be told to get out, but instead, after a moment, Diana said, 'Thanks.'

Encouraged, Sadie said, 'I suppose it's Charles?'

Diana's eyes went past her to the photograph.

'It's so unfair,' she said. She drew a sigh of pain, sat up, blew her nose again, and wiped her eyes. 'We were going to be married. He was a *good* person.'

'I know,' said Sadie.

'So why did he have to be killed? I don't understand any of it. All those years of growing up, and education, and training, and the Territorials, and becoming a good man and a soldier, and then he's just dead and gone, and nothing.' A sob hitched at her breath. She controlled it. 'Torn up and thrown away, as if he didn't matter. It's such a waste!'

'He went to fight for his country,' Sadie said. 'He fought to bring us peace.'

'But there *isn't* peace, is there? He didn't do anything. He didn't have time. He died for nothing.'

Sadie had thoughts she had never expressed, which existed more as shapes in her mind, and she struggled for the right words, afraid of hurting Diana even more, afraid anything like sympathy from her would be resented. She said, 'No, look, I don't think it was for nothing. Suppose – suppose the war is like a balance.' She held out her hands, like the two pans on a weighing scale. 'Suppose so much has to be given before peace can come again. Say it was a thousand lives before the scale went down.' She let one hand lower. 'Take just one away, and...' The hand came up level again. 'Do you see? Every single one matters. Charles gave his life, and it wasn't wasted. Maybe it had to be, maybe they *all* have to be, and in the end it will add up to

341

something very great, and then we'll understand.'

Diana looked at her carefully. 'Do you really believe that?'

Sadie met her eyes. She hadn't thought about it before, but now she had... 'I really do.'

Diana stared a moment longer, but then the tears welled up again, and she turned her head away. 'But he's still dead. I'll never see him again. He was *there*, and now he's gone.'

She also was unpractised at expressing her thoughts. It had never been required. How could she tell Sadie of the power of his presence, of how when she was with him he seemed more real than his surroundings? And how his absence was like a great, suffocating stone on her chest, making it hard to draw breath.

But somehow Sadie did catch a sense of her loss. It hurt her, like a gulp of icy air on a cold morning. 'He's with God now,' she managed to say.

'I don't think I believe in God,' Diana said angrily.

Sadie looked at her. 'You do,' she said. 'You just don't like what He's doing.'

'It doesn't make any sense!'

'Not to us,' Sadie agreed, but wisely didn't pursue this line. Theology was not her forte either. Religion, she always thought, was better felt than talked about. And she understood, at least, that Diana was beyond being comforted by words or ideas. Only doing something could help when you were that sad. She remembered how her sister had perked up a little when helping to prepare the hospital. 'Look here,' she said, 'why don't you come with me when I go and visit Lieutenant Piper?'

'Go to the hospital?' Diana said. She thought of all those wounded officers, wounded as Charles had been wounded, but surviving where he had died – surviving to remind her of everything, if she were foolish enough to go near them. 'I couldn't possibly!'

'You could!' Sadie said. 'Oh, please, Di, do come. The poor chaps get so bored, with nothing to think about but their troubles. Quite a few of them need letters written for them. I can't do them all. And there are a lot who would love to be read to, or simply have someone new to talk to. They've all heard each other's stories until they're sick of them. It would be *such* a good thing to do. Think how awful it is to be them, wounded and far from home and not knowing what will happen to them.'

'I don't think I could bear it,' Diana said. But Sadie simply continued to look at her steadily, and she knew she *could*. She didn't want to. It would hurt. But wasn't that just selfishness? Doing your duty was not always pleasant, but it oughtn't to stop you. It hadn't stopped Charles. She remembered his saying that he was not naturally a soldier. 'Do you really think it would help?' she asked.

'I *know* it would,' Sadie said. 'Just looking at you will make them feel better, poor fellows. So you will come? I'm so glad. Will you come this afternoon?'

'This afternoon?' Diana said in alarm.

'No sense in putting it off. Put some cold water on your face, and it will have gone down all right by then.'

That put Diana on her dignity. 'I'll look after my own face, thank you.'

Sadie was pleased, seeing this as progress. Better anything than lying weeping. She jumped up. 'We'll have to leave at two o'clock, so be ready, won't you? And wear something pretty!'

CHAPTER TWENTY

'Your sister's beautiful,' said Tom Piper, watching her as she walked across to Baring's bed, graceful in her simple blue cotton summer frock, her wheatfield hair gleaming as she passed through a blade of sunlight from the window.

'Yes, she is,' Sadie said.

'I don't think I've ever seen a more beautiful girl. It's sad, her fiancé being killed like that. She's very brave to come and visit us. It must bring back memories.'

'Better for her to do something than sit moping at home,' Sadie said, finding herself feeling unaccountably brisk about it.

Piper looked at her with faint amusement. 'You are the sort of person who would think that. I'm afraid a lot of humanity falls into the moping-at-home category.'

'It doesn't help,' said Sadie.

'Anyway, I hope you don't use that word to her. It's a great deal more than moping, you know.'

Sadie had nothing to say to that. Instead she

asked, 'Shall we get on with your letter?' She had learned a good deal about his family, who lived in some remote part of Northumberland. He liked to talk about them, and read aloud bits of their letters to him.

But now he said, rather listlessly, 'Oh, not now. I don't feel like it. Just sit and talk to me.' He was still looking at Diana, seated now at Baring's bedside. Baring was gazing up at her adoringly, his lips moving in a stream of talk. 'Tell me what's happening in the world outside.'

'Well, the new battalion marched in yesterday,' Sadie obliged. 'I hear the advance party complained bitterly about the state the camp was left in. But Mrs Cuthbert said Colonel Barry told her every battalion thinks they're the only one that keeps proper order. I felt a bit sorry for the new lot – they didn't have as big a turn-out as the last lot got when they left. But I suppose we'll be every bit as fond of them in time.'

'They don't know what they're in for,' Piper said.

Sadie thought about his hand. He never complained, or even mentioned it, but it must be terrible to be so young and to have lost something so essential. She was trying to think of something to say to distract him, when the moving sunlight finally cleared the frame of the window next to his bed and fell across his face. He moved his head away fretfully.

Sadie jumped up and said, 'Shall I pull the curtain over a little?' He didn't answer, but she did so anyway and, returning, examined him more closely. She knew when something was not right with a horse: there was a look about them, an un-ease, a glassiness to their eyes – it was an instinct more than anything. And that instinct was oper-ating now. There was something, she thought, not quite *right* about Tom Piper today.

'I say, don't you feel well?' she asked.

'I'm all right,' he said automatically, and gave her a smile, but it was rather feeble.

'I think you might have a temperature,' she said.

'Maybe I'm getting a cold,' he said.

'In July?'

'One of the nurses had one. Summer colds are the worst,' he said. She hesitated, looking down at him, and he moved his head again, that same, fretful movement. 'Don't hover,' he said. 'I can't stand being hovered over.'

It was the first thing even approaching a cross remark she had ever heard from him. She sat down; but she said, 'If you're starting a fever, you should tell the nurse.'

'I'm all right. Don't fuss,' he said. Sadie said nothing. He looked at her. 'I'm sorry. I didn't mean to snap. I do feel a bit under par. But it's nothing. Look, let's go on with the letter.'

'If you like,' she said.

'Read me what you've got so far,' he said.

She did so, noting as she read that he turned his head away again on the pillow, looking in the direction of Baring's bed, but before she had got very far, his eyelids were drooping. She read more slowly, lowering her voice, and when she got to the place they had reached, and paused, he did not stir. He had gone to sleep.

She got up quietly and left him, and went over to see if Lieutenant Perceval, who had a head wound and had lost an eye, would like to be read to. She kept glancing over to Tom Piper, but he did not wake again, though he moved a few times, restlessly, in his sleep.

When Sister Ryman announced visiting time was over, Sadie went to her and mentioned her concern for Piper. 'I think he might be starting a fever,' she said. 'He has a sort of look about him that I've seen in horses.'

'His temperature was up a little today. You would make a good nurse,' said Ryman.

Sadie said shyly, 'I just know horses. What do you think it means – the fever?'

Ryman glanced across at him and sighed. 'I'm afraid it may be an infection. One must hope not.'

'In the – amputation?' Sadie asked, trying to sound nurselike.

'It happens sometimes, I'm afraid. The men are wounded in such dirty conditions. But we'll keep an eye on him, and hope for the best. You must go now.' She looked across at Diana, who was still at Baring's bedside, but had three other officers, the ones who were mobile, standing in an admiring group at the end of the bed. 'Your sister seems to be popular. Will she come again?'

'Yes,' said Sadie, thinking, *I'll make her.*

'I'm glad. It does do them good to see outsiders.'

'Should I see if any of my friends will come?' Sadie asked.

Ryman considered her. 'If they are quiet, sensible young ladies, like you, I think it would be a very good idea.'

That evening Mrs Oliver, who was head of the hospital committee, called at The Elms. Sadie was going out of the room to leave her alone with Beattie, but she said, 'No, don't go, Sadie dear. This concerns you. In fact, I rather think you are at the heart of it. You and Diana. Where is she?'

'I think she's in the garden,' said Sadie. 'Shall I fetch her?'

'No, that's all right. You can tell her about it later. I had a call today from the chief medical officer at the fever hospital – I beg your pardon, I should say Mount Olive. Old habits die hard!' she added, with a smile.

'Is it about my visiting?' Sadie said anxiously, afraid some army protocol was going to be cited. 'Because I do think–'

'Oh, my dear, no need to look worried. He and the rest of the governing board think it's a splendid thing. Sister Ryman spoke to the matron and she spoke to him, and between them they have decided that having nice young ladies visit them is the best thing for the wounded's morale. And good morale, you know, aids recovery. So they've decided to extend visiting hours to the same time *every* day, and they've asked me to drum up some more recruits, "like those nice Miss Hunters", they said, to come and talk to the men, read to them, do little errands and so on.' She beamed. 'So you should be proud, my dear, because it is thanks to your good example.'

'Sadie is a good girl,' Beattie agreed. 'I don't

suppose you'll have time to go every day, will you, with your work at Highclere?'

'I'll go as often as I can,' Sadie said.

'Is it only *young* ladies they want?' Beattie asked Mrs Oliver.

'I think, given their average age, the officers will appreciate the young ladies most!' Mrs Oliver smiled. 'But the board wants *anyone* who is willing to visit. Of course people of our generation, Mrs Hunter, are already tremendously busy, doing such a variety of good works. But I did hope you would be able to spare one afternoon a week.'

'I'm sure I could,' said Beattie. 'We ought to get up a regular rota, so that everyone doesn't turn up at once, and someone's there every day.'

'Yes, exactly. I'm going to call a meeting of the hospital committee in the church room tomorrow evening for that purpose. Yes, I know that's the Sewing Circle's evening, but we can meet immediately afterwards, and as several of us will be there for that it will save travelling about. In the mean time, do make a note of anyone you think might be suitable – and willing. And you too, Sadie. Think about which of your friends would like to help.' She stood up. 'I'd like to get this on a really good footing because I have a feeling that our first hospital won't be our last. It's all quiet on the front at the moment, but I've heard rumours that there'll be a big push this autumn, and that's bound to mean more wounded.'

'Where would they put another hospital?' Beattie asked, walking her to the door.

'Oh, my dear, any big house,' said Mrs Oliver. 'Manor Grange. Coneysfield. And, of course,

Dene Park springs to mind.'

Beattie raised her eyebrows. 'Dene Park? Lady Wroughton wouldn't like that.'

'If the war goes on another year or more, as they're saying, we may all have to get used to many things we don't like,' said Mrs Oliver.

Sadie thought about Tom Piper all the next morning up at Highclere as she worked with the roan, trying to get him to pass various obstacles without napping. The whole group was going off at the end of the week to make room for a new intake, and Mrs Cuthbert was anxious that the black and the roan shouldn't let them down.

They broke off at lunchtime, and as they walked back to the stables, Mrs Cuthbert said to her, 'This afternoon, it would do them good to go out for a long hack together. They've had a lot of schooling in the last few days. The unbent bow, you know...'

Sadie looked apologetic. 'I wonder if you would mind awfully if I went home this afternoon.'

'Of course not,' Mrs Cuthbert said, though she seemed surprised. 'You are free to come and go as you wish. This is voluntary work, you know.'

'I don't like to let you down. But, you see, there's someone I'm worried about at the hospital. I'd really like to go and visit.'

'One of the officers? Of course, my dear, you must do as you think fit.' Mrs Cuthbert smiled to herself. 'I can't expect to keep you all to myself, especially when there are other attractions. An old woman can't compete with a young man – an officer, at that.'

'It isn't like that,' Sadie said, blushing.

'Isn't it? Very well, if you say so.'

'Really,' said Sadie. 'He's very nice, but I just write letters for him and talk to him.'

'Dear Sadie, you don't have to explain yourself to me,' said Mrs Cuthbert.

Having washed and changed, and sat through what for once seemed an interminable luncheon, Sadie set off at two to walk up to the hospital. Diana was not with her – she had other arrangements that day. The sun was hot and the steep hill seemed steeper than ever, as if Nature were conspiring to slow her down and hold her back. The old man in the entrance hall nodded permission to her without speaking, knowing her well enough by now. She ran up the stairs and pushed in through the ward doors. Her eyes flew to Piper's bed, and she felt a jolt of shock in her chest when she saw it was empty.

Sister Ryman came over with her rapid, clockwork steps. 'Looking for Lieutenant Piper? He's been moved to one of the side rooms.'

'Oh, I see. May I visit him?' Sadie asked.

'No, I'm afraid not. The doctor decided a further operation was needed. He went up to theatre this morning, so he's still recovering.'

'What – what sort of operation?'

'I'm sorry, I can't discuss it with you, as you aren't a member of the family. Perhaps you can visit him tomorrow.'

'If he wakes up, will you tell him–'

'That you came to see him? Yes, I'll tell him.' She glanced around. 'There are a number of other men who would be glad of some company, you know.'

'Yes – of course,' Sadie said, and looked round to see who else might catch her eye.

The sister had to be discreet, but the other men didn't, and when Sadie sat down by Apthorpe, who had lost both legs and had the bed next to Piper's, he told her what had happened. 'They had to take the arm off further up,' he said. 'The same thing happened to me. My left leg was only off at the ankle to begin with, but when the infection started, they had to take it off at the knee.'

'I didn't know. I'm so sorry.'

'Luckily that did the trick, or I wouldn't be here now. It's a damn' shame, though, for poor old Piper.'

'Where – how far?' Sadie found her mouth dry.

'At the elbow, I heard. Sounds a bit drastic, but if they don't take enough you can end up chasing the infection up and up – and losing. Better to deal with it once and for all.' He looked at her anxiously, and patted her hand. 'I shouldn't have told you. Young ladies shouldn't hear about things like that.'

'No, I'm glad you did. I'd always sooner know the truth, whatever it is.'

'I know. Piper thinks the world of you – tells us all what a splendid girl you are.'

'Does he?' she said, blinking back tears.

'Don't upset yourself,' Apthorpe said. 'He'll be all right. Look, if I can get along with no legs, he can manage with one hand.'

The poignancy of a man who had lost both legs comforting *her* did nothing to stop her wanting to cry. She did it with a manful swallow, stitched a bright smile on her face, and said, 'Can I do anything for you?'

'As a matter of fact, you can,' Apthorpe said. 'I'd be obliged if you could scratch my left foot for me. It itches most abominably, and I can't reach it.'

She looked shocked for a fraction of a second, before she realised he was teasing her out of her tears. 'Does it really itch?' she asked.

'All the time,' Apthorpe said. 'But I'm lucky. Some people have terrible pain in their missing parts. All I have is a terrible tickle.'

The following day, she presented herself again at the hospital, this time accompanied by Diana and Lizzie Drake. The list had not yet been compiled or the rota made out, but as Lizzie had expressed herself eager to help, thinking of her fallen cousin, Diana had arranged for her to accompany them. Lizzie was very nervous about what horrors she might see, and how embarrassing it would be to see a lot of strange men in bed. But Diana told her calmly that it would not be embarrassing at all, and that she must think of them, not of herself. Sadie was impressed that Diana had learned that for herself so quickly.

As they entered the ward, Sadie saw at once that Piper's bed was occupied again, and her heart lifted for an instant before she realised it was a stranger, a rather undersized young man with a heavily bandaged head and left arm.

Sister Ryman was coming towards her.

'Is Lieutenant Piper still poorly? Please, may I

see him?' Sadie asked, before she could speak. The sister's face seemed to bode the negative. 'Just for a minute. I promise I won't disturb him.'

'I'm afraid Lieutenant Piper died early this morning,' said Sister Ryman. 'I'm very sorry, my dear.'

The trees were in full summer leaf, and the woods were shady, sun-dappled along the rides. *The woods are lovely, dark and deep*, Sadie thought vaguely. She had picked up a stick without even knowing it, and swished it angrily at the long grass as she walked. I won't cry. I *won't*.

He had shown her a photograph of Dad, Mother, brother Michael and sister Polly, arranged, with him, in a line in front of their house – square, grey stone, with some kind of creeper across one side. The photograph had been taken the previous autumn, so the creeper was deep crimson, bright against the stone. They had a dog, too, a Labrador called Jet, though he wasn't in the photograph. She wished she had asked where he was. Sitting with the photographer watching them, she thought, in the perverse way of dogkind.

The father and mother looked nice people, ordinary and pleasant. She hoped they wouldn't blame themselves for not having made the journey to see him. He had told her that it was not possible for them to get away. They had been planning to come at the end of the month when school was out, and Tom Piper senior could take his annual leave. *Too late!* What terrible words. They would think of that always – that they had left it too late.

'But he still would have died,' she said aloud. She turned her face up to the trees to stop the tears leaking out. The leaves seemed to flicker in the sunlight. It was a cheerful sort of movement. *How can anything be cheerful when there are such injustices in the world?* He had lost his hand, then his arm. You would have thought that was enough. But then his life was taken too. *Unfair!* 'Why did you do it?' she demanded, her voice high with anger.

He had never complained. She had always believed that he felt he had given of himself in a good cause, and that the sacrifice was worth while. *But had he?* she wondered. He was brave, like all of them, but deep inside, was there no seed of resentment over his loss? He would never have told her, if there was. She remembered him saying, 'They don't know what they're in for.' The only time the mask had slipped? But perhaps it wasn't a mask. He had always seemed a practical person, not the sort to cry over spilled milk. Perhaps that was why she had liked him so much – because she was like that too.

'I liked him so much,' she told the indifferent trees. Her voice sounded bewildered. *Stupid girl! Did you think your liking someone would make them safe?*

No-one was safe any more. She thought of the girls who had been killed in the Zeppelin raid. They had just been coming back from the pictures, and then they were dead.

She walked on, the stick trailing from her hand, her anger dissipated. But that only left the tears closer. There was an emptiness in her mind where she had used to think about Tom Piper, and she flinched from touching it, like a sore place. But she wanted to think about him: she didn't want to forget him. How could he be dead? How could he suddenly just not be there? She walked faster, struggling to come to grips with the idea of death, which had never impinged on her before. He was so cheerful – so young, with all his life before him. *Unfair!*

Bobby arrived home, unannounced, like a whirlwind. 'I'm not here to stay,' he cried, dumping his kit bag in the hall and seizing Ada round the waist in a boisterous hug that made her shriek. 'I'm in transit, so I've only got a couple of hours, but I'm as hungry as a horse. Could you go and wheedle Cook for me, darling Ada, and get her to rustle up something?'

Released, Ada straightened her cap and apron and tried to straighten her dignity. 'Of course I will, Master Bobby. Would it be luncheon or tea you wanted?'

'Both. High tea, like they have in Scotland. Plenty of savoury and plenty of sweet.'

'But, Bobby, dear, what are you doing here?' Beattie interrupted, waving Ada away.

'Finished basic infantry training, and my company commander put my name forward for officer training. So I'm off to school, and you'll never guess where.'

'Where?' Diana asked dutifully.

He grinned. 'Oxford! Not only Oxford, but actually Balliol! They've set up an officer training school in one of the under-used buildings, and the instructors will be the old OUOTC instructors. It will be a veritable home-from-home for me. I've only just left the old place, and now I'm going back!'

'How nice for you, darling,' said Beattie. 'I expect there will be some of your old friends around, too. You'll be able to see them again.'

'According to what Colonel Hall says, I won't have time for any carousing with undergraduates – even if there are any left. I believe the ranks at Oxford are thinning fast, or they wouldn't have an empty house to donate for a school. Still, whatever leisure time I have, it will be nice to be back in civilisation.'

'Wasn't it civilised at Woldingham?' Diana asked.

'Far from it, as the seasick chap said when the steward asked him if he'd dined.'

'Oh, Bobby!' Beattie said reproachfully.

'Sorry, Mater. It's a wonder I'm not more coarsened than I am, living cheek by jowl with all manner of fellows, in primitive conditions, and doing things no gentleman would normally dream of. Digging latrines, Mother dearest – imagine! You will be glad to know your boy now has all the skills needed to dig a latrine a man can be proud of. And this from a man who didn't know the meaning of the word two months ago!'

'It doesn't seem to have done you any harm,' Diana remarked. 'You look very well on it.' He was leaner and harder, she could see that at a glance.

'Oh, they're very keen on physical fitness. Marching twenty miles in full kit – and I can tell you, it weighs a ton! Scaling a six-foot wall at the run, while carrying a rifle and pack. Anyone who couldn't meet the standard was transferred to the service battalion in the greatest ignominy. But your boy passed with flying colours.'

In record time, Cook produced a meal: an omelette and fried potatoes, a piece of cold meat pie, a ham that was in cut, with pickles, flanked by tomatoes and a dish of lettuce, a heap of bread and butter, a raspberry jelly she had made for the servants' supper, and the big fruit cake that was always on hand in the kitchen.

Ada said, as she finished laying it all out, 'Cook sends her apologies that she hasn't got anything more dainty, but you did say you were in a hurry.'

'Tell Cook it all looks delicious, and I'm far beyond wanting dainties. I'm a soldier now, with a soldier's appetite. You tell her she did just right.'

Sadie came in while he was quieting the first pangs of hunger, and rushed to hug him, and receive a smacking kiss with a hint of piccalilli. 'What are you doing here? Don't tell me you've been thrown out!'

'Oh, such faith in me!' Bobby said, grinning, and told the story again.

Sadie sat down beside him, turning her chair towards him. 'What's Woldingham like?' she asked.

'Lovely country. It's up on the top of the Downs, and the air is magnificent – worth a pound a sniff, at least. Pretty exposed, though, when the wind blows. I'm glad I wasn't there in winter. The advance party didn't even have huts to shelter in – some sort of foul-up with the builders. We were all hutted, of course, but even so, I can tell you, it can be pretty brisk washing at six in the morning, out of doors and in cold water. They have a sort of long wooden table with metal bowls let into it at intervals and we all stand there shoulder to shoulder, like pigs at a trough. I must say,' he added thoughtfully, as he reached for the ham, 'this communal living isn't for me. I'm glad I'm off to be an officer.'

'What are the other fellows like?' Sadie asked.

'Oh, a terrific bunch. We've got every sort – playwrights, poets, architects, lawyers. We've got an actor, Edmund Tennant. He joined with his brother, who was with a bank – foreign exchange. Speaks I don't know how many languages. They could have gone forward for officer training, but they decided to stay in the ranks. Thought they'd get to France quicker. Good luck to 'em!' He chewed and swallowed another mouthful. 'You know what's the worst thing about living together with all those men?'

'No, tell us,' said Diana.

'Feet,' said Bobby. 'I never realised before, but men have smelly feet.'

'*You* don't,' said Beattie.

'No, Mother dearest, I'm as sweet as a rose from top to bottom. But most chaps' feet have a fragrance all their own, and about one pair in six is a real stinker. And put them all together in a confined space, especially when those feet have got good and hot with marching all day ... I tell you, if pongs were noises, I'd be stone deaf now.'

All too soon he had to go. 'I wish I had time for a bath,' Bobby said wistfully. 'But I dare say facilities will be a bit less primitive in Oxford.'

'Will you be able to visit again?' Beattie asked.

'Quite possibly. One of the good things about Oxford is that it's not too far from here, and if I get a few hours off, I may be able to get home. On the other hand,' he added, dropping a swift wink to Sadie, 'the town's full of pretty ladies, so I may be too busy to come.'

'Don't you dare get yourself into trouble,' Beattie said, alarmed. 'You're too young to think about ladies.'

He kissed her. 'Fear not, Mother dear. I have my mind set on higher things.' He kissed Diana and Sadie. 'Give my respects to Papa. And tell the boys I'm sorry not to see them.'

The servants were lingering by the kitchen passage, and he went to say goodbye to them, too, giving Cook a smacking kiss of thanks, which made her blush. She pressed a package of sandwiches into his hand. 'For the journey,' she said.

'Bless you, Cookie darling,' he said. He was enough of a soldier now to know he'd be quite ready to eat them on the train, despite the large meal he'd just consumed.

Laura and Louisa had been several times to the Partridge–Gibson studio, which was in a tall house in Southampton Row. The other occupants were either artists or scholars of some sort, reflecting the presence nearby of the university and the British Museum. The whole house had a cheerful, informal, drop-in-and-chat atmosphere that Laura found unexpectedly beguiling. It was the sort of thing Louisa had been used to in her years of working with the suffragists, and Laura could quite see, now, why she had liked it so much.

Sylvia and Beryl – everyone was on first-name terms – had the drawing-room floor, with the tall windows that gave good light for their artistic endeavours, and since their rooms were the largest, it seemed natural for others in the house to gather there. Their parties – which Sylvia insisted on calling *soirées* – generally followed the same pattern. A number of people would be invited, the rest of the household would drop in, some of them bringing guests too, and the rooms would become hot and crowded. Evadne and Sybil, who lived downstairs and had a large kitchen, would provide food, drinks would be served in a harlequin variety of vessels, and talk and cigarette smoke would rise as the evening progressed until they seemed to displace all the air in the rooms.

Laura had never heard so much talk in her life. The first occasion had left her bemused and with a headache, and afterwards she had lain sleepless the whole night while threads of conversation repeated themselves in her head and wound about each other until the tangle looked like wool a cat had been playing with.

She had grown more robust now, and could not only survive the experience but even hold her own in an intellectual argument. The nice thing, she thought, about Sylvia's and Beryl's circle was that, while they argued vigorously on every subject, they never took anything personally. You could take an opposing position safe in the knowledge that there would be no unpleasantness or hurt feelings.

The people she met there were a mixed bunch,

some obviously poor scholars with patched elbows or struggling artists who headed straight for the food without apology, others quite well-to-do, with private incomes, well-paid jobs, or engaged in a line of artistic creativity that had a ready market. Sybil, for instance, wrote romantic novelettes under several pseudonyms, cheerfully called it 'my trash' and made a very decent living, while Evadne, who shared the flat with her, did nicely out of making figurines, which were reproduced in their hundreds by a pottery company in Clerkenwell. Before the war it had been shepherdesses and nymphs, but now she was bringing out a line of famous soldiers and politicians.

In this company Laura and Louisa were not the comedy turn, or objects of unseemly fascination. People were interested in their work, but not in a prurient way. So, despite having believed she preferred a quiet evening at home at the end of a day packed with incident, Laura found herself quite willing to unbend the bow in Southampton Row. And Louisa was quite simply in her element.

One evening in July Laura was sitting on the large and shabby sofa (one had to be an early-comer to get a seat there), having a discussion about the National Registration Act. It was a warm evening and the windows were open as far as they would go, letting in the street and traffic noises to compete with the voices within; even so, it would be intolerably stuffy later. Laura had provided herself with a paper fan for the eventuality. Nothing of that sort offended Sylvia or Beryl.

The National Registration Act had just been passed by Parliament. It provided for a form of census to be taken of all men and women be-tween fifteen and sixty-five. Twenty-nine million forms would be distributed, and had to be filled in on the 15th of August, giving age, address, occupation and details of any special skills.

Some Suffragettes among them remembered the last census in 1911, which they had attempted to wreck by staying out of doors, walking about the streets all night, hiding in outbuildings or gather-ing in the houses of census-resisters. One group kept each other company in Trafalgar Square, keeping a sharp look-out for policemen; another had hired a charabanc and had driven out to the middle of Wimbledon Common.

'But in that case, of course, we were objecting as much as anything to the fact that only a man could fill it in,' said Leland Brandt, who lectured at UCL, and had housed protesters on that night. With the census, the head of household was re-sponsible for completing the form and listing everyone under his roof. 'With this new registra-tion, every individual has to complete their own.'

'I find that awfully encouraging, don't you?' Sybil said. 'For the first time they're taking women seriously.'

'I wouldn't go that far,' said Sylvia.

'Well,' said Leland, 'they're at least acknow-ledging that women are a resource.'

'Charming compliment,' said Sylvia.

'Better than being told to go home and keep quiet,' said Grace Lattery, a tall, grey-haired doctor. A group of female doctors offering their services in August 1914 had been told just that.

'I think we're seeing the beginning of a new

thinking,' said Laura. 'As more and more men go into uniform, women will have to do their work, and the authorities are beginning to realise it, however unwillingly. Otherwise, the Registration Act would only cover men.'

'But is it true,' Sybil asked, 'that the Act is the first step on the way to conscription? I can't believe the government would really consider it. It would be very – controversial.'

'It would be more than that,' said a newcomer, reaching them through the crush just then. 'It would be shocking in the extreme. Sylvia darling, you're looking well. You know Erskine, don't you?'

Sylvia struggled to her feet to offer a cheek. 'Rupert, my sweet, what a treat! Of course I know Erskine. We played together in the nursery – stole each other's toys, at any rate.'

Laura looked up, and saw Rupert Wroughton, rather fantastically dressed in a velvet jacket with a silk scarf instead of a bow tie. Leaning against his shoulder was a very tall, rather pale young man with a languid air, correctly dressed in evening clothes, with a crimson rose in his buttonhole.

Sylvia performed introductions. 'Laura, do you know Rupert Wroughton? And Erskine Ballantine. Laura Hunter. Wait a minute.' She clapped a hand to her forehead. 'Of course you must know Rupert – your niece was engaged to his brother.'

Rupert's hands were in his pockets, so Laura didn't offer hers. 'I know him by sight, but we've never actually met,' she said. 'How do you do? My deepest condolences for the loss of your brother.'

'The condolences work both ways,' Rupert

said. His eyes had a strange glitter to them. 'The loss to *your* family is as great as to ours.'

'Not *as* great,' Laura demurred. 'I believe you were very kind to my niece while she was staying in London.'

He turned his head away, like a horse avoiding a caress. 'Not kind at all. Don't talk of it. I'm much more interested in this new Act you were talking about. It can't really mean conscription, can it?'

'My friends in the police force say it means just that,' said Laura. 'The government simply isn't raising enough men through volunteering. And with volunteers, they arrive when it suits them, which doesn't necessarily suit the army. The whole thing needs to be properly controlled. I'm afraid the war can't be run on the old amateur basis.'

'You have friends in the police force?' Erskine Ballantine queried, with a faint air of alarm.

Laura thought he looked drunk, though no smell of alcohol came from him. '"Colleagues" might be the better word,' she said. 'We don't visit each other's houses.'

'Laura's a lady-policeman,' Sylvia said proudly. 'She and Louisa–' she looked round. 'Oh, she's over there. Striking a blow for women's equality.'

'Well, that's not entirely why we're doing it,' Laura said, with a smile. 'Mostly it's tremendous fun. Much better than knitting socks for soldiers.'

Rupert grinned. 'You and Louisa, eh? And here I find you cosily ensconced with Sylvia on her sofa. How charming.'

He and his friend had an odd way of jumping

about from subject to subject, Laura thought.

'We met at a Bedfordite party,' she said shortly.

'Oh, everybody *interesting* meets Sylvia sooner or later,' Rupert said, with a knowing emphasis.

'Rupert, what are you plotting?' Sylvia said. 'Don't trust this boy as far as you can throw him, Laura, that's my advice. He's always up to something.'

'Gross calumny!' Rupert said, throwing up his hands.

'Well, you won't be able to idle about when conscription comes in,' Sylvia said sternly. 'That'll trim your sails for you.'

'We won't go,' said Erskine, without emphasis – almost drowsily. 'We'll have moral objections.'

'You'd better go and lurk with the Bedfordites, then,' said Sylvia. 'They're all madly anti-war.'

'Your drinks are better, darling,' said Rupert. 'On the subject of which...'

'In the next room, as always,' said Sylvia, and they wandered away.

'He's been very odd since his brother was killed,' Sylvia said, sitting down again. 'Poor boy, it hit him hard.'

'Were they very close?' Laura asked.

'Not that I ever knew,' said Sylvia. 'But he's certainly not been the same since.'

CHAPTER TWENTY-ONE

Mrs Farringdon, who was deputy chairman of the Rural District Council, recruited Beattie to the team handing out registration forms and collecting them in. They had to be given out in the week before Sunday, the 15th of August, and collected by the Wednesday following.

'Now, don't forget, it's the granite blue form for the men, and the white form for the women. Make sure you leave one for every member of the household, including the servants. And impress upon them that the section about any other skills they might have is important. Especially the retired men – oh, and any man who has changed his occupation. And tell the men *not* to list their wives under "dependants" because, of course, their wives will have their own forms.'

'That will ruffle some feathers,' Beattie said. 'Men are so touchy. And a lot of women won't want to fill in the form. They'll be used to their husbands handling everything of that sort.'

'I know, my dear,' said Mrs Farringdon. 'But you must *persist*. That's why we need *intelligent, patient* people like you to give out the forms.'

Beattie's first problem came with her own servants. Cook was not usually difficult, but she set her jaw at the sight of the form and would not take it, putting her hands behind her back. 'Master did the census just a few years ago. I remember it clearly.'

'This is something different. The government needs to know who everybody is and what they are good for. For the war effort.'

'I heard it's because conscription's coming in,' Ada said, eyeing her form nervously as though, like Moses' staff, it might turn into a snake in her hands.

'They're not conscripting women, surely to God!' Cook exclaimed. 'If women have to go and fight, that *will* be the end of the world!'

'Of course not,' Beattie said patiently. 'But there may be other things women can do at home to help.'

Cook looked mulish. 'I've got as much as I can do already, madam, cooking for everybody. I can't take on any more jobs.'

'I don't expect you'll be asked to,' Beattie said, understanding what Mrs Farringdon meant about patience. 'Just fill in "domestic servant, cook" where it says "occupation", and everything will be all right.'

Still Cook didn't take the form. 'I don't like it,' she said.

Beattie grew firm. 'I'm afraid you'll have to do it, under penalty of the law.'

'What penalty?' Cook asked suspiciously.

'A fine of five pounds,' said Beattie, sternly.

Cook sat down involuntarily. 'Five pounds! I haven't got five pounds!'

'Then you must fill in the form,' said Beattie, and this time Cook took it from her, and searched about for one last grumble, to save face.

'It'll be a fine thing, Emily filling in one of

these. Find out what people are good for? I'd like to know the answer to that one myself.'

Things were quiet along the front, and the army took advantage of the fact to deal with the matter of leave. Jack came home, preceded by a telegram, in which he instructed Beth not to try to meet him at the station. So she waited at home, walking from room to room, fiddling with things, uncertain as a bride. It would be the first time she had seen him since he was wounded, and she was unaccountably nervous.

He was to arrive at lunchtime, and when Mrs Beales had prepared a cold collation, she sent her out for the day so they could be alone together. Then she stationed herself at the front window, watching the traffic. Three times a taxi-cab slowing down gave her false hope. Then when a taxi did finally stop in front of the building, she had turned away to look at the clock and missed it. The doorbell ringing made her start so violently she bit her tongue.

She almost ran to the door, and there he was, in a uniform that looked strangely shabby and which didn't seem to fit him properly.

'Are you the lady of the house?' he said. 'I'm collecting for depraved and dissolute soldiers.'

'I'm sorry, I only give for handsome heroes,' she said. It was a clumsy imitation of their old manner and it made her eyes fill with tears.

'Oh, good Lord,' he said in alarm, 'no waterworks, please!'

'I'm not crying,' she said, closing the door behind him. 'How long have you got?'

'A whole glorious week,' he said. 'Not that it's nearly enough.'

'What would you like first? Food, or a bath?'

'Oh, food, to be sure. I need a bath, but I've been deloused, and breakfast is a distant memory. It wasn't very memorable to begin with. A bit of hard bacon, some stale bread, and a cup of brown water that disgraced the name of coffee. What have you got for me?'

'Mrs Beales put up a cold luncheon – chicken and salad and some other things. And I've a bottle of hock to go with it.'

'Angel! You think of everything. Lead me to it.'

She did, thinking with that same odd sense of awkwardness that they hadn't touched each other yet. No kiss had been offered from either side, not even a peck on the cheek. It was as if the Channel was still between them.

Perhaps the wine would help.

His appetite hadn't been affected, at any rate. She made a pretence of eating – her stomach was too unsettled to take much – and watched as he despatched his meal with rapid efficiency, drinking the best part of the bottle without her help. Only when they got to the raspberries and cream did he slow down. 'Glorious!' he said. 'My favourite fruit.'

'I know.'

'It must be a dream,' he said. 'We hardly see fruit of any sort from week to week, though I suppose they must grow it in France. Fancy, I missed the whole English strawberry season!'

She watched him as he ate, as they talked in-consequentially. It had been a shock when he first took off his cap. His hair was cut unbecomingly short, and it was going grey at the sides. There had been no grey last August. And perhaps it was the effect of the brutal haircut, but his face seemed quite gaunt. And though he smiled, the smile did not really reach his eyes. It took a lot of steady gazing at him for her to get used to it. He was like a stranger.

When he had finished with the raspberries, she poured him a brandy and went to the kitchen to make coffee.

'It's not as good as Mrs Beales's,' she said, returning, 'but I'll guarantee it's better than brown water.'

'Darling, it's in a cup at a civilised table. That makes it the best cup in the world.'

She poured for him and sat down. 'Was it very bad?'

A veil seemed to come down. 'Was what very bad?'

She waved a hand helplessly. 'The war. Ypres.'

'I wrote you letters about it.'

'Yes, but...' She sought words that would get through to him. He had told her *what* happened – or some of it. He had not told her what it had meant to *him*. 'I believe it was a close-run thing,' she said at last, hoping to cue him.

He made a strange sort of grimace. 'If the Boche had known at any point how stretched we were, it would have been a different story. Fortunately, whenever we were at breaking-point they seemed to get cold feet and backed off. And we were hell-ishly short of ammunition – counting out bullets like shillings.' He seemed to catch himself back.

371

'Quite a picnic, all in all,' he said lightly. 'You'd get yourself settled in one position, then have to go tearing off harum-scarum to reinforce some poor beleaguered company that suddenly found itself on the end of a Boche bashing. Then, as soon as it went quiet there, you'd be marched off to some other desperate fray. Military General Post.' He sipped coffee and seemed to hear himself. His tone changed and he went on jokingly, 'Trouble was your kit never caught up with you, so you'd none of those little luxuries that make life tolerable. And sometimes your rations couldn't find you, because you weren't where HQ thought you were. And as for sleep – well, we never caught up with *that!*'

'Oh, Jack,' she said, half concern, half reproach for putting her off.

'Oh, Beth!' he mimicked her. 'I told you in my letters. It was muddy,' he said. 'And noisy, my God! Those shells make such a racket. Like a whole hardware shop of pots and pans being thrown down a concrete staircase.'

'Can't you tell me, really, what it was like?' she pleaded.

'No, I really don't think I can,' he said. He sipped brandy. 'It's too long ago. I've had a lovely stay in a base hospital, and I've been out of the action ever since. I can't really remember Ypres. When I try to think of it, all I remember are the words in my letters. It's like the lines of a play. They don't mean anything when you're not on stage.'

She didn't understand, and looked at him, pained and enquiring.

'How did you get wounded?' she asked at last, quietly.

He made a restless movement. 'Didn't I tell you? I'm sure I told you. A shell went off nearby when we were marching back. A piece of shrapnel hit me amidships. That's all.' He stood up abruptly, as though he could not bear to sit there any longer. 'Let's not have any post-mortems. Put some music on. I haven't had any music for months.'

She put on a gramophone record without really knowing what it was. He sat down across the sitting-room with his brandy, but she could see he wasn't really listening any more than she was. When it got to the end of the side he stood up again and said, 'Is there any hot water? I'd like to take a bath.'

'I'll run it for you,' she said. 'Go and put on your dressing-gown.'

When the bath was full she went into the bedroom to tell him so and, moving quietly, walked in on him before he was ready. He jumped, and pulled the dressing-gown hastily round him, but not before she had seen, and was shocked. His white body was so much thinner, and between his ribs and his hip bone there was an ugly, puckered scar, like material clumsily cobbled together by someone unused to needlework.

He turned, tying the cord tightly, meeting her eyes with a look that was part wary, part hostile.

'Bath's ready,' she said. She tried to speak lightly but heard her voice wobble.

'Right,' he said. 'You don't need to come with me. I can manage alone.' He picked up his cigarettes and lighter and walked past her, entered the

373

bathroom and closed the door.

Beth sat down on the edge of the bed, not knowing what to do with herself. The sight of that wound was a horrible shock. She had known about it in theory, but seeing it made her realise exactly what he had lost. A flying piece of metal had cut into him. The integrity of his body had been breached. He was no longer, in that sense, whole. The thought of that metal ploughing through his flesh was an obscenity.

But, she realised now, the integrity of his mind had been breached as well. That was why he couldn't talk to her. He was not as he had been. He was not her Jack – not the man she had seen off to war.

She wanted to cry, but the pain was too deep. Would she ever be able to touch him again? Would they ever find a way back to each other?

She sat staring at her hands, her mind revolving painfully and uselessly, until the striking of a clock downstairs brought her back to herself, and she realised he had been far too long in the bathroom. The water would be cold by now, but he had not come out. A nameless dread seized her, vague shadowy thoughts of drowning and razors flitted like bats through her mind. She got to her feet and went to the bathroom door, listened, heard nothing, hesitated, afraid of provoking him to anger against her. Then she thought, *I am his wife. I have every right.* And she turned the knob and stepped in.

He was asleep. For a single instant she thought he was dead, he was so white under the unloving light from the bare bulb. His face looked sunken;

his head was resting back on the bath's rim and his mouth had fallen open in a horribly deathlike way. Her heart contracted so hard she felt it like an iron pain in her chest. But then he snored. Not dead, but asleep – too exhausted to wake even when the water got cold.

She seized a towel and went across, pulled the plug, and as the sound and movement of draining water disturbed him he opened his eyes in a drugged way and said, 'Eh?'

'You're at home, in London,' she said, afraid for his sanity. 'You fell asleep in the bath.'

'Ugh,' he said. His hands – *they* were still strong – gripped the edges of the bath and he heaved himself up. He seemed to be beyond any awareness of her seeing him naked. His ribs lay like bars across his body, lit from above; his genitals were shrunk and childlike from the cold water; the scar was like an evil, wry mouth that might suddenly say cruel things to her. She wrapped the towel around his waist and hid it and his tender parts at once.

She helped him out – he pressed heavily on her shoulder for balance. It was a warm evening, thank God, but he was shivery from the cold water. She grabbed her own towel and rubbed his back and shoulders and head while he dried the lower half. After a moment he walked out from under her hands without a word, passed into the bedroom, dropping the towel just inside the door, climbed into bed, and fell instantly back into the same heavy sleep.

When she had tidied the bathroom she went back to him, but he had turned and was sprawled

375

slantwise across the bed, face down, abandoned as a beached starfish.

There was no room for her there. She slept that night in the spare room – not that she slept much. She kept waking, not knowing where she was, or thinking she had heard him call out; would listen in the darkness until she heard him snore, or breathe. Some of the time she just lay there, staring at the invisible ceiling, thinking of her laughing, loving husband, wondering if she would ever see him again. A small part of her – which she hated because it was ungenerous – wondered if he had sprawled across the bed deliberately to stop her sleeping beside him.

It's the war, she told herself. *War changes people.*

Then she thought of Diana. *At least he came back.*

At the beginning of August the North Midland Rifles got orders for France at last, and David and Oliphant were given forty-eight hours' embarkation leave. Oliphant was going home. Unfortunately, his family had gone down to the country a couple of weeks earlier.

'So it's a ridiculous journey and I'll only just about have time to get there and back,' he complained, 'but I suppose it's better than nothing. At least I'll see them.'

'Would you mind if I came with you?' David asked.

'But your home is closer than mine. You'd have more time with your family than I shall have.'

David looked embarrassed, but only said, 'Please, Jumbo. I'm sure your mother wouldn't mind.'

'I'm sure she wouldn't. She's always liked you better than me.'

'Oh, rot!'

'Every mother wants a handsome son,' Jumbo said indifferently. He didn't in the least mind not being handsome, like David. He thought it would save him a lot of trouble in the long run. Good-looking people had expectations, and others had expectations of them. Anything he, Jumbo, achieved would be a nice surprise all round.

But he cared for his friend, and studied his reddening face carefully. 'Look here,' he said, 'if it's Sophy–'

'I know,' David said hastily. 'Humphrey Hobart. But a girl can change her mind, can't she? Lady's privilege, and all that.'

'She changes hers every five minutes,' Jumbo said disparagingly.

'There you are, then. And she hasn't seen me since I got my pips. That might make a difference. It would be awfully feeble of me not even to give it a try, don't you think?'

Jumbo shrugged. 'Up to you, old fellow. I can only warn you.' He sighed. 'I just don't know what you see in her.'

'Of course not. You're her brother.' A mischievous thought came to him. 'Just think of the way you feel about Bertha Dale.'

Now it was Jumbo's turn to redden. 'Miss Dale doesn't know I exist.'

The all-too-brief visit was almost over, and David had had no moment alone with Sophy. On the journey there, his spirits had risen, with the hope that the uniform and the new pips would out-weigh the advantage that Humphrey Hobart had by being on hand. The signals he had received were mixed. She seemed pleased to see him, greeted him with a handshake and a most becoming blush, and listened with smiling interest to his tales of their adventures on Salisbury Plain. On the other hand, Humphrey Hobart seemed to come into the conversation rather often. Some of this was doubtless due to Mrs Oliphant, who seemed to favour his suit, and explained at un-necessary length that his father had a very nice estate that he would inherit, that he was a fine rider to hounds and a most elegant dancer. When she expatiated on his virtues, Sophy listened complacently; however, she did not expound them herself, which David chose to believe meant she had not made up her mind.

After luncheon, David thought a walk in the garden might provide the ideal opportunity for him to speak; but when he suggested it to Sophy, Mr Oliphant jumped up, saying it was an excellent idea, good for the digestion, and that he particularly wanted to show David his new herbaceous bed. 'I know your father is very fond of a garden. You may take an account back to him when you next see him. My *Astrantia carniolica* from Finland has settled in at last and is doing beautifully. Of course, you've missed the flowers, but I think you'll see how vigorous it is. I'm afraid the garden was looking much better two weeks ago...'

David went with him perforce, thinking it was odd that, whatever time of year you visited, garden enthusiasts always said the garden had looked better shortly before you arrived. Sophy walked with them for a while, but then gently detached herself and wandered off, and he heard her from a distance playing a two-handed game of croquet with her brother. When he finally got away from the horticulturalist and hurried to find brother and sister, he discovered that a female friend of hers had called, and he was obliged to make a fourth in a game that lasted, tediously, until tea-time.

They were to leave that evening after an early dinner. His only chance would be between tea and dinner. Fortunately, while they were at tea, the sky darkened and a persistent sort of rain set in. Tea over, the female friend wished to depart, and Jumbo was required by his mother to hold the umbrella over her on her way home. Sophy said she was going up to the old nursery – which the younger folk had long used as a sitting-room – for a book. David, finding no-one was looking at him, seized the opportunity to sidle out of the room and follow her. Now, he thought, treading up the stairs in her wake, if only Jumbo dawdled, and especially as long as Humphrey Hobart didn't take it into his mind to visit...

Sophy was by the bookcase, trailing her fingers idly along the shelves as if searching for something to read, but as soon as he came in she abandoned the quest and went to sit on the window-seat, tucking a foot under her and leaning her cheek in her hand and her elbow on the windowsill. It was a very fetching pose.

As David approached, she sighed. 'How I hate a rainy evening! Nothing to do, and no-one will visit while it's like this.'

The background of streaming glass and wet trees against a low grey sky made her seem, to David, to be outlined in light. Her dress was of apple green, figured in white, high-waisted and rather flowing; her abundant hair was drawn into a large, loose knot at the back. She was like a pre-Raphaelite goddess, he thought. In her green gown, she could be Pomona: trees would flourish and become laden with fruit when she passed by. He imagined her barefoot, hair loose and flowing, stepping on the soft turf of an old orchard, perhaps with a wreath of blossom round her head.

'Come and sit down and talk to me,' she said, leaning forward and patting the other half of the seat. She stretched her white arm, then covered her mouth daintily with the back of her hand as she yawned. 'Sundays are so boring, aren't they?' And then she rested her cheek against her other hand, tilting her head over, and smiled at him.

He sat down, completely tongue-tied. How could he be worthy of such a creature? And yet he dared not let this chance pass. He wished he had something to present to her – a rose, a poem – that would declare his love without his having to find words. He thought of the poems he had written at St Monica's and shuddered. He could never have shown her those! In Latin, he thought, he might have expressed himself better; but Sophy knew no Latin.

'You're very quiet,' Sophy said. 'I expect you're thinking about having to go away. Poor David. But you look very nice in your uniform.'

'Do you think so?' he said eagerly.

'Oh, yes – especially now you're an officer.'

'I hoped you'd think that,' he said.

'Me? What is it to do with me?' she asked demurely, developing two dimples he hadn't noticed before.

'Everything has to do with you,' he said. 'Everything I do. Everything I think.'

'Really, David, I don't think you ought to talk that way to me.'

'I have to,' he said desperately. 'If I don't now, when will I have another chance? We're going to France, Sophy. To the war. We shall be in battle sometime soon.'

'So I imagine.'

'Won't that concern you?' David asked. 'Won't you care? I might be wounded.'

She turned her face away from him, so that he saw her profile as she looked out of the window. It was an exquisite profile, painted by Alma-Tadema on a particularly good day. The soft, dark mass of her hair, the white column of her neck, and the delicate little curls at her temple made him feel quite hollow with love.

'Of course I'll care,' she said softly. Then she spoiled it a little by adding, 'I'd care about any brave young man fighting for his country.'

David said, a trifle peevishly, 'I wonder you don't tell that to Humphrey Hobart. He isn't even in uniform.'

She looked at him now, delight dancing in her eyes. 'Why, what on earth has he got to do with it?'

'Your brother told me you were sweet on him. That you're walking out with him–'

381

'Freddie doesn't know what he's talking about. I'm not walking out with him. His mother and Mummy are very good friends, so of course I see him sometimes. He visits here and we visit there. We go for walks, and he takes me out in his motor-car sometimes.'

Hope leaped up in David's breast. 'So you're not serious about him?'

'I don't know. He *is* very nice. And it's nice to have someone to dance with, and to take one to tennis parties.' David scowled. He couldn't help it. Sophy went on serenely, 'On the other hand, there's something so manly about someone in uniform. I sometimes think Humphrey *ought* to have volunteered, like Freddie.'

'And me,' David urged.

'I can't say about you. You're not my brother.'

'I'd like to be something a great deal more than a brother to you,' David said. The words startled him when he heard them. Somehow, he had come to the point.

They seemed to surprise Sophy, too. The teasing look went out of her face, to be replaced with something thoughtful, perhaps searching. She regarded him gravely. 'I don't know what you mean,' she said.

'I think you do,' he said. 'You must do. Oh, Sophy, it can't have escaped your notice that I'm in love with you.' She didn't reply, but she didn't draw back. Encouraged, he reached out and took her hand, and when she didn't object, his heart surged with hope. How small and white it was, resting in his brown one! 'I've been longing to go to France ever since the war started, but the one thing I hate about going away is not being able to see you. I think about you all the time. I write long letters to you in my head, but in real life, the best I can do is send you my regards when Jumbo writes a letter home. My *regards!*'

'It's very nice when you do,' she said demurely. 'Freddie does pass it on, you know. He's a decentish stick for a brother.'

'We'll be in France in two days at the most. And all the time I shall be thinking about you being here, and me out there, and other fellows, who haven't volunteered, who can see you whenever they like, while I can't even–' He choked.

'David, what are you trying to say?'

He summoned his courage. 'If we were engaged, I could write to you properly, and you could write to me. And when the war's over, when I come back, we could get married. My father wants me to follow him into banking and it's a pretty decent career, so I'd be able to support a wife and so on. And we'd be so happy! Oh, Sophy, what do you say?'

She continued to look at him gravely. 'You haven't asked me a question yet. I can't answer the question until you ask it.'

He slipped off the seat and onto his knees in front of her, which happily brought his face on a level with hers. 'Sophy, I love you with all my heart. I've loved you since the first moment I saw you. You're the most beautiful girl I've ever met. If you'll have me, I'll give my life to serving you. Will you marry me?'

There was a silence, which seemed long and agonising to him. She searched his face, and he felt himself unworthy to be there, unworthy of anything but a rejection.

And at last she spoke. 'Yes,' she said. 'I will marry you.'

He had no words. He kissed her hand fervently, and then, seeing permission in her eyes, he kissed her lips. A pang shot through him. They were amazingly soft, and somehow she smelt of gardenias. He felt all sorts of passions surging up in him, felt himself grip her hand more tightly, his lips grow harder; and with an effort he pulled himself away before he lost control.

She was looking at him now with an expression that was almost dazed. 'Oh, David,' she breathed. 'I didn't realise...'

'Sophy,' he said. 'Oh, my darling!'

He wanted to kiss her again, though he knew it was dangerous, but she drew back a little and said, 'You'll have to ask my father's permission. But I expect it will be all right. I know he likes you.'

'We'd better go and see him now,' David said. 'There isn't much time.' Still holding her hand, he drew her to her feet, and looked down at her, smiling with triumph now. 'You're not going to change your mind?'

'What sort of a question is that to ask a girl?' she said, with a little of the old tease. And then, seeing something greater, stronger, more noble in his face, she grew serious. 'No,' she said. 'I shan't change my mind.'

It was not what Mr Oliphant wanted. Humphrey Hobart was a young man of property, quiet, steady, known to the family, in the same interest.

David Hunter was an unknown quantity. Of course, the Hunters were well-to-do, but that was not the same as land. David would have to earn his living. And he was going off to the front. That was a consideration. If Humphrey went, there was every chance he would have enough notice to marry Sophy first, and then she would be in possession whatever happened.

But he was a tender-hearted man when it came to his daughter, and if she loved the fellow (and one could quite see why she would: Humphrey could not hold a candle to him for looks, presence, physique – brains, too), he did not want to break her heart. There was no time to ponder the matter, as it stood – he must give his permission or withhold it before the boys went off to catch their train, he saw that. Well, well, David was a good boy. He had known him for years, through his son, and had seen nothing but seriousness of purpose and strong moral values in him. If Sophy wanted him, well, it would probably turn out all right.

And, of course, if he fell in France, that would resolve the matter anyway.

He stood up, shook his hand, clapped him on the shoulder, and said, very well.

David and Sophy were now licensed to spend a half-hour alone together in the back parlour saying goodbye, holding hands and kissing at intervals. 'I wish I had a ring to give you,' he said. 'I don't even have a signet ring. If I get a chance to, I'll buy something in France and send it to you, just for show, until I can buy you a proper one. Would you like that?'

'Yes, yes, please. Oh, but, David, I don't like to

think of you going into battle.' It had come home to her, since they had come downstairs. He and Freddie, both, were going to be risking their lives. There were casualty lists in the newspapers – not that she read them, but she knew they were there. People got hurt. People got *killed*. Hadn't David's own sister lost her *fiancé?* 'You will be careful, won't you?'

'Don't worry, I'm coming back to you, safe and sound – I'll see to that! We have our whole lives ahead of us. Do you think I'd miss out on that?'

She looked at him with renewed confidence. He was so tall, so strong, like a great Viking warrior. There was something indestructible about him. One simply couldn't imagine him any other way but brimming with life and health. 'You'll take care of Freddie, too, won't you?' she begged.

Time ran out, and the two young men had to take their leave. Nothing was said between them until they were settled on the train. By then a little of David's euphoria had evaporated. He felt – as Mr Oliphant had, though he didn't know it – that the shortness of time had worked in his favour. He had a sense of having scraped through by the skin of his teeth – a sense of disaster narrowly averted.

But Sophy was his, lovely Sophy! Nothing could change that. He would have to write to his parents. He was of age, and didn't need their permission in law, but he wanted it. He couldn't see any reason why they would object. And he must write to Antonia Weston – he looked forward to writing *that* letter. How pleased she would be for him!

He took out his cigarettes, and offered one to

Jumbo. Jumbo leaned forward to take the light David offered, and said, as he breathed out smoke, 'Well, old man. You did it.'

'You might sound a bit happier about it,' David said. 'Remember, you aren't losing a sister, you're gaining a brother.'

'You were already my brother,' Jumbo said.

David cocked an eye. 'Aren't you pleased? Do you think I'm not worthy of her? I wouldn't blame you if you did.'

Jumbo sighed. 'I suppose if I said she's not worthy of you, you'd black my eye.'

'No, but I'd wonder why you'd say something so mad.'

'Mad, yes, that's what it is. Love is a madness – don't the poets say so? And you can't argue with lunatics.' He saw David was frowning now, and went on more lightly, 'Pay no attention to me – I'm raving. Tired, that's all. All this travelling about. What I'd give for a decent bed and a long lie-in, breakfast on a tray, my bath run for me, and the whole day to do nothing in.'

'No chance of that for a while,' David said. 'It'll be standing-to at dawn and army rations until we beat the Boche. But seriously, Jumbo, you are happy for me, aren't you?'

'Yes, old chap,' Oliphant said. 'If you're happy, I'm happy.' Marriage was always a gamble, anyway, and the unlikeliest pairings sometimes worked out all right. There was never any point in wondering what fellows saw in the women they chose, he thought.

CHAPTER TWENTY-TWO

Beattie had plenty more doubts, questions and arguments to deal with on giving out the census forms. She rather marvelled at herself, going round from house to house, knocking on the doors of strangers, standing up to sullen men who didn't want her talking to their wives – and all with the composure of a Suffragette, she thought, with a wry smile. The war had certainly changed her. This time last year she had moved in such a small circle. The sort of people she was addressing on their doorsteps had been mere background scenery in her theatre – there to give verisimilitude to her daily drama, but not really relevant to her.

At the corner of Oaklands Road her territory met that of Mrs Fitzgerald, and she saw the rector's lady just coming out of a house a little way down. She gave her a nod, thinking it enough at that distance, but Mrs Fitzgerald raised her hand and hurried towards her.

'I see we are on the same mission,' said Mrs Fitzgerald. 'Have you had much difficulty? How tiresome people can be!' she continued, without waiting for an answer. 'It's a perfectly simple form to fill in, but some people make such a fuss.'

'They're not accustomed to filling in forms,' said Beattie. 'I suppose it's something we will have to get used to, if the war goes on, but most people have never had any sort of contact with officialdom. It makes them nervous.'

'Oh, I know!' Mrs Fitzgerald said impatiently. 'We see it all the time at the rectory. The number of people who come to get married, and tell us they have no birth certificate! It makes so much extra work for everyone. I've just had *such* a tussle with the Bedlingtons' gardener. Said he wasn't going to tell the government *anything* about himself, thank you very much. That it was none of their business. Or mine. I was obliged to remind him sharply that there was a war on, and it was *everyone*'s business to make an effort.'

'Their gardener doesn't live there, does he?' Beattie said. 'Surely his form will be delivered to his home. You didn't need to approach him.'

'Oh, I dare say he might get a form at home,' said Mrs Fitzgerald, 'but I thought it best to tackle him anyway, as he was there. I could see he would be a hard case.'

In fact, Beattie thought, *you couldn't help interfering.* But she cancelled that thought with a reproach to herself for being unchristian, and said, 'Well, I must get on.'

'Oh, by the way, Mrs Hunter,' said Mrs Fitzgerald, catching her back with a touch on the arm, 'I must tell you about my dear nephew, Adolphus. I had a letter from him to say that his commanding officer thinks so well of him, he is putting him forward for a commission.'

This, Beattie realised, was not at all 'by the way' but the reason Mrs Fitzgerald had stopped her in the first place. She listened patiently to a recital of Mr Beamish's virtues, his quickness to learn, his perfection of execution, his immense popularity, his inborn powers of leadership. But when she got to the unprecedented quickness of his promotion from the ranks, some inner imp drove her to produce Bobby, sent for officer training after a mere six weeks' basic training.

Mrs Fitzgerald was taken aback. Her eyes narrowed; but she recovered and found a smile that managed to be both triumphant and patronising. 'Ah, but your Bobby was in the Officer Training Corps, wasn't he? That gave him an advantage. My Adolphus had to rely on his *natural talent* for soldiering. Now I must be off, Mrs Hunter. Delightful as it is to chat, I have my duties to attend to.'

Beattie watched her go, shaking her head in wonder at how the rector's wife could manage to make being in OTC seem like cheating, and her own delivery of census papers a higher form of activity than Beattie's.

David's letter came by the afternoon post, and was waiting for her when she got back, too late for tea. It looked as if there had been none served in the drawing-room – everybody must have been out. She put her hat and gloves on the hall table and took the letter through to the morning-room to read it.

It was full of unpleasant shocks. First, that his battalion was going to the front – indeed, by the time she read this, he said, he would already be in France. So it had come, the thing she had been dreading! The process of training, which had seemed interminably long to him, had been her safeguard. She would have been glad for him to fail every test and stay in training for ever. But once he had gone to officer training school, she had known that he would not fail. The army, Edward told her, was desperately short of officers; and he was David, who really had the qualities of leadership Mrs Fitzgerald imagined in her nephew. He had chosen not to join the OTC at school, preferring intellectual pursuits to physical, as his father had before him, but had he done so, there was no doubt he would have excelled.

I don't want you to be an excellent officer, she thought. Excellent officers were brave, led their men into the thick of battle, and got killed. *I'd sooner you were a coward and lived.* But it had come. He was in France, and soon, when the summer lull was over, he would be in action.

There was a second shock. She had been wondering why he had not had embarkation leave. Now she read that he had chosen to go to the Oliphants' instead of coming home.

The third shock explained the second. 'I am engaged.' For an instant blind fury gripped her. Sophy Oliphant, his friend's sister, that viper in the bosom! She must have tricked him. He could not possibly love her – could not know her well enough. She was a child, a chit.

Besides, what man fell in love with his friend's schoolroom sister? Her *being* Oliphant's sister ought to have made him immune – he had seen her in plaits, in pinafores, with *spots!* The magic, the beguilement that captured men's fancies, ought to have been missing.

'I know I don't need your permission now I am of age, but I hope I will have your blessing. More,

I hope and trust you will be delighted for me, and welcome my Sophy into the family with all your heart.'

As fury ebbed, Beattie felt a moment of weariness. She thought of the Wroughtons, the agonising social occasions, trying to join like with unlike; the minefield of wedding preparations. *I can't go through it all again!* Of course, this time it was the Oliphants who would have to arrange the wedding. But sitting through dinner with them, finding things to talk about! Pretending to embrace the girl, when she really wanted to drive a stake through her heart!

And at the end of it, David would be lost to her. Her precious, her beloved, the love of her life, would belong to another woman, who would receive the love and confidences that ought to be hers.

She came back to the present to realise that she had crushed the letter into a ball in her clenched hand. She straightened it out gently, tried to stroke away the creases with a finger. It was *his* letter, his words; his hand had held the pen. And who knew how many more there would be?

She shook away the thought. He would come back. He would be safe. No Charles Wroughton, he. He was quick and clever and full of energy. Wroughton she could imagine stumbling, not nimble enough to get out of the way. David, her salamander, would thrive in the fire, and he would come back. But, oh, not to her!

Because of the collection of the census forms, the annual holiday in Bournemouth could not be arranged for the usual time. Instead, the rooms were taken from the 21st of August. Last year, everyone had been too excited and matters too uncertain to go away. But this year they were settling into the rhythms of the war. Beattie was tired, and could see that Sadie was rushing between her horses and the hospital visiting – and sad, too, because of the death of the nice young officer she used to visit. Being Sadie, she did not talk about it, but Beattie saw it.

Diana was still in mourning, of course, though Beattie thought the visiting had helped her a little, enabling her to see a bigger picture. Still, it would do her good to go away somewhere that did not remind her constantly of her loss. The boys were not so afraid this year of missing something, and remembered the delights of Bournemouth, the sea and the sand, with longing. And, of course, the servants had to have their holiday.

Cook was going to her sister in Folkestone, and would take Emily with her. Emily didn't usually enjoy these visits, but she had heard there was a large army camp near Folkestone with the result that the town was full of soldiers; and while she was no Ethel, she thought their presence might add to the fun.

Ada was going to stay with her cousin, who had a farm on the far side of Gosford. Helping on the farm was harder work than housemaiding, but it was holiday enough for her to see a different view from the windows, hear different conversation, and enjoy someone else's cooking.

Ethel would not tell anyone what her plans were. To begin with, she had none. Though she complained vociferously about her work, the idea of leisure, when it became reality and not fantasy, rather frightened her. She did not like walking or reading, and everything else cost money. She had no friends, and was not good at making them. And, besides, where could she go? To lay out money on bed and board was out of the question. But to stay here and admit she had nowhere to go was equally impossible. She had no option but to adopt a lofty secrecy.

It didn't occur to her to discuss her problem with Eric: she had never had a spark who was interested in her welfare, or one in whom she could confide. But the worry of it made her so moody that he was finally driven to worm it out of her. Having confessed, she waited for him to laugh at her; but he looked serious and said, 'I'll give it some thought. Don't worry, we'll work something out.'

The word 'we' in that context so surprised her that she had nothing to say. They went into the Electric Palace at Westleigh, and she was so distracted by wondering what it meant that she did not get the full enjoyment out of Theda Bara in *A Fool There Was*, and even missed the dialogue card that said, 'Kiss me, my fool!', which made most of the audience gasp with its louche directness.

The next time she saw him, he had a solution for her. 'You know the Swan Hotel in Westleigh?'

'Of course I do,' Ethel said. 'What about it?'

He told her one of the chaps of his acquaintance in Westleigh – he worked in the signal box – was called Danny Carroll, and his mother was the pastry-cook at the Swan. 'And I remembered he told me once that they take on temporary staff in August, so the regular staff can have their holidays. Well, I asked him if they're hiring now, and he told me his mum said they're short of waitresses in the restaurant.'

'Waitresses?'

'Yes, don't you see? It's the perfect solution for you. You'll have somewhere to go, and you'll get paid into the bargain. Tips, as well. A pretty girl like you ought to do especially well for tips.'

The idea of pay *and* tips was attractive. 'But I've never been a waitress,' Ethel objected.

'You've served your family in the dining-room. It can't be that different – except you might have to move a bit quicker.' He grinned. 'Anyway, you're smart as a whip – you'll pick it up in no time. Why don't you pop along and see the manager, before they get someone else and you lose your chance?'

'Oh, I don't know,' Ethel said doubtfully.

'The best bit is, you'll be able to come and go as you like, when you're not working. No having to ask permission to go out. And since I live in Westleigh...'

She felt the irksome burden of gratitude fall on her shoulders, and rallied. 'You think a lot of yourself, Eric Travers!' she retorted. 'Don't flatter yourself I have to spend every spare minute with you. I have other admirers, you know.'

'Of course you do – thousands of them! Well, it's up to you – it seems like a good idea to me, but if you've got a better...'

She hadn't. She went to see the manager, and invented a story about being between jobs, and some spurious waitressing experience. He didn't believe her, but he was impressed by her prettiness and liveliness, and was desperate in any case, having lost two of his waiters to the recruiting sergeant, and having staff holidays to cope with.

'All right, the job's yours. There's a room vacant, if you want to live in–'

That was welcome news to Ethel. She nodded.

'You've got a black dress, I take it? Black stockings and shoes. We provide cap and apron. Show me your hands. No warts or bitten nails? Good. Make sure you keep 'em clean. Breakfast is six thirty to nine thirty, lunch is eleven thirty to two thirty and dinner is seven to nine. You'll work two of the three shifts every day. You keep your tips, bar the ten per cent that comes to me. Any questions?'

Ethel had none. She was still calculating that she would have at the most six hours' work a day, and the rest of the time to herself. If Eric's shifts worked out happily, she could see a lot more of him. And there would be something – quite a bit, if the tips were good – to add to her savings account, the money she was putting by for the day when she could get out of domestic service and into a new life. Some girls called it bottom-drawer money or trousseau money, but to Ethel it had always been her running-away money.

The manager was looking at her curiously, wondering what her story was, hoping she wouldn't cause him trouble.

Ethel came back from her reverie, caught the look and wondered about the living-in bit. She hoped he wouldn't cause her trouble.

Edward did not go to Bournemouth. The later than usual date happily meant he had missed his club's annual closing and would be able to stay there for the two weeks.

'Won't you come down at all?' Beattie asked, seeing the answer in his face.

'I don't think I shall be able to, but we'll see. Perhaps the middle weekend.'

He looked at his wife with compassion. He knew how much she had been upset by David's going to France, however inevitable it had been, but he hoped that would be offset to some extent by pleasure in his engagement to be married. It was nice for her, he thought, that David had picked a girl they knew, rather than coming home with a stranger. And the Oliphants were decent people, people of their own sort. The strains of trying to mingle with the Wroughton set would not be a feature of David's nuptials.

'You look tired, dear,' he said. 'You need a thorough holiday. Just enjoy doing nothing for a fortnight, and put everything out of your head.'

'I will,' said Beattie, 'if you promise to come down that weekend.'

'If I possibly can,' he said. Catching a Saturday-afternoon train down and an early Monday-morning train back left too little time there to make it worth all the travelling – and trains these days were not what they had been before the war. But he saw it was important to her, so he said, 'I promise.'

Sadie *was* tired but, all the same, she didn't want

to leave her work at Highclere. They had just received a new batch of horses, apparently gathered up from all over the country, and this time they seemed completely unbroken.

'They're scraping the bottom of the barrel,' Mrs Cuthbert said. 'The army's sucked in all the possibles and now they're sending us the impossibles.'

'There'll be so much to do,' Sadie said. 'Couldn't I come and stay with you, instead of going to Bournemouth?'

'No, Sadie dear, I couldn't ask it. And I think your mother would be quite upset.'

'She wouldn't mind,' Sadie asserted.

'I'm sure she would! No, a family holiday is a good and necessary thing. And we don't need you so much in the early stages, anyway. You know we promised your father there would be no rodeos for you.'

'But I can do other things – handling them, getting them used to being groomed, led exercise.'

Mrs Cuthbert was adamant. 'In any case,' she said, 'Captain Casimir told me they were sending us some extra help very soon, and I expect it will come while you're away.'

It came before Sadie left, and did nothing to settle her mind. It was just one man, Private Higgins, who was regular army but unfit for combat. 'Can't do the marching,' he said. 'I'm a martyr to me feet.'

Sadie didn't like the look of him. He was bony and pale, with a pinched, sly, adenoidal sort of face, and small eyes, usually narrowed against the smoke from the cigarette that was always glued to his lower lip. He had about him the ingratiating air of the dog that fawns in front of you, then slips behind you to bite your heels. The small eyes were cold, and she was afraid he would be cruel to the horses.

And then there were the officers she visited at Mount Olive. Anne Carruthers said she would be sure to visit them for her, but though Sadie was fond of Anne, she didn't think she was a real substitute. She didn't have a great deal of conversation, and had a tendency to giggle.

Edward found the two weeks strangely restful. The club was dedicated to his comfort, with none of the competing demands that were inevitable at home. If he sat down to read the newspaper, no-one would disturb him until he wanted to be disturbed, for the bringing of coffee or a drink. If there was a disaster in the kitchen, or one of the servants had an ailment, he would not hear about it. He could sit alone at dinner if he wanted, and no-one would dream of trying to talk to him. On the other hand, if he wanted company, it was there to be had, in masculine form, charged with proper masculine conversation. He would not like it for a permanency, of course, but for two weeks it was a very pleasant change.

London had not emptied as it used to in August before the war, but it had thinned a little, which meant it was easier to get a taxi or a table. The news from the war was not good. At the Paris conference, Lord Kitchener had made what Lord Forbesson, who had been there for the War Office, called 'the devil's compact' with the French commander, Joffre.

'It was all done in private talks away from the table,' Forbesson said, with a shake of the head, 'walking about in the garden. It should never have been allowed. Trouble is, K speaks perfect French – better than his aides. Means they can't keep a collar on him.'

Edward was taking a glass of sherry with him in the drawing-room before dinner. Forbesson was hosting a dinner for colleagues from his other club, which was closed for its annual refurbishment, but they had not arrived yet, so he was happy to pass a quiet half-hour with Edward.

'The conference had been going so well,' Forbesson mourned. 'Everything as smooth as you like. All in agreement. No new major offensive on the western front until next year, when we shall have enough Kitchener men ready, and the eastern front not to be given up, but just maintained. And then off he goes with Joffre – that dashed old libertine, with his smiles and his charm and urbanity – and the next thing we know, K's back with a whole new agreement.'

'And what was that?' Edward asked.

'Joffre apparently wasn't prepared to wait until next year for an offensive on French soil. And Kitchener wasn't prepared to mark time in the Dardanelles. So in return for permission for an attack in the peninsula, K agreed to a new joint offensive on the western front this autumn, and even said Joffre could choose the place and the time.'

'Ah,' said Edward, 'was that how it came about?'

The action in the Dardanelles – a new landing at

Suvla Bay, with diversionary attacks at Anzac and Cape Helles – had been a disaster. The diversions had worked, but the officer commanding at Suvla Bay had delayed consolidating the advantage. The Turks had discovered the ruse, scrambled back to the position and dug in on the high ground. The British had suffered heavy losses – the 32nd Brigade was virtually wiped out – and the stalemate in Gallipoli was unchanged.

'So now we're committed to a joint attack on Joffre's terms?' he said.

'That's right,' said Forbesson. 'Can't give you too many details, of course, but I know you can keep your mouth shut. It'll be in September for sure and somewhere around the coal-mining district, near Lens.'

'My boy's battalion's just gone out to France,' Edward said.

'Well, he's in good company,' said Forbesson. 'About a hundred battalions have gone out since July.' He finished his sherry. 'Let's hope they're ready.' A servant came to tell him his guests had arrived, and he stood up to take his leave.

Aeneas Palfrey was similarly orphaned, his family having gone to Brighton for the whole month – though that journey was much shorter and he contrived to go down most weekends. Edward met him for dinner one evening. They went to the Savoy, for a change from club food, and Palfrey was a little shocked when, having been conducted to their table and handed the menus by a waiter, a waitress came to take their order. When she had gone, he said to Edward, 'Now I've seen it all! Whatever next? Females serving you in Turnbull & Asser? Have they got females in your club yet?'

'Not yet,' Edward said. 'We've got a lot of very old servants, too old to join up. And a few boys – though I suppose we'll lose *them* if conscription comes in.'

'You say "if"?' Aeneas said alertly.

'The government doesn't want to bring it in, of course. I believe they'll have another try at voluntary enlistment this autumn. But most of the fellows I've spoken to think it's inevitable. You're thinking of Donald?'

'I don't know how I could possibly manage without him,' said Aeneas. 'And there are my skilled machinists. I suppose,' he added doubtfully, 'women could be taught their work, but how long would it take, and how much disruption to production would there be? Don't you think,' he appealed, 'that as I'm on a government contract, I could get a dispensation?'

'I'm not the man to ask,' Edward said. 'Certainly you can try. I mean to fight like the dickens if they try to take my secretary.'

'Damn the Boche,' Aeneas said gloomily. 'It comes to something when war starts to affect life back home. Like the damned blackout and the Zeppelins – though we haven't seen so much of *them* recently.'

'Short summer nights,' Edward said. 'They don't get enough cover of darkness to get here and back again.'

'Is that it? Then I suppose, now the days are drawing in, they'll be back again. Civilisation itself is under attack, my friend! Do you know, when the memsahib popped into Selfridges the other day, there was a *girl* running the lift? A girl! In a sort of page-boy uniform above and a skirt below.'

'*Ruat caelum!*' Edward said, but with a grin – catching sight of which, Aeneas started to grin himself.

'Oh, well,' he conceded. 'Perhaps the heavens can withstand a female lift attendant.'

The waitress approached and addressed Aeneas. 'I'm very sorry, sir, but the Dover sole is off.'

'*Off?*' Aeneas yelped.

'I'm sorry, sir. We have some very nice turbot instead.'

'No Dover sole? The Boche have gone too far this time!'

'It wasn't the war, sir,' the waitress informed him. 'It was just an unusual number of gentlemen ordering it, and we've run out. But the turbot is very nice, sir.'

'Very well, bring me turbot. And cyanide for two afterwards with the coffee,' he added, when she had gone.

After dinner, as the evening was fine, Edward went with him along the Embankment to Charing Cross to catch his train home. They walked slowly, smoking cigars, enjoying the mild air and the movement of the river. Twice they were approached by young females wondering if they were lonely.

The second was so young, and looked so starved, that Edward gave her a florin to go away. 'There's a pie stall under Waterloo Bridge,' he told her, and watched her scurry off.

'There's more of that these days than there used to be,' Aeneas said.

As they passed Cleopatra's Needle, there were shadowy shapes engaged in close wrestling down in the well. The male shapes were in uniform. Edward thought of his sister, and shook his head. The war was changing things fast – too fast for the likes of him and his brother-in-law.

Having seen Aeneas to the station, he found himself restless, and took a leisurely stroll back, through Trafalgar Square and up the Haymarket. The theatres were letting out, and he had to move to the outer edge of the pavement to avoid those issuing from the Theatre Royal. In the press he thought he glimpsed a face he recognised, though he could not for the moment think who it was. And then a small figure wriggled clear, and came towards him with a beaming smile.

'I thought it was you I saw over the 'eads,' she said, extending her hand.

Edward bowed over it. 'Madame de Rouveroy,' he said. 'What a pleasant surprise.' He looked around to see whom she was with, and she laughed. 'I see you, Edward, you think I must have someone to escort me, but I am alone. Is it very shocking for a lady to go to the theatre alone?'

'It's not for me to say,' Edward said.

'But you think it is, I can tell. But consider, I have no-one, and one must go to the theatre. It is a condition of life, *n'est-ce pas?*'

Edward managed quite well to live without the theatre, but he bowed again, allowing the conceit. 'Was it a good play?' he asked.

She made that little *pfft* explosion of the lips that was so entirely French. 'The title was the best thing about it,' she said, and showed him the programme. The play was called *Elegant Edward*. 'Naturally I was put in mind of you. *Et voilà, vous voici!* Is that not magic?'

'Magic indeed,' he said, smiling. It was impossible to look into her lively, expressive face and not smile. 'As you are alone, may I secure you a taxi, or escort you anywhere?' he asked.

'We shall see. But, first, what are you doing here alone, my friend?' she asked. 'You were not at the theatre also?'

'I was taking a walk and happened to be passing,' he said. 'My family is on holiday by the seaside, so I am living at my club. I am at your disposal, if you would like me to see you safe home.'

'You may do more than that,' she said, tucking her arm firmly through his and starting along the street. 'Bad plays make me hungry. To tell the truth,' she laughed, '*all* theatre makes me hungry, because it reminds me of my dancing days when one spent so much force and there was never enough to eat. So I must have some supper, and you may have some with me, if you will? I know a charming little restaurant in Shaftesbury Avenue where the wine is French and the food is *à merveille*, but not at all expensive.'

He hesitated no more than a second. He had pretty much walked off the dinner with Aeneas, and it would be unkind to force this gregarious creature to eat alone. 'It will be my pleasure, Madame,' he said.

'Good,' she said, as if she had never much

doubted he'd accept. 'But indeed you must call me Élise. We cannot take the supper together as banker and client. We must take it as friends, and friends do not call each other "Madame", *hein?*'

'Very well,' he said awkwardly, 'Élise.' The word sounded strange in his voice and felt stranger on his tongue. But she laughed as if she knew that, and gave his arm a little squeeze, and suddenly his shyness fell away – he didn't really know why, except that she was so easy and natural, as if they had known each other since the schoolroom.

Anyway, there could be no harm in taking a client out to supper. He took clients for meals all the time, even if they were generally male.

David wrote to Antonia Weston:

We are billeted at a farm about ten miles from the line – out of range of the guns, but we can hear them grumbling like summer thunder in the distance. The men are helping with the harvest, which makes a change from digging and drilling, but we're still desperately keen to get into the thick of it. The good news is that we are to have our turn in the trenches next week, and though this is apparently a quiet sector, at least we shall be manning the line. And there are rumours flying around that something bigger is building up, and will come off soon, and that we shall be part of it. I pray we will! For all our light-heartedness, we know this is a great and glorious venture. The Hun is the tool of Darkness, spreading his vile stain over Europe, and we are the army of Light, fighting in the name of freedom to cast him back. It's good that it is almost here at last, after all the prep-

406

aration. I can't describe to you the elation I feel. I know the others feel it too. I see it in their eyes, and the noble cast of their expressions. As I write, I think of you at home in your quiet village, the peaceful green fields and hills, the woods, the streams. All this the Hun would despoil, as he has despoiled France, if we did not defeat him. We have seen a little, on our way here, of the beastly destruction of war. It shall never come to England – I pledge my life to that.

CHAPTER TWENTY-THREE

Ethel eyed Sadie with interest. 'There's someone to see you, miss,' she said. 'A soldier.'

Sadie was puzzled. Was it someone from the hospital? 'An officer?' she asked.

'No, miss,' Ethel said. 'He's waiting down by the gate. He wouldn't come in.'

'Oh,' said Sadie. 'Well, I suppose I'd better see what he wants.' It crossed her mind then that it might be Higgins with a message from Mrs Cuthbert – but, then, why wouldn't he say so?

At the gate was a khaki-clad figure who looked faintly familiar. He snatched off his cap as she approached, and grinned uncertainly, as if unsure of his welcome, though his eyes searched her face hopefully. 'Have you forgot me, miss?' he asked.

Now she knew him. 'Victor Sowden?'

''Sright, miss.' Gingerly, he took the hand she had instinctively offered, and let it go again as though afraid of damaging it.

407

'I hardly recognised you,' she said. 'You look so different.' Though no taller than her, and still skinny, he had filled out in the arms and shoulders with muscle, and his face had lost the half-sullen, half-sly look. The strange bumpiness of it had gone, too – he would never be handsome, but he looked like a normal member of the human race now. His hair, which had always had an odd tuftiness, as though it grew in patches, was cut soldier-short, but was even and springy. 'I think you must have grown two inches,' she concluded.

He grinned more comfortably now. 'I reckon I have, miss. The grub's okay in the army, and there's plenty of it. Seconds, if you want.'

His drunken, barely employed father and thriftless mother had probably never put enough food on the table for growing boys, she thought. It came to her with a sudden sense of shame that perhaps the bumpy face of old had been the product of his father's knuckles, and could it be that his hair had been tufty because clumps had been pulled out in the course of paternal attacks? Sowden senior was known to enjoy 'teaching a lesson' to weaker mortals when he was drunk.

'But what are you doing here?' Sadie asked.

'Leave, miss,' Victor said promptly. 'We're off to France.'

Sadie did not want to dent his excitement, but she knew the rules. 'You're not old enough. Soldiers can't serve abroad until they're nineteen, and you're only thirteen.'

'Fourteen now,' he said. 'But it don't matter. *They* don't know that.' She looked at him doubtfully. He could have passed for sixteen, perhaps, but no more. 'Any rate,' he added, 'they don't care. I reckon the sergeant's twigged me, but they need me, so he won't say nothing.'

'What is it you do that's so important?' she asked.

'Battalion transport,' he said, with enormous pride. 'Horse-handler and driver, me.'

'So you got to work with horses after all! I'm so pleased for you.' It occurred to her that the transport section would probably not be called on to man the trenches, so perhaps his being under-age didn't matter. Perhaps the all-seeing sergeant had taken that into consideration.

'Yeah, miss,' he said. 'It's what I always wanted. I drive 'em in the wagons, and I get to look after 'em as well – grooming 'em and feeding 'em and such. I like that. There's this horse, Nobby, he's my special favourite. When I go to see him in the morning he whinnies at me, like he's saying hello. He knows me, see.'

'Of course he does,' said Sadie. 'Horses always know which people love them.'

He looked embarrassed at the word 'love'. He said, 'They're all smashing, all the horses, but Nobby's my favourite.'

'So you're on your forty-eight embarkation leave?' she said. 'Have you been to see your mother and father?'

His face closed down. 'I don't want to see them. And they don't want to see me, neither. Good riddance to bad rubbish, that's what me dad said when I joined up.'

'I'm sure he didn't mean it,' Sadie said automatically.

'He did,' said Victor, with certainty, and she was afraid from what she knew that he was probably right. 'I've just been up the school to see me brother, Horry. Waited till they came out for play-time and talked to him through the railings. He'll be twelve next month so he can leave school. I told him he ought to join up, same as I did. There's nothing for him here. Then I come to see you.'

'That was nice of you,' Sadie said. She was touched, never having realised she had made an impression on him.

'You like horses,' Victor said simply. It was answer enough for him. 'Anyway, I'd better be off. Don't want to miss me train.'

'No, that'd never do,' Sadie said. 'Well, good luck to you. I know you'll do well, and I'm sure everyone will be very proud of you.'

'There ain't no-one who cares,' he said, without self-pity

'*I* shall be proud of you,' she amended.

He blushed, but held her gaze steadily. 'Truly, miss?'

Yes,' she said, and because it had got embarrassing, she added lightly, 'I quite envy you – seeing France. Don't suppose I ever shall.'

A thought visibly came to him, like a light-bulb above his head. 'I'll send you a postcard,' he said, evidently pleased by the idea. He resumed his cap, drew himself up and gave her a salute, supported by a wide grin, and was off down the road at a smart march. It was nice, she thought, that the war was doing good to someone.

David's letters to Sophy were very different from

his letters to Antonia; and the reverse was true. Antonia's letters were about St Hugh's, the current batch of soldiers and officers, a digest of the news from England, and her own thoughts on the war. There might be a message from her father, generally with some philosophical point to mull over, and a recommendation about what he should be reading (impractical, if he hadn't brought the books with him). They were full, meaty letters that he re-read over several days, and answered at length.

Sophy's letters in her large, elaborate hand contained the best English an expensive governess could instil, full of words but short of matter. She wrote about her social engagements, domestic affairs, the health of various friends and members of the family, and what the weather had been doing. It reflected, he saw, the difference in their lives: Sophy's so feminine and protected, Antonia's almost like a man's in its exposure to events. He found Sophy's gentle epistles infinitely endearing, especially the ingenious ways she found of filling out the paucity of subject.

When he wrote back to her, he said very little about the front or his military activities, guessing they would not interest her. What she wanted to read – and what he was happy to write – was how much he was missing her, how he thought of her constantly, and his memory of her sweetness, her loveliness, her many perfections, and his dedication to making her proud of him.

To Antonia he wrote:

This part of the line is quiet, what the regulars call 'a

411

cushy billet'. Nothing but the occasional exchange of machine-gun fire across no-man's-land to tell you the Germans are there. The enemy is the subject of intense speculation, since all we see of them is a distant line of sandbags and the occasional muzzle-flash. What are they up to over there? Are there ten thousand of them, or ten dozen, or ten? Our adj opines that the whole front line has been abandoned and is now held by a caretaker and his wife. The caretaker does the occasional firing, while his wife lets off the flares!

We have been issued new rifles and have been training with them, marching, to get used to the weight, and target practice. Otherwise it is all digging – twelve thousand yards of new trenches have to be created. We have to dig at night as the Boche have balloons up during the day. The engineers lay out the line with tape and we file out after dark and dig. The strange thing is that the enemy must be able to see in the day what we have done the night before, and could easily get the range of the new line. They could practically wipe us out with machine-guns if they wanted, but for some reason they do not fire. A few shells come over, and there is the constant nuisance of snipers, but nothing worse. Still, I cannot express how exposed and naked one feels when a Very light goes up and one is suddenly illuminated like Vesta Tilley at the Hippodrome. One can almost hear the sniper smacking his lips.

He added the next day:

Yesterday something horrid happened. We had done our usual digging during the night and had some hours of sleep. Then I had to take a party to repair the frontline trench where the parapet had been broken by a shell.

One of my men, Logan, had climbed up to put the new sandbags in place, which the others were handing up to him. I hadn't noticed his position until I heard sniper fire. Then I saw him and shouted to him to get down, but he was not quick enough. A bullet blew his head open. I feel horribly guilty about it. The men are in my charge and I let him down. The first man in the battalion to be killed, and he was one of my own. The captain has been kind enough to say it wasn't my fault, and these things happen in war, but I shall have to write to his parents and have no idea what to say. It's the first time I have been so close to death, and what shocks me most is how little there is to it. A man's skull seems no stronger than an egg-shell, and he can pass from life, which seems so large and undeniable, into the nothing of death in a split second.

Later I found something like herring roe on the shoulder of my tunic, and realised it was poor Logan's brains. Is that all we are – an egg-shell full of gruel? Will my own death be so small and unimportant? I have pledged my life to the service of my country, in the cause of freedom, but what does Logan's death mean in that context? Please, dear friend, write me something to help me to understand it.

Ethel was routinely peeved when Eric asked her if she could change her evening off. 'I'm doing driver training, you see,' he said, 'and I'll be going up and down to Liverpool Street in the cab learning the ropes.'

'I thought you'd passed your driver's test,' she objected.

'That was for the steam locomotive,' he explained. 'Now I have to learn the electric engine so

I can drive on the underground section if they ask me. It's all to the good,' he added soothingly. 'I'll get an extra few shillings for being trained on both, and there'll be lots more chances for overtime.'

'All very well,' she sniffed, 'but what am I supposed to do while you're gallivanting off playing with your trains?'

She never managed to rile him. He only grinned at her and said, 'You'll be too busy to miss me. But see if you can change your night off to next Wednesday, and come up to London. You could meet me at Liverpool Street station when I get off duty, and we can go and have a bit of supper together, see a show or go to the pictures.'

She was partly mollified. 'You know I got to get back, though.'

'If you get a train around eleven you'll be home by midnight.'

'Midnight? They lock the back door at ten, and I can't ring at the front.'

'I bet you can wheedle someone to let you come in a bit late,' he said. 'After all, there's a war on. And you're a grown woman.'

'That's right!' she said, remembering her recent stint as a waitress. 'It's time they realised things have changed. I'm not a heathen slave, to be locked up when I'm not working. I can come and go as I please.' It was a delightful thought, but in reality she didn't fancy standing up to the missus and telling her that. She dismounted her high horse. 'I bet I can get round Emily. Cook goes up to bed at ten o'clock, and she sleeps like a log, so she'll never know what time I came in, s'long as Emily keeps her mouth shut.'

Emily was thrilled to be taking part in a conspiracy. Ethel had no difficulty in changing her evening off – Ada rarely went out anywhere – and she approached Cook very soberly and respectfully and said that she wanted to go up the West End, and expected to be back by ten, but if it happened that she was a teeny bit late, it wouldn't matter, would it?

Cook said. 'I can't sit up all night waiting for you to come home so's I can lock the door.'

'No, of course not,' Ethel said humbly.

'And Ada needs her sleep too, so don't you go asking her.'

'I don't mind,' Emily piped up, taking the cue. 'I'll sit by the fire a bit after you've gone up.'

'You!' Cook exclaimed. 'Think I'd trust you to lock up? You'd be leaving everything open for burglars to walk in.'

Emily pouted. 'Ah, you're always so mean to me. I can do it. I've seen you do it a thousand times. Bolt the top and bottom and turn the key, put the guard up round the fire and turn the lights out.'

Cook wavered, and Ethel added, 'I'll be there to check she does it right. Any case, I'll prob'ly be back by ten. But you know how the trains are. It's just in case, that's all.'

Cook gave in. 'But don't you be later than ha' pas', if you *are* late. And don't make a noise coming in. And don't let master or the missus see you on the stairs.'

'And don't *you* go falling asleep,' Ethel said fiercely to Emily, when they were alone, 'because if I have to wake you up to get in, I'll skin you!'

'Ah, I won't! Where are you going, anyway? Is it something nice?'

'Never you mind.' Seeing Emily's face fall, she thought she had better sweeten the bargain, and said, 'You do this right for me, and I'll give you – two bob.'

Emily beamed. 'Two shillin's? It must be a special evening, then.'

On the Tuesday everything was almost ruined: that night two Zeppelins made their first appearance over London since July, and attacked the docklands of the East End. Rotherhithe, Deptford and the Isle of Dogs were hit, and the next morning it was said that eighteen people had been killed, including one whole family from a poor street in Deptford, father, mother and three children.

'Oh, those poor people! It's a sin and a shame! Those wicked Huns!' Cook exclaimed, as she fried kidneys and bacon. 'Whatever is the world coming to? You're not going up London tonight, Ethel, not after this.'

Ethel just managed to stop herself saying, 'Don't be daft,' which would not have gone down well with Cook. She controlled her temper with an effort, and said, 'It's a terrible shame for them, but I won't be going to that part.'

'That's not what I mean. Suppose they come back?'

'They won't,' Ethel said. 'They never come two nights in a row, 'cause the defences'd be ready for 'em.'

'Defences? They didn't do much good last

night!' Cook cried.

'Well, they was took by surprise,' said Ethel. 'They'll be looking out for 'em now. Which is why they won't come. And, like I said, I'm not going down the docks. What d'you think I am – a stevedore?'

'Never mind that, you watch your lip,' Cook said, distracted. 'Where *are* you going, as a matter of fact?'

'West End,' Ethel said promptly. 'To the pictures.'

'Ah, that's nice,' Emily said helpfully. 'She'll be safe enough in the picture house, sure she will. And they've never bombed the West End, right enough.'

Cook waved a distracted hand. 'Oh, all right, if you must, you must. Don't know why you can't go to the pictures in Westleigh, though.'

'Because Eric's working, and if he has to come back to Westleigh to meet me it'll be too late for the pictures.'

'You getting serious about this Eric?' Ada asked, with a curious look.

Ethel tossed her head. 'Maybe I am, and maybe I'm not. We'll see.'

She met Eric under the clock when he came off duty, and after a brief discussion they took a bus to High Holborn and the Empire, where they were re-showing *The World, the Flesh and the Devil* in Kinemacolor, which Ethel had never happened to see. It was a gripping melodrama about a plot to switch the babies of a poor family and a rich family; with such meaty emotional fare and a small

417

packet of chocolates, plus a newsreel and a short comic film, they passed a happy couple of hours.

Despite the chocolates, 'I'm starving,' said Ethel, when they came out.

'That's all right,' said Eric. 'I've got it all planned. There's a little restaurant behind Barts Hospital – where the nurses go when they're off duty, so it's quite respectable. And nurses being always hungry, they do a nice little supper there for half a crown.'

'All right, but I daren't be too late,' Ethel said.

'I know. It's only five minutes' walk from there back to the station and there's a train at ten to eleven. We've got plenty of time.'

The supper *was* good – a warming hot-pot for what had turned out to be a slightly chilly evening, followed by treacle sponge and custard. Eric watched his companion packing it away with a fervour equal to that of the pair of nurses at the adjacent table. He liked to see a girl with a good appetite. He had gone out once with a girl who picked daintily at everything under the impression it was more ladylike and it had driven him mad. Ethel, for all her fanciful ways, was plain and simple where it mattered. 'More pudding?' he asked her, when she put down her spoon, comfortable in the knowledge that she would not look coy and say, 'I have to think of my figure.' It didn't seem to matter what she ate, she always stayed slender as a willow. He supposed she burned it off with her temper.

'No thanks,' she said. 'We prob'ly ought to think about going. What time is it?'

He pulled out his battered watch with the steel

418

case. 'Nearly half past ten.'

She looked alarmed. 'We've got to go! We'll miss the train!'

'No, we won't. It's only five minutes' walk. Miss!' He paid the waitress, helped Ethel on with her coat, and they were out into the street, where the sooty smell of fog and the haloes round the street lamps gave an autumnal feel.

'Hullo,' said Eric. 'Look at that!' The sky was criss-crossed with searchlights, sweeping back and forth.

Ethel craned her head. 'What's it for?' she demanded nervously.

'There must be a Zepp warning,' he said. 'Soon as they cross the coast, they send a warning to the AA units. Don't worry. It's probably nothing. I expect they're bombing the east coast again – poor things.'

'Let's hurry,' Ethel said. She slipped her hand under his arm and they set off briskly towards the station.

The first explosion came from the north and west of them. The boom of it made Ethel jump and grip Eric's arm painfully. 'It's them!' she cried. As the rattling cough of the guns began their answer, she stared up into the sky, and tripped over a paving stone.

'Watch where you're going,' he admonished, holding her up by her arm. 'They're a long way off. Must be Golders Green, Finchley, somewhere like that.'

But there were more explosions, which seemed to be coming closer. Glass chattered in the windows of the tall building beside them and a fine dust fell from somewhere. Another explosion was so close they could feel the ground press upwards through their feet.

Now there were shouts and whistles blowing. Someone ran across the top of the street, and paused to shout at them, 'Hey, you! Zeppelins coming! Get under cover!'

'Don't stop. We're nearly at the station,' Eric urged, as he hurried her along. 'We'll be safest down the Underground. Can you run?'

Ethel didn't answer, but she ran when he did, clutching her hat with her free hand, fear tight in her throat. There were other people running, more shouts, another explosion. It was definitely closer. 'Where *are* they?' Ethel cried. 'Why can't we see them?' It was like being hunted, not knowing how close they were.

Eric glanced over his shoulder, and saw a red glow of fire go up. 'That was somewhere over Holborn,' he panted. 'They're south of us now.'

Holborn? But they'd just been in Holborn! A shriek was jerked out of her as two thuds came in quick succession, followed by a leaping wall of flame behind the buildings to the right.

'Oh, my God, was that St Paul's?' Eric cried.

Someone else was running alongside them, now, a little man in a cap and muffler who was overtaking them. 'No, guv'nor, they didn't get it,' he panted. 'You can see it be'ind the flames. That's them ware'ouses gone up. Bastards!' And he was past them, sprinting like the hare before the greyhounds.

A lot of people were around them now, most hurrying or running in the same direction.

'There's the station!' Eric panted, as the roof rose up behind the brick walls of the workshops and yards surrounding it. 'We'll be all right in a minute.'

And then someone shouted, 'There it is! Oh, my Gawd!'

High above them, a long silver cigar hung in the sky, horrible, unnatural. Two probing spotlights converged on it – swung past it – swung back and pinpointed it. The ack-ack guns spoke angrily.

'They've got him!' someone shouted. 'Now they'll give him what for!'

More spotlights converged, cutting through the red glow in the sky, turning the silver cigar yellow, and from every direction the guns spoke. The massive naval guns at Woolwich boomed like giant's thunder.

'Kill it! Kill it!' a woman's voice shrieked. 'Blow it to bits!'

'What if it comes down on us?' Ethel panted.

'He's turning,' Eric said. 'They're driving him off.'

Now they were by the station, running towards the entrance, and there were people, taxis, omnibuses idling by the kerb as passengers poured off, seeking the safety of the station. Eric and Ethel were slowed by the press of bodies, and Ethel, in a panic to get under cover, screamed, 'Get out of the way!'

'It's all right,' Eric shouted into her ear, over the noise of engines, guns and voices. 'We're safe now!'

Laura and Louisa had not been on duty on the

421

Tuesday, but a note had come round to the house early on Wednesday asking them to undertake an extra duty that evening. Laura telephoned Sergeant Webster, their superintendent. 'We need a lot of extra hands,' he told her. 'The Zepps probably won't come back, but there'll be crowds out hoping to spot one, and you know what that means. Prostitutes, pickpockets, drunks. We need extra patrols to keep people moving. Get 'em off the streets, if possible.'

'Where do you want us to patrol?' Laura asked.

'Round Liverpool Street station. There's thousands of daft people round Bishopsgate and Shoreditch, just the sort to go out in the street gawping. Just keep going round and through the station. Keep the pedestrians off the roads, keep the entrances clear, generally keep things moving.'

'Right, Sergeant. I understand.'

'You'll have the Boy Scouts to help you. And I'll have as many regular patrols out as I can, so if you need help you can use your whistle.'

'Yes, Sergeant.'

'But try not to need help, there's good girls,' he concluded.

The area to the east of Liverpool Street station was packed with slum streets as well as factories, warehouses and workshops, so the population there was dense. The two women got curious looks and blatant stares as they began their slow walk through the station. They had grown used to being a familiar sight on their own beat; here they were a novelty again. A constable patrolling past the entrance as they came out onto Liverpool Street gave them such a jerk and stare it was a wonder he didn't rick his neck. Then a slow grin came over his face.

'Well, if that don't beat Banagher!' he said. 'I'd heard about you lady-policemen but I never thought I'd see one.'

'Didn't you know we were coming?' Laura asked.

'Now you mention it, the sarge did say something. But I didn't take it in properly. Well, I suppose any help's welcome. You got your orders?'

'To keep people moving, keep the roads and entrances clear,' Louisa said promptly.

'Right. I got half a dozen Scouts directing traffic, and if the bloody Zepps don't pay us a visit we should have a quiet night.'

'Anything in particular you want us to do?' Laura asked.

'Just do your usual – whatever *that* is,' he said. He gave them a long, disbelieving once-over, nodded curtly, and walked on.

It was a pretty routine sort of evening, except for being on unfamiliar ground. They reassured decent citizens, answered questions as best they could, quizzed a couple of girls who looked too young to be out, sent a few drunken soldiers in the right direction, and scared off a number of suspicious characters who were lurking, waiting for the opportunity to pick pockets. There did seem to be a lot of people wandering aimlessly about the streets, many of them looking up, and their numbers were added to considerably after closing time when the pubs emptied. But since nothing seemed to be happening, a lot of them began to drift away and the unnatural crowds were thinning.

And then the bombs started to fall.

Ethel didn't know what had happened. There was a terrible, awful noise, that turned into a terrible, awful silence. Something lifted her off her feet and threw her through the air, which was hot and prickly, and then the ground came up to meet her. She had an instant of pain in her back and shoulder, then something heavy but strangely thick drove the air out of her. Blackness swirled around her. Her arms stung as though attacked by bees. She heard a sort of tinkling like a gigantic box of nails being spilled on the pavement and then she was gone into the darkness.

When she came back to being her again, there was a roaring sound in her ears that made it hard to hear anything else; through it, as if distantly, she could hear voices shouting, screams, whistles, and a crackling sound that seemed to go with a smell of burning paint. Something big and squarish and heavy was lying on top of her, making it hard to breathe. Her arms hurt. She tried opening her eyes. It was dark, but there was flickering light, like firelight. The street lamps seemed to be out.

Why am I lying in the street? she wondered. *Has there been an accident?* She thought of her stockings, her best stockings that she had put on for – for some reason. She hoped they hadn't got torn. Her face seemed to be wet. She tried to put her hand to it to see what it was, and found she couldn't move her arm. Panic seized her. '*What's happening?*' she screamed, but her voice sounded faint and weak. '*Where am I?*'

A face loomed over hers, and someone shouted, 'This one's alive!' then said to her kindly, 'Don't worry, love, we'll get you out.' *Out? Out of where?* 'Hey! Give me a hand here!'

There were feet scuffing the pavement around her, and the loom of men, and then the thing lying on top of her was lifted and she could breathe properly again, though the air was bitter and unsatisfying. Now she could move her hand she touched the side of her face and saw her fingers come away bloody. 'I'm hurt,' she said, and her voice came out like a whimper.

Another face above her – a woman's, middle-aged, firm, the sort used to organising things, the sort that took no nonsense from the likes of her. 'Let me see,' said the face. Cool fingers touched her head, parting her hair, making her wince. 'Hold still,' said the face. There was a sharp pain, which spurred Ethel to sit up in protest.

'Ow!'

'You had a piece of glass in your scalp,' said the woman. 'Keep still while I see if there's any more.'

The fingers were in her hair again. *Where's my hat?* Ethel looked about in amazement at a scene from an insane person's dream. There was something burning behind her, smelling horribly of rubber and paint, throwing a ghastly red light over the scene. It flickered and reflected off a million pieces of glass, which seemed to have been spread over every surface, like a poor man's diamonds. By the kerb beside her there was a giant, wounded, twisted jumble of metal that made no sense to her at all, and there were twisted bits of metal and other debris amid the carpet of glass.

And all around there were people, many lying down on the pavement, others kneeling or squatting beside them. She turned her head in a slow circle of amazement. She saw a policeman gesticulating to some people, while a woman with her hair falling down screamed and tugged madly at his arm without effect. She saw a Boy Scout in uniform, standing with his mouth open and an expression of horror on his face, as though he had been turned to stone. She saw a woman in a fur coat giving a drink from a flask to a man propped up against a lamp-post, which seemed to be leaning at a strange angle. To her left an arm, in a sleeve, was lying on the pavement as though someone had been assembling a tailor's dummy there and left a bit out. The voices all around fused into a wall of noise, which was punctured here and there by sharper sounds – a police whistle, an ambulance bell, a woman sobbing, the cascading tinkle of glass.

'Have you got a hanky, dear?' said the woman attending to her. Ethel stared at her blankly. 'Never mind,' said the woman. 'Mine's reasonably clean. Here, now, give me your hand. Right, just press that there, like that. You've got a cut scalp but I don't think it's too bad. Do you think you can stand up?'

'What happened?' Ethel managed to ask at last.

The woman's lips thinned. 'Zeppelins. They dropped bombs on the station. Three or four at least. Two buses were hit.'

'Buses?' Yes, she remembered buses. She had been hurrying towards them. No, not towards them – past them, to get to somewhere.

'You were lucky,' said the woman, grimly.

With her help, Ethel got to her feet, swaying weakly. Her head seemed to be ringing like a bell in a steeple. As well as losing her hat, she discovered that the sleeves of her coat were shredded as though with a knife, and her arms were stinging with cuts. And her precious stockings *were* torn.

She saw now that the people lying down were injured. There was blood, and terrible wounds. Some of them were dead. And the arm was not from a tailor's dummy. Tears of shock burst from her eyes, and her knees gave way.

Someone in a nurse's uniform came then, took her arm on the other side from the woman and supported her. 'Let's get her into the station. We're setting up a first-aid post there,' said the nurse.

Ethel was helped across the pavement, over the crunching layer of glass, and in through the entrance to the station.

'What's your name, dear?' the nurse asked.

Ethel stared at her wildly. 'I don't know!' she cried.

'Shock,' said the nurse, wisely. 'Sit her down over here, that's right. Would you like to get her a cup of tea? The wagon's over there. Three spoons of sugar.'

Ethel found herself seated on a bench while the nurse felt her all over. She was too tired and confused now to mind. There was something important she had to remember, but she couldn't catch hold of it. The nurse removed the handkerchief from her head and wound a bandage efficiently round it; looked at the cuts on her arms and pronounced them superficial. The first lady came back with a mug of tea and put it into her hands. The nurse put a blanket round her shoulders.

And then somehow they were both gone. Time seemed to have flickered, because the tea was halfway down the mug and she didn't remember drinking it. Time. What was the time? The train, she remembered, left at ten to eleven. It was important she caught it. She wasn't sure why. She had been running to catch the train. *They* had been running to catch the train. *They!*

Memory flooded back, and she cried out. A man in the uniform of a special constable came hurrying over. 'Are you all right?' he asked.

'Eric!' she cried. 'Where's Eric?'

He seemed to understand her. 'Were you on the bus with him, love?'

'Not on it. We were just passing. Trying to get to the station. To get the train.'

'Eric what? What's his name?'

'Eric Travers.'

'And what's your name?'

'Ethel – Ethel Lusby.' It came to her with an effort.

'All right, Ethel Lusby, you sit tight and I'll see what I can find out.'

She drank the rest of the tea, staring around her with a sense of waking up – except that the nightmare seemed to be going on. There was organisation now – people being attended to, stretchers taking some away, blankets covering others right up, right over their faces. How would they be able to breathe? she wondered vaguely.

And then a voice that sounded familiar. 'It's

Ethel, isn't it? Mrs Hunter's housemaid? I thought I recognised you.'

She lifted her head, like one tormented beyond enduring, and saw a strange figure, a female but in some kind of dark serge uniform and hat. She had a smear of blood on her cheek but didn't seem to be wounded. She was smiling in a troubled way. 'Don't you know me?'

Ethel's mind lurched, and she said, 'Miss Hunter. Master's sister.' She tried to stand up, but Laura pushed her gently back down.

'It's all right. Just rest. What are you doing here?'

'I was with my gentleman friend. My evening off. I don't know where he is,' Ethel said. Her eyes went past Laura and saw the special coming back. '*He* said he'd find out.'

'All right. Sit tight.'

Laura straightened up, and put herself between Ethel and the special. They seemed to have a long and muttered conversation. Then she turned back. Her face was horrible with pity. 'It seems he's one of those they've taken to hospital. Barts. He was quite badly wounded.'

The information didn't seem to fit anywhere inside Ethel's head. 'I want to see him,' she said.

'Oh, you won't be able to see him tonight,' said Laura, firmly. 'Besides, you're quite shaken up yourself. We'd better see about getting you home. I think you'd better spend the night at my house – it's too far to Northcote. Don't worry, I'll send them a telegram to say you're safe.'

Ethel had nothing to say to that. She couldn't think properly, or work out what questions to ask, or remember what anyone had just said to her. Her thoughts kept stopping short, uncompleted. She couldn't tie the ends of anything together.

'Don't worry,' said Laura. 'You'll feel better in the morning, when you've had a sleep.'

Ethel let the thought of that carry her away, like strong arms. There was something else she should be thinking about, but it kept slipping away from her. She felt very, very tired.

CHAPTER TWENTY-FOUR

The damage, it seemed, had been done by just one Zeppelin, which had dropped bombs on Golders Green, Bloomsbury, and Lamb's Conduit Street, where the walls of the Dolphin pub had been smashed in and two men killed. Several textile warehouses behind St Paul's had been bombed, causing such fierce fires that twenty-two fire engines were needed to fight them and a fireman had lost his life. Barts Hospital had lost 1,200 panes of glass in the blast when Bartholomew Close was hit. The Admiral Carter pub was shattered, killing two men, and a whole row of houses opposite was demolished. Coleman Street and Portpool Lane had been hit, and four small children killed. Moorgate and Finsbury Pavement were bombed; there was not a single unbroken window in Moorgate.

And then, passing over Liverpool Street station, the Zepp had let go four bombs. One hit the railway lines, the others fell in the street outside, and two had hit buses, killing crews, passengers and bystanders. In all, twenty-two people were killed and eighty-seven injured. Huge amounts of property were destroyed. The anti-aircraft guns had fired to the best of their ability, but the airship had been too high for them to reach. Because of the fog, only six defence aeroplanes had been able to take off, and none had even come within sight of the enemy. One had been destroyed on landing when its own bombs had detonated, killing the pilot.

Most of this Laura had learned before Ethel woke up, which was around noon on the Thursday.

For a moment Ethel didn't know where she was. She was terribly thirsty, her head ached and she felt bruised all over. She put her hand up to her head, felt the bandage. Her arms hurt when she moved them. She opened her eyes. She was not wearing her own nightdress, and there were scratches on her hand; and this was not her attic bedroom, but a posh one with flowered wallpaper and a large mahogany wardrobe, and there was a green silk eiderdown on the bed...

For an instant she thought she must somehow have gone to sleep in the mistress's bed, and struggled up with a cry of alarm. But this was not the mistress's bedroom either.

And then Laura came in, and memory flooded back. Liverpool Street – the bombs! It was little comfort to remember.

'What...' she croaked.

'Oh, good, you're awake,' said Laura. 'I expect

431

you'd like a cup of tea. I won't be a minute.'

Ethel had an unwelcome period of leisure in which to assemble more of her memories, so that when Laura came back with a tray, her first words were 'Where's Eric? How is he?'

'Drink some tea first,' Laura said firmly. 'You must be thirsty. And I've brought you a couple of aspirins, because I'm sure you have a headache.'

Ethel was used to doing what she was told, when she was told in a voice like that, so she let herself be helped to a sitting position, meekly swallowed the aspirins, and sipped at the tea.

Laura drew a chair up to the bed. 'Just to put your mind at rest, you have a lot of shallow cuts on your arms, and a deeper one in your scalp, but none of them needed stitches and you'll be right as rain in a day or two. It seems the bomb that hit the motor-bus as you were passing blew one of the seats straight out, which knocked you down but shielded you from the debris. My friend Miss Cotton and I brought you back here last night and popped you into her bed, and you've been asleep ever since. I sent a telegram to your mistress last night, so they know what happened, and that you're with me, and safe. When you feel up to it, you can have a bath, and we'll find some clothes for you, and then you can go home.' She smiled kindly. 'Does that answer most of your questions?'

'Yes, miss,' Ethel said. 'Except...'

The smile became kinder – worryingly kind. 'Yes, of course. Your friend – Eric Travers, is that the name?'

'Yes, miss.'

'I'm afraid he wasn't as lucky as you. That seat shielding you probably saved your life, but he was hit by debris. He was very badly injured. He was taken to Barts Hospital, but I'm afraid he had no chance. He was dead when they got him there.'

In fact, Laura reflected, he had been dead already and had been taken with the other dead straight to Barts' morgue. That was what the special had told her, but she had thought it better to keep it from Ethel at the time. His injuries had been so severe they had needed to look in his pocket book to identify him.

'I'm so sorry,' Laura said. 'It's a dreadful shock to you, I know.'

Ethel said nothing, stared straight ahead with a slightly puzzled look. *Eric, dead?* The words didn't seem to make much sense to her. 'He's a train driver,' she said. 'He'd just come off work.' Laura nodded. 'He's learning to drive the electric engines as well, so he can do the whole Metropolitan Line. That's why we were at Liverpool Street. We went to a show at the Empire, then had supper at a restaurant behind Barts, where the nurses go.'

'Restaurant? In Bartholomew Close?' Ethel nodded. That was where the bomb had destroyed the Admiral Carter. The restaurant, which had been next door, was no more. If they had been there any later, they might both have been killed. 'You had a lucky escape,' Laura said.

'Lucky?' Ethel said dully. *Was Eric really dead?*

'I'm sorry,' Laura said again. 'I'll leave you alone for a bit. I expect you want to cry.'

But Ethel was too angry to cry. *Why him?* she demanded of the indifferent ceiling. He was a good man. And she had started to trust him, started to think maybe everything was going to be all right. She'd been worried about him going to war, taken badly his hints that he envied those who had volunteered. She'd thought if he stayed at home, being an engine driver, he'd be safe. The joke was on her. *I suppose You think that's funny?* she cried angrily at the Presence above the ceiling. *You got a nasty sense of humour!* God had it in for her, tried to put a spoke in the wheel of any plan she got up to better herself. *Well, I'm not going to let You win! So You can stick that in Your pipe!*

Eric, nice Eric, blown up by those rotten Zepps, those rotten Germans. It was a rotten, *rotten* trick!

And then the tears came.

Beattie received back her white, silent maid with sympathy, and told her not to overdo things for a few days. In the servants' hall, she knew, Ethel would be fêted. She was aware peripherally that there was a small but constant stream of back-door traffic, and that tea-parties were being presided over by Cook so that the story could be told in style. A genuine Zepp victim with a first-hand story to chill the blood was the most exciting thing that had happened in months.

Nula, doing some mending in the sewing-room, told her it was the best thing for Ethel. 'Helps to keep her mind off. Ada thinks she really was fond of the chap. She'd been going out with him longer than any of the others.'

'It's a bad business,' Beattie said. 'What a dreadful way to die.' Laura had given her details she would not pass on. Apparently the man had been

434

almost decapitated by flying debris.

'Making a fuss of Ethel's a good thing for Cook, too,' Nula added. 'She'd be scared out of her wits about the Zeppelins if she wasn't too busy with Ethel to think about it.'

'This is a horrible war,' Beattie said feelingly. 'It's making horrible people of us all.'

'Ah, no,' said Nula. 'Cook's really sorry for her. I didn't mean–'

'I have to go,' Beattie interrupted her. 'I have a meeting of the hospital committee.'

It was not Cook she had been thinking of. As she walked down to Manor Grange she reflected on her own reaction to the news of Ethel's disaster. She was truly sorry, of course, for her loss, and the fellow concerned had seemed, from all accounts, to be a good man. But her first thought had been that deaths come in threes. *Lord Dene, Sadie's lieutenant and now Ethel's beau.* David was at the front and, according to Edward, a big push was imminent. David's battalion would probably be involved. Her David, her son, would be going into battle soon. *Lord Dene, Sadie's lieutenant and now Ethel's beau.* Deaths come in threes, so perhaps David would be safe. Her first feeling had been relief.

It had been a ridiculous thing to think, the merest superstition, with no basis in reality. But when what you loved was in jeopardy, and you had no means to affect the outcome, superstition was all you had. Crossing fingers, lucky heather, horseshoes, St Christopher medallions – weren't they all just another way of praying? *Please, God, not mine! Don't take my son!* Did prayer work? Self-evidently not for thousands and thousands, whose sons had already died. Sons and husbands and brothers. So you were left with superstition. Which would not work either.

But we are what we are, poor helpless creatures, Fate's playthings. Cross your fingers, pray – and know yourself. Was there a mother in the land who, offered the choice, *Your son or someone else's?* would not secretly and urgently pray, *Take the other, not mine?* She had wished no harm to Ethel's train driver, but if he had closed the circle and saved her son, she would not want him back.

She walked on unhappily to her meeting, thinking, *War is making us horrible.* Perhaps there was something for her to do at the hospital that would make up for that. Just a little.

On Sunday Frank Hussey came to visit Munt, and to be invited to take his dinner with the other servants.

Munt was not officially employed at The Elms on a Sunday, but he was usually there on Sunday mornings, while his wife went to church. He was always happier in his shed than at home, and he didn't hold with God – or, at least, with churches. God he regarded with grudging respect for the growing things, the miracle of flowers, plants, trees and such-like – oh, and bees, though he thought He had slipped up a bit with greenfly, slugs and that sort of cattle. Got a bit carried away, you might say. And what He was thinking of when He got on to pigeons, cats and Germans... Still, he reckoned he and God were on reasonable terms, on the whole. Like him and Mr Hunter. Mr Hunter provided the wherewithal, and left

Munt alone to do his job, which was pretty much what God did when you thought about it.

No, it was church he couldn't stick, all that starch and nonsense, vicars telling you what you could and couldn't do, women in silly hats poking their noses into your business, to say nothing of all the kneeling and standing, up and down, up and down, and the hard pews to make your bones a misery. His wife tutted and told him he'd go to Hell, but he reckoned God had a bit more sense. Better to be in a garden with sweet growing things than a dusty, mouldy church – and he'd tell God the same if he had to, when he met Him.

So it was from Munt that Frank Hussey learned what had happened to Ethel. Munt had no liking for Ethel, and told it straight, without any curlicues of sympathy to spoil the line of the story. He did, however, say it was a pity, because from what he had heard the chap was a decent sort who was having a good influence on 'that flighty piece'.

'Yes, it is a pity,' said Frank, thoughtfully. 'It's the sort of thing that could set a girl on the wrong path.'

Munt gave him a gleaming look. 'Only if she's on the path already. You can't make a silk purse out of a sow's ear – nor vice versa.'

Frank smiled. 'Oh, I don't know. You can try, anyway.'

'You can make an idiot of yourself,' Munt said. 'Want to see how them chrysants have done, what you brought me cuttings of last year?'

There followed an agreeable interlude devoid of women or talk of women as they discussed the merits of pinching out and which wood made the best stakes.

Emily had seen Frank arrive and had told Cook, and when he didn't come straight up to the house, Cook got more and more impatient, and finally despatched Ethel down the garden to enquire if he was coming in for his dinner.

Frank found Ethel pale and listless. He had seen the same blank look of shock once in the eyes of a man knocked down by a motor-car. As they walked back to the house together, he said, 'I'm very sorry about your young man. That was a terrible thing.' Ethel said nothing. He went on, 'You must think of him as having fallen in battle. He's just as much a casualty as any man at the front.'

That got through to her. The blankness dissolved. *And that's supposed to comfort me, is it?* she thought bitterly. Anger was the only thing that made her thoughts bearable. 'Oh, he'd have gone to the front sooner or later,' she said. 'He was talking about volunteering anyway.' She felt herself beginning to shake, and gripped the anger tighter. 'He didn't *have* to go. Driving trains is important work. But he wanted to. Unlike *some* people I know!' Her hot eyes, turned up to him, said, *Why aren't you dead instead of Eric?*

'I'm helping the war effort in my own way,' he said mildly.

'Is that what you call it? Some people have another word for it.'

'Cowardice, you mean?' he said. He saw it shocked her, hearing the word out loud. 'Oh, I'm not afraid – not more than any normal man would be.'

438

'Then why don't you go?'

He looked at her kindly. 'You don't get to know everything all at once in this life.' He stopped just outside the back door and laid his big, hard hand over hers. She became very still. 'I just want to say to you how very sorry I am, and that if you ever need any help, you should come to me. I'll do anything I can for you.'

'What sort of help do you suppose *I'll* need?' she demanded. She couldn't bear his kindness. She needed scorn, anger, because otherwise she would see again the blood, the wounds – that arm, just lying there. In her nightmares, it was Eric's arm. She had been lucky, they said, protected from the explosion. Just under the surface lay the unendurable question, *What had it done to him?*

'Anything at all,' Frank said, as if she hadn't spoken. 'You've got a friend in me, and I'll always help, if you need it.'

She met his eyes and bit off the hard thing she was about to say. Just for an instant she felt warmth from him; for that instant she didn't feel so alone. Then it passed, and she pushed past him without a word, and went in.

At the meeting of the hospital committee, Mrs Oliver proposed getting up a concert for the wounded officers at Mount Olive. 'It's the least we can do,' she said. 'We can't nurse them or mend their wounds, but we can entertain them, and the poor things do get so terribly bored.'

'I was just about to propose the same thing myself,' Mrs Fitzgerald said quickly, 'A concert. Songs and recitals and so on. I'm sure we can find enough talent in Northcote to get up a programme.'

Mrs Oliver was accustomed to dealing with the rector's wife's attempted *coups*. She produced, with magnificent timing, a sheet of paper on which she had already written down suggestions and the names of possible performers.

'I think we should form a sub-committee and call it the hospital entertainments committee. We won't want to stop at one concert. There are many other things we could do to beguile their weary hours. And as they recover and leave, others will be coming in. We have an *ongoing* duty to Mount Olive.'

'In my view–' Mrs Fitzgerald began.

Mrs Oliver overrode her firmly: 'Now, finance. We shall certainly need some money, and I'm afraid our people are getting rather jaded with the constant appeals for funds. We should call upon our younger people to involve themselves, bring some fresh faces and new ideas into it.'

'I was just about to say that,' said Mrs Fitzgerald.

As a consequence, Diana found herself walking up to Dene Park one still, warm September day. The concert idea had come at just the right time for her, when the initial interest of visiting the wounded officers had begun to lose its power to charm away her sadness. She had agreed readily to take part in the concert, to serve on the sub-committee and to help to raise funds.

The biggest item was securing the use of a piano. 'We could manage unaccompanied,' Mrs

Oliver had said, 'but it would be rather dismal. And it would be such a wonderful thing for the men to have use of at other times. We need a small upright piano that could be got up the stairs and be wheeled between the wards. If we could secure a long-term loan that would be the best thing of all, but we may have to purchase an old unwanted instrument.'

As Mrs Oliver had happened to mention that Lady Wroughton had just returned to Dene Park from Scotland, Diana had swallowed hard and offered to go and see her. She remembered, as she walked up the interminable drive, the last time she had done so. Then it had been high summer; now the chestnuts were beginning to turn, with rims of gold and bronze to their green, the sky had a soft, autumn pallor, and there was a smell of wood-smoke on the air. The indifference of Nature to man's suffering was brought home to her. The year turned, taking her further away from him with every passing month. The leaves would fall and winter would come, and next spring he would not be there to see them unfurl again. The vastness of it all dwarfed her. She felt very alone.

At the house she sat on the same hard little chair while the footman went away to enquire, and was fetched at last to the same green parlour, where the countess, still in black, sat on the same sofa. But the blank stillness had gone out of her. She looked old, older than she had when Charles was alive, but she was active again, cold and fierce. Diana thought of a hawk, perched high and ready to stoop.

'What is it you want?' she asked at once. Diana

441

found her mouth dry. 'Speak up!' the countess snapped. 'If you had married my son you would have been expected to know how to address anyone at any time without hesitation. Modesty is one thing, woolly-mindedness quite another. You should have assembled your thoughts before you entered the room.'

Diana felt a flash of resentment. 'I have come as the representative of the hospital entertainments committee,' she said clearly.

The countess gave a grim quirk of the lips, which might charitably have been interpreted as a smile. 'So you have some spirit left in you? You've come to ask for donations, I suppose. For what other reason does anyone come to the Park now? What do you want money for?'

'We are planning a concert for the wounded officers at Mount Olive. They get bored with nothing to do. Many of them are bedridden and–'

'Time hangs heavy on their hands,' Lady Wroughton finished for her. 'They should count themselves lucky.'

'I'm sure they do,' said Diana, stung to their defence. 'But it's hard for them. Many are in pain, some have lost limbs and don't know what the future holds, and all have lost friends. A concert would give them something else to think about.'

The countess eyed her with interest. 'You've changed since I first met you. You seem to have – grown up.'

Diana met her eyes. She didn't say, 'I've had to,' but it was in her face. And it was the countess who looked away.

'Well, well,' she said. 'What exactly do you need

money for? Singers presumably don't charge for their voices.'

'We need a piano, or the use of one. An upright, that can be wheeled from ward to ward. If we can't secure the loan of an instrument, we may have to buy one.'

'I imagine,' the countess said, with a bitter look, 'that there are instruments in many homes that will not now be wanted.'

'Yes,' said Diana. 'Perhaps.' And she had the wisdom to say nothing more.

The countess was silent for a long time, her eyes fixed on the distance, obviously deep in thought. At last her attention returned, and she studied Diana without hostility – it almost seemed with a touch of kindness. 'You *have* changed,' she said. 'You were always a pretty girl, but you have something more now. I wish–' She stopped, and Diana had the mad idea that she had been going to say, *I wish Charles could have seen you.* She went on, 'There is an upright instrument in the old governess's room.'

'May we borrow it?' Diana asked.

'You may have it. I donate it permanently to the hospital committee.'

'Thank you, your ladyship. You are very kind.'

'No, I'm not. It is never used.'

'Everyone will be very grateful, all the same,' Diana said, and managed a small smile, which seemed to surprise her ladyship.

'Well, well,' she said again. She looked ill at ease, and Diana stood, thinking she should remove herself as quickly as possible. But the countess said, 'You are going?' Diana didn't answer, unsure what she should say. Lady Wroughton went on, 'Will you come again?'

Now Diana was surprised. 'Your ladyship?'

'I would like you to visit me,' said the countess. It seemed to have been hard for her to say, and Diana couldn't frame an answer quickly enough. The countess went on, 'I – I have photographs I would like to show you. Of Charles, when he was younger. Some things of his you might like to see. Will you come?'

She's lonely, Diana thought, then thrust the thought away as absurd. How could the Countess Wroughton possibly be lonely? She might summon friends any time she wished, assemble a house party, go to London and be in a crowd of her own sort. The invitation was something else. She didn't know what. It didn't *seem* like a trap to humiliate her... At any rate, there was no refusing it. 'Of course,' she said. 'I'd be honoured.'

Having secured the assent, the countess became brisk. 'Very well. Come next Tuesday. At three exactly. You shall tell me about the plans for the concert, and we shall have tea. I will give instructions about the piano. You may send a cart at any time.' She rose and went to the bell. 'Good day to you.'

The interview was over.

Since his release from hospital after being wounded, Jack had been in a quiet sector, one of the famed 'cushy billets', in Picardy near the river Somme, but in September his battalion was moved back to Ypres.

When battle approached, the censors were

444

careful about allowing anyone at the front to tell his people back home exactly where he was, in case the information got into the hands of the enemy, who might deduce battle strategy from it. However, once the action started, the men were given 'green envelopes', in which they could write whatever they wanted, in case it was their last letter. On the 21st of September the bombardment began that was to smash German defences in advance of the big attack, and the green envelopes were given out.

It is to be the biggest barrage ever, and ought to soften up Fritz nicely [Jack wrote]. *By the time you get this, I am sure you will know exactly where the battle is taking place. I, however, shall not be there. There are to be two diversionary attacks, and we are to form one of them, so I'm sorry to say I shall be back on my old beat, a place I had hoped never to see again. Our orders are to convince the Boche at all costs that it is the main assault, so we must attack and keep on attacking regardless of casualties. My darling, I hope you will not find the phrase 'sacrificial lamb' springing to your lovely lips! This is where we break the Germans and end the war, so no effort will be too much. My belongings are all packed and sent into store, and I feel a strange lightness, like setting off for a walk in the country with nothing to carry. Do not worry. This is a foolish instruction, but truly, try not to. It is all luck, you know, and there is good as well as bad. Believe in the good, believe I shall come back to you, and I shall do the same. It's all there is.*

The battle began on the 25th of September, near

445

the city of Lens, centred on a mining village called Loos. Thus much was known at home. Now there was only the waiting.

The concert at Mount Olive was a good way to occupy the mind. Rehearsals were going on, at the church hall, the village hall and in private houses. The programme was still in a state of flux.

'Mrs Carruthers is keen for the children from the village school to take part,' Sadie told Captain Luat, one of the new intake she was visiting. The idea of the concert had taken a firm hold in the wards. It had certainly given the men something new to think about.

Luat was ghastly pale and his face was lined deeply, like an old man's. He had lost both legs when a shell fell on his column as it made its way towards the line to relieve the company in the front trench. He was Sadie's particular concern, because his wife had died in childbirth the previous year, which meant he had no-one to visit him and nothing good to think about. 'That sounds a nice idea,' he said.

'A nice idea perhaps,' said Sadie, 'but think of the pitfalls! Miss Snoddy says they'll never stand still for long enough.'

'What are you going to do in the show?'

'Me? I'm just a lowly worker behind the scenes. I don't have any talents.'

'Not singing? Or playing something?'

'If you'd heard me singing you'd know better than to ask that.' Sadie grinned. 'I suppose I could recite something,' she added, 'but only if they're very short of acts to fill the programme.'

'But your sister,' he said, looking across the

room to where Diana was sitting by a bed, writing a letter to dictation. 'She must be in it. I expect she sings like an angel.'

'She sings a bit, but she's better on the piano.'

'She's very beautiful, isn't she?' said Luat.

'Yes,' said Sadie.

The piano was collected from Dene Park, and Diana much praised for securing it. The piano tuner, Alfred Clewlow – cousin to the chimney sweep – volunteered to tune it for no charge. Beattie had secured the promise of Dame Barbara Woodville to give an opening address. And at Mrs Fitzgerald's suggestion, the camp at Paget's Piece was canvassed to lend some soldiers both for fetching and carrying, and to add some male voices to what otherwise was too female an effort.

That was how Ada met Corporal Armstrong. She had taken a message from the mistress to the rector's wife at the church hall one evening, and arrived to find him in charge of six volunteers, who were there to rehearse a choral piece, and half a dozen miscellaneous helpers. They were crowded into the morning-room, waiting to be told where to go, and Ada had difficulty in getting through the door, since the corporal had little choice but to be standing with his back to it.

'Hullo!' he said jovially. 'Room for one more on top! Mind the stairs!'

She flushed, but saw kindness, not mockery in his eyes. 'I've got a message for Mrs Fitzgerald,' she said.

'Well, she's not here yet, as far as I can see, but come in, come in. Join the party, the more the merrier.' As she squeezed herself into the room, he

447

gave her a very frank look-over and seemed to like what he saw. 'Well, you're a sight for sore eyes,' he said. 'Stuck in that camp with nine hundred soldiers, I can tell you any woman is a welcome relief. But when it's a smart, pretty young woman like you – all I can say is, it must be my lucky day.'

Ada blushed at being called 'young' and 'pretty', and wished she had Ethel's ready tongue for dealing with such nonsense. 'Oh, get on with you!' was the best she could manage. The other men were looking at her and grinning.

'I'm dead serious,' the corporal said. He stuck out his hand. 'Len Armstrong's my name. In charge of these monkeys, for my sins. And what might yours be?'

'Ada Cole,' she said, taking the hand timidly.

He held on to hers rather longer than a hand-shake warranted. 'Ada,' he said. 'Now that's a name I've always been partial to. Most partial. It's a pretty name for a pretty woman. And what are you doing here, Miss Ada Cole? Have you come to rehearse, along with these monkeys of mine?'

'Oh, no,' Ada said. 'I've just brought a message from my mistress, Mrs Hunter. I'm head house-parlourmaid at The Elms, just down the road.'

'A parlourmaid!' he said, as though she had just bestowed a rare treat on him. 'Cream of the crop, parlourmaids! I bet you've got a beautiful singing voice as well.'

Ada blinked. As a matter of fact, she had been known at school for her singing voice. Nobody had asked her to sing since she had left school, too many years ago to remember, and nobody had ever heard her, either. She sang over her work, because she enjoyed it, but if anyone approached she stopped. She suspected a tease; but the corporal was looking at her with nothing but interest. 'Why d'you say that?' she asked shyly.

'I can tell from the way you speak. There's music in your voice. I'm half Welsh, me, and we can always tell. You ought to get yourself in on this concert party.' He dropped her a wink so swift she couldn't be sure it had been there at all. 'That way we'd get to see each other again.'

Ada felt her face grow hot, and needed to beat a retreat. 'I'd better go and find Mrs Fitzgerald,' she said, and made her escape. Outside she put her hands to her cheeks, and listened for mocking laughter, but there was only an upsurge of chatter. *Monkeys?* she thought. *He was making a monkey of me!* She straightened her shoulders, and went looking for the rector's wife.

She found her in the church hall with a number of performers assembled, gave the message and mentioned the soldiers in the morning-room.

'Oh, that's where they've got to,' said Mrs Fitzgerald. 'I've been waiting here for them. Go and fetch them for me, will you?' Ada hesitated, and she continued, 'Are you staying to help? I hope so. We have a great deal to do.'

'As a matter of fact,' Ada said, astonishing herself with her boldness, 'I wondered if I could be one of the singers.'

'*Can* you sing?' Mrs Fitzgerald asked, her eyebrows rising.

Now was Ada's chance to back down, back away, save herself from foolishness and exposure.

'Yes, I can,' she said. She gulped, and added, 'If the mistress doesn't mind.'

'Oh, she won't mind, not a bit,' said Mrs Fitzgerald. 'And we are short of singers for the choral pieces. I'll try you out, and if you can sing, Mrs Hunter will be delighted for you to join in, I have no doubt. Just run and fetch the soldiers in here, will you? I can't start the rehearsal without them. I do hope they'll behave themselves,' she added to herself, turning away.

Ada hoped so too.

CHAPTER TWENTY-FIVE

Beattie's suffering was intense, but it was not long. Sooner than she had dared to hope, she received a field postcard: *I am quite well.* Alive, at any rate! Thank God, thank God! But the battle was still going on, according to the newspapers. She was not out of the wood yet.

A field postcard for the mother; a letter of love, reassurance and longing for the fiancée; but it was to Antonia Weston that he wrote in detail.

Preparations were extensive – we were even taken to walk about a scale model of the battlefield! Though when it came to it, it didn't prove to be as much help as hoped. We went up to the line the night before the attack. It was pretty cramped in the trench. The men had to sit each between the legs of the man behind, like kids in a bath! We were to be the second wave. A and B

Companies were to take the German front line and C and D were to go through them and take the second. Parties were out in the night cutting the wire in front of our lines so we could pass through, then we had sixty yards to cross to the German wire, which would, we hoped, be cut to pieces by the barrage. Oh, those guns! They had been brought up as close as possible, and the noise was simply indescribable. When they stopped, you went on hearing them, ringing in your ears.

The moment of attack was like a dream. There was fog and smoke, so visibility was poor. We had the Jocks on our right, and some madman was playing the bagpipes, and that wailing coming out of the fog added to the unreality. I thought beforehand crossing no-man's-land would be hell, and thought I would be afraid, but when it came to it, there was no time for fear. It was a hell of destruction – a mass of holes and debris and dead men everywhere, our men. When we got to the wire, they were lying in heaps. The guns hadn't managed to cut it, and they were sitting ducks while they tried to cut it by hand. We went through the gaps they'd made, and thanked our luck we had not been in the first wave.

We got to the German front line and the rest of A and B were mopping up, mustering the prisoners. There were dead Germans everywhere. We went through to the second line, but it was almost empty. They must have run for it, and the few that were left didn't seem inclined to fight, for they surrendered as soon as we fired. Then a message came up that the Jocks had hit Loos so hard, the Germans were in flight back to their reserve line. The Jocks were in pursuit, and we were to follow and support them. We advanced through the outskirts of Loos. The village was wrecked, heaps of rubble with a few walls standing up in them. The most amazing thing was that we saw civilians, heading the other way, mostly old people, but I saw a woman with two small children. She was limping badly. Why they had hung on there I couldn't imagine. There must have been a dozen or more.

Beyond Loos it got more difficult. Without landmarks it was hard to know which direction we were going. I believe now the Scots had gone too far to the right, chasing the Germans. At any rate, we found ourselves under fire from one of their heavily fortified pit villages. That was pretty terrible, as there was no shelter. We lost a lot of men then. The order came for us to dig in on the reverse slope of Hill 70, and then it was just a matter of holding on and waiting for reinforcements. However, they didn't come. Sometime in the afternoon the Germans counter-attacked and drove the Jocks back to us. We held on together for a time, but when darkness came we were ordered to fall back on Loos, where we spent the night. It had been raining all day, and was cold, and our quartermasters didn't manage to get food up to us, so we had only the remains of our iron rations. Rather dismal!

The next day orders came up to retake Hill 70. The Germans were now dug in at the top of the hill and commanded the slopes with machine-guns. We didn't know that until we charged. The Jocks were ahead of us and went down like mown grass. Then we came in for it. It was awful. I saw men just flopping down like rag dolls. We took the front line, but there was a redoubt from which they could fire on the trenches, and eventually we had to retreat – those of us that were left. We fell back on Loos as darkness came, and during the night we were relieved and told to move *back. We were very tired by then. I have only a vague memory of our scarecrow battalion trudging along the dark road, while working parties, limbers, ambulances and staff cars passed us going the other way. There were military police stationed to guide us, or we should never have found our way in that featureless and wrecked terrain. We were guided to a field about six miles behind the line, and it took us nearly twenty hours to cover those six miles! There was soup waiting for us but most were too weary to eat, and simply lay down on the bare earth and slept.*

We were paraded the next day in our reduced numbers. Four in ten of us were missing, and all but five officers. Jumbo, thank God, is here and unharmed. It was only when I woke up and went to wash as best I could that I discovered I had been wounded. It was a scalp wound, and had bled pretty freely, but as it had not run into my eyes I had not noticed. I think I may have discovered an alternative to hair oil!

The battle goes on, and I don't know how it will turn out, but we have done our part, and have gone now into billets to recoup. What are my feelings now I have seen my first battle? Mostly relief and gratitude that I have come through. Memories are vivid but so fragmented it all seems like a dream. One thing – the heavy loss of officers means I am now acting captain and in command of C Company.

Diana's visit to Lady Wroughton became the first of a regular train. In a curious way, she came to enjoy them. The countess did not say much, and her face was not built to express pleasure, but at the end of each visit she ordered Diana to return at the same time next week. The pattern was always the same. They met, after that first day, in the countess's private parlour – the overstuffed and slightly shabby room Beattie had visited. She would ask Diana how the concert was coming along. Then tea would be brought – always a very good tea, though Lady Wroughton did not take much of it – and while Diana ate, the countess would show her some object or photograph from Charles's past, or tell some anecdote about him.

They were strange little vignettes, which Diana remembered afterwards almost like dreams. The cluttered room, the tea tray, the hiss of the spirit lamp and the smell of warm muffins, the rigid woman turning some object over and over in her thin hands, the harsh aristocratic voice chipping away at the silence. It was as though, Diana thought sometimes when she was alone, she was trying to keep him alive by delving back into his childhood. But Diana, who had never known him as a child, found it only wore away her memories of him, took him further from her.

One day, for something to say in a silence, Diana asked the countess if she would come to the concert. Her ladyship recoiled as though she had been struck, and Diana, embarrassed, could only stumble on. 'It would mean so much to everyone if you would. The men would regard it as an honour, especially as – as your ladyship has lost – has made such a sacrifice...' She managed, thankfully, to stop, and waited, shrinking, for the inevitable sharp retort.

But the countess seemed to be thinking, and at last she said, almost as if to herself, 'Perhaps I might. I could speak to the men, shake their hands. I need not wait once the music starts.'

Diana was about to thank her, but as it hadn't seemed to be directed towards her, she hesitated to interrupt. The countess was silent again, and then looked up sharply, as though rediscovering that she was not alone. She examined Diana thoroughly, but Diana was growing used to these inspections, and neither blushed nor shrank.

At last the countess spoke: 'I shall be going up to Town next month for a few weeks. Would you care to come and stay at Wroughton House? I shall have various engagements to which you might accompany me – parties and so on. And there is the theatre, and the opera. I expect Wroughton and I shall give a dinner – you might help with that.'

Diana could not have been more surprised if her ladyship had kissed her. Stay at Wroughton House? Be taken about by Lady Wroughton? It was the attention – though she had not realised at the time – that ought to have been paid to her when she was Charles's intended. What was the meaning of it now? Her mind scrambled about, trying to see the reason, or the trick, or the hidden insult.

The countess stared. 'If you are unwilling, say so at once. You perhaps,' she added sourly, 'do not anticipate much pleasure from my company.'

There was something under the tone that Diana could not fathom. If it had been anyone else, she would have thought, as she had before, *She's lonely*. But she must answer. She couldn't see how she could refuse, so she said, 'I would be delighted to come, ma'am. It's a great honour to be asked.'

'Yes, it is,' said Lady Wroughton.

'I must ask my parents' permission,' Diana added.

'Of course,' said the countess, waving the idea away. 'But they will give it.'

And, of course, Diana knew they would.

The concert was a great success. Sadie was not called upon to recite, as there were others, if not more skilled, at least more willing. Augustus Ellison gave *The Pied Piper of Hamlyn* with great gusto, one of the soldiers did *The Shooting of Dan McGrew*, and the Frobisher twins chanted 'The Boy Stood on the Burning Deck' in perfect unison, in matching white dresses and red hair ribbons.

James Lattery played the violin – a real treat, because he was a genuine artist – and Edith Farringdon played the flute somewhat less well in duet with Harold Woodwick on the piano. The primary-school children sang 'Five Eyes', and 'London Bridge Is Falling Down', arranged by Miss Snoddy and accompanied by Diana on the piano. The mixed choir sang sea shanties and English folk songs. There were piano recitals of varying skill, and Diana accompanied several solo singers. Miss Snoddy accompanied the choral pieces. And the programme ended with all the performers singing 'Land of Hope and Glory' together.

The whole thing was performed twice, once in each of the two larger wards. It went down so well that the mobile patients followed the act from one ward to the other, while the bedridden thought themselves hard done by to catch it only once.

The committee had managed to secure several

bigwigs to give countenance to the event, including Dame Barbara Woodville, Mr Whiteley, MP, and two senior officers from the camp. Lady Wroughton duly made her appearance, went round every bed, shook hands and spoke a few words to each man, and gave each a present of a box of cigarettes, but departed before the singing started.

And finally the performers served the audience with tea.

'Well,' said Corporal Armstrong afterwards, when they were clearing up, 'that went a treat, didn't it?'

'Yes,' said Ada. 'I think the gentlemen enjoyed it.'

'Oh, they did, there's no doubt – and I was right about you. You sing like an angel.'

Ada blushed. 'Oh, I don't! Get on with you!'

'Well, you sing very nicely, at any rate,' he amended. 'It's a shame to hide your light under a bushel.'

'I did enjoy it,' Ada said, with a sigh. Now it would be back to the usual routine, and singing only when no-one was listening. 'It'll be hard, not having it to look forward to.'

Armstrong winked. 'I wouldn't be too sure of that. I've heard a rumour that our CO had a chat with your CO–'

'With who?'

'The lady in charge. What's her name? Oliver, is it?'

'Oh, yes, Mrs Oliver. What about?'

'It seems they both think it would be a shame to waste all this fine co-operation and hours of

457

rehearsal. They're talking about putting on another performance in the village hall for everyone to come to. What d'you think of that?'

Ada's face lit up. 'You mean, we'd do it all again?'

'That's the idea. What d'you think?'

'I think it's grand!'

'So do I. Especially as rehearsing gets me off other duties. And–'

'And?' Ada asked, not managing to meet his eye.

'And I have a chance to see you.'

'Oh, get away with you!' was all Ada could say.

Edward was up in Town late on the 13th of October, having been with others from the banking world to a meeting at the Treasury to discuss the raising of treasury bills and exchequer bonds to fund the war for the following year.

When he came out of the meeting, his head felt thick: so many figures, so many words, so much smoke from so many cigarettes. It was after half past eight, and he had had no supper yet. He decided to walk across St James's Park and up the Queen's Walk and go to his club for something to eat before he went home. It was a misty but temperate evening, and he needed to stretch his legs. The air in the Park smelt pleasantly of damp earth; the lamps, with their tops blacked out, threw down fuzzy yellow pools of light on the path.

He heard the first crashes as he approached Piccadilly – the heavy sound of bombs falling in the distance, to the east. The sky over there was

458

criss-crossed with searchlights, and even as he turned about on the spot, looking up, the White-hall searchlights came on and began sweeping the darkness above him.

A policeman was talking on the telephone in the police box at the end of the walk. Edward stopped and asked, 'Another raid? Are we to expect them over here?'

'I can't say, sir,' said the officer. 'It seems three Zeppelins crossed the coast, then split up. One went south, one north, and I think we know where the other went. That's the docks catching it again, poor devils. My advice to you, sir, is to get under cover.'

'Yes, Constable. I'll do that.' He didn't want to add to the man's troubles. The streets were busy with the usual evening traffic, and as soon as the word went round, people would pour out to see if they could catch a sight of London's tormentors. It was said that there was as much danger from glass and shrapnel falling on those who came out to look as from actual strikes by bombs.

He was walking quickly along Piccadilly when a tremendous explosion made the ground shake under his feet. There followed a heavy rumbling, the sound of a building collapsing, and shouts and screams coming from somewhere up ahead and to the right of him. The glow of fire rose up in the sky. There was another explosion, and another. 'It's somewhere over the Strand, St Martin's Lane – that way,' said a man beside him.

'Oh, my God, they're bombing the theatres,' said someone else.

Figures in evening dress were pouring out of the

Ritz. People were coming up out of the Underground station while others were trying to get down there, making a struggling mass in the entrance. Women were screaming, men were shouting, there was a wild babble of voices. People ran in conflicting directions, like ants from a broken ants' nest.

The next crash seemed to come from further north. In his mind's eye, Edward drew the line of the attack, from the Strand through theatreland and up Charing Cross Road. It led directly to Soho Square. Before the thought was even completed he was running, pushing his way through the milling bodies, dodging across roads between traffic, cursing those who impeded him, cursing most of all the vile Hun, who thought it fair game to attack helpless, unarmed civilians in their own homes.

He crossed into Soho, and the narrow streets were even more crowded. There were little restaurants and clubs everywhere, and tenements above them, and people were pouring out in alarm, some of the women in tears, clutching favourite possessions, shouting for loved ones they'd become separated from. A group of men was smashing street lamps. He heard someone shout, 'Put that fag out! D'you want them to see you?' A man grabbed at another's cigarette and they started to struggle, hitting wildly at each other.

A shout was passed from person to person: 'They got the Lyceum! The Lyceum's been hit. There's hundreds killed!'

A woman moaned, 'We're all going to die!'

Edward was finding it hard to breathe. She was

fond of the theatre. Had she been at the show there tonight? Another explosion. How far away? It sounded further off – towards Holborn, perhaps. Was it heading eastwards, the Zeppelin? Would it return?

And now at last he was in Soho Square, and the crowd was thinner, and he could run. The street door was open. He pushed past a cluster of staring, chattering people and ran up the stairs two at a time. He hammered at the door, forgetting in his agitation that there was a bell. It was opened, and she was there, staring up at him with wide eyes. Solange was at the end of the passage behind her, hunched and with a shawl over her head, as though that would protect her from the bombs.

'You're all right! Oh, thank God, thank God,' Edward gasped.

She was trembling. 'It is like the shells all over again. When they shelled Lille. It is so terrible! It is the Zeppelins?'

'Yes,' he said. 'I think they are moving east.'

'Am I safe, then?' she asked, as though he would know the answer, as though he could protect her.

'I don't know,' he said.

There was another explosion. The glass in the windows shivered, and the cups on the kitchen dresser chattered, and she flung herself against him. He thought this one was further off, though. 'I think they're moving away,' he said. His arms were tight round her, her face was buried in his chest.

'Don't leave me,' she said, muffled by his overcoat.

'No,' he said. 'I won't leave you.'

461

The fighting at Loos went on, subsiding on the 28th of September and resuming when the Germans counter-attacked on the 3rd of October. Ground was gained, ground was lost. The action surged this way and that. There was a renewed offensive on the 13th of October that was close to success but faltered for lack of armaments. On the 18th it died away again. General Haig thought it might be possible to attack again in early November, and there were discussions with Joffre, who was anxious to press on, but the weather was worsening: heavy rain was making the going impossible, fog was hampering spotting, and the German artillery had recovered and was shelling the ground heavily.

The front line had been pushed forward and the Germans forced backwards; but the cost had been heavy – some sixty thousand casualties, of whom nearly eight thousand were dead. Two thousand officers had been killed or wounded. But the New Army had won its spurs in its first battle: the men had fought like tigers and had held steady under withering fire.

Jack emerged unscathed from the diversionary attack at Ypres, and wrote home to Beth:

All is quiet now on the line, or as quiet as it gets. The weather is atrocious, and unless it changes out of all reason, I don't believe there will be any more action this year. On both sides we will dig ourselves in and hunker down until spring, in this strangest of all wars. The men are terribly anxious about the news of the Zeppelin raids. It seems hard when they are risking their lives over here to keep their families safe at home. I hear the last raid was the most destructive so far – they are saying forty people killed in London alone. Thank God you weren't in it. Perhaps the bad weather will put a stop to them, too. Write soon and tell me what you are doing. I am safely back in Poperinghe for now, where I am in search of a really good bath – not as easy as it sounds. I have saved the last bar of soap you sent, and mean to do the thing properly.

The action at Loos was chewed over for many weeks. There was no doubt that on the 25th of September, the British had won a great victory, had smashed through the German line, gained ground and held it. Lord Forbesson was of the opinion that Lens would certainly have been taken if only they had managed to get the reserves up in time. Lord Henry Hastings said that the advance into Lens would not have been halted if German machine-gun nests had been knocked out by artillery. Others cited the failure of the initial barrage to cut the German wire completely; the problems of spotting, caused by fog and heavy rain; the difficulties of communication – the carefully laid telephone wires had been cut by the shelling.

Even so, it had been a triumph, and could easily have been an even greater one, and it showed what the British could do. It was a beginning, to be built upon, towards the ultimate victory. Sir Douglas Haig was the hero of the hour.

It helped to distract attention from the failure in the Dardanelles, where the stalemate had not been broken, the troops clung to a narrow rocky coast with no hope of dislodging the Turks up above, and sickness and disease were taking a terrible toll – dysentery, blood poisoning from infected insect bites, heart disease, skin disease, exhaustion and debility. How would it even be possible to supply the men through the winter on that storm-lashed, dangerous coast? The questions got into the newspapers, and public opinion became engaged. Evacuation began to be talked of.

Diana was enjoying her stay at Wroughton House more than she had expected to. The countess never appeared before noon, and sometimes not until after luncheon, so Diana had the mornings to herself, and usually spent them with the cousins in Kensington. She felt herself to be living a curiously double life, so comfortable and home-like were her mornings with the Palfreys, so very different her afternoons and evenings.

She was taken to visit Lady Wroughton's acquaintances in a variety of grand houses, at luncheon parties, tea parties and *soirées*. It was strange to be introduced to these exalted companies by the countess as her protégée, to find herself accepted almost incuriously as though she had a right to be there. The gatherings in themselves were elderly and dull, but it was novelty enough for Diana to be in such different surroundings.

At the dinner parties there were generally young people present as well, and there was usually dancing afterwards. Diana was in demand as a partner, rather like in the old days, before Charles. At a distance of six months, it did not seem wrong to dance. Everybody these days knew someone who had fallen. Life had to go on.

There were visits to the theatre and the opera. Lady Wroughton enjoyed plays but disliked music in any form, and it was apparent that she went to the opera purely as a matter of form. One afternoon they went to the House of Lords to listen to a debate. It was so warm in the gallery Diana found herself nodding off. But tea afterwards with the earl was pleasant. They were joined by several of his colleagues, one of whom, Lord Teesborough, knew her father, spoke highly of him and engaged her in friendly conversation.

She was a little surprised not to see Rupert. She knew he was at Wroughton House, but he seemed to live a completely separate life, not appearing at any meals. She met him for the first time at an exhibition at the National Gallery. She had been taken there one afternoon by Lady Wroughton and Lady Teesborough, and they bumped into him in the crowd. He was accompanied by a tall, rather pale young man, whom Diana recognised as the person she had seen him with in Piccadilly, that time when she was shopping with Mary.

'Oh, hello, Mater,' Rupert said without enthusiasm.

'I didn't know you were going to be here,' the countess replied.

'That was rather the point,' Rupert muttered, then turned a dazzling smile on Lady Teesborough. 'Aunt Mary, how lovely to see you! You're looking younger and more beautiful every year.'

'Don't flannel,' she said, offering her cheek.

'You know Erskine, don't you? Erskine Ballantine?'

'I've met his father, but never him,' said Lady

465

Teesborough. 'How do you do, young man? How do you know my godson?'

'Oh, bumped into him somewhere, don't-you-know,' Ballantine said, looking very ill at ease.

'He is the son of Courtland Ballantine, the MP,' Lady Wroughton explained to Diana. 'Mr Ballantine – Diana Hunter.'

'Who was to have married my brother.' Rupert completed the introduction. He gave her a flashing look. 'I hope you're enjoying your taste of the high life?'

Diana wasn't required to answer this as Lady Wroughton broke in: 'I never see you at home,' she complained to her son, 'so while I have your attention: you are to come to dinner on Saturday. I have invited several young people, and you may dance afterwards in the Long Gallery.'

'I'm afraid I'm already engaged to dine with Erskine,' Rupert said quickly. Diana saw Ballantine's look of surprise, and guessed that the countess did, too, because her lips thinned.

'You may bring Mr Ballantine, but you *will* be there, Rupert. And you will remain at least until midnight. It is my particular wish.'

'Oh, very well,' Rupert said sulkily. Then he gave Diana a sharp look. 'Will you still be with us, Miss Hunter? I do hope so. I long to dance with you again, as we did at Dene Park. But perhaps you do not dance any more – I was forgetting your broken heart.'

Diana recoiled at his obvious intention to wound. The last time they had met he had been friendly and attentive. She could not keep up with his changes of nature.

466

Lady Wroughton said briskly, 'Of course Miss Hunter will dance. And so will you. Mark me, Rupert. I do not want to see you sitting out, or lounging in corners in your usual stupid way. It's time you started to address your duty.'

She gave him a look so ferocious that Diana guessed the last sentence had some special meaning; Rupert looked as though he knew what it was. For herself, she couldn't guess. She was glad when the countess moved away. She remembered the last time she had danced with Rupert: she had come away with a bruised hand.

Laura had gone alone to a fancy-dress party in Bloomsbury, as Louisa was at a family dinner with her aunt and brother. The party was given by friends of Sylvia and Beryl, who lived in the two lower floors of a tall house in Bedford Way. There had been no Zeppelin raids since the 13th of October, and everyone was hoping that the foggy weather would keep them away. Nevertheless, the invitation had said that the party would be held in the basement, just in case. Some people had gone to great lengths with their costumes, including one ingenious fellow who was clad in silver paper and claimed he had thought they were all supposed to come as Zeppelins. Sylvia and Beryl were both dressed as Tommies. Grace Lattery was Florence Nightingale. Leland Brandt caused the greatest stir by coming as a harem girl, and Laura noted that he made a very passable female in his long black wig. He seemed to have quite good legs under the semi-transparent baggy trousers.

Laura rather disliked fancy dress, not caring to

make a fool of herself. She wore a red skirt and a grey blouse and, with the aid of a plaid shawl, passed herself off, when anyone asked, as Grace Darling.

She was deep in conversation with a pleasant young man in toga and chaplet when her shoulder was smartly tapped, and she turned to find Rupert grinning at her. He was in white tie and tails, and was accompanied by Erskine Ballantine, similarly clad.

'I'm glad to see you've made such an effort,' Rupert said. 'Who are you meant to be?'

'Grace Darling,' Laura said.

'I wouldn't have recognised you without your boat,' he said. 'Couldn't you at least have brought an oar for verisimilitude?'

'I don't think you have the right to lecture me,' she said, 'when you haven't come in fancy dress at all.'

Rupert opened his eyes wide. 'What *can* you mean? Erskine and I have gone to great trouble. Can't you see? I've come as *him,* and *he's* come as me!' He roared with laughter. 'And where is your lovely other half?' he asked at last. 'Your *alter ego?*'

'Miss Cotton is otherwise engaged,' Laura said. 'Family matters.'

'Ah, families, the great scourge of mankind! Wouldn't it be heaven if we were all grown in laboratory bottles and decanted by scientists at twenty-one?'

'I don't know. I enjoyed my childhood,' Laura said. 'Do you know John Sampson?' Introductions were performed. 'Mr Sampson's an engineer. He's joining the sappers at the end of the month.'

'Thought I'd get in while there's still a choice,' Sampson said. 'Don't want to wait for conscription and be sent into the Poor Bloody Infantry.'

Rupert looked distinctly uncomfortable, while Ballantine seemed to turn a shade paler, and clutched his sleeve. 'There's not going to be conscription,' Rupert said. 'The government wouldn't dare bring it in. Take my word for it.'

Sampson shook his head. 'I'm afraid you'll find you're wrong. In any case, don't you think it's up to us to do the right thing? I'd have volunteered before, except that I've been working on something I felt was important for the country.'

'My brother did the honours for the family,' Rupert said. 'Went to the front and got himself killed.'

'I'm sorry,' said Sampson. He was clearly going to say more.

But Rupert cut him short. 'We have a house guest at Wroughton House,' he said to Laura. 'Your delightful niece.'

'Diana? Yes, I had heard. I saw her at my sister's house in Kensington the other day, and she told me all about it. I hope she's having a nice time.'

'Do you think she ought to?'

Laura frowned. 'You mean because of her fiancé – your brother? Well, of course she was very upset – I'm sure she still is – but life has to go on. And while we're at war, I think it is everyone's duty to keep cheerful, or at least to appear so. Don't you agree, Mr Sampson?'

'I do. Morale is very important to the war effort.'

'Oh,' said Rupert. 'Well, as long as she's only *pretending*, I suppose it's all right. How well do

469

you know her?'

Laura was puzzled. 'Diana? She's my niece. I'm very fond of her.'

'Doesn't always follow,' said Rupert. 'I have aunts I rarely see.'

'We're a close family,' Laura said. 'I know Diana very well.'

'Do you?' Rupert said thoughtfully. 'Do you really? And it follows, then, that she knows you *very well*. How interesting.'

Laura couldn't follow his meaning. 'I know she was devoted to your brother, if that's what worries you,' she tried.

He seemed to come out of a train of thought, and gave her a gay smile. 'Oh, I'm not worried – not a bit! We're dedicated to enjoyment – aren't we, Erskine? Eat, drink and be merry, for tomorrow we die. Don't you think that's frightfully pertinent in wartime? After all, a Zeppelin might be approaching at this very moment, and we could all be blown to bits five minutes from now.'

Laura said, 'Now there's a nice, cheerful thought. And here I am with an empty glass.'

'Allow me,' Rupert said, took her glass, and slipped away through the press of bodies, closely followed by Ballantine.

'What a very odd fellow,' Sampson said. 'And that chap with him ... I'm sure I've seen them before somewhere.'

'They seem to have latched on to Sylvia and Beryl and their set,' said Laura.

'Ah,' said Sampson, as if that explained it, but he said no more, so Laura was left with the mystery.

Though Diana had assembled much of her trousseau before Charles fell, the dinner at Wroughton House on the Saturday strained her wardrobe to the limit. It was much more formal than she had expected. Lady Wroughton scared her by saying she would send her maid to dress her on the evening. 'She will come to you before me, so you must be in your room before the dressing bell.'

Pickering had a rather downtrodden air when in the countess's company but, separated from her, was quite formidable enough to make Diana's mouth go dry and give her two left feet. She dressed Diana's hair in silence, then surveyed her coolly and said, 'It's quite fitting for you to be simply dressed, miss, but it is a formal occasion, and you should have some jewellery.'

'Um,' said Diana. 'I really don't–'

Pickering interrupted her: 'Her ladyship guessed how it was, and sent something for you to wear.' From her pocket she took a velvet-covered box, placed it on the dressing table and opened it. 'It's not the full set, of course,' she said.

'Oh,' said Diana.

She thought them beautiful. They were no prince's ransom, not the contents of a fairy-tale treasure chest, not fit for a queen, but they were splendid enough to her. A necklace of amethysts and pearls, very delicate and pretty, accompanied by matching earrings and a bracelet. When Pickering had put them on her, she thought they went beautifully with her lavender gown. 'They bring out the colour of your eyes, miss,' Pickering said kindly, seeing how pleasure had brought a bit of colour to Miss's cheeks.

'How very kind of her ladyship,' Diana said. 'Please thank her for me when you go up.'

'Which I must do now,' Pickering said. 'Now sit quietly, miss, until the bell, and don't untidy yourself.'

The first person she saw when she went down was Rupert, and her heart sank. He came straight to her and said, 'Miss Hunter! How nice you look. Beautiful, in fact. I'm glad to see you ready to enjoy yourself again. My brother wouldn't have wanted you to shut yourself away for ever.'

Diana didn't know whether he was being sincere or ironic. She said, 'Thank you,' in what came out as quite a bewildered tone.

'I am to take you in to dinner,' he said. 'I asked my mother particularly. And I hope you will dance with me afterwards. Now, let me introduce you to people. I shouldn't like you to feel at all at a loss.'

Smiling, he offered his arm. She took it and let him lead her forward, a large question mark in her mind. *Did he mean it? Had he changed again?* And, most of all, *What was he up to?*

CHAPTER TWENTY-SIX

On the 11th of October Lord Derby had been appointed director general of recruitment, and shortly afterwards had put forward his scheme, a last attempt to avoid conscription. The National Registration in August had established that there were almost five million males of military age who were not in uniform, of whom 1.6 million were in occupations that should be protected – essential to the nation or involving scarce skills. They were listed with an asterisk, their occupations 'starred'.

Under the Derby Scheme, men could either volunteer at once, or attest their willingness to serve when called upon later. Those who attested were given a day's pay and sent home, with a grey armband bearing a red crown to wear, to show they had volunteered. The promise was made that married men would be called up only when the source of single men was exhausted.

There was a national effort to make the scheme a success. Posters were put up everywhere. Some made use of the Zeppelin threat, showing the London skyline with a searchlit Zepp hanging above it, and the words, IT IS FAR BETTER TO FACE THE BULLETS THAN TO BE KILLED AT HOME BY A BOMB. There were posters showing a soldier with a bandage round his head and a wooden crutch under his arm, and the words, HE DID HIS DUTY. WILL YOU DO YOURS? The popular music-hall artists, Harry Lauder, Marie Lloyd and Vesta Tilley, incorporated recruitment songs into their acts. On the 12th of October, the Germans had executed the nurse Edith Cavell in Brussels for helping Allied soldiers to escape, and the popular outcry was used for all it was worth.

But while more than two million men did come forward and attest, the numbers were disappointing. Thirty-eight per cent of single men and fifty-four per cent of married men not in starred occupations failed to register.

'It's a damned shame the scheme hasn't answered,' Lord Forbesson told Edward at the club one evening. 'Now we'll have to bring in conscription.' The Military Service Bill had already been drafted, just in case, and was ready to go. 'There will have to be an appeals process, of course,' he went on. 'I foresee endless arguments and unpleasantness.'

'How will it work?' Edward asked.

'There'll be a military-service tribunal for every town or district. Men will be able to appeal on the grounds of work of national importance or medical unfitness. Or domestic hardship – I suppose we have to include that. Chap who's the sole support of his aged mother and six dependent children and so on. Trouble is, that sort of thing can be stretched a hell of a long way. The tribunal officers will have to be pretty canny to sift out the malingerers.'

Edward almost hated to bring it up, but he said quietly, 'What about conscientious objectors?'

Forbesson sighed. 'Oh, yes, those too. We'll have to allow for those. Damned difficult to distinguish between a genuine conscience and someone who just wants to wriggle out of his duty. But they won't get out of service altogether. There are plenty of things they can do to help the war effort, without carrying a gun.' He emptied his glass. 'Another? Or are you toddling into dinner?'

'As a matter of fact, I'm not dining here,' Edward said. 'I have an engagement.'

'Ah. Well, another time.'

It was a raw evening, and Edward pulled his

scarf tight in the neck of his overcoat as he went out into the freezing fog. It was not a long walk. He had gone over Élise's finances again a week ago, and explained that she could afford to move to a nicer apartment, but she had said that she was quite happy where she was. 'Solange and I are comfortable, living in a small way. And who knows what lies around the corner? One must be prudent. No, we are happy here. And it is convenient for your office.'

Yes, that was true. He went there once a week, to supper, ostensibly to discuss her investments, though he knew in the uncomfortable part of his brain that he did not need to do that weekly. But she was all alone in the world, and was not attention to his clients' welfare part of his duty? He went there after the office, and they had supper and talked. He enjoyed their conversations so much! They flowed like free rivers, full of interest and laughter and discovery. They talked, that was all. There was nothing wrong in that, was there? Yet he had not mentioned it at home. He just said he had to work late, and it was something that happened often enough for no-one to be curious. He had not told anyone that he visited Madame de Rouveroy regularly. He wasn't sure why.

The Bedfordites, including Sylvia and Beryl's circle, were in a state of ferment about conscription. 'I refuse to kill another human being,' said George Morgan, firmly. 'They can't make me carry a gun.'

'Of course they can,' said Leland Brandt, 'if it's the law of the land.'

475

'There'll be an appeal system,' said Laura. 'If you can think of an honourable excuse. I believe flat feet are popular.'

'It's all right for you,' Rupert said crossly. 'You women won't be called up. You might be a bit more sympathetic.'

'You can appeal on the grounds of conscience,' said Louisa, 'though I do think it's too bad, considering how all our friends and relations are out there fighting for our freedom.'

'Not my freedom,' said George Morgan. 'I never asked them to go.'

'Poor argument,' said Laura. 'You'll get the benefit of the freedom they win, whether you asked them to or not.'

'I don't care,' he said. 'War is a terrible thing, and killing other people is murder. Doing it for your country makes no difference.'

'If everyone refused to go, there'd *be* no war,' said Ballantine.

'Ah, well, unfortunately, darling,' said Sylvia, 'the Germans don't feel that way, so we can either sit down and let them kill us, or fight it out.'

'That's exactly the point,' said Morgan, hotly. 'They know we'll fight, so *they* do. Someone's got to stop it somewhere.' It was an argument that came up over and over again.

'Well, they can't make you fight,' Sybil soothed him, 'so don't get upset.'

'They can put you in prison,' Brandt said provokingly. 'That's in the legislation. If you resist conscription, they can put you in jail.'

'Is that true?' Ballantine asked anxiously.

'Yes, but they probably won't,' said Laura. 'It

wouldn't suit them to have to waste manpower guarding a lot of prisoners. I believe the idea is that objectors will be given non-killing things to do. Like stretcher-bearers or ambulance-drivers.'

Rupert laughed harshly. 'Excellent thought! Stretcher-bearing is the most dangerous job in the army, everyone knows. Kill off the objectors as quick as you can, that's the idea.'

Ballantine was hurt. 'You needn't sound so happy about it. You'll be in the same boat.'

'Not me,' said Rupert. 'I shan't take the risk. I shan't resist conscription – I'll rely on the pater to find me a safe billet where the guns can't reach me.'

'You think he can?' Laura asked.

'Of course,' Rupert said calmly. 'Sir John French is a personal friend. Pa will fix it. I'm the only heir. If I go west, the whole bally estate will go to some deadly cousin.'

'Hm,' said Sylvia. 'I wouldn't rely on that too much, Rupert darling. That was all very well in the days of volunteering, but once conscription comes in, the whole war will be on a different footing. There'll be none of that "I'll do you a favour if you'll do one for me."'

'You'll see,' said Rupert. 'It's a cushy billet for me – and I have other plans, too.' He looked thoughtfully at Laura as he said it, and she wondered what was going on in his mind.

On the front, the winter weather had set in, and there was no prospect of further action. After a period of rest, David's battalion was back to normal trench duty, this time on the far left of the Loos battlefield. The monthly rotation was three days in the front line, three days in support and three days in reserve, then back to billets. It took a day to march up and a day to march back, so they were out behind the line for more than half of the time. But everywhere in that flat land it was muddy, and even in billets it was hard to get clean and stay clean. And the days in the trenches were depressing. The weather was raw, frequently foggy, and the view, of slag heaps and cranes and small, ugly pit villages, had been unlovely even before it had been torn by artillery fire. Now, with the mist hanging in low banks over the cratered mudscape, and clinging in ragged wisps to ruined buildings and derelict machinery, it had a gloomy, uncanny air.

And that was reckoning without the dead. They lay all across no-man's-land, just where they had fallen. There was no possibility of bringing them in. The bodies lay in swathes, where they had been felled by machine-gun fire, almost tidily, like corn cut down by the scythe. In the damp weather they were beginning to decay, and the smell hung around the trenches as a grim reminder.

It was David's job, as acting company commander, to try to keep his men's minds occupied, but it was hard, with nothing to do, to stop them staring at the bodies that were spread in front of them every day. They couldn't help knowing that they would lie there all winter, and perhaps longer – perhaps for ever – until they sank unmarked into the mud and were lost. Already there was a saying, when it was very quiet: 'as quiet as the Loos dead'.

And it was cold. No snow yet, but the night

frosts were killing, and in the trenches where you couldn't move around much you felt it most. The women at home were knitting for their lives, and parcels of gloves, stockings, mufflers and even helmets were being distributed up and down the line. The regiments took on a homely, unmilitary aspect. David's battalion had a quartermaster with some ingenuity, who had foreseen the problem of winter in the trenches, and had ordered fur jerkins to keep the men warm. Some were goat and some were sheepskin, many were pony-skin and some even came from cows, and all were imported from South America where they had been hastily and imperfectly cured. But worn fur-side-out over the khaki tunic, they kept out the cold, even if, as David wrote to Antonia, his company now resembled a band of mountain *banditti*.

An Allied conference was convened in Chantilly on the 6th of December, to try to forge a common strategy across all the fronts of the war. Representatives were there from France, Italy, Serbia, Russia and Britain, including Mr Asquith, Sir Edward Grey and Lloyd George. On the return journey, in the dining car, these three had a conversation which, even if it was meant to be secret, soon ceased to be. The rumour was soon rife in military and government circles that Sir John French was to be replaced as commander-in-chief, and the job was to go to the man of the moment, Douglas Haig.

'One can't help feeling sorry for French,' Edward said to Warren, the day after he had first heard the news. 'The fifteen months that he's been commander-in-chief have seen war as no-one's ever waged it, and on a scale never seen before.'

'Everyone's had to learn as he went along,' said Warren. 'I suppose that applies to the commanders more than anyone.'

Edward nodded. 'He must feel angry and resentful at being replaced – but, in his heart of hearts, I can't believe he'll be sorry to come home.'

Diana was home. The Wroughtons were staying a little longer in Town, then going on to Norfolk for the Christmas period, with an expected stay at Sandringham. She felt oddly as though she had been dismissed, like a temporary maid who was no longer needed. But she was happy to be home.

She had the concert to involve herself in. A string of colds and sore throats had prevented its immediate reprise, so it had been decided to give the performance for the village in December. There were more rehearsals, some new items added, and the arrangements to be set up: decorations in the village hall, tickets, chairs, ushers, refreshments – plenty to keep everyone occupied. Diana had agreed to do all the accompanying, to give Miss Snoddy more leisure to police the children, in whom the excitement of performance was beginning to mix with the excitement of Christmas approaching.

As the concert was to be performed on a proper stage, someone suggested there should be a backdrop. It was sketched out on the backcloth by Peter Bentley, son of Lord Bentley, who was studying art in London, at least until conscription plucked him away, and he did a very fine snowy village scene of cottages and shops and muffled figures. Volunteers did the painting, under his direction. Sadie found it great fun to crawl about on her hands and knees with a brush and a pot. Nailer almost disgraced her one day. He had followed her to the hall, managed to slip inside, and ran across the cloth to get to her, leaving a trail of paw-prints. But Peter Bentley thought they looked rather artistic – it was lucky he had run across the snow at the bottom rather than the sky – and decided to leave them.

'A lucky let-off for you,' Sadie told the dog. 'Now you'll have helped with the concert too.'

Nailer seemed unimpressed. He had tried to lick his paws clean, and was thoughtful for several hours afterwards.

The concert ended with the singing of two carols by cast and audience together – 'Hark the Herald Angels' and 'Once in Royal David's City' – after which the rector climbed onto the stage, thanked the performers and said a prayer. Then, after the singing of 'God Save The King', there were refreshments for all.

Corporal Armstrong eased his way through the crowds with a cup of tea and a slice of cake for Ada, and stood beside her, chatting pleasantly.

'So it's all over,' Ada said wistfully.

'Yes, more's the pity,' said Armstrong. 'It's been a very nice little interlude.'

'I suppose that's what it was,' Ada said. 'After all, there's a war on. We shouldn't forget that.'

'Not much chance of forgetting it,' said Armstrong. 'I don't wear khaki because it matches my

481

eyes, you know.'

He said funny things sometimes. She didn't know whether to laugh or not. 'I suppose you'll be going off to the front sooner or later,' she said instead.

'Trying to get rid of me?' he asked.

'Oh, no, I–'

'Don't worry, we'll be here for a few weeks yet. We've a bit more training to do before we're ready – I reckon we'll be around until spring. If that means anything to you.'

Ada didn't know how to answer. Just then one of his men caught his attention and he turned his head to talk to him, so she had a moment to look at him unobserved. He was no Lionel Barrymore, that was for sure – but, then, she wasn't Mary Pickford. He was middling in height, rather scrawny, probably in his late forties. He had been a regular and had been recalled to train the New Army intake. His hair was no-coloured, his eyes were a faded blue, his features just ordinary. But he was amusing to talk to, though she often didn't understand his jokes. And he had a way of smiling at her that made her feel special. When all was said and done, he was the first man who had ever shown any interest in her. She was even more ordinary than him, so why should they?

He finished his conversation and turned back to her so quickly that he caught her staring at him. She went red.

'Admiring my good looks?' he said, with a grin. 'They were after me for Hollywood, you know, but I said I'd sooner stay here and fight the Jerries.'

'Oh, get on with you!' she said, alarmed that he

had so accurately echoed her thoughts.

He grew serious. 'Look here, this jamboree'll be over any minute, and you'll be dashing off, and we might not get another chance to make arrangements.'

'What arrangements?' she asked.

'Why, to see each other again,' he said, raising his eyebrows. 'How about walking out with me? I know I'm not much of a catch, but you seem to like me all right, and there is a war on. How about it?'

A warmth of pleasure flooded through her at the thought. A man of her own! She had never supposed it would happen to her. 'I'd like that,' she said. 'But – how can we manage it?'

'Well, my lass, you get time off, don't you? And I get time off. As long as we can match the two up, the world is our oyster.'

Cook said, 'But you don't know anything about him.'

Ada had expected Cook to be as pleased as she was, but she had nary a smile. If *she* was doubtful, Ada wondered whether she should be, too. 'His name's Len,' she said falteringly. 'He comes from Essex. From Leigh-on-Sea. His dad was a fishmonger, but he didn't like the smell of fish so he went into the army.'

'What – give up a good business for the sake of a smell? A bit finicky, isn't he?' said Cook.

When she put it like that, it did sound odd, but Ada had heard it from the horse's mouth. They had lived in the flat above the shop, and Len had described so vividly what it was like to wake up and go to bed with fish every day, how the smell got in your clothes and your hair, that she'd almost ended up smelling it herself.

'And why isn't he married? A man of his age! There must be something wrong with him.'

'He was sweet on a girl at school, but she married someone else,' Ada said. Though the girl – Nelly – hadn't said so, Len had been sure she had turned him down because of the smell. He had become convinced it clung to him no matter what he did, so he'd decided the only thing to do was to go right away, from Nelly and the fishmonger's shop. He had joined the army, causing a rift between him and his parents, which had hardly been healed before his father died. The shop had been sold, and his mother had gone to live with his sister and her husband – who had a good job at a printing works in Southend and, said Len with a grin, smelt of ink, if you liked that better.

He had made such an interesting narration of it that it had not occurred to her for an instant to doubt it. But she could not reproduce his story or his style to Cook. She concluded lamely, 'The army was his life.'

Cook sniffed. 'Well, you know your own mind, I suppose. But if it was me...'

Ada felt her wonderful new happiness being taken away from her. 'But what am I supposed to do?' she cried in anguish.

Cook shook her head. 'I don't know the fellow. And you're a grown woman. I'm just saying be careful. He's a soldier from a camp down the road, a stranger who wasn't here a few months ago and won't be here in a few months' time. I'm thinking about your welfare, that's all.'

'He's nice,' Ada said.

Cook got up with a shrug. 'Time to get that leg of mutton in the oven. Emily – have you done the potatoes yet? And where's Ethel? She can help with the vegetables.' She turned back to Ada. 'She's no use to man nor beast since that chap of hers got killed. I liked her better the way she was before, for all her lip. At least she had a bit of vim about her.'

The implication, Ada felt, was that having to do with chaps was a mug's game and always led you into trouble of one sort or another. She went off to lay the dining-room table with her head down and her heart sore.

Cook stuck capers into the leg of mutton with gloomy savagery. Everything was changing, and she didn't like it. She and Ada had been together for over twenty years, and their lives had not altered in that time, bar the move from London to Northcote. Life was like that, before the war. Nothing ever happened, nothing ever changed, you knew where you were, and where you would be next year.

And your life would have been instantly recognisable to your mother, your grandmother, your great-grandmother. There was a magnificent solidness to the world – by which she meant England; a dignity, a worth. If a thing was right, it was right – why would you ever change it?

But now, just in one year, everything was as different as could be. Young men went off to war and got killed. People got blown up in their own streets, in their own beds. New words were being

485

flung about. Routines couldn't be relied on. There were strangers everywhere you looked. And women in particular were doing things you could never have imagined. Skirts above the ankle bone – and where would *that* end? Going about unchaperoned. Eating in restaurants. Getting jobs – men's jobs! Miss Sadie – very well, she'd always been a bit of a tomboy, but she'd have grown out of it. Now she was *training horses for the army!* Poor Miss Diana, widowed before she was even married, reading books to men with no legs! The mistress out and about all the time with her committees – before the war she'd hardly stirred out of doors, any more than any of them had. Everything was upside down, everyone was out of their place, nothing could be depended on.

And now Ada – Ada of all people! – wanting to walk out with a man she hardly knew. She and Ada had been like two halves of a walnut. What would happen to her, Cook, if Ada changed? What if she went away? *Why can't things be the way they always were?* She threw the impassioned plea to Heaven. *I hate change. I hate it!*

When the excitement of the concert was over, there was Christmas to look forward to, and the hope and anxiety about who would be able to get leave, who would be coming home. Beth wrote to say that Jack was lucky this year, and would be home on Christmas Eve. They would have their Christmas Day alone together, but would be at the Palfreys' on Boxing Day, and as the Edward Hunters had been invited too, they would see each other there.

David wrote to say his leave would be after the New Year. Jumbo's was from the 28th. The Oliphants were to stay in London so that he did not have so far to travel, and would stay on for David.

Beattie received the news that he would spend his leave with the Oliphants with bitterness, but knew it was inevitable, now he was engaged. He said that he would come out to Northcote on one of the days, and bring Sophy with him. She was expected to be grateful for such bounty! From Bobby there was no word. He had been having too much fun in Oxford, she assumed, to write. She supposed he would come home when his leave fell, without bothering to tell them beforehand. That was Bobby's way.

The village was determined to make a fuss both of the Tommies at Paget's Piece and the wounded officers at Mount Olive. Collections were made and working parties set up. There was a box for each Tommy containing cigarettes, chocolate, some extra treats like tinned sardines or meat paste, and a couple of useful presents, like knitted fingerless mittens and a pocket knife. The army would provide a special Christmas dinner of roast pork, but the village meant to send plum puddings, nuts and sweets to augment the feast; Dagnell's, the brewery in Westleigh, promised a bottle of beer or stout for each soldier; and Hetherton's Hygienic Bakery was to give boxes of cream buns to have with Christmas tea.

For Mount Olive, the hospital committee was planning a dinner of turkey – a farm in Gosford was providing the birds – plum pudding and mince pies (made in various Northcote kitchens), with cheese to follow, and wine and port from the cellars of the wealthier residents. There would be Christmas cake (Hetherton's again) to go with the ham tea that would follow the singing of carols by a mixed choir.

Sadie was kept busy, combining the usual hospital visiting with preparations for the Christmas feast; and there were lots of little extra errands to run for the officers, who wanted to send presents home but were unable to get out and buy them. And there was still her work at Highclere.

One day she was patiently accustoming a bay gelding to having his feet handled, running her hand down a leg, picking up the hoof, and rapping it with a small hammer. This particular animal didn't mind the picking up, but objected every time to the rapping, and only endless repetition and kind words would work the miracle.

She straightened up and stroked the bay's neck. A shadow crossed the straw as someone came to the open door behind her. She assumed it was one of the grooms, but before she could turn, hands came round from behind her and covered her eyes, and a voice said, 'Guess who it is?'

Her heart jumped. She whirled, making the horse jerk its head and snort, and only just managed not to fling herself at him. 'Captain Courcy!'

'You don't seem to have the idea of this game. You're supposed to guess *before* you turn round and see.'

'I recognised your voice,' she said, her face open with delight. Some monitor at the back of her mind told her not to show her pleasure too keenly, but she ignored it. 'I'm so glad to see you! What are you doing here? Is it leave? How long have you got?'

He was smiling, seeming to examine her with almost as much interest. 'Yes, it's leave. I volunteered to take it early so as to let an officer with a family have Christmas itself. I couldn't get up to see my father anyway – it would have taken the whole leave just to get to Edinburgh and back. So here I am.'

'Where are you staying?' she asked.

'With me,' said Mrs Cuthbert, appearing behind him. 'Horace and I have plenty of room. I invited him the moment I realised he was homeless.'

Courcy grinned. 'Not exactly homeless, but very grateful to be saved from staying in a hotel.'

'And you shall have your Christmas,' Mrs Cuthbert said. 'Goose and plum pudding and everything nice. We'll do it on Tuesday, to give you time to recover. It makes no difference to us which day, so we might as well have the pleasure of sharing it with you.'

'You're far too good to me,' he said.

'Sadie doesn't think so,' said Mrs Cuthbert, with a twinkling smile, and Sadie was annoyed to feel herself blush.

'I've just had a thought,' Mrs Cuthbert went on. 'If Sadie can bear the idea of eating Christmas dinner twice in one year, perhaps I can persuade her to come on Tuesday, too. It'll make it more of a party. Will you?'

'I'd love to – if they don't mind at home,' Sadie said.

'I don't suppose you notice it, being here every day,' Courcy said to Mrs Cuthbert, 'but I see a difference in Miss Hunter. I know it's only been a few months. But she's changed.'

'Oh, I see it,' said Mrs Cuthbert. 'She's growing up. I think she's going to make a very handsome woman.' Sadie turned her face away in embarrassment, and Mrs Cuthbert laughed. 'She doesn't like to be talked about. But you must ask her about her work up at the hospital. It was all her own idea, to visit the wounded officers and relieve their boredom with chat, and reading, and games and so on.'

'Do you really do that?' Courcy said. 'I'd like to hear about it.'

'I'm sure she'll oblige you,' said Mrs Cuthbert. 'After all, the returning hero must have everything he wants.'

'I'm not sure about the hero part, but I can tell you what I'd really like right now.'

'Yes?'

'A ride. A normal hack, on a normal horse, one that isn't sick or wounded. Through normal countryside, that isn't ruined and pockmarked and churned up by war. You can't think how beautiful England looked from the train – especially the last bit, through Middlesex and Hertfordshire.'

Sadie loved Mrs Cuthbert anyway, but she loved her ten times more when she heard her say, 'Well, there's no difficulty about that. Take your pick of horses, and Sadie shall go with you.'

'You choose for me,' Courcy said to Sadie. 'You know them and I don't. And will you really come with me? I'd like to hear about your hospital work.'

'I'd like to hear about what you've been doing in France.'

'Jolly good. That's settled, then,' said Mrs Cuthbert. 'And take your time – don't hurry back. Have a good long ride. It'll do the horses good.'

Now what, Sadie thought, as she turned away, *is she looking so pleased about?*

Bobby arrived on Christmas Eve, unannounced, and just when the fellow from Gosford who had brought the Christmas tree was complaining that it would not go through the door. Bobby dumped his bag, sprang into the fray with enthusiasm, and had the thing safely in place, upright in its bucket of sand and firmly tied before anyone properly knew he was there.

'Organisation,' he said. 'That's all it needed.'

'It seems you've turned into an officer while we weren't looking,' Diana said. 'I can just see you ordering people about in the trenches.'

'Is that all I get by way of a greeting?' he complained. 'Ulysses returns after long wanderings...'

'I'm glad to see you,' Sadie said, and enveloped him in a hug.

'That's more like it,' he said. 'Is there anything to eat? I'm starving.'

'Now I *know* you're home,' Diana said.

'Luncheon will only be half an hour,' said Beattie. 'Can you wait?' She was noting everything about him, seeing changes in her boy, who was rapidly turning into a man.

'I could get you a piece of cake,' Ada offered, 'to keep you going.'

'Darling Ada, thank you – and a cup of tea. I've had nothing since the crack of dawn when they hauled us out of bed. You can't think how much I'm looking forward to lying in tomorrow.' A comical expression of alarm crossed his face. 'Oh, my goodness, it's Christmas Day, isn't it? I do hope you children won't be dashing into my room at five o'clock to show me your stockings.'

'I don't know who you mean by "you children",' Sadie said. 'There's only Peter, and even he's nine.'

'Did you bring us all presents?' Peter demanded.

'What a question to ask!' said Bobby, but with a grin. 'Be careful with that bag – you might break something.'

'Was shopping nice in Oxford?' Sadie asked teasingly.

'You'll have to wait and see,' he said. He gave her a thoughtful look. 'But you ought to have warned me you planned to grow up so fast as soon as my back was turned.'

Two people in just a few days, Sadie thought. *Am I really changing?*

They went through to the dining room, to the fire, where Ada brought Bobby tea and cake. He looked around him as he ate, like someone waking from a long dream. 'I'm glad everything's the same. I hope you won't get a sudden urge to change the wallpaper or re-cover the chairs, Mum.'

'I'm too busy for things like that,' Beattie said.

'I'm glad to hear it. We soldiers like to come home to familiar things.'

'So tell us your news,' said Diana. 'And try not to spit crumbs.'

'I never spit. Look, cake's all gone now, anyway.'

'I don't know why you couldn't tell us you were coming,' she went on, being very elder-sisterly. 'Oh, wait, don't tell me you got sacked! David was always warning you'd get sacked from school but you seemed to escape by the skin of your teeth.'

'Sacked be damned!' Bobby said indignantly. 'Oh, sorry, Mater. I mean, be *blowed*. I've passed everything with flying colours. I'll be gazetted in January – what do you think of that?'

There were congratulations and praise. 'I knew you'd be good,' Sadie said. 'You *look* like an officer.'

'So when do you go to the trenches?' William asked.

Bobby looked very pleased with himself. 'No trenches for me, my boy. A higher fate is reserved for Second Lieutenant R. D. Hunter. Literally higher. I shall be looking down on those poor fools, like David, stuck in the trenches for the whole war.'

'What are you talking about?' Diana said impatiently.

'What have you done, Bobby?' Beattie asked sternly.

'I've transferred to the Royal Flying Corps,' he said, grinning, as William, who had always been fascinated by aeroplanes, gave a wild whoop, and Peter jumped up and down in excitement. 'I'm going to be a pilot.'

The fact that it was Christmas Day did not alter the routine in the trenches. There was the stand-to at dawn, and David's company, which was holding the front-line trench, was ordered to

493

send five rounds of rapid fire across no-man's-land, 'to wake the buggers up'. What a way to greet the Saviour's birthday! In his head he sang,

Hail smiling morn,
That tips the hills with gold,
Whose rosy fingers ope the gates of day...

The day before, the routine shelling had died away as darkness fell, and the ensuing quiet had finally been invested with the sound of someone over in the German lines singing 'Stille Nacht'. The Germans kept Christmas Eve far more than Christmas Day. The sound carried well on the frosty air, and it gave David goosebumps listening to it. But the singing stopped abruptly in mid-verse, as though someone had closed a door. David imagined an officer stamping along and shutting the fellow up.

Stand-to was followed by breakfast and kit-cleaning. The quartermaster had sent up bacon for breakfast, and the officers had clubbed together to buy sausages for everyone, so at least it was a good one.

Major Tiverton came along afterwards and, offering David a smoke, said, 'Orders are we're to keep up slow fire all day. And any minute now–' A shrill whine and a rattling crash interrupted him as a shell went overhead. 'I was about to say,' he resumed, 'that our artillery is going to be shelling the enemy intermittently. They'll probably retaliate, so keep your men alert. We don't want any accidents.'

'Yes, sir,' said David.

'I think the powers that be are extremely

anxious to prevent any fraternisation. You know what happened last Christmas.'

'I read about it, sir.'

'Strictest orders nothing of that sort is to happen this time.' Tiverton smoked reflectively for a moment, then said, 'We had someone from Brigade over yesterday. He seemed struck by the Loos dead – well, there's not much else to look at out there. He said we must avenge them, kill two Germans for every one of our dead.' He shrugged. 'Orders is orders, Hunter, but...'

He left the sentence unfinished. David knew what he meant. The purpose of war was to defeat the enemy's forces, not to exact revenge on individual soldiers. Warfare was bloody enough as it was, without such attitudes making it bloodier.

In the afternoon, just as dusk was gathering, word came along the trenches that one of the men in D Company, over on their left, had been hit in the head by a sniper's bullet, and had died shortly afterwards.

'On Christmas Day!' David heard a soldier say resentfully. 'Some bloody Christmas present!'

The sun sank redly against a pink sky, and the frost started to glitter on dark surfaces. It was very still, not the least sound out there, no bird, no dog, no man. It began to get very cold. 'Too cold for snow,' said one of his new lieutenants, hopefully.

There was cold roast pork sent up for supper, with hot potatoes. In his dug-out, David had a bit of cheese left, and some nuts and chocolate he had brought in with him, so it wasn't a bad Christmas dinner, all told.

Afterwards they lit up cigarettes. There were a

few minutes still before rounds, but conversation seemed to have dried up. It was strange, he thought, to be Captain Hunter and in authority over these lieutenants hardly younger than himself. But war was essentially an absurdity – he was learning that. Hooper, the youngest of them, just nineteen, was looking rather blue, no doubt thinking about his family and Christmases at home.

'Give us a song, Hooper,' David said, to distract him. 'What's everybody singing back home these days?'

So Hooper, who had a mild, sweet voice, put his cigarette aside and sang:

'Keep the home fires burning
While your hearts are yearning.
Though your lads are far away
They dream of home.'

It was a rather melancholy tune, David thought – not exactly calculated to get the toes tapping or the knees up. But it was a tune you would remember, and it was easy to sing. And it spoke to something inside you, here in your dugout by the light of a candle stuck in a beer bottle.

He remembered last year, when they had said it would all be over by Christmas. Well, they *would* win – there wasn't a doubt about that – but they knew now it was going to be a long, hard grind.

'Turn the dark cloud inside out
Till the boys come home.'

And when would that be? he wondered.

This Large Print Book for the partially sighted, who cannot read normal print, is published under the auspices of

THE ULVERSCROFT FOUNDATION